# PRAISE FOR *TO FETCH A FELON*

"Two paws up! First in a wonderful new series. . . . Take one smart—albeit somewhat reluctant—amateur sleuth, Emma Reed, add an idyllic English village setting, colorful characters, a puzzling mystery, and a talking corgi . . . and you get the perfect mix of all things cozy."

— *New York Times* bestselling author Sofie Kelly

"Effortlessly blends a woman's drastic midlife career and environment change with a solid murder mystery and a dash of paranormal pet communication. . . . Unique and intriguing and full of heart." —Criminal Element

"A promising debut for dog lovers, who'll delight in the clever talking corgi and his charming owner."

—*Kirkus Reviews*

"Absolutely delightful. I cannot wait for the next installment. Highly recommended!" —Open Book Society

"The perfect cozy launch—I loved Emma and the other characters in Trevena. The setting is lovely, and Oliver is a delight. . . . A not-to-be-missed book for those who love cozy mysteries as well as for dog lovers."

—The Neverending TBR

D0044289

# Murder Always Barks Twice

## JENNIFER HAWKINS

**BERKLEY PRIME CRIME**
New York

BERKLEY PRIME CRIME
Published by Berkley
An imprint of Penguin Random House LLC
penguinrandomhouse.com

ISBN: 9780593197103

First Edition: August 2021

Printed in the United States of America
1  3  5  7  9  10  8  6  4  2

Book design by George Towne

*To all the dogs, big and small,*
*who have helped make this dark year brighter*

# 1

·········

"YOU ARE *KIDDING* ME!"

Emma Reed jumped, scattering the tea leaves across the polished oak bar.

"No, no, wait, Daphne, say that again!" Pearl Delgado pressed her finger against one ear and held her mobile phone closer to the other to shut out the B&B's background chatter. Emma glared at her and swept the spilled Ceylon leaves into the bin.

Pearl jerked her chin toward the tea leaves and mouthed *"Sorry!"*

Around them, the great room of the King's Rest Bed & Breakfast bustled with activity. The third seating for afternoon tea was well under way. Scents of warm butter, vanilla, sugar and tea filled the air. Customers clustered around tables, enjoying slices of cake, finger sandwiches and Emma's rapidly-becoming-famous-around-the-village scones. It was a pretty good turnout, considering this was a dampish spring day on the Cornish coast with the tourist season only just starting up.

Once, the King's Rest had been a tavern and a hideout for smugglers. Now it was a popular bed and breakfast run by Angelique Delgado and her daughter Pearl. Every morning, its U-shaped oak bar served as the staging area for a (truly amazing) breakfast buffet. Three afternoons a week, it was also the place where vintage teapots were filled with select blends to be enjoyed alongside treats furnished by Reed's Tea & Cakes.

Just now, Angelique herself was behind the bar, helping Emma fill the latest round of tea orders, and eyeing her daughter. Pearl continued to listen intently to whatever was being said on the other end of the phone.

"You're sure about this, Daph?" said Pearl. "No, no, I'm do . . . that is . . ." Pearl looked up to see Emma and her mum, staring back at her. "Hang on just a tick." With the phone still pressed to her ear, Pearl hurried down the back hallway toward the office.

"Now what do you suppose that was all about?" Emma asked.

"Girl stuff," Angelique said. Angelique was a broad, tall woman with dark brown skin. Her family had emigrated from Jamaica when she was a girl and she still retained a hint of her original accent. This morning, she wore her black braids swept into a heavy coronet. She had a strong face with high cheekbones, and brown eyes that could look straight through you. This skill probably came from raising four children all while running a successful business.

Angelique and Pearl had invited Emma to open her tea-room inside the B&B almost eight months ago. Emma (with Oliver) had left the mad world of London finance to settle in Trevena village. At forty-five, she had decided it was finally time to live out her dream of opening her own tea shop. She'd originally planned on finding a space of her own. Pearl, however, had stepped up with a new idea to help Emma, diversify the family business and make use of space in the B&B that sat mostly empty during the day.

Emma and the Delgados had spent the winter refurbishing the great room and orchestrating the "soft launch." Winter in Cornwall had turned out to be everything Emma had heard—gray, cold, filled with squalls and storms, including waves that broke so far up the beach, the B&B's car park flooded. When Emma's brother quizzed her about it during Christmas, she'd been within an inch of deciding to chuck it all and moving back to London.

But then Henry'd shaken his head and said, "Still don't understand why you'd want to throw over a good career and go mucking about with something as silly as cakes."

Which sent Emma straight back to Trevena with renewed determination to make her silly cakes into a success.

Now, spring was turning to summer. Reed's Tea & Cakes was up and running. They served cream teas on Fridays, Saturdays and Sundays, with plans to ramp up as demand grew. In addition to the sit-down service, they had a bakery counter for those who wanted a nice cuppa and a sweet treat to enjoy at one of the tables or take home.

When the takeaway counter and tea service were happening at the same time, it could get a bit mad, but Emma wouldn't trade her new life for anything. Baking cakes and tarts, serving perfectly brewed pots of tea and inventing new varieties of finger sandwiches were Emma's idea of the good life. As a bonus, she got to have her corgi, Oliver, with her all day instead of having to leave him at home or with a dog-sitter.

"So who's Daphne?" Emma asked Angelique. Along with cakes, curiosity was Emma's defining trait.

"Daphne Cochrane. She's been friends with Pearl since they were girls." Angelique checked the temperature readout on the electric kettle and filled the quirky cabbage leaf pot. "Probably she has some life-and-death gossip about the girls up at uni."

"Should I go follow Pearl, Emma?" Oliver, the final, furry—and extremely vital member of the service team was currently snuffling around the floor mats, attempting to zero in on Pearl's otherwise invisible footprints. "I can find out what she's doing!"

"Not now, good boy," said Emma. "We'll let Pearl have her space."

Oliver plumped down on his hindquarters and scratched his ear and sneezed. "Okay, Emma."

Reflexively, Emma glanced to see if anyone else had noticed anything . . . odd in this little exchange. There was nothing outwardly unusual about Oliver. He looked to be a standard white and tan Welsh Pembroke corgi, with all the usual off-the-chart levels of cuteness. But to Emma, Oliver spoke—perfectly intelligible, Welsh-accented English that nobody else heard or understood.

Being able to talk with their dogs was a trait that tiptoed through Emma's family. Of course, nobody ever actually said anything about it. At least not where they might be overheard. Except maybe by the dogs.

Oliver was the only animal Emma could understand. That was disconcerting enough, thank you very much. She loved her loyal, intelligent, boisterous, occasionally hyper-active corgi, but she did not feel a need to communicate with anybody else's pet or the local wildlife.

Of course, the situation did have its drawbacks. Oliver might talk, and he might be extraordinarily well-behaved by corgi standards, but he was still very much a dog. He saw the world from an entirely different angle than Emma, or any human. That, in turn, meant Emma could sometimes have a hard time understanding what Oliver was actually talking *about*.

Just now, Oliver was back to sniffing the trail only he could detect. "Nope, nope, nope. Kitchen, here, kitchen, upstairs . . . nope . . . ooo . . . what's that?" Nose to the floorboards, he trotted out into the main seating area. He did not get very far before one of the guests reached down to give him a pat, which he accepted with a happy, full-bum wag.

Angelique set the tea tray she'd just finished on the bar for their server Becca to pick up. "Oh, Emma, I've been meaning to ask, have you finalized our menu for during the du Maurier festival? We should be getting a good lot of foot traffic those days. I want to put it up on the website as soon as possible to lure them in."

Like a lot of villages, Trevena's summer calendar was filled with fetes and festivals, and the season kicked off in just over two weeks.

"Just about there," Emma told her. "But I'm worried about whether we've got enough help for the extra seatings we've planned."

Angelique added the matching cups to the tray she had set out. "I've made some calls, but let's sit down this evening, all right? Daniel won't be back until tomorrow, so the evening is clear." Pearl's husband, Daniel, ran a fishing and tourist boat that took campers and holidaymakers out to the islands off the coast.

"Great."

Before Emma could add anything else, the door from the car park opened to let in a middle-aged man in a blue work shirt.

"Oho," murmured Angelique. "You'd better take this one, Emma."

Emma attempted to roll her eyes. Why was that so much harder to do when she was blushing?

Emma reached the glass bakery counter about the same time as the new guest did. He made a show of stopping short and bowing for her to go first.

This time Emma did roll her eyes.

"Hullo, Brian." Emma took her place behind the case of cakes and buns. Oliver, of course, came over to check out the new arrival.

Brian Prowse ran Trevena's one-car taxi service, and was also the local mechanic and vintage car salesman. He was a fit man going gray at the temples with a snarky sense of humor, bright blue eyes and an infectious smile.

"All right, Emma?" said Brian. "Busy day? And hullo to you, Oliver." Brian bent down and rubbed the corgi's head.

Oliver sniffed at Brian's boots. "Dirt and asphalt and oil," he reported. "And that collie dog. And coffee."

Emma listened to her dog with half an ear. Brian had straightened up and turned his sunny smile on her. Since she'd come to Trevena, Emma and Brian had fallen into a bantering friendship, and she had to admit he could give her tummy the sorts of warm fluttery feelings she'd thought she'd left behind in adolescence.

*No, I do not have to admit that,* Emma told herself sternly. *I do not have to admit it on any level.*

"What can I get you?" Emma asked him. "Apple cake?"

"If you would, please. I just can't seem to stay away from it."

Emma pulled the cinnamon-scented loaf out of the case and cut a slice to package up. As she did, Angelique picked a couple canisters of tea off the bar and brought them to the takeaway counter, placing them into the appropriate gaps on the new shelves full of similar tins. The move reminded Emma of nothing so much as when her mum would casually come into the living room to tidy up when Emma had a boyfriend over.

Brian noticed too. He grinned at Emma and leaned both elbows on the counter.

"Are we still on for tomorrow?" he asked softly.

Emma leaned in close. "You do know I've never done this before?"

"What, you mean never?"

"Not even once."

He touched her hand. "I promise I'll be gentle."

"All right, the pair of you," said Angelique. "If you're trying to shock the old lady, you're going to have to do better than that."

They all laughed. "So what is really going on?" asked Angelique.

"Emma's thinking of buying a car," said Brian. "I told her to stop by tomorrow and I'd show her what's on offer."

"Yes, I'm sure you did." Angelique's tone was far too bland.

Brian laughed, paid and said goodbye. Emma's gaze followed him as he walked out the door.

"Well, *somebody* works fast," remarked Angelique.

"What?" Emma blinked. *Focus,* Emma. "Oh, come on, Angelique—he just really likes my apple cake."

"Is that what the kids are calling it these days?"

Fortunately, before Emma had a chance to say anything rash, Pearl came back into the dining room. She had a kind of dazed look on her face, like she'd been spending too long in the sun.

"Pearl?" said Angelique as her daughter reached the counter. "Is everything all right?"

"I don't know, Ma."

"Well, what was it Daphne had to say?"

Instead of answering her mother, Pearl turned to Emma. "Em, have we got an extra table for tea?"

"Should do," said Emma. "We were only about half booked. For how many?"

"And it's on today? I mean, the cakes and all? They're all on point, yeah?"

Emma pulled back, confused.

"Pearl," said Angelique. "What's going on?"

Pearl looked at the room; people were beginning to steal glances in their direction. She straightened up and smoothed down her apron. She also gestured frantically toward the kitchen.

Emma nodded at Becca. The server returned a quick salute, indicating she and her sister, Bella, had everything in hand. Reassured, Emma followed Angelique and Pearl into the kitchen. Oliver, of course, was not going to be left out and scampered to catch up.

"All right now, Pearl," said Angelique. "What is it?"

"Is anything wrong?" added Emma.

"Not yet," Pearl said. "Only I've just been told the governing board of the Daphne du Maurier Literary and Appreciation Society is going to walk through our door in about ten minutes."

"And they want tea?" prompted Angelique.

"They want more than that." Pearl turned to Emma. "Em, how would you feel about helping cater Trevena's biggest annual tourist festival?"

# 2

........

"AH. ERM. UNK." REPLIED EMMA.

"What is it, Emma? What?" barked Oliver.

"Slow down, Pearl," said Angelique. "What is it you're talking about?"

Pearl held up her phone. "The Daphne du Maurier Literary Festival just lost its caterer, and Daphne said her aunt is in a real pickle."

"Chicken would be better," mumbled Oliver.

Daphne du Maurier was one of Cornwall's best-loved authors. Her most famous books, *Rebecca* and *Jamaica Inn*, brought a steady stream of tourists to the southwest every year. Emma had been looking forward to the festival since she moved here. Not only did it celebrate her absolute all-time favorite writer, but every single tea service had been booked solid for the entire festival weekend. She'd added three extra seatings, and they'd still had to start a waiting list.

Her only worry up until now had been how to keep up with the increased business and still find time to visit the festival herself.

"Your friend is involved with the festival?" asked Emma.

"Not her. Her aunt," said Pearl. "Daphne's aunt is Marcia Cochrane," she added. "She owns Truscott Grange, and they host the du Maurier festival every year. They always get Weber's Catering from over in Treknow to do the food. But Daphne says this year Weber's pulled out."

"Pulled out?" echoed Angelique, shocked. "With barely two weeks to go?"

"I know, right?" said Pearl. "Anyway, Daphne and her mum and Marcie were down here for tea last week. I told her that we were looking to expand the B and B's catering operation, and between that and Emma's lemon drizzle cake, they decided they want to talk to us about filling in."

"Emma?" Oliver poked her in the calf with his surprisingly hard nose. "Is everything okay, Emma?"

Before Emma could say anything to anybody, the kitchen door swung open, and Becca rushed in. "Oh, sorry, everyone. I just, um, Emma, we've got a party of six wanting a table. Where should I put them?"

"That's the board," said Pearl.

Angelique immediately swung into action. "Put them in the private parlor, Becca. I'll be right out. Pearl, find us some notepads and pens. If they want to talk business, we need to be ready. Emma, we might be needing an extra treat or three for our special guests."

Angelique fixed her professional smile onto her face and breezed out of the kitchen with the air of a lead actor making her entrance. Pearl gave Emma a quick thumbs-up and followed, leaving Emma alone with Oliver.

"Right then," said Emma. "It's game on."

"What game?" Oliver bounced up and down on all four feet. "Where? Should I get the ball? I can get the ball, Emma!"

"I wish it was that kind of game."

The kitchen was currently laid out in its teatime assembly line. Trays of sandwiches, scones and biscuits and cake slices waited, along with a row of tiered cake stands and dishes of jam and clotted cream. All anyone had to do was read the service ticket and arrange the guest's chosen selections on the stand. Emma, being who she was, also kept a checklist beside each tray so they could tick off which treats had gone out the door. It gave her a running tally of what varieties were most popular with Trevena's tea fanciers.

But Angelique was right. If the board of the Daphne du Maurier Literary and Appreciation Society really was being seated in Angelique's private parlor, they should be given something that was not on the regular menu.

The problem was she had maybe ten minutes to make it happen.

"What's good, Oliver?" Emma headed for the fridge. "What have we got?"

"Chicken!" announced Oliver unsurprisingly. "Also biscuits."

"Also whipped cream!" cried Emma, spotting the carton of double cream.

"Yes! Yes!" Oliver bounced and wagged behind her.

Emma pulled out the bins of chopped chicken and watercress. She grabbed lemon, mustard and mayonnaise to go with it. She also got out the cherries she had marinating in kirsch for tomorrow. And the extra chocolate sponge she'd baked this morning, because along with checklists, Emma firmly believed in having backups for her backups.

Emma felt her baking adrenaline humming in her veins. Down by her ankles, Oliver barked encouragement and stayed on the alert for any stray bits and crumbs that might drop into corgi range.

A few minutes later, she had a fresh chicken salad to spread on thin slices of whole wheat bread. She whipped the double cream in the stand mixer with mascarpone and drizzled in the kirsch-laced cherry juice.

Pearl came into the kitchen.

"What have we got, Pearl?"

"Becca's putting the pots together now. Full cream tea for five. How can I help?"

Under Emma's direction, Pearl arranged the sandwiches and sweets on their stands. Emma added the chicken salad, little squares of the lemon drizzle cake, each topped with an extra dollop of clotted cream and a smidge of candied lemon peel, as well as the fresh rounds of chocolate cake and whipped cream with a boozy cherry in the middle.

"What are we calling those?" asked Pearl as Emma set down the last cakelet.

"Black Forest minis," said Emma promptly. "I've got these." She picked up a stand in each hand. Pearl got the other two. "Showtime! Stay put, Oliver."

Oliver didn't answer because his mouth was full. Emma had slipped a bit of chopped chicken into his kibble bowl to help keep him in the kitchen.

Emma followed Pearl out the door. Quickly.

# 3

THE B&B'S PRIVATE PARLOR WAS A COMFORTABLE ROOM just to one side of the common area. Back in the day, it had been reserved for ladies who might stay at the tavern. Now it was used for larger groups of guests, like wedding parties and family reunions.

Or the board of a local literary society.

The board members had ranged themselves down either side of the long table at the center of the room. There were two men and four women, each with their cups and their individual pots of tea already in front of them. Angelique sat at the foot of the table nearest the door with a notepad and pen.

"Ah, and here is our own star baker, Emma Reed." The smile she gave as Emma and Pearl entered was ever so slightly strained. *Uh-oh.*

"Good afternoon," Emma said to the seated guests. She and Pearl set the cake stands down on the table. Emma was pleased to hear the intrigued murmurs and at least one "Lovely!" She did note that the woman at the head of the table—a thin, aging blonde—just looked at the tiers of sandwiches and sweets and frowned. Even from this distance, Emma could smell her hair spray and rose perfume.

*Uh-oh. Again.* Emma glanced at Angelique, but Angelique's face was set in a smooth, professional facade.

"Emma"—Angelique indicated the woman sitting to her right—"this is Marcia Cochrane. She hosts the festival."

"Please, call me Marcie. Everybody does." Marcie turned to shake hands with them both. "Lovely to meet you, Emma, and you as well, Pearl."

Marcie's hands were calloused and the nails were well-kept, but they were stained. Emma wondered if she was a gardener. She was certainly no delicate lady. Marcia Cochrane was a strongly built woman with mournful brown eyes and creamy skin that was just starting to take on a summer tan. Her waving auburn hair was cut into a neat bob and held back by a plain white headband. Emma's imagination immediately pictured her in a tweed skirt with a shotgun under her arm and spaniels at her side. In reality, she wore a dark green blouse and crisp black slacks.

"You must forgive us for descending on you like this," Marcie went on.

"Not at all," said Pearl. "We're delighted to have you." She smiled to include the entire gathering, even the sour-faced woman at the head of the table. The woman frowned and Emma felt a pinch of sudden irritation.

The man next to Marcie stuck his hand over his shoulder for Emma, then Pearl, to shake. "Ned Giddy," he told them. "And yes, I'm Giddy. Go ahead, say it. Everyone does."

Ned Giddy was the kind of mild, glasses-wearing, mostly bald man who seemed mystically drawn to the minutia of running small social groups.

"I wouldn't want to be conventional," replied Emma.

"Neither would I, if I could help it." He smiled, and blinked rapidly. "But I'm afraid, despite the name, I'm really rather boring."

"Nonsense," said the woman across from him. She was older than Emma, proudly gray haired with a pink and freckled face. Truthfully, she looked like she should be cast as somebody's biscuit-baking nan in a family drama. "Ned, you are many things, but you are not boring. You should hear him read *Jamaica Inn*. His interpretation of Francis Davey is absolutely chilling. I'm Tasha Boyd, by the way. I've had your tea, Emma, and I adore your rosemary and walnut scones. So tender! This is my husband, John." She put her hand on the shoulder of the cheerful man beside her, who was the very picture of the stolid Cornish countryman.

"Delighted," said Emma to them both.

"And this is our president"—Marcie gestured toward the thin woman at the head of the table—"Caite Hope-Johnston."

Caite Hope-Johnston did not offer to shake hands, nor did she smile. She was thin as a reed and had a face that suggested she was quite comfortable with enforcing the rigid self-discipline it took to stay that way. Emma guessed that she and Caite were about the same age, but the skin around the other woman's eyes was smooth and unmarked as if freshly ironed. Neither her chin nor her forehead betrayed a single wrinkle. Makeup and manicure were likewise faultless. That, even more than her perfect pink St. John twinset, and pearls, told Emma that this was a wealthy woman, and like most wealthy women she was used to getting what she wanted.

"We were just telling Mrs. Delgado that we have a business proposal we'd like to discuss," said Marcie. "Won't you both join us as well?"

"Thank you." Emma pulled out a chair between Ned and Caite, leaving the one next to Angelique for Pearl. "Just for a minute."

"Yes—of course you're in the middle of your day," said Marcie. "We do understand."

At her end of the table, Caite coughed. "I should think that any proper caterer would be pleased to make time for potential clients."

"Well, Caite, you have to agree, this is a little sudden." Marcie helped herself to a chicken salad sandwich and one of the cucumber and butter ones that were a teatime staple. "In fact, we should probably explain the full situation now."

"Marcie's right, Caite." Tasha seemed to prefer prawn to

chicken and did not wait to help herself to the ginger scones. "We're in a fix, and we have to act."

"I see I'm outnumbered." Caite's smile was tighter than Emma's budget at the end of the month.

"Good heavens!" cried Ned Giddy suddenly. He was staring at the bitten sandwich in his hand. Emma's heart stopped as he turned his drooping eyes toward her. "Ms. Reed, this may be the first time in my life I've had a cucumber sandwich that was not insipid!"

Emma could breathe again. "Thank you, Mr. Giddy."

"Ned," he said cheerfully. "I am always on a first-name basis with anyone who makes a good sandwich." He helped himself to two more cucumber, and a chicken salad, and a prawn.

Ned Giddy was most definitely Emma's type of guest.

Pearl took one of the notepads off the stack beside Angelique and uncapped a pen. "Perhaps you can tell us about this fix?"

Ned and both Boyds looked from Marcie to Caite and back again. Caite stared at Marcie. Marcie stared at Caite.

Marcie spoke first.

"Well, as you may know, the Daphne du Maurier Literary Festival has always partnered with Weber's Catering. This year, however, there were some problems . . ."

"What kind?" asked Angelique.

Marcie hesitated. At her end of the table, Caite smiled just a little. "Well, Marcie? This is your meeting."

"A payment was missed," cut in Tasha quickly. "The matter was looked into and cleared up."

Emma, who had spent over twenty years in the finance industry, felt all her internal antennae stand straight up.

"It was due to an unfortunate oversight," said Marcie and she looked straight across the table at Caite. "Or perhaps one should say *lack* of oversight."

"Yes." Caite looked back at Marcie, her brows arched ever so slightly and the tiniest curve on her perfectly glossed lips. "Perhaps one should."

"We were hoping that Weber's would take into account

how long they and the festival have had a smooth working relationship, but they made a different decision," Marcie went on. "Much to everybody's disappointment—"

"And surprise," put in Caite. She was still smiling, but the expression did not reach her eyes or her forehead.

*I think I'll just take a dislike to you now and avoid the rush.* Emma glanced at her partners. Angelique was clearly not pleased at this little exchange. Pearl was looking positively grim, and Emma couldn't blame either one of them. The rest of the board seemed to be trying to concentrate on their tea. The clinking of china sounded tinny and awkward in the silence.

"Caite, I'm sure we don't need to go into society politics right now," Marcie said.

"I just want to be clear where the situation stands," replied Caite loftily. "You should all be aware that despite Marcie's enthusiasm, the rest of the board is not prepared to turn over so much responsibility to an organization with no proven experience. I understand you've only just opened, Ms. Reed?"

"Reed's Tea and Cakes has been open for four months," said Emma. "And I'd agree that would be a concern, except for the fact that the King's Rest has been involved in event catering and planning for well over two decades."

Caite lifted her chin. "A grandmother's birthday party here and there is *hardly*—"

Angelique did not let her get any further. "Pearl," she said crisply, "would you please get the catering packets?"

"Yes, of course." Pearl rose and went to the antique sideboard. She brought out a stack of neat folders stamped with a replica of the King's Rest's sign—a canopied bed with a crown and scepter in the center. She handed them around to the board members and came back to sit beside her mother.

"Now, if you will look at the first page, please," said Angelique.

The board dutifully flipped open their folders. Caite frowned at what she saw. Her forehead didn't shift at all.

"The first is the letter of appreciation from Lord and

Lady Jordan-Arrow for our work on their youngest daughter's wedding," said Angelique. "The second page is the thank-you for coordinating the New Year's banquet for the Greater Cornwall and Devon Historical Society, also on short notice. It was only a week that time, I believe, Pearl?"

"Just barely a week," Pearl confirmed. "Two hundred guests and a plated dinner."

Caite stared at the papers like they might bite.

"And I'm sure some of you know that we have been catering the annual Trevena Fete for the past three years," Angelique went on pleasantly. "Did you have any other questions about our event planning experience, Caite?"

"Well." Caite folded her hands on top of the copies of Angelique's letters. "I'm simply surprised to find a decent caterer available on short notice. I'm sure you understand." Her smile was thin and purely cosmetic. "But there's still a question of the quality of Ms. Reed's . . ."

"Have you tried one of these, Caite?" Tasha Boyd held up one of the Black Forest minis. "Divine!"

Caite's plate was empty and devoid of crumbs. She hadn't touched a thing.

"Normally, I'm opposed to any rush decision." Ned blotted his mouth with his napkin. "But these are extraordinary circumstances. "Perhaps we should vote?"

"*Perhaps*," said Caite acidly. "We should not be pinning too much on a premade afternoon tea. *Perhaps* we should get a serious proposal and a cost breakdown first. This may be an emergency, but the reputation of our festival is still at stake." She stared right down the table. "Don't you agree, Marcie?"

Marcie flushed pink. Everyone else was looking at their plates.

Emma looked to Pearl and Angelique. They looked back. Emma nodded.

"Of course you would want to review a menu," said Angelique. "And we would be happy to provide an opportunity for you and the board to do so. When would you be available?"

"Caite," said Marcie. "We don't have time . . ."

"Because of your mismanagement, Marcie. A fact I assure you the rest of the board is profoundly aware of."

"There really is no need for all this," murmured Ned.

Caite arched one perfectly shaped brow. "Isn't there?"

"No," said Marcie. "I told you—"

"But that's just it, Marcie. You haven't told us anything."

Marcie's cheeks reddened. She was obviously not somebody who enjoyed participating in any kind of scene, especially not in front of strangers. Emma had the feeling that Caite Hope-Johnston knew that and was using it.

Emma could tell from the set of her jaw that Angelique felt the same way.

*And we've had* quite *enough, thank you.*

"How soon would the board be available for a tasting?" Emma snagged a notepad and pen for herself.

"I'm sure we could be available Friday," said Marcie. "But I would never expect . . ."

Friday. Today was Wednesday. "Friday will be just fine. Four o'clock?"

"I can be here then," began Tasha. "But—"

"Oh no," said Caite smoothly. "We should have the tasting up at Truscott Grange. After all, that is where the festival and the masquerade ball will be held. We have to make sure the food can be properly presented on the premises."

"That's really not necessary, Caite," said Marcie.

"But I *insist*," said Caite. "We need to be sure that your new partners can work under the specific conditions presented by the grange." She paused. "May I remind you that the board still authorizes the funding? And we have not yet approved anything." She glowered at the remaining members of the board. The Boyds looked at each other and sighed. Ned took another cucumber sandwich.

"At the grange will be just fine," said Emma calmly. "What is it you'll be needing from us, should we be selected for the festival?"

"The luncheon for the speakers, the snacks for the speakers' break room and the sweet and savory canapés for the fancy dress," Marcie told them, and Emma heard the unspoken thank-you in her voice.

"All right," said Emma. "If you could just email us with the numbers for each, we'll give you a menu and cost estimates. If those meet with the board's approval, we'll have a tasting on Friday to finalize the choices. Four o'clock would . . ."

"Eleven," counted Caite. "This is an *extremely* busy time for the board, as I'm sure you understand."

"That will be fine," replied Emma.

"We can finalize the details at that time," said Angelique.

Caite's little frozen smile said *we'll see.* "Now, if you will excuse us? We have other business we should be discussing."

Angelique and Pearl gathered notepads and folders. So did Emma, but more slowly. When the others were heading for the door, she deliberately went around the table and reached her hand out.

"I trust we'll be able to show you that the board has made the right decision in contacting us."

Caite's hands stayed on the table, and she turned her big blue eyes up toward Emma,

"I will be perfectly honest with you, Miss Reed, I expect the entire business to be a spectacular failure." She smiled and leaned close to whisper. "And I'm very much looking forward to it."

# 4

.........

EMMA, ANGELIQUE AND PEARL WERE BARELY HALFWAY across the great room, when Marcie caught up with them.

"I do apologize for Caite," she said. "She's just so anxious for everything to go right. This has all been very upsetting."

She said it smoothly, like she was used to apologizing for other people. She clearly didn't like it, but she did it, because somebody had to.

Emma found herself wondering about Marcie, and about Caite. How did they get to this point? There was clearly an ongoing war between them, of the particularly polite drawing room sort. What had happened? It had apparently involved some cash going missing. But how . . . ?

Usually, when Emma got thoughts like this, she admonished herself for too much curiosity. Her need to know things that were not necessarily her business had been getting her into trouble since she was a little girl. This time, however, she had a perfectly legitimate interest in the answers.

"That's quite all right, Marcie," Angelique was saying. "We understand this is a difficult time."

"Thanks," said Marcie. "I wish I didn't have to lay our

problems on you, but at this point we have very little choice. Canceling the festival . . . well, it would just be a disaster, especially this year."

"Why this year?" asked Pearl before Emma could.

Marcie's cheeks reddened. "Sorry, slip of the tongue. Any year would be bad, but there's some personal things going on as well, and well . . . we'll see you Friday. I know you'll put everybody's doubts to rest for good and all. Thanks again." She hurried back into the parlor.

"Right," said Angelique as soon as the door closed. "My office, I think."

"Right behind you," said Emma.

At least she would be as soon as she'd had a quick look round the great room to make sure everything was still going smoothly. The last few guests were lingering over their half-empty cups, and Becca and Bella clearly had everything in hand.

With Oliver's able assistance, of course.

"Emma!" He bounded up to her. "I tried to get in but you forgot and shut the door! I was worried! Are you okay?"

"Yes, yes, good boy." She bent down to give him a good patting and also so she could answer him more easily without being overheard. There were strategies to talking to your talking dog in public. "It was just one of those boring human things where everybody sits around talking."

"Oh, that's all right, then." He wagged at her. "Where are we going now?"

"Office."

"More talking?" Oliver drooped with his entire body.

"Just a little." She straightened up. "You can come this time if you want."

Oliver shook himself, and he did follow along.

They didn't get very far, though. The door from the car park opened and a young, suntanned woman in running shorts and a Manchester United football jersey strode in.

"Can I help you?" Emma asked, automatically falling into hostess mode. The girl, however, was a little distracted.

"A corgi!" she exclaimed, and immediately crouched

down and held her hands out. Oliver darted forward, sniffing and licking, and, of course, wagging his entire bum.

"Flowers and green," he reported. "Very healthy, takes lots of walks, and peanut butter and dust and there's a dog! A mutt, I think, and what's that? That's new . . ." Oliver drove his wet nose into the center of her palm.

"Oh, he's a darling!" cried the young woman. "Is he yours?"

Emma laughed. "He is, and his name is Oliver."

"Hello, Oliver! Who is a very good boy, then?"

"All corgis are good boys," Oliver answered. He also licked her chin. "Except the girls."

"Okay, Oliver, enough." Emma pulled him back gently but firmly. "Were you coming in for tea?" she asked.

"Me? Oh, no. Sorry. I'm looking for Pearl. Is she . . ."

Pearl must have heard something, because she came up the corridor just as the girl was straightening up.

"Daphne!" Pearl shouted. "What are you doing here? They're still in there!"

"I know, I know, no worries."

"What if they catch on that you tipped us off . . ."

"They won't," she said with careless confidence. "We were going running this afternoon, remember? I'm just here to pick you up."

Daphne Cochrane was tall, with curling, dark hair that was pulled back in a bright pink scrunchie. But Emma could see the strong resemblance to her aunt in her dramatic dark eyes and her snub nose. The shorts and football jersey emphasized her broad, athletic build. Her trainers were new and top-drawer.

Pearl stared at her friend, sorting out what she'd just said. "Oh, yeah. Right. Running. I remember now."

"Nothing to see here, then, is there?" said Daphne easily. "Hullo, Mrs. Delgado!"

Angelique, of course, had come to see what was keeping Emma and Pearl.

"Good to see you, Daphne," said Angelique as they

shook hands. She also gave Pearl the tiniest bit of a side-eye. "How is university treating you?"

"Oh, you know me, always on the edge of disaster, at least according to Mum. But we're taking the team all the way to the finals this year."

"Rugby?" asked Emma.

"Football," said Daphne.

"Daphne's the best goalkeeper we've had in years," announced Pearl. "Daph, this is Emma Reed. She's the genius behind Reed's Tea and Cakes. And you've already met Oliver and . . ."

But Daphne was looking over Emma's shoulder. "Oh, sugar."

Emma knew what she was going to see before she even turned her head. The private parlor door had just opened and the board was filing out. Despite her previous nonchalance, Daphne's breezy air dampened considerably when she saw her aunt.

"Daphne," said Marcie, "I didn't know you were here. Everything all right?"

"Oh, um, yeah, course. I didn't even see your car out there. Hullo, everybody." Daphne nodded at the board. "Just came down to get Pearl. We were planning on a run this afternoon."

"Oh."

"Well, Marcie." Caite's thin smile didn't shift a single millimeter. "Isn't this your niece? I had no idea she and Pearl knew each other."

Daphne returned her own thin, steely smile. "Oh, wow, Caite. Love the new hair color. Looks great on you. On the beach in ten, Pearl, yeah?" she added.

"Erm. Right. Just as soon as I get my gear. Pearl pointed back toward the office.

"Great. See you back at the house, Aunt Marcie! Tell Mum I'll be home for tea!" Daphne whisked out the door. She was, Emma assumed, hoping to get out of there before anything looked too fishy.

But it was too late. Even the Boyds were not looking particularly happy.

"I do so love seeing a close-knit family," said Caite. "It's inspiring."

Marcie sighed. "And I'm sure you'll be letting us know all about it, Caite, but not in front of the whole village, all right? Pearl, Angelique, Emma, thank you for a lovely tea. I'll get you those numbers. We look forward to your proposal."

The board filed out with more backward glances than Emma was comfortable with. She was also suddenly keenly aware of the half-dozen guests still picking at the remains of scones and biscuits, not to mention Becca and Bella standing behind the bar, pretending to be putting away the teacups.

Angelique sighed and gave her daughter a sardonic look. Pearl shrugged and tried to assume an innocent expression. It didn't work. Angelique crooked her finger, and Emma, Pearl and Oliver followed single file into her office.

The office was crowded but neat as a pin. The old-fashioned partners desk that Angelique and Pearl shared took up most of the room. There was also a line of wooden filing cabinets. The radio-receiver set she used to keep in touch with her husband, Daniel, when he was out on the boat occupied the corner by a window that overlooked the B&B's lovely gardens.

"Well." Angelique dropped into the chair on her side of the desk and slapped her folder and notepad down in front of her. "That was . . . interesting."

"Do you have any idea what the story between Caite and Marcie is?" Emma pulled up the smaller guest chair. Oliver immediately assumed one of his favorite positions, sprawled on the floor, with his chin on her toes.

Angelique shook her head. "Village politics, mostly."

"The Hyphenated Caite's new money," said Pearl, settling into her own chair. "Married rich a couple of times. Buried the first, divorced the next. She thinks that the Cochranes look down on her, because they're the old landed gentry. At least, that's what Daphne says."

Emma shook her head. She'd seen this sort of thing more than once during her career in finance. It seemed ludicrous for anybody to care how long a family had been rich, but there it was. Whether a family's money was classed as "old" or "new" could make a difference in some circles. It could also breed all kinds of resentment.

"Never mind the pedigree of the money for now," said Angelique. "There's a more important question we need answered before we go any further." She typed something into her desktop computer, then picked up her mobile and entered a number.

"Emma?" Oliver nosed her shoe tops. "Is the talking almost over?"

Emma rubbed Oliver's ears.

"Hullo, Holly?" Angelique said into her phone. "It's Angelique at the King's Rest. Yeah . . . Good, yeah. Listen, you won't believe this, but I've just had the board of the du Maurier Literary Society in my parlor. They're saying they need a new caterer for the festival this year, and I just wondered . . . yeah? I see . . . yes, yes . . ."

Emma picked Oliver up and held him on her lap. Obligingly, he snuggled up close. Pearl reached out and rubbed his chin.

"All right," said Angelique. "Thanks for taking the time, Holly . . . Yes, yes . . . Ta. You too." She hung up.

"Was that Holly Weber? What did she say?" asked Pearl immediately.

Angelique shook her head. "That Weber's Catering walked out on the festival because they were having trouble getting paid. She said the initial deposit payment had failed to clear, and then so did the second one, and when that happened, Marcie apparently lost her temper and said the trouble must be on Weber's end."

Pearl frowned. "That doesn't sound like Marcie."

"Holly said that too," said Angelique.

"But she didn't say anything about a problem on their end?" asked Emma.

Angelique shook her head. "She said she didn't want to

tell me what to do, but she really strongly hinted that maybe we didn't want to get involved this year."

"This year?" Pearl repeated. "Why'd she say that? Is something different this year?"

"That I don't know," said Angelique. "And she wouldn't tell me. But if there were chronic problems with the festival, we would have heard well before this."

"You would think that," agreed Pearl. "So whatever this is, it's safe to assume it's recent. The festival's been going on for years, though. Why would it blow up this year?" She drummed her fingers on the desktop.

"Maybe we're overthinking it?" suggested Angelique but not very hopefully. "Maybe it really was some kind of a mistake."

Emma considered this, but then she shook her head. "If it had only happened once, I'd say maybe. Deposits can take time to clear, even with online banking. But twice? That's either negligence or—"

"Or somebody's been dipping in the funds," Angelique finished for her.

"So, you're saying you don't want the job?" Pearl sounded resigned. Emma was ready to agree. Catering the du Maurier festival would be great publicity for her tea shop and the King's Rest, but she did not like this business with money going missing. She especially did not like it with the board being so evidently unwilling to address the problem, whatever it was.

No one wanted to turn down a plum job, but getting tangled up in money troubles and client rivalries was always a bad idea.

*Been there, done that—the T-shirt fell apart in the wash.*

But to Emma's surprise, Angelique swiveled her chair so they faced each other squarely. "Would you really be able to get a tasting menu together by Friday?"

"Emma can do anything!" yipped Oliver.

Emma patted his back. "I . . . I'm not sure," she confessed. "I'd probably have to park myself in the kitchen, for say, the next forty-eight hours."

"Done," said Angelique. "How about the cost estimates?"

"That should be easy once I have a sample menu. Say, late tomorrow?"

"Ma?" said Pearl. "What's going on?"

When Angelique answered, her voice was steely. "There's something else at stake here besides the festival. Our reputation." She paused to make sure she had Emma and Pearl's attention. She did. Even Oliver had sat up on his haunches and cocked his ears toward her. "The exposure and prestige will be a wonderful boost for our catering business, and the tea shop, but I've dealt with clients like this before. If we do not give the board a good presentation, the Hyphenated Caite is just the sort to start a whispering campaign against the King's Rest and Reed's Cakes. I am not going to let that happen. We are going to put on the best show that board has ever seen. Then, if they can't meet our terms, *we* will be the ones to turn *them* down."

# 5

·········

RELUCTANTLY, EMMA CALLED BRIAN TO POSTPONE THE AP-
pointment to come look at cars.

"But I washed my best shirt and all!" he protested.

"It's not you," she said. "It's me." Briefly, or at least as
briefly as she could, Emma explained about the du Maurier
festival and what she was rapidly coming to think of as the
audition.

"Oh, Hyphenated Caite's on the case, then?" he said.
"Woman's a menace."

"You don't say?"

"I do, and so would just about anybody else. It's a shame
too. Her family's old Trevena, like mine, and she used to be
a sweet kid."

"Old Trevena but new money?"

"Not the best combination for a comfortable village
life," he said. "We tend to dislike abrupt changes."

"Like short of a couple of decades or so?" suggested
Emma blandly.

"There now, you're beginning to get the picture," answered Brian, equally bland.

"What happened to her, do you think? I mean, to make
her change?"

Brian considered. "Disappointments, mostly," he said. "Then trying too hard to make up for them. Her dad died when she was really young too, so that didn't make anything better. So, listen, do you need any help for this thing on Friday? I'm champion at hauling bins. Or if you need a ride up to the grange . . . ?"

"As much as I hate to say it, we're covered. Genny Knowles is coming along to help, so we'll be taking her van."

"Oh," said Brian, and this time, it sounded less like joking and more like genuine disappointment. Emma's stomach did that little fluttery thing. Again.

*Stop it,* Emma ordered her stomach. Her stomach didn't listen.

"Well," said Brian, "you'll call and let me know how it went, yeah? I'll be crossing my fingers for you. Very hard to hold a spanner that way, but I'll manage."

Emma laughed and agreed she would call, and they settled on Monday, which was her next day off, for her to come look at cars. Truth be told, she would have loved to talk more, but she was already starting to feel the time slipping by. She had her misgivings about actually taking this job, but she couldn't argue with Angelique's reasoning.

It was time to get to work.

IT WAS STILL TIME WHEN THE OLD CARRIAGE CLOCK IN THE great room struck nine. A full day later.

"We've got it!" Emma's shout rang around the otherwise empty kitchen. She brandished her spoon in the air. The lime and ginger cream was delicious. "Perfection!" she shouted.

For once, Oliver did not answer. He'd heard it all before.

Outside, it was pouring. Emma had her music playing, and was humming along to Belle and Sebastian. It had been a busy day, not to mention a fraught one. She should have been exhausted, but instead she felt energized. Good cream tended to have that effect on her.

Right after the tea with the festival board, Emma had in fact parked herself in the kitchen with her notebooks, her suppliers' lists and her copy of du Maurier's *Rebecca*. From three to five, she'd scribbled notes. By four o'clock, the board, as promised, had emailed the expected numbers for the luncheon and the masquerade. Emma allowed herself a full five minutes to wonder what on earth she'd gotten into. From five o'clock onward, she'd baked, and sautéed, and simmered, zested, pounded, rolled, cut and whipped.

Around seven, Genny Knowles had come by with her oldest son, Josh, to take over the usual prep work for the tea shop. Genny had been Emma's first friend in Trevena. Usually, this time of night found her closing up her chip shop, the Towne Fryer, which she owned and ran with her husband, Martin. But because of the tasting for the board, Genny had agreed to come down with Becca and help run the takeaway counter.

While the mother-son duo worked on the cakes and buns on Emma's daily list, Genny also helped Emma taste and dissect her festival menu. Too much cinnamon. Not enough zest. Maybe some toasted walnuts? Or would hazelnuts be better? A sprinkle of salt just at the end maybe? Definitely the garlic-chive compound butter for the seafood salad.

By the time Pearl and Angelique came in to say good night, Emma had pushed her sample menu with cost estimates into their hands and gone on creaming butter and sugar.

At around eleven, however, Genny had put her foot down and said Emma had to get some sleep or she would be "no good to anybody for anything." Emma wanted to argue, but Oliver was already bonking her calves with his nose, trying to herd her toward the door.

"Bed for you," he said. "Walks in the morning. This way, Emma."

"You're ganging up on me," she muttered, but she didn't resist. Much.

Back home, Emma dutifully showered and put on her pajamas and lay in bed, with Oliver snuggling up beside her. But even the rain on the cottage roof failed to lull her to sleep. Her head was too full of questions of flavors and textures and all the problems of execution. If she got too elaborate in her efforts to impress the board, it would all collapse into chaos on the day and . . .

And Oliver was snoring and the rain was clattering against the slates and at some point Emma slid into an uneasy dream that involved sinking slowly into a froth of whipped egg whites.

At six a.m. Thursday morning, Emma was back at her station with a fresh to-do list and a mug of industrial-strength tea. Genny, thankfully, brought her Irish setter, Fergus, along with her, so Oliver had a friend and was getting (a little) less underfoot.

At ten a.m., Pearl burst into the kitchen. "Emma! The board's approved the cost and the menu plan!"

Emma cheered and Genny cheered and Oliver barked and zoomed back and forth. Then, Emma got back down to sifting flour into the sponge mixture. Now they just had to get through the tasting.

Josh ran the takeaway counter that day like a champ, which was not surprising since he'd grown up in the family chip shop. By the time they closed up for the day, Emma was ready to consider hiring the cheerful teenager.

But she was not ready to leave. The lime cream angel cake still wasn't right.

"Just a little more tweaking," she said, when Genny left.

"Just one more batch," she said when Angelique and Pearl left.

"Almost there, Oliver, good boy," she said around ten o'clock.

Now it was midnight. Oliver was sprawled out on his back beside his kibble bowl, snoring. Emma had a row of delicate angel cake slices in front of her, each one filled with lime and passion fruit curd and topped with a lime cream flavored with ginger syrup. As a final touch, she topped it with a sprinkle of salt and sugar crystal mix.

Now, they were all lined up neatly next to the rows of modernized Victoria sponge slices. Emma took up a fork and plunged it into the nearest slice of angel cake. Crossing the fingers on her free hand, she tasted. The cake melted slowly on her tongue, sweet and tangy and with just the final lingering sensation of heat from the ginger.

"I'm a genius!" she shouted.

"What!" Oliver barked and rolled up onto his feet. "What! Where! What!"

Emma laughed.

"What? What?" Oliver shook his ears. "What?"

"Oh, I'm sorry, Oliver." She rubbed his back and neck. "I didn't mean to wake you. I was just excited."

"Something tastes good?" He sniffed at her hands. "Lime and ginger and butter and more lime and tea. You drink too much tea. You need to get more sleep."

"I know, I know, and we're going home just as soon as the place is cleaned up. I promise."

"You promised before it got dark," he whined.

"Want to try some cake?" She put a square of plain angel cake in his bowl.

Oliver dipped his nose and gave her a look that said distinctly that he knew she was distracting him, and that he did not approve at all. He also trotted over to his bowl and started munching on the cake.

Emma made some final notes and ticked off the last item on her to-do list. They could print off copies of the menu plan tomorrow before the meeting. Bella would be on hand to serve the board, while Becca stayed behind and helped Josh run the takeaway counter. Angelique and Pearl would be at the table, and she'd be in the kitchen, handling the plating and any last-minute details. She tapped her pencil.

"Maybe . . . Ow!" She jumped. Oliver bonked her shin.

"Time to go, Emma. No more maybes."

"Yes, yes, okay. But I need to clean up." She grabbed the nearest mixing bowl and headed for the dishwasher.

That was when a sharp, fast and entirely unexpected knock shot through the kitchen.

# 6

"GAH!" SHOUTED EMMA, WHICH REALLY WAS A PERFECTLY logical response. The metal bowl flew out of her hands and clattered to the floor.

Oliver zoomed to the kitchen door and started barking. "Here! Here! Somebody's here!"

"Yes, Oliver, I hear it too," Emma wheezed. She also picked up the bowl she'd dropped and set it on the counter.

"Sorry, Emma." Oliver dipped his muzzle. "Instincts."

Emma took a deep breath and tried to will her heartbeat to slow down. She also went and looked out the window.

It was still raining like it had no intention of stopping anytime this decade. Emma snapped the outside light on and peered through the window.

Marcie Cochrane, slightly bedraggled, looked hopefully back at her.

"What in the world!" Emma fumbled with the lock and threw open the door. "Marcie! Come in out of the wet! What's going on?"

Oliver barked helpfully to reinforce the invitation and the question.

Marcie stepped inside, blinking a bit in the light. Water sluiced off the brim of her shapeless black rain hat and dripped from the hem of her coat.

"Oh! I'm sorry," she said, noticing the water puddling on the kitchen tiles. "I should . . ."

"No, don't worry about it," said Emma quickly. "Here, hang up your stuff." Emma pointed her toward the row of hooks by the door.

Oliver snuffled around Marcie's Wellingtons. "Mud, mud, rain and a dog!" he mumbled. "A mutt, I think. Yes! The same one the running lady knows. And petrol, because she's been in the car, of course, and . . ."

"What brings you out at this time of night?" Emma asked. She also checked the water level in the electric tea-kettle and opened the tin of second flush Darjeeling she'd purloined from the stockroom.

"I'm sorry to be here so ridiculously late, I should have called first, but, well, I was passing, and I saw the light on and I thought maybe Angelique was still here . . ."

"Oh, no, just me," Emma told her. "Everybody else has gone home for the night. Look, let me get you a cuppa. You're practically blue!"

"I don't want to be any trouble," said Marcie, plainly on reflex. But she also shucked off her coat and hat. Water sluiced off the brim as she hung it up.

"It's no trouble. Kettle's already hot." Emma added an extra spoonful of tea leaves to the Brown Betty pot and poured the water in.

Marcie set her handbag on the steel counter and climbed up on the kitchen stool. She looked exhausted. She didn't have her headband on, and the rain had plastered straggling locks against her cheeks and forehead. She shoved them back, making her dangling gold earrings swing and glitter in the bright kitchen light.

Emma also noticed how Marcie's eyes were all puffy and accented by dark rings. It looked like she hadn't been getting much sleep either.

*And possibly not enough to eat.* Marcie was staring openly at the rows of cake slices.

"Is this for the tasting?"

"Yes. Would you like to try? I don't want to prejudice the jury, but I've been experimenting and I'd love an opinion." Before Marcie could object, Emma picked up the spatula. "Angel cake or Victoria sponge?"

"They both look marvelous."

"Thanks." Emma used the spatula to set the Victoria slice on a plate. She also poured a cup of tea. "Wouldn't be a proper British gathering without Victoria sponge, yeah? I've added cardamom and lemon to the cake, and mixed some black pepper and balsamic with the strawberry coulis. No, pick it right up. We need to see if it's going to hold together or splosh all over the place."

Marcie picked up the bit of cake and ate it in two bites. Emma held her breath. Oliver nosed around Marcie's stool in case of crumbs.

"Mmm . . ." groaned Marcie. "Oh, my, that's delicious! You're a marvel!"

Emma was able to breathe again. "Thank you. Obviously, we don't have the staff to do canapés for a hundred, but we can do the slices. I was thinking if we went with a high tea sort of theme, we could have carts and tables—we could rotate the selection throughout the night, starting with the savories and going for the sweets. It would help increase the party circulation, and the guests could sample as they mingled and . . . Are you all right?"

Marcie was blinking at the trays, her face and jaw tight. *She wants to cry.*

She didn't, though. She just pressed the edge of her hand under her nose, as if to hold off a sneeze. "Yes. Yes. I'm fine. That sounds lovely. I—I so very much wanted this to be perfect, but so much has gone wrong."

Emma felt her curiosity trying to burn through all her politeness. She was dying to ask Marcie about the catering deposits, and about why this year was different for the festival, and what she was doing out so late on such a foul night. But the woman was so plainly looking for distraction and comfort. Emma felt rotten for wanting to keep the conversation on the festival and its problems.

"Well, any long-running event can have an off year," she said to Marcie. "It'll be better next time."

"Yes. I'm sure you're right." Marcie shook herself and forced some brightness into her voice. "So, Emma, are you a du Maurier fan?"

"I love du Maurier," she said.

"I knew it!" Marcie grinned at Emma over her mug. "You can always spot another one. Which books are your favorites?"

"Well, *Rebecca*, of course, and I have a real soft spot for *Jamaica Inn* and *My Cousin Rachel*. What about you?" she asked curiously. "How'd you start reading du Maurier?"

Marcie smiled. "Well, if you live in Cornwall, you can't really avoid her, can you? To tell you the truth, for the longest time, I thought of her as just someone my nan read. But then, I don't know, I was home from uni, and . . . I think I'd had a fight with one of my brothers. I've got three, you know. We've always fought like cats and dogs." Oliver barked. "No offense." Marcie leaned down and rubbed his chin.

"Cats start things," said Oliver.

"He accepts your apology," Emma said.

Marcie smiled in the amused and tolerant way people did when Emma told them what her dog was saying.

"Anyway." Marcie sighed. "I suppose I must have been bored, and sad and . . . well, growing up can be hard, can't it? I picked up *Rebecca* and I was . . . enchanted. Transported. I really identified with the narrator. I felt like here was somebody who really understood what it was like to be alone and to want something for themselves, even if everybody said they couldn't have it."

Emma nodded. It was a powerful pull.

"It's strange, though." Marcie frowned at the remains of her tea. "The older I got, the more I started sympathizing with Mrs. Danvers. Oh, not because she tries to drive the narrator out, but can you imagine what it must have been like being her?"

"Well, she didn't have it easy, that's for sure, but she did try to kill the narrator."

"Yes, well, she was desperate, wasn't she?" Marcie wrapped both hands around her mug. Her voice shook. "And heartbroken. And who wouldn't be? The person she loved, for better or worse, had been murdered. And what was left for her after Rebecca was gone? She was going to spend the rest of her life taking care of a house that would never really be her home. Not really." She shook her head and took another swallow of tea. "Sorry," she gasped. "That's just me going on. Anyway. As you can see. I'm a bit of a—what do they call it?—fangirl." Marcie's hands tightened around her mug of tea. "You'll make this work, won't you? The festival and everything? It has to be perfect."

"We'll certainly do our best."

"Promise me."

"Yes, of course. Marcie . . ." Emma hesitated. "Is there anything special you're worried about? It would be a big help if we knew what we have to look out for."

"No, no, nothing like that. Really. But I am glad you mentioned looking out for things." She reached into her bag and pulled out an envelope. "Will you make sure Angelique gets this?" When she saw Emma's inquiring look she added, "It's the deposit check. From my personal account."

"The deposit?" said Emma. "But the board hasn't even given us the contract yet."

"Oh, they will." Marcie tried to sound nonchalant. It did not go well. "With all that's happened, I just wanted . . . I wanted Angelique, and you, of course, to be certain that you would get paid."

Emma stared at the envelope on the counter. A wave of concern prickled down her spine. She was an ex-banker from a family of accountants. She liked order, and paperwork, preferably signed and with the copies all neatly filed away. She did not like checks passed hand to hand after dark. Especially when some other checks had already bounced.

"Thanks for the thought, Marcie," she said. "But I know Angelique would prefer a check from the society's account. Otherwise, it will complicate her own bookkeeping, yeah?"

"Oh," Marcie murmured. "I hadn't stopped to think . . . Well, yes, of course you're right."

She stuffed the envelope back in her bag. Emma couldn't miss the way her hand shook.

"Well, thank you so much for the tea and cake." Marcie zipped her bag shut. "I should be getting home."

"Are you sure?" Emma said. "It's still raining hammer and tongs out there."

"Oh, never you fear. I'll make it all right." Marcie bundled herself into her mac and pulled her hat down over her disarranged hair.

"Well, see you tomorrow, then."

"See you! Oh, and when you get to the house, you come round the back, all right? I'll make sure the kitchen door is open for you."

"Good night, then."

Marcie smiled, took a deep breath, squared her shoulders and made a great show of marching boldly out into the rain. Emma stood at the closed door, watching through the window while the other woman climbed into the black BMW.

"What's wrong, Emma?" Oliver whined.

"I don't know, corgi me lad. I really don't know."

Outside, Marcie Cochrane drove away into the dark.

ONE OF THE THINGS EMMA HAD LEARNED OVER THE COURSE of the past year was that a life of tea and cakes was not all beer and skittles. Especially when it came to getting up in the morning.

In Emma's new normal, she and Oliver were up at five. They were dressed and/or brushed and heading down to the King's Rest by six. Breakfast and tea—lots of tea—would happen while working up the day's first batches of scones and biscuits, and getting the buns that had (hopefully) proved overnight into the oven.

This morning, though, Emma not only had to get herself washed and brushed and decent, she had to pack her suit bag, find her portfolio with the menus she'd printed out last night and her good ballet flats, all while arguing with a discontented corgi.

"No, Oliver."

"But, Emma . . . !" Oliver trotted behind her as she crossed the hall from the bathroom to the bedroom and then hurried downstairs to the parlor.

Normally, Nancarrow cottage was Emma's haven of quiet and comfort. Since she'd moved in last summer, she'd thrown herself into refurnishing and repairing the former holiday cottage, doing everything she could to turn it into the cozy home of her dreams. The tacky seventies era furnishings had been replaced with lovely Arts and Crafts–style chairs and tables, not to mention a Victorian era chaise lounge. After some serious price-sharing negotiation with her landlords, the avocado-green kitchen had been fully updated. Now, the cottage and Emma were both living their very best lives.

This was hard to remember just now as she was running around trying to find the extra pencils, and the last page of notes she'd made while leafing through *Rebecca*—

"You might need help." Oliver poked his nose into her calf. "I can help! You know I can!"

—while at the same time Oliver was making it perfectly clear that he was not going to take this business of her going off on her own for a few hours lying down.

"Look, Oliver"—Emma crouched down and rubbed his chin—"this is going to be one of those boring human things with everybody sitting around and talking."

"But it's a new place!" he whined. "There might be something you need me to find out for you. Or . . ."

Emma sighed. Ever since they had helped solve Victoria Roberts's murder, Oliver had become very much enamored of the idea of himself as canine sleuth extraordinaire.

"I know you're disappointed, but that's the way it's got to be." She kissed him on the nose and straightened up. "Don't worry. You'll be fine. Josh and Becca are both going to be at the shop today, so you won't have to be alone. And as soon as I'm done at the grange, I'm taking this afternoon off. We'll have a walk and we'll nap and we'll grab some sandwiches at the co-op and have dinner on the beach."

"But, Emma . . . !"

There wasn't time for another argument. Emma straightened up. "Look at it this way: you'll be keeping an eye on the King's Rest for me. You don't want that fox thinking he can just get into the garden anytime he wants, right?" This was something of a low blow. Oliver's ongoing feud with the local town fox was a very serious matter, by corgi standards.

"Oh, I suppose," mumbled Oliver. "He's been back, you know. I can tell. He likes to sneak in around the side where they keep the wheelie bins . . ."

Emma smiled and let the corgi chatter flow over her. She also found the last page of notes inside her portfolio, right where she'd left it. She tucked in the extra pencils, and grabbed her handbag, and suit bag, and her umbrella, because it was probably not done raining out there yet.

"Here we go, Oliver," she said. "If we can pull this off, we can do anything."

"You can already do anything," said Oliver staunchly. "Except about the fox."

Emma laughed. "That's why I have you, corgi me lad."

TODAY, OLIVER REALIZED, WAS GOING TO BE A CHAL-lenge. That was okay. Corgis were noble warrior dogs. His ancestors had sailed with the Vikings and his brother corgis guarded the queen wherever she went. A corgi never turned a challenge down.

The question was, how could he convince Emma that she should not go to this new place alone? Something strange was going on with the Rain Lady—What was her human name? Oliver sneezed and shook his ears. *Oh! Marcie!*

Something strange was going on with Marcie, and Oliver didn't like it.

Humans tended to be at certain places at certain times—home, shop, village, beach. New route, and new patterns, well, of course they happened. Everybody strayed sometimes. But there was something about her turning up so suddenly in the rain and the dark that was not right. It made Oliver restless.

It was just getting light outside. Oliver trotted beside Emma as they headed down the hill through the fresh, chilly morning into Trevena. The rain had washed the walks and the cobblestones almost clean of all the smells except for water and mud. He could barely even pick up the traces of the night animals that roamed the streets while the humans slept. A few humans had been out already, and Rosco the Jack Russell terrier had been here, and the annoying cat called Cream Tangerine, but not for long. Cats were fussy about wet feet.

But they weren't the only ones who had been here.

"Genny's ahead of us," Oliver told Emma. "And Josh . . . and Fergus!" Fergus was the big, easygoing Irish setter who lived with the Knowleses.

"There, see?" said Emma around yet another huge yawn. "You'll have plenty of company."

Oliver sneezed, and kept his nose to his cobbles. He didn't need company. He needed to find a way to convince Emma to take him with her.

They always went in the kitchen door first thing in the morning. As soon as Emma pulled the door open, a rush of wonderful smells engulfed Oliver—butter and cheese, tomato, tea, coffee and bacon. Especially bacon. There was a crowd of his favorite people too—Angelique and Pearl, of course. *And Genny the Fish Lady!* He charged in, barking and sniffing and wagging and listening to everybody laugh, until Emma called him back and told him to calm down.

"My goodness, girl!" exclaimed Angelique to Emma. Angelique was working at the stove, frying up a most delicious-smelling mix of bacon, onion and peppers. "How late were you here last night?"

"I think it had turned into this morning. But that's okay. I'll be fine." Emma climbed on the stool, rested her elbows on the counter and leaned her forehead on her arms. "After a gallon of coffee."

"You sure?" said Pearl skeptically. She put a big mug of coffee down in front of Emma. "You are not going to be helping the cause by mixing up the sugar and the salt."

"That's why we label the bins," mumbled Emma. "And I'll be fine."

"Well, we'll be right there in case you're not," said Genny. "Come on, let's get loaded up. If I know Emma's menus we're going to need every minute to get things done."

Oliver barked. Emma lifted her head and also drank the coffee. "Are you saying I overplan?"

"It's possible you might be something of a type A personality, yes," said Genny. She was one of their best friends. Her son Josh was a fine, young human, and Fergus was an excellent and friendly dog.

*And around here somewhere* . . . Oliver was sure he caught the distinctive scent of Irish setter in the layers surrounding the kitchen. It was a little muddled this morning. Usually, Genny smelled like fish and hot oil. This morning, she smelled like hot oil and butter and vanilla and spices from all the baking.

The kitchen was warm enough that Oliver was already starting to pant. Maybe it would be better if he went outdoors.

*No. I need to stay with Emma.*

"I'll have you know I am perfectly realistic when it comes to my schedules," Emma was saying.

Pearl and Angelique looked at each other. Angelique patted her hand. "If you say so, dear. Do you have your checklist?"

"How did . . ."

"You always have a checklist, Emma." Angelique flipped open Emma's portfolio. "Ah. Here it is."

"Numbered the bins too," Genny reported, looking at the stack of tubs on the counter nearest the door. "Very handy."

Emma sniffed, and drank more coffee. "When we have the entire board of the literary society at our feet, you will no longer mock my organizational skills."

The door from the great room swung open, bringing with it the scents of a young male human.

Oliver barked and zoomed over to greet him.

"You all right in here, Mum?" asked Josh. "Only I was going to open the counter . . . Hello, Oliver! Good boy!" Josh always smelled of the out-of-doors and fish and seawater and sunshine and dirt. He laughed when Oliver bounced. He also snatched a bit of bacon out of the pan and held it up for Oliver to snap at.

"Hey!" shouted Angelique. But she was already too late. *An excellent human.*

"And people think I'm the one who spoils Fergus," grumbled Genny.

"You can get yourself out of my kitchen, young man." Angelique waved her spatula at him. "Go do something useful."

Josh, who could be very obedient for a young human, hurried out, but he also paused to kiss Angelique on her temple. "You know you love me!"

She swiped the spatula toward him, but not seriously. Josh pushed open the door again. Oliver zoomed out ahead of him. It was important to check the great room and make sure nothing was wrong there.

Not only was nothing wrong, Fergus was lounging in front of Emma's cake counter.

"Oliver!" The big dog heaved himself to his feet.

"Fergus!" Oliver bounced over to greet the Irish setter. He was slow, like big dogs were, but that wasn't his fault. He was cheerful too and always ready to chase down a trail or investigate new corners. Since Emma and Genny spent a lot of time together, Oliver and Fergus had become good friends.

Fergus dropped down to Oliver's height so they could sniff and nip and get to know each other all over again.

"Okay, you two!" called Genny, bringing out a tray of buns. "Take it outside!" She kicked open the door to the garden as she passed.

"Come on, Oliver!" huffed Fergus, heading for the door.

Oliver felt his bum wriggle, but he also remembered how worried he was about Emma.

"Be right back!" He zoomed into the kitchen.

Emma was still on her stool. Angelique was cracking eggs into a bowl. Oliver trotted over to Emma.

"Right. So," said Angelique. "Pearl, Becca and I will meet you and Genny at the grange after breakfast service is over, yeah?"

"Yeah," agreed Emma, but she was not happy. "There's

something you should know, Angelique. Marcie Cochrane showed up last night."

"Did she? What for?"

"She wanted to give you a personal check for the catering deposit. She said she wanted us to feel confident we would get paid."

"What did you tell her?" demanded Angelique.

"That I was sure you'd rather wait for an official check from the society account."

"Well, thank heaven for that!" said Angelique. "What could the woman have been thinking? We can't take her check for work we're doing for the literary society."

Emma rubbed Oliver's back, but it didn't make him feel any better. Ears drooping, he headed back out through the great room, out the side door and into the garden. Fergus was nosing around the tables and chairs, probably looking to see if anyone had dropped anything tasty.

But Oliver stretched out on the brick terrace and put his paws over his nose.

"What's wrong, laddy?" Fergus nosed Oliver's neck.

"Emma's leaving," Oliver grumbled. *And she won't* listen!

"Ah, now." Fergus flopped down beside him. "They always do that. You're the one as says how they always come back."

"This is different. She needs me. There's something wrong. I know there is. *She* knows there is."

Fergus waved his tail and huffed and snuffled at Oliver's ears, to make sure he was serious. Oliver could tell Fergus agreed with him that all this was bad. But what could they do? Out past the gate, he saw Genny's little white van back up to the kitchen door. They'd gone for rides in it before. It smelled like cod, and haddock, and potatoes.

Emma would be leaving very soon.

"What am I going to do?" Oliver whined.

"Patience." Fergus nudged him. "You have a very smart human. Not as smart as mine, maybe, but very smart anyway."

Oliver huffed. He didn't want to get into an argument about humans now. He wanted a way through that gate and into that van. There was a pretty big gap at the bottom of the gate. He'd tried to get through it before. Maybe if he dug just a little . . .

"Oliver." Fergus nosed him. "I know what you're thinking, lad. It's a bad idea."

A pair of guests came out from the B&B, with cups in their hands. They smelled like salt water and laundry soap and coffee and breakfast. They were talking to each other and looking at their phones at the same time. They walked through the gate and let it swing shut behind them.

Oliver's nose and ears shot up. He hadn't heard the gate latch snap. That happened sometimes, and when it did, that gate was even easier to push open than the swinging door into the kitchen.

"Now then," cautioned Fergus, "take it easy."

Oliver laid his chin back down on the ground, but his ears stayed tilted forward. On the other side of the gate, Genny got out of the van. Then Emma opened the kitchen door, and she and Genny started carrying bins and piling them into the back.

Both Emma and Genny went back into the kitchen. The door closed behind them.

They didn't come out.

The little van's cargo door was open.

"I'm going," muttered Oliver.

"All right, if you insist." Fergus climbed onto all fours.

Oliver trotted toward the gate. He paused and listened. All the human sounds were muted. He bonked his nose against the gate. The gate swung slowly outward.

Oliver ducked through. Fergus slid through after him. Keeping low, Oliver crept past the kitchen door. He could see Emma, Pearl, Angelique and Genny all standing inside, talking, like humans did.

They did not look at him.

Oliver eased over to the van. He stretched up to put his front paws on the step platform. There was a pile of tubs with labels. There was also a plaid blanket, and some cables and other human things.

He backed up and measured the distance with his eyes and all his instincts.

"What," huffed Fergus, "are you doing?"

"Getting in."

This was not going to be easy. But a noble warrior corgi did not give up. There might be hidden things in this new place where Emma was going. There might be other dogs, or cats, who could be rude and needed to know they were dealing with *his* special human.

"Better get on then. They're moving in there."

Oliver charged the van and *jumped*.

He landed in the cargo compartment, yelped, slid and skidded, banging into the bins and toppling sideways.

"Very graceful," barked Fergus. "Little shaky on the dismount."

"Like to see you try it." Oliver pushed himself to his feet, shaking his head.

But Fergus cut him off. "I gotta go! You hide!" Oliver heard the gravel clatter as Fergus took off running.

Oliver shoved his nose under the plaid blanket, sprawled down and paddled and wriggled until he was covered. It was dark and stuffy, but that didn't bother him. The blanket smelled of dust and grass and assorted humans. He sneezed.

What if Emma saw Fergus and wondered where Oliver was? What if she went looking for him to say goodbye? Oliver flattened himself against the floor of the van. What if she called for him? He'd have to answer, or she'd get worried.

Oliver rubbed his nose. *This is for Emma. I'm not being bad. This is for her.*

Oliver heard human footsteps. The doors slammed shut. Oliver panted happily. The van had obviously been used to transport fish and he was surrounded by good, interesting smells. Genny and Emma climbed into the front seat. He couldn't see them from under the blanket of course, but he knew them both by their smells.

He panted, resisting the instinct to bark and let Emma know he was here.

The floor vibrated as the engine started up. He smelled exhaust.

Oliver put his chin on his paws. *It'll be okay, Emma. You'll see.*

# 8

· · · · · · · · · ·

"SO, YOU WANT TO TELL ME ABOUT IT?" SAID GENNY AS SHE shifted the van's gears.

Emma was lost so far down the tunnel of her own thoughts she actually jumped. "About what?"

"About whatever's making you make that face, and don't tell me it's just because you didn't get enough sleep last night."

They'd left the center of Trevena behind and had turned onto the winding road heading up into the hills. The traditional cottages gave way to detached and semidetached houses, and then to thick hedges and old trees that turned the road into a green tunnel.

Genny's little van was an old Ford Transit, a squared-off machine with shocks long overdue for replacement. Despite the seat belt, Emma kept one hand on the dash to steady herself. The roads out this way alternated between tarmac, gravel and dirt.

Emma lifted her hand to run her fingers through her hair, but at the last minute remembered all the time she'd spent wrestling it into a braid this morning. She was in loose slacks and a casual black blouse because she'd be cooking, but she had her blazer and good flats in her suit bag so she'd look businesslike when it was time to face the board.

"Well, I didn't get enough sleep last night," Emma grumbled. As if to prove it, she cracked another enormous yawn. Angelique made her coffee strong enough to stand a spoon in, but it had barely taken the edge off her exhaustion. "But, no, that's not the problem."

"So what is it?" Genny kept both eyes on the road. Their section of Cornwall was still very much the countryside, and the narrow roads were made even more claustrophobic by being hemmed in by hedges and earthen berms.

"I was just thinking how troubled Marcie looked when she tried to give me that check last night," Emma said. "I don't know . . . it made me nervous."

"So it was the check that made you nervous?" Genny eased the van around a turn. "Not the fact that she showed up at the back door well after closing on what can only charitably be called a dark and stormy night?" A fat raindrop smacked against the windscreen. "Speaking of . . ."

"Yeah, there was that too," admitted Emma. "It's just . . . I just overreact when something unusual happens and it involves money. Leftover instincts from the bank, I think."

"Well, after twenty years running a chippery, I can tell you that's called a survival instinct. You don't really think Marcie was up to something, do you? Like making off with the society's funds?"

"If I did, I wouldn't be here now. But I'll tell you what, Genny, I'd bet Nana Phyllis's chocolate cake recipe that Marcie knows what's really going on and she is not happy about it."

Genny whistled. "Well, if you're right, this could be a very interesting board meeting." They bounced over a pothole. "Did you hear something?"

Emma listened. "What kind of something?"

"I thought I heard an extra squeak."

THE RAIN WAS FALLING STEADILY BY THE TIME THEY TURNED onto the private road leading through Truscott Park and up to Truscott Grange. Emma looked out at the acres of idyllic, if rain flattened, meadows.

*More like heading into a Jane Austen novel than anything by du Maurier.*

That impression lasted until they pulled up to the stone wall with its elaborate wrought iron gates. Truscott Grange sprawled against the dark hillside, all dramatic gables and arched windows. The manor house had two long wings stretching out from its main entrance. To Emma, it looked like the house was trying to hold back the looming hills. As they pulled up into the graveled courtyard, Emma found herself expecting a flock of crows, or even a solitary raven, staring down from the roof peaks.

The gravel driveway curved around the house, probably making a full circle.

"Marcie said we should pull around the back," Emma told Genny. "She'll have the kitchen door open."

"Servants' entrance," said Genny. "Got it."

Genny shifted the van into low gear and steered it gently forward, sloshing through the puddles. She followed the drive toward the house's east wing. *Literally, they have an east wing,* Emma thought, delighted despite her misgivings. She could not wait to see inside this place.

They rounded the first corner. She leaned forward, trying to get a clearer view of the grange's details. She'd always loved dramatic old houses. *Downton Abbey* was her favorite show, right after *The Great British Bake Off.*

They rounded the second corner. The gardens came into view, and another gravel courtyard, and what looked like an old carriage house.

*I wonder . . .* Emma turned her gaze toward the bushes and flower beds beside the house. And she saw a lump on the edge of the drive nearest the house, right beside the drooping shrubbery.

"What's that?"

"What!" Genny put on the brakes. This time something definitely squeaked. It also whined.

"What the . . ." Emma twisted around, trying to see into the little van's cargo compartment. She saw the bins, and she saw the old plaid blanket and—one familiar, and muddy, paw.

"Oliver!" Emma shouted.

Oliver sat up. The blanket he'd hidden under slithered down to his shoulders.

"Sorry, Emma!"

"What am I going to do with you!" she wailed. "Genny . . ."

But Genny wasn't paying attention to her. Genny was staring out the windscreen. "Emma," she said quietly, "I think we've got other things to worry about."

Emma stared out the window too. The lump she'd seen was a pale bundle, sprawled across the edge of the drive. It looked a bit like someone had dropped an industrial-sized sack of flour.

Except it was too big to be a flour sack. And the wrong shape.

"Oh no," breathed Emma. She scrabbled with her seat belt and the door handle. "Oh, no, no, no, no!"

"Emma!" barked Oliver from the cargo compartment. "Emma, what's wrong!"

But Emma was already out of the van and sprinting forward. But the faster she ran, the slower she seemed to be moving. It took forever to reach the bundle. It took even longer to kneel down, and turn it over, and see Marcie Cochrane's eyes staring up into hers.

# 9

. . . . . . . . . .

IT ONLY TOOK A FEW FRANTIC HEARTBEATS TO SEE THAT
Marcie could not possibly be alive. Her face had been badly
smashed in. Hoping against hope, Emma grappled at her
cold wrist to try to find a pulse. As she did, she couldn't
help noticing Marcie was wearing the same clothes as when
she'd shown up at the King's Rest last night. They were
soaked through. She must have lain there for hours. Emma's stomach twisted tight. Marcie must have come right
home and . . . and something. Emma stood up slowly, rub-
bing her palms on her slacks. She felt like the world had
dissolved into a gray fog. There was nothing left but her
and Marcie, and the rain.

"Oh my God!" gasped Genny and just like that, the
world jerked back into place.

"It's her! It's her! Emma! Emma!" Oliver was barking.
Emma reflexively stepped backward herding him away
from the body.

"I'm calling the police!" Genny pulled her mobile out of
her pocket.

*But someone in the house must have already called,*
thought Emma, dazed. *But, no, because they'd be out
here . . .*

Nobody inside this huge, beautiful Gothic house knew Marcie was dead yet.

"Up there!" Oliver jumped and pointed his muzzle at the sky. "Look! Look!"

Emma's gaze snapped up. Overhead, on the third story, one diamond-paned window stood open. The long dark curtain flapped in the chilly breeze.

Reflexively she gauged the way the body lay.

"Oh." She pressed her hand over her mouth. "Oh, Marcie."

Oliver whined and huddled against Emma's leg. Emma swallowed and wiped uselessly at her face.

Genny was nodding as she talked into her mobile. She ended the call and turned back to Emma. "Raj Patel is on the way." Raj was Trevena's one and only police constable. "The ambulance is coming too. We need . . ."

All at once Oliver whipped around. "Who's there!" he barked.

Emma slapped her hand across her mouth to stifle the squeak, but when she turned, it was to see a shaggy, thoroughly wet, flop-eared, mostly brown dog of uncertain breed loping across the lawn. He must have caught scent or sight of something because he was still several meters away when he broke into a gallop, straight for Marcie's corpse.

Emma tried to make a grab for him and missed. He wasn't wearing a collar. The dog sniffed at the body and then plumped down on his hindquarters, lifted his muzzle and howled to the sky.

This of course set Oliver barking again. Any words he might have had were entirely lost to the pure emotional need of letting the world know something was terribly wrong.

And the world answered.

The grange's side door flew open and a pale, dark-haired man in khaki trousers and a yellow polo shirt stormed down the steps.

"What the hell is going on out here?" he demanded. "Dash! Quiet!"

Somewhat to Emma's surprise the mutt obeyed.

The man turned to glower at Emma, but the effect was spoiled by the fact that he kept having to blink against the rain falling into his eyes.

"Now who in the—?" he began, but Genny interrupted.

"Frank!" Genny started forward, arms spread like she wanted to herd him back into the house. "Oh, Frank, I'm so sorry!"

"What for? What?" But then he saw the body, and all the color drained out of his face. "Oh my God. Marcie? Marcie!"

He dashed toward her, splashing straight through the puddles.

"No, don't!" Emma ran forward to try to put herself between the man—Frank—and the body. "I'm so sorry, but she's dead."

"Dead!" He reeled backward.

"We can't touch anything. I'm really, really sorry."

"But that's my sister!" Frank shouted. Now Emma could see the resemblance. To Marcie and to Daphne. This man had a broad build and a broad face. His thick brows framed the same dramatic brown eyes.

"Just who the hell are you?" he demanded of Emma.

"This is Emma Reed, Frank," said Genny. "And we need to get inside, okay?"

"We can't just leave her there in the rain!"

Emma winced. She understood. It felt indecent.

"We have to," said Genny gently. "Just for now. The ambulance is on its way. Please, Frank." Genny gestured toward the open window in the top story.

He looked, then swallowed hard, wiping at his face.

"Come on, Frank," said Genny gently. "Let's get inside."

"Yeah, yeah, you're right, okay. You . . ." He blinked at Emma. "You'd better come in too."

"Thanks." Emma turned to the dogs. "Come on, Oliver. Bring Dash."

Oliver got to his feet, shaking himself. "Dash, come on, Dash," he barked.

The bigger, older dog woofed heavily and didn't move.

But Oliver, displaying all his tenacity, not to mention his herding instincts, stuck his long nose right under the other dog's bum. Dash woofed, offended, but he did stand up. He looked, Emma thought, to be some sort of pointer-collie mix, with a milk-chocolate brown coat and random splashes and spots of white.

"This way, this way." Oliver nudged the dog toward the door. "Come on. Emma says we need to be inside. This way."

Reluctantly, Dash responded to Oliver's promptings and let himself be persuaded into the house.

"Good boys," Emma murmured as she followed the dogs inside.

Emma found herself in a fairly modest foyer with a floor of black-and-white tiles. Obviously, this space had been intended for use by servants back in the day. There were umbrellas in a stand by the door, along with coats on hooks and a row of galoshes and Wellingtons. A plain wooden stairway rose on the left and a padded green door opened to the right. Ahead of them stretched a windowless hallway, with dark wooden paneling up to the chair rail. Above that, the plaster walls were painted a deep minty green. At the very far end Emma could just glimpse the grander entry hall.

Emma shivered and wrapped her arms around herself. Despite the hallway, and the door open to the rain, the little foyer was quickly filling with the smell of wet dog. The big mutt, Dash, slunk to Frank's side and crouched there, head and ears drooping in dejection.

Frank stepped away from the dog. Emma tried not to frown. Who stepped away from a sad dog?

"Genny." Frank wiped at his face. "You said you called the ambulance?"

"Yes. They said they'd be here in just about fifteen minutes. The police are coming with them."

"The police!" Frank exclaimed. "What for?"

Emma and Genny glanced at each other. "You know they'll have to look around, Frank," said Genny.

Frank turned a sickly green. "Oh, God. Yes, well, of course, no, but . . ." he stammered.

He didn't get any further. Footsteps clattered overhead on the stairway. Everyone's attention jerked around, including the dogs'. Oliver ducked forward, putting himself between Emma and any potential new threat. Dash was on his feet too, all alert.

"It's Running Lady!" barked Oliver.

And so it was. Daphne thudded down the stairs. She had on black leggings and a loose pink tunic today.

"Dad?" she said as she saw Frank. "Did you find out what the . . . Oh, hi, Genny, and . . . Emma, isn't it?" she said as she registered their presence. "I didn't know you were here already. Where's Pearl?" She stopped on the lowest stair and looked from one of them to the other. "What's wrong?"

"Um, Daphne." Her father covered her hand where it rested on the newel. "Sweetheart, I'm afraid there's been an accident."

"What do you mean an accident?" She stared past Frank to Emma and Genny. "What's going on?"

"Come on, I . . . we need to find your mother too and Gus and—"

"No!" Daphne snatched her hand away. "We are not going anywhere! You're telling me what's going on!"

That was when they all heard the sirens. Daphne glowered at her father, and then she jumped right off the stair and charged for the outside door. Oliver and Dash both yipped and ducked sideways. Emma and Genny fell back. Daphne ran out into the rain.

Frank swore and bolted after her.

She hadn't gone more than two meters when she stopped and pressed both hands over her mouth.

"Oh my God," she breathed against her palms. "Oh my God. That's . . . that's Aunt Marcie!"

"Daphne." Frank caught up with his daughter and took hold of her gently. "I'm really, really sorry. I . . ."

Daphne ignored him. "Where's Mum?" she demanded. "I need to find Mum."

"I . . ." began Frank again. But Daphne pushed past him and ran inside, barreling down the corridor like nothing was going to stop her. Frank followed as far as the threshold, and stopped, swaying uncertainly.

"I . . ." He swallowed. "I don't know what . . ."

"Go after her," said Emma. "We'll meet the police."

"Yeah, yeah, thanks." Frank strode into the dimly lit corridor after his daughter.

It was only a minute later when the village police car, a tiny electric vehicle, came whizzing up the drive with the ambulance right behind.

# 10

...........

AFTER SOMEONE DIED, EMMA KNEW, THERE TENDED TO BE a lot of activity, but not for everybody. Right now, all she, Genny, Oliver and Dash could do was stand and watch.

The two women and the two dogs clustered in the grange's side doorway; and all peered out together to see the EMTs confirm with PC Raj Patel that Marcie was dead. Once that was done, Raj directed them to help him set up a small tent, made from parts pulled out of the back of his car, over her.

The dogs, perhaps showing more sense than their humans, soon tired of the show and retreated to a corner of the foyer. They snuffled and nipped in a sort of desultory version of the usual canine getting-to-know-you ritual and then finally curled up together. Emma and Genny, though, stayed where they were and watched as PC Raj looked up at the open window. They watched him make notes and talk on his radio and take pictures with his phone.

Emma couldn't help noticing how the body lay right at the edge of the gravel drive, and wondering about the open window overhead. Marcie must have fallen out and landed badly. Emma swallowed. The whole scene was reminding her of something. Several somethings, in fact, and none of them were any good.

It wasn't all standing around, though. Death also required phone calls. Genny called her husband, Martin. Emma called Angelique.

"Oh, poor Marcie," Angelique breathed when Emma gave her the news. "Are you okay, Emma?"

"Yes, yes, fine," Emma lied. Angelique's silence radiated disbelief, even through the phone. "Well, not really, but I will be. I've got to stay here for a while, but Genny's here too. I'll be back as soon as I can."

"All right. I'll tell Pearl. Oh, dear." Emma could picture Angelique pressing her fingertips against her eyelids the way she did when laboring over a particularly difficult work schedule. "I knew Marcie had troubles, but I never thought . . . not this."

"It was some kind of accident," said Emma. "I'm sure of it."

"I hope you're right," Angelique said seriously.

They hung up and Emma stared out at the rain. She was so lost in thought, she didn't notice Genny come stand right beside her.

"So, are you thinking what I'm thinking?" asked Genny quietly.

"I'm thinking that window overhead was big enough for a person to fall out of."

"Oh, were you?" There was not a lot of confidence in Genny's words.

"Yes," said Emma firmly. "I'm thinking Marcie must have been opening the window, or leaning on it, or something gave way and she fell."

"And had bad luck on how she landed," said Genny. "Because, I mean, it isn't that high up. She could have just as easily been hurt instead of killed."

"Bad luck happens," said Emma. *There might have been a big rock, or, or something.*

Only she hadn't seen large rocks in the drive when she rolled Marcie over.

*That still doesn't mean anything.*

*I hope you're right,* she heard Angelique say again. Angelique plainly thought this tragedy might not be an accident.

*So what does she think?* Emma sucked in a slow breath. *Well, what are* you *thinking?*

Emma remembered Marcie as she'd last seen her; the way Marcie had smiled so sadly over her shoulder and the too cheerful singsong way she'd said her goodbye. The way she'd talked about wanting to make sure things were taken care of, and that everything was perfect. Uncertainty nibbled at the edges of Emma's thoughts.

"You know, it's normal, when somebody . . . goes . . . out a window, you just naturally wonder whether they jumped."

"Or were pushed," said Genny.

"Genny!"

Genny held up both hands. "Don't blame me. You were thinking it too. I could tell."

"I was not!" protested Emma. "Well, okay, I was, but that's only because . . . because . . ."

Emma felt her frown deepen. There was something nagging her about that conversation with Marcie. But it seemed to be stuck in the back of her mind and she couldn't dig it out.

"Because why?" asked Genny.

Emma shook her head hard. "What I don't understand is why didn't anyone find her before now? She's been there a good long while. Why wasn't anybody in the house looking for her?"

Before Genny could answer, Oliver got up from his spot beside Dash and trotted over to them. He also shook himself, scattering water everywhere.

"Dash is sad," Oliver told Emma. "He liked Marcie Rain Lady. There aren't always a lot of humans here, he says, and she was his favorite."

"Oh, Oliver." Emma bent down and hugged him. He was wet, but so was she, so it didn't matter. "I'm sorry. I really am."

Genny touched Emma's shoulder. Emma straightened up and saw PC Raj was trudging up the drive.

Raj was a tall, wiry young man. His grandfather had emigrated to Great Britain from New Delhi as a boy back in the fifties and had become the first constable of Southeast Asian heritage in Cornwall. Emma knew Raj as a serious person who regularly took prizes in the Cornwall bike marathons, flew kites on the beach with his little nephews, and loved lemon poppy seed cake.

"Emma, Genny," Raj greeted them. Rain streamed off his plastic-covered hat and bright yellow raincoat. "I'm sorry we're going to have to ask you to wait in the house awhile. I've had to call for a detective."

"Oh," breathed Emma. "Oh, I mean, surely, it must have been an . . . accident?" It was obviously a very old house. Things broke, including windows.

"We don't know anything yet," Raj told her. "I do have a few questions, though."

Emma and Genny both steeled themselves as Raj pulled out his notebook. "Can you describe the scene when you arrived?"

So Genny told him about pulling around the corner of the house and seeing "the bundle" on the edge of the drive. And Emma told him about turning the body over to see if there was any chance Marcie might still be alive. They told him the time they arrived; they told him about the dogs and about Frank, and about Daphne.

As Raj was noting all this down, the crunch of tires on gravel cut through the sound of the rain. Emma squinted at the long drive and saw a silver Saab rolling up toward the house.

Oliver, eternally curious, and completely indifferent to both rain and the smell of wet dog, made to lunge forward. Emma caught his collar just in time.

"Go on over to Dash, Oliver." Emma shooed her corgi back. "He needs a friend."

Whether or not this was strictly true, Oliver accepted it with a wag and went to curl up beside the deflated mutt.

Raj, in the meantime, muttered under his breath and ducked back out into the rain. He hurried toward the car, putting up his hands to motion *stop!* The Saab did stop, and the driver's-side window slid down.

Caite Hope-Johnston stuck her head out.

# 11

. . . . . . . . . .

"WELL," BREATHED GENNY. "THIS SHOULD BE INTERESTING."

Between the distance and the rain, Emma could only hear the clipped, displeased rhythm of Caite's speech, not the actual words. She didn't hear Raj's reply either, but she did hear Caite shriek. Caite shoved the car door open so fast Raj jumped back. She climbed out into the rain, with a complete disregard as to how it was straightening her carefully styled blond waves—or soaking her blouse through her open, plaid mackintosh. She strode toward the house with impressive turn of speed, considering her wedge-heeled sandals, ignoring the mud as completely as she ignored the rain.

Raj stood stunned for a second, then he ran ahead. He circled in front of Caite, hands out, motioning for her to stop, just like he had when she was driving.

Oliver thrust his nose forward like he was hoping to catch an interesting scent.

Raj was clearly talking. Caite stood where she was, hand on her stomach, listening. Then, slowly, she turned around, and limped back to the car, like one of her straps had suddenly come loose. When she drew level with the Saab, she slammed one hand on the bonnet for balance, bent over and vomited.

"Plot twist?" said Emma feebly.

"I'll say," murmured Genny.

"That is not good," mumbled Oliver.

Raj patted Caite's back awkwardly and tried to hand her a handkerchief. She just shook him off and straightened up. Caite gestured toward the house. Raj shook his head.

"Should I go out there, Emma? I'm already wet." Oliver wagged hopefully.

"Not yet, good boy," she breathed.

Dash barked once.

"Dash says he should go. He says Marcie needs him."

Emma swallowed and went to rub Dash's ears. The mutt's wet, fringed tail slapped the tiles in a slow rhythm. As she did, Emma suddenly heard Marcie's voice speaking from memory. *You'll make this work, won't you? . . . It has to be perfect.*

Marcie who was a du Maurier superfan. And all at once Emma realized what the open window and the fallen body made her think of. It was a scene from *Rebecca*—a scene that detailed an attempted murder.

Now Emma felt like she wanted to be sick. Because she and Marcie had talked about the book, just last night.

Outside, Caite climbed back into the car, backed and turned and drove away. Raj shook his head again, wiped at his face and started trudging back over to the doorway.

At the same time, Emma heard footsteps coming from behind. She and Genny turned and the dogs sat up, all equally startled. A woman strode determinedly up the corridor from the main house. Frank followed right behind, obviously unhappy but just as determined.

"That's Helen Dalgliesh," Genny murmured to Emma. "She teaches up in Manchester. She's also Daphne's mum, Frank's ex and Marcie's best friend."

"That's a lot," breathed Emma.

"You got that right," murmured Genny.

Helen Dalgliesh was dressed with casual elegance in a fitted green top and cream trousers and ballet flats. Like her daughter, Helen was a tall woman, with a wealth of curling, dark hair. She had slanting, hazel eyes in a sharp face with a long, crooked nose. Those eyes at the moment were puffy and red and her nose dripped. She'd obviously been crying.

Genny moved forward and expressed her sympathies, and introduced Emma.

Helen held her chin up with an angry stubbornness. She clutched a crumpled tissue in one hand.

"I came to see if you needed anything," she announced. Her voice was raw.

Before either Emma or Genny could answer, Frank got round between them and Helen. "Helen . . . come on. You shouldn't be here. You should be in with our daughter and the rest of the family."

"Now is *exactly* the wrong time to tell me where to be," Helen snapped. Dash heaved himself to his feet and came over to Helen, whining and wagging his tail. Helen put a hand on the mutt's head reflexively.

Raj had reached the door in time to hear this exchange. Oliver headed toward the constable, obviously ready for another good ankle snuffle. Emma scooped him up quickly.

"I wasn't going anywhere!" The corgi squirmed.

"I'm so very sorry for your loss," Raj said to Helen and Frank. "I promise we won't be here any longer than necessary."

"When can I see Marcie?" asked Helen.

"We'll be arranging that as soon as we can. I know this is all very upsetting, and I'm sorry but . . ."

Frank squared his shoulders in a way that Emma guessed meant he'd decided it was time to take charge. "Look, Raj, what do you need from us, eh? I'm sure Genny and . . . um . . ."

"Emma," said Emma. "Emma Reed."

He looked down at her like he was trying to remember something, and the something didn't quite turn up. "Right. I'm sure Genny and, erm, Emma don't want to be hanging around here, and the family . . . good God, you *have* to give us some time."

"It's just a little bit longer, Mr. Cochrane," said Raj. "I promise. The detective is already on her way."

"The . . . ?" Frank pulled back. "I mean, no offense, but having you here is bad enough. How can we need a detective?"

"It's regulations," said Raj. Emma wondered if this was true, or if Raj was just saying it because it was the reply for which there was no argument. "Believe me, if there was a choice, I wouldn't have called in."

It was easy to see the implications of this settling into Frank's mind. Helen's as well. But their reactions were complete opposites to each other. Frank's face went pale. Helen's on the other hand, flushed, but whether it was from anger or fear, Emma couldn't tell.

"Do you know what time Marcie got in last night?" asked Raj.

"No, but I went to bed maybe ten thirty, and she wasn't home then, so it must have been late." He paused. "In fact, everybody was out late that night. My brothers, Bertram and August, they weren't home either. Helen was, of course, and our daughter, Daphne."

Raj made notes about all this. "And you didn't see her this morning?"

"Well, no," admitted Frank. "But that wasn't unusual. Marcie was always up with the chickens. She'd get herself a cup of tea or something and shut herself up in her office to take care of business. Sometimes we wouldn't see her until lunchtime. Especially during festival season. Isn't that right, Helen?"

Helen nodded in agreement, but she didn't look happy about it.

"But I don't want to say it, but we—" Frank gestured to indicate himself and Helen and maybe the rest of the family. "We can pretty well guess what happened, can't we? My sister's been depressed, and then, well, things have been going wrong and—"

"Marcie was *not* depressed." Helen cut him off. "Stressed, yes. Disappointed, yes. But not depressed."

*Disappointed about what?* Emma bit her lip to keep the question from popping out. Now was most definitely not the time.

"Gus said—" began Frank.

"Gus doesn't know his arse from a hole in the ground!" Helen's face flared bright red. "God!" She pressed both hands against her cheeks. "I'm sorry. I shouldn't have said that."

"It's okay," said Raj. "This is awful. I know. I do. But we have to follow procedure, and that means I can't leave, or let anybody else leave, until the detective gets here."

"Maybe Genny and I could wait in the kitchen?" suggested Emma. "We wouldn't be in anybody's way there, yeah?" *And we won't be making things even more awkward for the family.*

Everyone looked at Raj. Raj sighed and rubbed the back of his neck. "I guess that would be all right."

Emma got the feeling he mostly wanted to reduce the number of people standing around getting angry and impatient.

"Helen? What do you think?" Genny asked.

Helen blinked. "Yes, certainly. Fine."

Emma's curiosity itched. Badly. There was so much going on here. Frank said his brother Gus had said Marcie was depressed. Except Helen didn't think so. Emma knew that family members could easily miss the difference between someone going through a bad patch and someone experiencing full-on depression. But then Helen said that Marcie was stressed.

*Stressed and disappointed. About what?*

She looked out at the rain, more than a little ashamed of herself. Frank had just lost his sister. Helen had lost her friend. Poor Daphne was beside herself and here she was, letting her brain run on like Marcie's death was her problem to solve.

*I just wish there was something we could do.* An idea hit. *Maybe there is.*

"We could make some lunch," she suggested. "That's what we came here for. I'm sure . . . I'm sure everybody's going to need something."

Helen looked startled. Frank looked oddly relieved. "That's an excellent idea. Thank you. And perhaps some tea? I know I could use a cuppa."

"Of course," said Genny. "You leave it to us."

"And maybe you could look after Dash?" he suggested.

"We'd be glad to," said Emma.

"Yes! Yes!" barked Oliver. He nosed Dash in the side. "Come on, we're going downstairs. Come on!"

"I'll take you." Helen took a step toward the padded green door Emma had noticed earlier.

"No, I'll do it," said Frank. As soon as the words left him, Helen turned on him. This time there was no mistaking the anger that put the color in her cheeks. But Frank was ready for it.

"Helen, listen," he said before she could open her mouth again. "I know I'm not the person you want here, and I also know I'm not the person Daphne wants. That's my fault. I know that. But she needs you right now, not me. What I can do is show Genny and, um, Emma where to go. You take care of our daughter." He touched her elbow briefly. "And yourself. All right?"

Helen looked up at him, and for a moment, Emma thought she was going to start shouting. But whatever she saw in his eyes, it seemed to drain the anger out of her, at least a little.

"Yes," she said. "Yes, all right."

"Good," said Genny. "I'll meet you round back then. And don't worry, Raj. I'll go round the other way."

"Thank you." Raj faced Helen. "Maybe you could take me to the rest of the family? And anybody else who was here when Ms. Cochrane was found?"

Helen nodded and set off down the hallway toward the center of the house. Raj tucked his cap under his arm and followed.

Frank and Emma looked at each other. Oliver sniffed at

Frank's shoes. "Mud," he mumbled. "And something else, I don't recognize that, wood, grass, petrol and something . . ."

Frank stared at the corgi, and stepped back. "Sorry," he said when he saw Emma's face. "I don't get on with dogs well. I'm allergic."

"Oh," said Emma. "Right. Come on, Oliver, leave it."

"He doesn't smell allergic," muttered Oliver as he came back over to Emma's side. "He just smells grumpy."

"Right," said Frank. "Well. This way then." He opened the padded green door and started down a dim flight of stairs to another long, dim corridor. Dash, clearly feeling he was about to be left out of something interesting, got to his feet and followed, leaving a trail of muddy paw prints on the tiles.

But there was nothing to be done about that either. Emma and Oliver followed Frank farther into the silent house.

# 12

TRUSCOTT GRANGE HAD BEEN BUILT IN THE DAYS WHEN THE actual work of running a house was kept as far out of sight as possible. That meant that where a more modern house would have a cellar, the grange had a warren of rooms and pantries for storage, sewing, laundry and, of course, cooking.

The kitchen was huge by modern standards. It had been built not just for one cook but for half a dozen. The oak-topped kitchen island stretched right down the center of the room, roughly long enough to be a runway for small aircraft. The cooktop had been installed right in the middle, with no less than three ovens underneath. In addition to the door they came through, there was another door out to the car park and three more at the opposite end of the kitchen, leading to destinations unknown.

A massive, elaborate cast-iron stove that to Emma's (not very expert) eye looked like it was brought in sometime during the Victorian era still stood against one wall. Evidently, somebody had decided that it wasn't worth the trouble of trying to get it out again when the modern cookers were installed. Now it was a place to put decorative copper pots and whimsical sugar bowls. Other, more functional counters lined the walls under the cupboards. There was an industrial-sized refrigerator, an entirely separate freezer and a double sink large enough to give Dash a bath in, never mind Oliver.

The windows looked out just about nose level with the gravel courtyard/car park. She could tell that was Genny's van parked outside, but all she could actually see were the tires and the undercarriage.

Oliver, of course, had to go into zoom mode, zigzagging around the kitchen, shoving his nose into every corner and mumbling about smells and asking questions. Dash just loped to a spot beside the door to the outside where somebody had put down an old blanket. He flopped down and put his chin on the floor.

"Well"—Frank gestured to include the entire kitchen— "here it is. Pantry there"—he pointed to one of the three distant doors. "Got its own loo there"—he pointed to a second door. "There used to be bells and so on, but now we all just text each other. How's that for modern?" He tried to smile and almost managed it. "I don't suppose . . ." he began. "Did Raj say anything to you about what he thinks happened? I mean, to Marcie?"

"No. I mean, he couldn't, could he. Not yet."

"But it . . . you saw it," he said. "I mean, you saw the open window. I mean, I don't want to say it, but did it sound like he was thinking there's something . . . wrong?"

Emma felt her brows knit. "Do you think there's something wrong?"

"She's dead—of *course* there's something wrong!" Frank snapped. Then he sighed. "That wasn't fair. It's just, there've been . . ." Suddenly Frank seemed unable to look at her. He looked at his shoes, at the counter, at the windows. "It's what I was trying to tell him. There've been problems lately, and Marcie's been . . ." He stopped. "Well, when she wasn't home for dinner last night, I was worried. I tried to text, but she didn't answer."

Outside, Genny was walking carefully down the stairs

from the car park carrying three stacked bins. There was a low thud, thud as she kicked the door to be let in.

Emma scurried to open the door. Genny stood at the foot of the steps, almost hidden by her stack of bins. Emma grabbed two off the top. Frank came over and grabbed one of Emma's.

"Marcie did stop by the King's Rest late last night," said Emma. "She had a check to drop off for Angelique."

"She did?" Frank put the bin on the counter. "I don't suppose you know where she was before that?"

Genny wagged her eyebrows at Emma. Emma shooed her away.

"No, sorry. She didn't mention it." Emma paused, and wrestled with her curiosity for a few seconds. Curiosity won. "I guess she didn't say anything to you either?"

Frank shook his head. "No. We . . ." He sighed. "Feels a bit like airing the dirty laundry in public, but I expect you'll hear soon enough." He looked at Genny. Genny busied herself with pulling Emma's checklist out of the portfolio and pretending to read it over.

"My sister and I did not get along very well," Frank went on. "We fought over my divorce from Helen and never really made it up."

"Oh, I'm sorry."

He shrugged. "I sometimes think our parents did her a disservice when they left her the grange. It kept her locked in here, isolated from the real world. She didn't . . . she didn't understand people very well, or how things actually work. She had control of a lot of money and I always worried somebody was going to take advantage, if you know what I mean."

Emma thought about Marcie facing down Caite in front of the board. She hadn't struck Emma as someone disconnected or out of her depth.

"But she never married?"

"Only one of us who didn't. Considering how that all worked out, maybe she understood people better than I thought. No." He sighed. "She had her house and her books, and the festival every year, of course. That seemed to be enough. I did think . . . I do think . . . maybe it wasn't the healthiest life. I should have said something sooner, but I'm only here for the occasional weekend these days and . . . I guess it was easier to believe she'd muddle through somehow." For a moment, Frank stared out the windows, seeing nothing but the thoughts inside his own mind. Then he shook himself. "I'd better get upstairs. I'm sure Raj will have some more questions and, well, my brothers and Helen, they don't get on. It could get ugly. Uglier. We'll be in the sitting room, I'm sure, when that tea's ready. Turn left out the door, take the stairs at the end of the hall, then turn to your right, go under the landing and then straight on 'til morning."

Emma assured Frank she'd find it, and he left. Emma watched him go. She didn't even realize how long she'd stood there staring at the swinging door until Genny put a hand on her shoulder.

"Well, that wasn't at all awkward, was it?" Then she saw the look on Emma's face. "Hey. You all right?"

"No, not really," Emma admitted. "I was thinking about Marcie coming to the B and B last night. I knew she didn't look good, and when she was talking about tidying up loose ends, I . . . I really should have known something was wrong."

"How? You'd only met her once before, for about five minutes. What could you possibly know about her?"

"I knew she was upset," Emma said.

Oliver, having completed his investigations of the far end of the kitchen, bounded back over and flopped down in front of Dash, so they were nose to nose. Dash's tail swished against the flagstones.

"Poor old thing," murmured Emma.

"He's sad," said Oliver. "And hungry. There's kibble in . . . here!" He zoomed all the way back down to the door that Frank said was the pantry. "Unless you brought chicken? Chicken is always helpful. Or steak. Steak would be excellent."

Genny gave him a wan smile. "You know, I don't think I've ever heard a dog yip as much as Oliver does."

"You should hear him when it's just the two of us," said Emma. "We should probably get started on the tea and sandwiches. I'm going to see if there's any dog food in here."

Emma pulled open the pantry door. Inside was what amounted to a walk-in closet filled with boxes, bags, bins and canned goods. Sure enough, there was a big bin of dog kibble and a battered ladle clearly meant to be used as a scoop.

While Genny started opening Emma's labeled and numbered bins, Emma filled a bowl with kibble and another with water and put them down for Dash. She gave him a pat on the head. He looked up at her mournfully.

Oliver hurried back over and plunked beside him, snuggling close and also looking seriously up at Emma. "He's still sad."

"Well, maybe this will help cheer him up." Emma pulled the smaller container of roast beef out of the bin marked #1, and shredded a slice into the kibble bowl.

Dash immediately scrambled to his feet and stuck his whole face into the bowl, wolfing down the meat and wagging his tail at the same time. Oliver barked in semi-outrage, and shoved his muzzle in as well.

"I'm being used," said Emma.

"I could have told you that," said Genny, which was true, although not terribly helpful.

Like any good British household, the grange had an electric kettle on the counter, just waiting to be filled. While it heated, Emma helped Genny ferry in the neatly labeled bins full of ingredients and stack them on the central counter by the cooktop.

One of the cupboards held both cups and pots. There was a tray as well. The tins beside the kettle were both simply labeled "Tea." Both held loose leaves. One was definitely Earl Grey, the scent unmistakable. The other looked and smelled like an oolong that had gone a bit stale.

She chose the Earl Grey and spooned leaves into the pot. When she finished, she looked up to see Genny watching her. "What?" she asked.

"You're making faces," said Genny.

"Sorry. It's just, I thought of something earlier. But it's really stupid."

"How stupid?"

"Have you ever read *Rebecca*?"

Genny chuckled. "Of course I've read it. I'm Cornish. It's practically a statutory requirement."

"Do you remember the scene where Mrs. Danvers tries to talk the narrator into—"

"Jumping out the window," Genny finished for her. She also drew herself up straighter. "Oh, lord."

"Yeah," agreed Emma. "I was thinking about that scene, I mean, here's this old house, and there's the open window, with poor Marcie below, and she was such a du Maurier fan. I mean, it almost—I don't know—it felt staged."

"Well, when you put it that way." Genny stopped, and now she was the one who frowned. "But, Emma, in the book, there's somebody else there, trying to talk the narrator into jumping. You're not suggesting . . . ?"

"No," said Emma firmly. "It was just something that came into my head. And now I'm putting it out of my head, because nothing about it makes sense in the real world."

"I agree," said Genny.

"I mean, if you really want to kill yourself—"

"Or if somebody else wanted to kill you—" Genny interjected.

"You don't set up a scene from your, or their," she added quickly, "favorite book."

"Especially when it's only a third story window, and you're more likely to end up in the hospital than the grave," said Genny.

"Right. If you really want to end it, or somebody wants to end it for you, you go find a nice quiet cliffside. We've got plenty to choose from."

"Yes. Exactly." Genny nodded.

"So, really, never mind what Frank thinks—we've got no reason to believe it was anything except an unlucky accident."

"I mean, it's not like that time last summer with Victoria, is it?" Genny added. "Something was so very clearly off there. We knew it from the beginning."

"Yes," agreed Emma.

"And there's nothing at all off, or missing, or anything like that this time," added Genny.

"No. Nothing. That we know of," said Emma.

"Right," said Genny.

"Right," said Emma.

The electric kettle beeped. Emma turned gratefully back to the tea things. She didn't want to be thinking like this. She wanted to believe it was an accident, and that she was just being overly dramatic, as usual.

"Well," she said briskly, "I'm just going to get this tea up to the family."

"And I'll get going on the sandwiches." Genny checked the list. "We've got the beef and horseradish, the chicken and cress and the seafood salad, yeah?"

"Yeah. And let's make them big. No one's going to want anything fussy. Same with the cake slices." Emma had baked the extra sponges last night. They just needed to be assembled and cut.

"Good idea," said Genny. "And much better than standing around wondering if there's some kind of back way to the upstairs from here. Because looking around before the police get here would be bad."

"Emma." Oliver came over and put his paws up on the counter, or tried to. "There's a stairway. Over here. This way."

"You're kidding," said Emma.

"Huh? Yes, of course I'm kidding," said Genny. "I never would. Not before the police, anyway. Besides, how would it look if the detective showed up and caught us?" Her eyes lit up. "Do you think they'll send that woman from last summer—what was her name . . . ?"

"Constance Brent," said Emma. "I don't know." There'd been no chance to ask Raj.

"Well, I hope it is her."

"So do I, she was really good."

"And she was willing to talk to you," added Genny. "You can let us know what's really happening."

Emma ignored this. She just set five cups and the pot on the tray.

If Genny was disappointed by Emma's lack of enthusiasm, or answer, she didn't let it show.

"Can you find your way?"

"Erm," said Emma.

"I can!" Oliver bounced on all fours. "This way!" He zoomed back toward the door they'd come through.

Emma sighed and picked up the tea tray. "If I'm not back in three days, send help."

# 13

......... .

AS IT TURNED OUT, DASH WAS ONE OF THOSE DOGS WHO
could not stand to be left out of anything. Emma and Oliver
were barely halfway down the hallway before the mutt was
loping along behind and then shoving his way in front so he
could climb the stairs at the end of the hall, stepping right
over Oliver.

"Hey!" barked the corgi. Dash replied with a low huff
that sounded suspiciously like a laugh.

There was a green baize door at the top of the stairs, like
something straight out of *Upstairs Downstairs*. Emma
eased her way past the dogs and pushed through. And
paused for breath as her inner thirteen-year-old went into
squeals of rapture.

This door opened onto the main entryway for Truscott
Grange. It was a perfect picture of old-fashioned elegance.
A glass and gilt chandelier lit up the hall full of dark paneling and marble tiles. The grand wooden staircase branched
to the left and the right, circling together overhead to create
an indoor balcony that Juliet could have brooded on for an
entire evening. Massive, gilt-framed oil paintings hung on
the walls. Arched doorways opened to the left and the right

of the stairs, while the dimly lit central corridor passed straight underneath the balcony.

*Turn to the right,* Frank had said, *and straight on 'til morning.*

As it turned out, she didn't need the directions. She just followed the dogs, who followed their noses. They led her under the balcony and down the broad hallway. Rooms—whole suites, actually—opened on either side. Emma couldn't resist taking a peek inside as she passed. The results though, were disappointing. She saw grand rooms, but they were mostly empty. What furnishings there were had been covered in white sheets. Overall, it looked like a convention of very sedate ghosts.

As much as it disappointed her inner thirteen-year-old, the adult portion of Emma's mind saw the practicality of it. A house like this would take a small army to maintain. Just the thought of all the dusting made her want to go lie down on her chaise with a plate of biscuits.

But it was all very quiet, and a little bit sad.

Except for the voices she could now hear coming from behind the closed door directly in front of her. Those were not sad at all. Those were angry.

"You should have told us!" shouted a man.

Emma froze in her tracks. The cups rattled on the tray. The teapot sloshed ominously.

"Told you what, exactly?" That was definitely Helen. Her tone was brittle and icy.

"That something was wrong! You must have known! You were the only one she ever talked to!"

"Yeah, and I wonder why that was!" snapped Helen.

"I knew." A second man's voice, filled with acid and sadness. Emma didn't recognize it. Maybe it was one of the other Cochrane brothers.

"I tried to tell you," the second man was saying. "But you were too busy being chummy with your boardroom buddies . . ."

"How would you know anything, Gus?" That was Frank.

"It's not like she talked to you any more than to the rest of us."

*I should do something,* Emma told herself. *Like knock. Yes. I should knock.* She moved forward, nudging both dogs aside.

"At least I tried to help!" shouted Gus.

"Okay, okay, we're all upset. What Marcie's done is a horrible shame, but it's no good yelling . . ."

"Oh, shut up, Bert," said Frank. "We don't need you trying to take over just yet."

*I should knock,* Emma told herself again. *If I don't knock soon, this is going to look like eavesdropping.*

"What's that supposed to mean?" demanded Bert.

"Like you don't know!" sneered Helen.

"As it happens, I don't." Bert again. "So why don't you just tell me straight out?"

*You shouldn't eavesdrop on a family that's just had a shock.*

Dash nosed disconsolately about the bottom of the door.

"That's enough, Bert," said Frank sternly. "None of this is Helen's fault."

"Bit of a change of tune for you, isn't it?" drawled Gus.

"Gus, you're not helping," said Helen wearily.

"Maybe I'm done helping. My therapist says I spend too much time trying to fix other people's problems. He says—"

"Oh, God!" groaned the other man. "Not *now*, Gus!"

"Emma?" Oliver bonked her calf. "Are we going in, Emma?"

"Half a tick, Oliver." Emma shifted position to get away from Oliver's nose. That this brought her a little closer to the door was purely accidental.

Gus evidently was not going to be deterred. "At least I'm getting some help. You might try it sometime! Maybe then you wouldn't—"

"Oh, this should be good," said the third man. "Here's little Gus, all ready to take charge, because he's so sure Marcie left him everything!"

Oliver scratched his chin. "Is this eavesdropping? Because you don't like eavesdropping."

"It's not," she said. "I'm listening for a pause."

"Oh. Okay then."

*I really shouldn't lie to my dog.*

"I don't know anything about that," shouted Gus. "And I don't care!"

Oliver slunk forward, snuffling at the gap between the door and the carpet. Dash whined and pawed at the wood. Emma held her breath, but nobody in the room seemed to have heard. "Oh, yeah, right," said Frank, his voice brittle. "You spent all those years sucking up to her for nothing, yeah?"

"Just because I liked my sister—oh, sorry *our* sister—" growled Gus "who is now *dead* in case you'd forgotten!"

"How could I forget it! We've got the police crawling all over the front lawn!" Emma pictured Frank stabbing a finger toward the door. "And they're going to start asking some really interesting questions, aren't they. Like, Bert, how come you're so quick to say Marcie jumped?"

"Because it's obvious she jumped!"

"Oh, *is* it?"

Emma felt the hairs on the back of her neck stand up.

"Listen, all of you," said Bert. "We need to get ourselves together. Things are bad enough." Bert's voice was cold and far too calm. "And if we sit here arguing like idiots, someone is going to think something's *really* wrong in this family, and they'll start asking awkward questions. Do you want that, Frank?" His voice took on a knife's edge. "Or you, Helen? With Daphne right here in the middle of it all?"

Silence fell, thick and heavy.

"Is that a pause?" Oliver cocked his head.

"Yes." *Besides, if I just stand here any longer, the tea is going to be too stewed to drink.*

Emma juggled the tray so she could free up one hand, knock on the door and shoulder her way in.

Everybody in the room stopped in place in a frozen tableau that would have done any BBC costume drama proud.

The sitting room itself was lovely, light and airy. Or, at least, it would be on days when the weather cooperated. One entire wall was lined with arched windows that looked across an expanse of garden that had been beaten down by the recent rain. A stand of ancient walnut trees stretched their branches toward the leaden sky.

*And there's your crows,* thought Emma, spying the birds circling the walnuts and strutting across the grass underneath.

Helen stood beside an oval marquetry table that was stacked with publicity brochures and posters for the upcoming festival. She still clutched her tissue in her fist, which she had raised to shake at a slim, bald man. He was the perfect image of the country squire with a gray-streaked beard and a pair of baggy tweeds to go with his loose button-down shirt.

He was also a match for Frank and for the third man. The third man had the same face, the same large dark eyes, dark hair and square, solid build that Emma was beginning to recognize as a Cochrane family trait. This man, though, had clearly been putting in some extra time at the fitness center. Muscles rippled under his green polo shirt, and his tan was far too even, and far too early, to be natural. Which got Emma wondering just how natural that rich dark hair color was.

At the same time, Emma couldn't help noticing Daphne was missing from the family group.

"I'm, erm, sorry to interrupt," said Emma, "but we thought maybe you would like some tea."

Oliver and Dash came in with her, of course. Oliver immediately got busy exploring as much of the room as he could get to. Dash went and nosed around the bearded man and then Helen.

Helen recovered first. She patted Dash and started forward, hands out for the tray.

"Thank you, Emma. I'll just . . ."

"No, I've got it." Frank hurried past and took the tray. "Thanks, Emma." Helen gave him a slightly confused sideways glance.

"We're making some lunch as well," Emma told them. "Sandwiches and cake."

Dash was snuffling around Frank's ankles, and Oliver joined him there. Frank stepped back, awkwardly. "Go on, go on now," he said to the dogs.

Helen lifted the tea tray out of Frank's hands and set it on the oval table beside the brochures.

"Thank you," she said to Emma. "I'm sure we'll all be glad of something to eat."

"Sounds like a splendid idea," agreed the bearded man. Emma thought he must be Gus.

"Well, we had the food, and it's no good letting it go to waste," she said, very aware she was making pointless small talk but somehow unable to help herself.

The tall, tanned man was staring at them all.

"Oh, sorry," said Frank. "This is, erm . . ."

"Emma Reed," said Helen. "Emma, this is Bertram Cochrane"—she indicated the tanned, muscled man—"and his brother August." The bearded man nodded. "And you've already met Frank, of course."

Dash, followed by Oliver, switched their attentions from Frank's shoes over to Bert's. Bert looked down at the dogs, hiked his tidy trouser legs just a little and stepped back. "Helen—"

"Oh, so sorry," said Emma. "Oliver, Dash, come on, both of you. Out you go."

Oliver barked once. Dash shook himself and gave a grumble, but both dogs let themselves be shooed out the door. Emma closed it and turned back to the family. Bert looked surprised. He had clearly expected her to leave as well.

"Emma is, was, well, is, I suppose, going to help cater the festival, after Weber's pulled out," Helen told Bert and Gus. "At least, that was Marcie's plan."

A dark look flickered across Bert's face. "Well, that's very good of you, Emma, especially on such short notice."

"We were going to do a menu tasting today for the board . . ." began Emma.

"Oh!" groaned Helen. "The board! I forgot! I'd better ring Caite . . ." She dove for the phone lying on the sideboard.

Which meant Helen didn't know about the scene with Caite out front. Emma wondered if any of the family did, and if it mattered.

"Thanks again, Emma," said Bert. "We're looking forward to those sandwiches."

It was a dismissal. Emma didn't move for a moment, although she wasn't sure why, except that something in Bert's manners seems to suggest he expected some gesture of respect, or immediate obedience. Or both.

"We'll bring up lunch as soon as it's ready," she said.

Bert smiled, putting a veneer of politeness over his very obvious irritation. "Sorry to be so much trouble. It's good of you to help out."

He did not mean a single word of it.

"Thanks," said Emma, because there was nothing else she could say, and because there was nothing else to do, she turned and she walked out of the room.

She was sure she felt Bert's gaze on her back the entire way.

# 14

AS SOON AS THE DOOR WAS SHUT, EMMA LEANED AGAINST
the wall and let out a long, soft sigh.

That was when she noticed neither Oliver nor Dash was
anywhere in sight.

"Oh bloody . . ." she grumbled. "Oliver!" she hissed.
"Oliver! Where are you?"

Not that she was really worried, but it was a big, strange
place, and it was a bad time for an unauthorized corgi to be
skulking about in places which might soon be declared a
crime scene.

*No, no, no,* Emma told herself firmly. *That's not what's
happened here.*

Except at least one other person was clearly thinking
about it. Emma wondered if Frank knew something, or had
seen something.

*But it still doesn't make any sense! Because if you really
wanted somebody dead, pushing them out that window
made no more sense than the idea of trying to kill yourself
by jumping out of it did.*

*Unless you weren't thinking ahead. Unless you weren't
trying to kill them. It could have been a fight, or something,
and somebody got pushed, and fell and . . .*

*And I have got to stop thinking like this. I don't know anything!*

"Oliver!" Emma called in a hoarse stage whisper. She also moved farther up the hallway. She didn't want the family to hear her. There was no need to make this any more awkward than it already was.

There was no answer. Emma swore again and tried to think what to do.

Down in the entryway, the front door opened. Someone came through, umbrella first.

*Daphne?* Emma hurried toward the foyer.

The person, a woman, leaned out the door and shook her umbrella. Even from this awkward angle, Emma could tell it wasn't Daphne.

Detective Chief Inspector Constance Brent of the Devon and Cornwall police had arrived.

Constance was a tall, strongly built, stern-faced woman. Emma had privately vowed never to get into an arm-wrestling contest or a poker game with her. She kept her bleached hair in a short, spiky cut and, at least the times Emma had seen her, wore practical trousers and jackets with commodious pockets. Today, she also wore a rumpled trench coat and broad-brimmed felt hat that gave her the air of someone who'd just walked out of a classic noir film to put the finger on a stool pigeon.

*Or something.*

Emma had met Constance last summer. A local woman had been poisoned, and Emma had been the one to find that body too. She'd also helped solve the case, a fact which still made her a little dizzy.

"Well, Emma Reed." Constance sighed and stuck the umbrella into the brass stand by the door. "I thought we'd agreed you were not going to make a habit of this."

"Sorry."

"PC Patel says you found Ms. Cochrane."

Emma nodded. "Me and Genny Knowles."

Constance took her hat off and hung it on her umbrella handle. "And you were here at Truscott Grange, because . . . ?"

"We're helping cater the Daphne du Maurier Literary Festival."

"We being you and Genny Knowles, or so I'm told." Constance frowned. "Doesn't she run the chip shop?"

"She's just helping out. The main team was going to be me, and Angelique and Pearl Delgado from the King's Rest. Today was the day we were supposed to present the tasting menu to the society board, but . . ." She waved helplessly at the front door.

"So where're the rest of your team?"

"Angelique and Pearl stayed behind to do breakfast service at the B and B. They were supposed to meet us here afterward. I'd come ahead with Genny to get started. She's in the kitchen. I had just been taking the family some tea."

Constance's jaw moved slowly back and forth.

"So, let me get this straight," she said. "A lot of literary types were converging on a grand country house ahead of the village festival, and suddenly one of them has turned up dead. Is that right?"

"In a scene that kind of echoes one in the dead woman's favorite novel. Yeah," said Emma. "Sorry."

Constance sighed sharply. "Just please tell me nobody here's a mystery writer."

"Not that I know of."

"Good." Constance hitched her bag strap up on her shoulder. Constance carried a handbag that would have fit Oliver and two or three of his younger cousins comfortably. "I need to talk to the family. I can find you where? The kitchen?"

"Yeah," agreed Emma. "As soon as I find Oliver. He's gone missing."

"Of course the corgi's here too." Constance rolled her eyes toward the ceiling. "Well, give him a scritch on the back for me."

"And, erm, there's something else you should probably know."

Constance raised one pale brow. "I am all ears."

"I, um, might have been the last person Marcie spoke to."

Constance blew out a long sigh. "Of course. All right. You do not leave this house until we've talked, yeah?"

"Yeah," agreed Emma.

"Right." Constance headed down the corridor, back and shoulders straight. Emma watched while she knocked on the sitting room door. It was Frank who opened it. Constance disappeared inside and Emma was alone again in the dim and silent corridor. The skin on the back of her neck prickled. Without Constance there, the house suddenly felt too heavy around her, like someone had just tightened the lid down further.

*And where on earth is Oliver?*

OLIVER WAS STARTING TO WONDER THE SAME THING.

Obviously he knew where he was *now*. Corgis did not get lost. But the line between where one was and where one had been did sometimes get a little tangled.

When Emma shooed him and Dash out of the room that had the other humans, Oliver was a little disappointed. He sniffed the closed door and thought about barking, but that would be rude.

"Humans," mumbled Dash. "'S truth. Well, what do we do now?" He scratched one floppy ear.

"Wait?" suggested Oliver. *A corgi is patient. Emma will be out soon.*

"Maybe." Dash nosed around the floor. "Or try the kitchen. Maybe there's more food. I like your human. She's a good human. You're lucky."

Oliver pushed his nose against Dash's shaggy brown side. He was starting to like Dash. He was easygoing and might be fun at another time, when he wasn't sad.

Dash shrugged Oliver off and started nosing around some of the other doorways.

That seemed like a good idea. There was plenty to investigate. This place was *big*, and it was fascinating. There were almost as many smells as the park outdoors. Oliver found himself snuffling along the floorboards, following the ripples and layers of scent into a side room almost without realizing it. This house had so many corners and shadows. There were smells of polish and vinegar and dust, and so many people had been in and out of here recently, people with dogs and cats and that was definitely a pig there and . . . was that a sheep?

When Oliver lifted his head, Dash was nowhere in sight. Oliver had gotten so distracted, he hadn't noticed him leaving.

Oliver hesitated. He knew he should wait for Emma, but he also knew that Dash was very sad. He didn't want the big dog to be alone.

*Emma will understand. Emma always helps our friends.*

Oliver followed Dash's fresh and clear trail to the foyer. Hallways stretched out in either direction. Dash had gone down the one on the left, and now he was at the base of the stairs, searching around the baseboards. His tail waved steadily. All at once, he thrust his nose forward. "Huh. Huh. Who's that? Huh? Who's that?"

Oliver put his nose down and sniffed. Quite a few humans had been through here recently. Some of the scents seemed familiar, but there were too many and they were too new for Oliver to identify individuals. He picked up perfume, soap, sweat and coffee, cats and dogs. There was plenty of mud and rain too because of the weather.

Dash, though, had picked out one smell in particular. Oliver could tell by the way his floppy ears and restless tail both pricked up. The bigger dog started up the narrow stairway.

"Where are you going?" asked Oliver.

"Upstairs."

*I know that,* thought Oliver a little impatiently. "Why?"

"Because something's wrong," Dash growled. "I don't like it."

Oliver gave a small whine. Emma might be done with the other humans by now. She might be worried if she couldn't find him.

At the same time, this might be important. If there was

something wrong in this big, strange house, Emma should know about it.

There was one problem. The stairs were steep and there were a lot of them. This wasn't like getting into the van where Oliver could get a running jump. Dash had long legs and climbed up with no problem. Oliver, though, hopped, and heaved and wriggled, scrabbled, scrambled and hopped again. But a noble corgi did not give up. Even when he was panting on the landing.

Dash didn't stop at the first landing. He kept going all the way up to the top of the stairs. By the time Oliver got there, he had to flop down on his belly and spend a long time panting. He wished someone had put a water bowl here. He'd mention it to Emma. The humans in this house were not very organized.

The corridors were narrower up here and the ceilings were lower. Dash stood at the first doorway with his nose against the crack by the floor. Dash scratched at the door. Slowly it swung open, and Dash started to bark. Someone, a human, squeaked.

Oliver jumped to his feet.

Dash had discovered an office-type room. Emma spent a lot of time in places like this. There was a desk, and a lot of books, and a computer. A woman hunched behind the desk. Both hands covered her mouth. She smelled like rainwater and sweat, acrid hair spray and that stuff called "perfume"— which on her was more like dead otters and roses than anything else—and she was very startled.

"Who? Who? Who?" barked Dash.

"No, Dash, it's me! It's me!" The woman slapped the computer lid shut and ran out from around the desk. "Come on, shhh, shhh, good dog!" She crouched down and tried to rub Dash's head and ears, but she was still scared. Dash felt it, and he kept barking.

Oliver barked too. "Here! Here! Somebody's here!"

"No, no, no!" she groaned. "Stop it, you little bi—!"

"Who? Who?" barked Dash.

The woman swore and jumped to her feet. She scuttled past them both and disappeared down the back stairs.

"Showed her!" growled Dash triumphantly. "She doesn't belong here!"

"I need to get back to Emma," Oliver told him. "I need to tell her!"

Dash shook his ears. "You can't tell humans this. They don't understand."

"Emma understands." Oliver turned his bum toward the bigger dog, ignoring Dash's huffing. As he did, a new scent reached him.

*Emma! Emma and . . . LOBSTER!*

# 15

EMMA WAS NOT AN EXPERT IN ETIQUETTE. HOWEVER, SHE did know that when people were trying to adjust to a tragic death, at the same time as they were trying to deal with the police, pretty much the last thing the guests should be doing was wandering around calling for lost dogs.

At the same time, she did not want to leave Oliver to his own devices. She wasn't actually worried he'd get hurt or anything while he was inside, but there was no guarantee he'd stay inside. Oliver could be very quick on his paws, and the grange had a lot of doors.

*Time to try something else.*

Emma ducked down into the kitchen.

"What's going on?" Genny barely glanced up from spreading softened butter on squares of whole wheat bread.

"Missing corgi." Emma scooped some of the chopped lobster they'd brought for the seafood salad into a bowl. "Need bait."

Back in the main entrance hall, Emma whistled softly and shook the little dish of lobster meat.

"Oliver?" she whispered. "Oliver!"

Hallways stretched out in three directions. Nothing moved in any of them.

*Upstairs?* Emma started climbing the sweeping staircase to the second floor.

"Oliver!" she stage whispered when she got to the landing. She shook the bowl. "Come on, Oliver!"

"Emma!"

Emma's head jerked up. Oliver and Dash both galloped out onto the landing one floor up. Well, Dash galloped, Oliver sort of scampered.

"Emma! Emma! I saw something! It's important!" he barked.

Dash also barked, and started loping down the stairs. Oliver stopped, and focused, and started hopping down, stair to stair as fast as his stubby legs could manage it.

"There was a woman"—*hop*—"in an office"—*hop*. "Dash says"—*hop*—"she shouldn't be there! Ooh, what's that!" Oliver finally reached her side and stretched up on his hind legs, trying to see over the rim of the dish she carried. "Is that lobster? I smelled lobster! What an excellent idea!"

"What are you talking about, Oliver?" Emma put the dish down. "What did you see?"

"A lady, all perfume and hair spray! She was in the office room. She wears too much perfume. It makes her smell like dead otters and bad roses. You should tell her."

Emma thought furiously. Oliver had clearly seen someone. Someone who smelled like perfume and hair spray, but didn't have a name. This wasn't Oliver's fault. He was a dog. He might talk to Emma, but smells were a lot more important to him than words, and a lot more memorable. Little things like human names, clothing or hairstyles were afterthoughts.

This was a lady with a strong artificial smell. But dead otters? Really?

How does he even know what dead otters smell like? Emma shook herself. *Focus! What could that mean . . . ?* What was in perfume?

*Musk!* Oliver must mean it was a musk perfume. And hair spray.

Realization hit and Emma covered her mouth. When she had control of herself again, she asked, "Oliver, was this the same lady we saw earlier, outside, in the rain? The one who got sick by the car?"

"Yes, yes! The sick lady!" Oliver put both his front paws on her knee. "What?"

Emma was swallowing a laugh. "Nothing. Her name is Caite Hope-Johnston and, yeah, she does wear too much perfume. Where did you see her?"

"Dash went upstairs, all the way up. He said something was wrong, and he went to the office room. She was there, standing at the desk, only when Dash barked she stopped and she tried to get him to be quiet." Oliver paused. "Dash doesn't like her very much."

Emma took a deep breath. She also took both Oliver's front paws in her hands. "Okay, Oliver, this is important. What was she doing at the desk? Was she looking in a drawer or . . ."

"She was typing, on the computer thingy." Oliver dropped back down on all fours.

Emma let go of his paws and stood up straight.

Oliver darted back to the bowl of chopped lobster, but it was too late. Dash had already licked it clean.

"That was not sporting," said Oliver.

Dash licked the corgi's nose. This time, Emma couldn't help laughing. But that didn't ease the spinning sensation inside her.

Caite Hope-Johnston snuck back into the house *after* Raj had sent her away. And she was in Marcie's study and doing . . . something with Marcie's computer. Barely an hour after she'd found out Marcie was dead.

*What on earth could she have been after?*

Emma looked up the stairs. *No. No. I should not go up there. I should wait for Constance. I should tell her. I should . . .*

"Oh, good, you found him!"

Emma jumped. Oliver barked. Genny stood at the door to the basement stairs, holding a big plate of sandwiches.

"Yeah, sorry." Emma leaned over the rail and stage whispered. "I guess Oliver wandered off upstairs somewhere . . ."

"Oliver followed Dash and discovered something very important!" Oliver barked.

"Let me get these two back to the kitchen," said Emma quickly.

"Great. I'll drop these off." Genny hefted the tray with the sandwich platter. "You can start in on assembling the cakes, all right?"

Emma agreed and shooed both dogs down the stairs. But not without a backward glance.

*What could Caite have been* doing?

Back in the kitchen, Dash flopped onto his blanket by the door, clearly exhausted from his explorations. Emma determinedly took herself over to the bin with the sponge cakes. Oliver followed and plunked himself down on his hindquarters beside her.

This morning, Emma had carefully wrapped the fresh sheets of angel cake in cling film to keep them from drying out. Now she unwrapped them just as carefully. She also brought out the small tub of lime and passion fruit curd filling and the cartons of cream and mascarpone, and the bottle of ginger syrup for the frosting.

"Emma." Oliver looked up with pleading eyes. "It was important, right? About the perfume lady?"

*I will not even think about going upstairs,* she told herself. "Yes, Oliver. You did great."

Fortunately, there was a stand mixer right on the work counter. She wanted to get the cream whipped before she started in on cake assembly.

"Do you want to see the office room?" Oliver yipped hopefully. "I can show you."

Emma thought about Constance Brent upstairs, questioning the Cochrane family over tea and Genny's sandwiches. She thought about how Genny was probably on her way back right now, unless, of course, Constance decided to keep her for questioning as well . . .

Either way, Emma would not have a lot of time. Plus, of

course, wandering around the house was a bad idea, even if there wasn't any kind of official investigation starting just yet. Anyway, the Hyphenated Caite might have a perfectly legitimate reason to be here, after being told by the police she couldn't come in. Besides, Emma had a job to do. She'd promised people cake and she'd already left Genny to make all the sandwiches. Emma could not let the side down for the sake of her own curiosity.

Emma resolutely opened the carton of double cream.

"Emma!" Oliver bonked her shin with his nose.

Emma sighed and closed the cream. "To heck with it. Oliver, where're those back stairs?"

"Here!" Oliver darted to the back corner of the kitchen. Dash barked once, but declined to get up from his spot next to the outside door. At least for now.

Emma yanked the back stairs door open, only to find herself face-to-face with Constance Brent.

# 16

· · · · · · · · · · ·

"GOING SOMEWHERE, EMMA?" THE DETECTIVE ASKED CHEER-
fully.

"Erm," said Emma.

"We'll take that as a yes. Come on, you can sit down and
tell Auntie Constance all about it." She brushed past Emma,
heading toward the kitchen island.

"Uh, right." Emma followed the detective back to the
counter. "Tea?" she asked reflexively.

"Had mine, thanks. But you go ahead." Constance
dropped her handbag onto the counter and climbed up on
one of the tall stools. "That looks like it's going to be some
amazing cake."

"It's an angel food sponge with lime and passion fruit
curd. Go ahead and try some."

Constance picked up a spoon and dipped out a bit of
curd. "Wow!" she said as she tasted it. "I think I'm glad I
don't live in Trevena. I have enough of a sweets problem."

"Thanks." Emma checked the water level in the kettle
and reached another teapot out of the cupboard—a Staffordshire ware painted with pansies and buttercups. She
also glanced at the door to the main stairs.

"Something wrong?" asked Constance.

"I was just wondering where Genny is," admitted Emma.

"I asked her to wait so I could talk with you privately." Constance pulled a black notebook and a mechanical pencil out of her bag. "Since we're old friends, we'll start with the hands, all right?"

"Oh. Yes. Right."

Emma had been ready for this. Constance wasn't like any detective she'd ever seen on television, or in her (very limited) experience with police in the real world. She liked to keep the people she questioned very much on their toes.

She also read palms, and tended to lead with that during her interviews. Emma suspected that it got people confused, which then got them to underestimate the detective. Emma also suspected Constance knew that.

Emma stretched out both hands toward the detective. "How's my Heart line?" she asked.

"Looking good. Strong." Constance cocked her head. "Anything I should know?"

"Not yet." Emma started spooning Earl Grey into the pot. "Anything I should know?"

Constance raised one brow. "Not yet."

"Emma! Tell her about the perfume lady in the office room!" barked Oliver eagerly.

"Okay, Oliver," murmured Emma. "Good boy."

Oliver dropped back, disappointed but resigned, and went over to investigate Constance's practical brown shoes.

Constance gave his head a quick pat and then clicked her pencil once. "How about you tell me what happened this morning?"

"Erm." Emma finished pouring the fresh water into the pot and put the lid on.

Constance sighed. "Seems to me I've heard that 'erm' before. What's wrong?"

"Before I tell you about this morning, I, um, should probably tell you about last night."

Now both of Constance's brows arched. "Why's that?"

"Remember how I told you I might have been the last

one to talk to Marcie? She came round to the King's Rest last night, late, to see me. Well, actually it wasn't me. She was there to see Angelique, but Angelique had already gone home."

Constance looked at her steadily. Emma found her words drying up. She looked toward the windows. Outside, the rain had finally stopped; she could see Genny wandering between the courtyard puddles, arms folded.

Genny turned toward the window and saw Emma watching her. She gave a little wave and a thumbs-up. Emma gave one back. Constance looked at the window, and then looked at Emma. Emma, guilty, let her hand drop.

"It's all right," Constance said. She also clicked her mechanical pencil again. "Believe me, I want this finished too. These cases . . ." She shook her head. "They're hard on everybody. So, we'll start with last night. Marcie Cochrane came to see, only not you, actually it was Angelique she wanted. Go on."

Emma did. She described Marcie coming to the B&B, how she tried to give Emma the check, and how she was so concerned about everything going perfectly.

Then Emma described coming up the drive to the grange, and following the drive around the house, and seeing the body.

Constance's jaw tightened. "And you're certain the window was open?"

"Yes. I remember seeing the curtains blowing in the breeze."

"Did you notice anything else at the time?"

"Um, no, not then."

"But?"

"Um, well, when I went to take tea to the family, I noticed Oliver had wandered off."

"Oliver followed Dash and made an important discovery!" Oliver reminded her.

Emma chose her next words carefully. "I couldn't find him on the main floor, so I went upstairs, and I heard barking and I saw somebody running out of Marcie's office. I think maybe they were using the computer. I thought I heard typing."

"Did you see who it was?"

Emma firmly resisted the urge to cross her fingers. Constance would notice. Constance was like that.

"I *think* it was Caite Hope-Johnston. She's the president of the Daphne du Maurier Literary and Appreciation Society. The ones who are putting on the festival."

Constance considered her notes. Then, she considered Emma. Emma, to her shame, turned away quickly and poured water into the teapot.

"I've heard that name already today," said Constance.

"She came to the house earlier. Raj stopped her from coming in."

"Yeah, that's it." Constance's gaze was still too steady for comfort. "Anything else?"

Emma set the pot down, defeated. "Well, I don't know if it's relevant . . ."

"We won't know until you tell me."

So Emma told her about the problem with the catering deposits going astray and causing Weber's to pull out of the festival.

"Seems like you know rather a lot about what's been going on with this festival," said Constance. "What exactly was Marcie's part in it?"

"She was the society treasurer, and that meant she took a lot of the blame for what happened with the money."

"Of course," agreed Constance.

"But she was also a huge du Maurier fan, and apparently she really poured her heart into the festival and the fancy dress every year."

"So she had something she was looking forward to?"

"Yes," said Emma. "She did."

*Or did she?* Emma remembered Marcie's anxious expression and how she said, *You'll make this work, won't you? . . . It has to be perfect.*

That had sounded more nervous than expectant.

"All right." Constance's voice cut across her thoughts. "I

think that's everything for now. Thank you for your cooperation." She stowed her notebook and pencil back in her bag.

"Are you, that is, do you—"

"Emma." Constance cut her off. "I value your intelligence, you know that, right?"

"Erm. Yes?"

"Good. And because you are an intelligent person, you will have realized we are at the very beginning of what could be a painful investigation. And since you know this, I also know you were not just about to ask me what I think happened. Were you?"

"No?" tried Emma. "I wouldn't do a thing like that?"

Constance nodded. "That's right. You wouldn't. Now, Oliver." Constance bent down and gave Oliver's chin a good rub. "You take Mum home. We'll call if there are any more questions." Constance shook her hand. "And, Emma?"

"Yeah?"

Constance's grim expression softened. "I'm sorry you had to be in the middle of this. It's not easy."

"Thanks."

Still softly, she said, "So don't make it harder than it has to be, yeah?"

Emma swallowed. She also nodded. "Yeah."

Constance slung her bag strap on her shoulder, gave Oliver another quick pat and headed out through the door to the main stairs. The door swung silently shut behind her. Emma sucked in a deep breath.

"Are we going home, Emma?" Oliver wagged hopefully.

"Soon, Oliver, I promise."

Dash grumbled and huffed.

"She does so!" Oliver growled.

"What was that?"

"Dash said I told you so. He thinks you wouldn't understand about Perfume Lady!"

"Oh. Well, you can tell Dash I do understand, but I have to pick my battles." Emma went to the outside door and pulled it open.

"All clear!" she called to Genny.

Genny hurried down the steps to give Emma a huge hug. "Oh lord!" she exclaimed. "Could that have been any worse?!"

"Um, actually, yeah."

"What?" exclaimed Genny. "Do you know something?"

"I know something very strange happened."

"And you will tell all!" Genny glowered at her to emphasize the seriousness of this order.

Emma wanted to, but before she could even get started, the door to the back stairs opened.

*Constance?* Emma straightened up abruptly.

But it was Daphne who peered tentatively around the door. Her air of buoyant confidence had been scraped away, and the young woman who faced them now looked raw and fragile.

Genny moved first. She wrapped Daphne in a strong hug. Daphne, however, made no move to hug her back, and Genny quickly let go.

"I'm so sorry about this, Daph," said Genny.

"Yeah, well." Daphne wound the end of her ponytail around one finger. "It was never going to be . . ." She stopped and shook her head. "Are you guys heading back to the B and B?"

"That was the plan," said Emma. "Just as soon as I've got the cake together."

"Take me with you?"

# 17

..........

THE DRIVE BACK TO TREVENA WAS QUIET, AND A LITTLE crowded. Daphne rode between Emma and Genny. Oliver sprawled across their laps.

When they reached the King's Rest, Genny let Emma and Daphne out in the car park. She wanted to get home to Martin. She told Emma to let Josh know he needed to come home as soon as possible.

Emma promised she would. Then she let herself and Daphne in through the kitchen. Daphne probably shouldn't be walking through the great room just now. News traveled fast through Trevena. It was possible that Marcie's death was already being discussed over the takeaway counter.

They found Pearl in the kitchen, scrolling through something on her mobile. As soon as she saw Daphne, she dropped her phone and folded her friend in a huge hug.

"I'm so sorry, Daph!"

"No, I'm sorry," Daphne told her. "I shouldn't have dragged you into this."

"Hey!" Pearl pulled back just far enough to give her a gentle shake. "You didn't drag us into anything. Nobody could have known this would happen."

As soon as Pearl said this, Daphne's face twisted up tight.

"I could," she gasped. "I should have. This is my fault!"

As soon as Daphne said it, all the strength seemed to drain right out of her. She collapsed onto the kitchen's stool and started crying.

"Oh, Daph!" Pearl wrapped her arms around her friend's shoulders.

Emma grabbed the box of tissues off the windowsill and set them down by Pearl, who pulled one out and pressed it into Daphne's hand so she could wipe her cheeks. The door from the great room opened, and Angelique came in, followed by her husband, Daniel.

Pearl looked up at her parents, and there was one of those moments of near-telepathic communication that happens in tight-knit families. Daniel put a hand on Angelique's shoulder, and nodded at Pearl. He was a tall, broad, kind man with calloused hands and dark, weathered skin. He kept his hair and his beard trimmed short and usually dressed in work clothes—a blue shirt, corduroys and stout boots.

Both parents went quickly out the way they came, and Emma hurried after them.

The great room was blessedly empty, except for Josh behind the cakes counter.

"Daphne's just having her cry out," Emma told the Delgados. "Things are not good up at the grange."

"No surprise there," breathed Angelique.

"What can we do?" asked Daniel.

"Well, Genny wants Josh to get back to the Towne Fryer. I can close up the counter after he's gone."

"I'll tell him," said Daniel.

"And I'll get Daphne some tea," said Angelique. "She could probably use it."

"Good idea," agreed Emma.

Daniel gave Josh the news. The boy went pale. He was plainly eager to hear the details, but he didn't ask questions.

At least, not too many. He just texted his mum, grabbed his cap from off the coat hook, and headed out the front door.

While Angelique started the tea, Daniel and Emma wiped down the counters and put up the Closed sign. Oliver, sensing the tension in the air, paced methodically around the room, ears and nose straining to detect any changes. When Fergus loped in from the garden, Oliver barely seemed to notice, and the Irish setter went out again in what seemed to Emma must be a bit of a huff.

"Tell you what," Daniel said as Angelique set the teapot on its tray. "I'll go home and start dinner, yeah? You and Pearl take your time here."

"Thank you, you good man." Angelique gave her husband a peck on the cheek.

Back in the kitchen, the worst of Daphne's storm had faded. Pearl had found a second stool and now the two friends sat side by side with a stack of crumpled tissues piled between them.

Angelique poured out the tea and passed round the cups. Emma swept the tissues into the trash.

"Ta," croaked Daphne.

"Now, my girl," said Angelique. "This is as bad as it can be, but you can't blame yourself. You don't know what was in Marcie's heart."

"We don't even know . . . what happened," added Emma.

"But that's just it. I can. I do." Daphne swallowed and wiped at her face with the heel of her palm. Pearl handed her another tissue, and she wiped her nose.

"Me and Mum came up early this year because I was turning twenty-one, you know? Mum said Aunt Marcie had asked if we could celebrate my birthday at the grange. Said it was special. Wouldn't have been my first choice, but, you know. Family." Daphne shrugged. "Anyway, after dinner, Aunt Marcie . . . she took me aside. We went walking in the park. She said she had something she wanted to tell me." Daphne took a long swallow of tea.

Oliver trotted over and flopped down beside her. Daphne looked down. Oliver rolled over onto his back and wriggled.

Daphne returned a bare ghost of a smile.

"Aunt Marcie said . . . she said now that I was old enough to make my own choices, she wanted to know whether I wanted Truscott Grange—house, land, the lot."

"You mean, as an inheritance?" asked Emma. Daphne nodded.

"Well, of course it would be you, wouldn't it?" said Pearl. "Who else would there be?"

"There's some cousins somewhere, I think, but, yeah It's pretty much all down to me," Daphne drew in a long, shaky breath. "Aunt Marcie said she wanted me to have a choice in whether to inherit. She didn't, you see."

"I didn't know that," said Angelique.

"Yeah, well, it's not one of those things you talk about, is it?" Daphne took another swallow of tea. "Seems my grandparents decided to put Marcie in charge of the estate because they were afraid the boys might make a hash of things. And they told Marcie it was going to be her responsibility to keep the place together for all of them."

"When did they die?" asked Emma.

"My grandparents? A while ago now. Car accident. I was just a kid."

"That's sad." Emma tried to imagine what Marcie would have gone through, losing her parents so suddenly and knowing they were trusting her to take responsibility for the whole family.

"Anyway, Aunt Marcie said if I wanted the grange, she'd keep on, you know, to make sure it was there for me and my kids, if I had any. She said she'd teach me how to manage the estate too, or would help to hire somebody. All that stuff. She said she'd already talked the whole thing over with Mum, and Mum agreed with her."

"What did your dad think?" asked Emma.

Daphne stared at her tea. "She didn't ask him. Said she'd kept it secret because Dad and the uncles were still all shirty about the fact that it was Marcie who got left the estate and they were all put on allowances. She didn't want them giving me and Mum any extra grief."

"You know, that's a lot to dump into your lap," said Pearl.

"Yeah, it is that." Daphne drank more tea. "I was pretty mad at first at Mum and Aunt Marcie both. I mean, you know, why not at least warn me what was coming?"

"I'm sure they were trying to do their best," said Angelique.

"Yeah, I know." Daphne twisted the end of her ponytail around her finger and tugged. And then seemed to notice what she was doing and let it go. "At least, I knew once I started thinking about it."

"So, what did you say to her?" asked Pearl.

"Not even a real question, was it? Me and Mum didn't live at the grange, but we're out here at least once every year, and I've got eyes. I saw how hard Aunt Marcie works, worked, trying to take care of that place. She never got to go anywhere or have any kind of life for herself. It was all about Truscott Grange and she always had to worry about money and stuff, because the uncles were such prigs and fought back on using the house as a wedding venue or anything that might actually help the place pay for itself, you know? Even gave her grief every year about the du Maurier festival. 'It's our home!' they said"—Daphne put on a remarkably good imitation of her uncle Bert—"'not some bloody tourist attraction!' But it's not like any of them ever tried to help her either. They didn't even *live* there, not even Dad. They just all got off on the idea of being a bunch of poshos with a country estate and all. So they'd turn up on the weekends, hang about, complain and leave it all for her to manage. It wasn't fair."

Emma winced. Her relationship with her brother, Henry, could be rough at times, but he'd never let her down when she really needed him, and they'd always pulled together for the family. She couldn't imagine what it would be like to be shouldered with all that responsibility, and all that blame.

"Not fair" didn't even begin to describe it.

Emma thought about Marcie the night she'd sat right

where Daphne was, talking about the fictional housekeeper, Mrs. Danvers . . . *She was desperate, wasn't she? And heartbroken. And who wouldn't be?* . . . She was going to spend the rest of her life taking care of a house that would never really be her home. Not really.

Emma frowned at her tea.

"There was no way I was setting myself up for that," Daphne said. "And there was no way I was going to make her hang about playing housemaid one second longer. So I told her flat out I didn't want any of it, and that as far as I was concerned she could lock the doors and chuck the key in the pond if that was what she wanted."

"Wow," said Pearl. "That's brave. Not sure I could have walked out on a whole grand estate."

"How did Marcie take it?" asked Emma.

Daphne's eyes went distant as she remembered. "She got all quiet at first, and then she said, 'That's what I thought. Well done, Daph.'"

Angelique nodded. "That doesn't sound to me like a woman who's been disappointed."

"Yeah." Daphne sniffed. "That's what I thought then. I mean, the whole idea was I could set her free, you know? Now she could sell the place, or give it to the National Trust, whatever, but she'd finally have her own life. I was sure I'd done the right thing." Her chin quivered. She tugged her ponytail again, hard. "And then . . . and then . . ."

"We still don't know what happened," said Angelique. "You cannot blame yourself."

"I hate to ask this," said Emma. "But has anybody found a note?"

"Not that I know about. But I read this thing where they said most suicides don't actually leave a note. That's for the movies and stuff." Daphne swallowed again. "Uncle Gus said she'd been depressed. More than usual. I thought it was because of all this . . . stuff going on with the festival. She was so big on responsibility and the Hyphenated Caite was being even worse than usual this year. But what if that wasn't it? What if she really wanted me to take over the grange?

What if she thought I was . . . all those years keeping the place up for me and I just told her to chuck it and she . . ."

"Oh, Daph," cried Pearl. "I'm sure that's not what happened!"

"How can you be sure?" Daphne snapped. "I'm not!"

Daphne jumped off the stool and slammed out the door to the car park.

# 18

. . . . . . . . . . . .

OLIVER RUSHED UP TO THE DOOR AND BARKED. BUT THEN stopped and slunk back to Emma's side.

"I should go get her." Pearl started for the door.

"Give her a minute, Pearl," said Angelique. "She just needs to get herself together."

Pearl stared at the door, clearly torn, but in the end she turned back to her mother and Emma.

"Emma . . . you were there," Pearl said. "Do you . . . do you think Marcie really jumped?"

The thought of Caite using Marcie's computer after her death rose up again. But so did the thought of Marcie driving around the district so late (by Cornish standards) on a miserable night. Where had she been? If she'd wanted to give Angelique her payment, why hadn't she at least called ahead to make sure Angelique was there?

And why draw on her personal funds? Marcie was the society's treasurer. She could just check the account balance anytime and make sure the money was there.

Emma found her mind backtracking to the bounced catering checks. Just how much money had gone missing from the du Maurier society?

"I don't know," she made herself say to Pearl. "I mean,

personally, I still think an accident is the most likely explanation." *Just maybe not as much as I did this morning.*

"I don't suppose you—" But she cut herself off. "I should check on Daphne," Pearl said, and before either of them could stop her, she hurried out the car park door.

"You know what almost happened there," said Angelique. "She wanted to ask if you could talk to that detective."

"Wouldn't have done any good," said Emma. "I already got warned off." Then, much to her embarrassment, she cracked a huge yawn. "Oh, sorry!"

"You should go home and get some rest," said Angelique. "I doubt you've slept more than five hours for the past two days."

"Yes, yes." Oliver stretched up to put his paws on her knee. "It is time to go home, Emma!"

Emma wanted to argue, but found she couldn't.

"Do you want a ride?" asked Angelique. "I could take you."

"No, thanks." Emma climbed off the stool. "The walk'll do me and Oliver good. And I can stop and check in on Genny on the way, if she's still at the shop."

"Good idea," said Angelique. "And—"

That was when the kitchen landline rang. Angelique muttered a highly creative curse on the head of whoever had such terrible timing, but she went over to answer it anyway.

"King's Rest, how can I help you? Oh, Mr. Whaling. Yes, I have the order ready. If you can just . . ."

Emma found her bag and waved goodbye. Angelique waved back. "Yes, yes. The same as last week. Yes."

"Come on, Oliver." Emma held open the kitchen door, and let Oliver out ahead of her.

Daphne and Pearl were still standing in the car park. Both girls had their heads down and were talking softly to each other. They saw Emma and Oliver, or heard them, and both looked a little startled and a little guilty.

Emma put on a friendly smile and waved.

"Um, Emma?" said Pearl.

"Yeah?" Emma stopped in her tracks. Oliver plopped down on his hindquarters and scratched his chin.

"I . . . that is, Daphne wants to ask you something."

Uneasiness prickled up Emma's spine. "Okay."

"Pearl just told me about last summer," said Daphne. "About when Victoria Roberts died."

*Uh-oh.*

Oliver, sensing Emma's mood shift, bonked her calf and whined in wordless concern.

Daphne was taking a deep breath. "I was wondering, if maybe you could . . . you know . . . have a look around about Aunt Marcie?"

Emma forced herself to remain quiet and just keep breathing. Oliver looked up at her, full of concern, and gave her an encouraging bum wag. What she really wanted to do was scoop him up in her arms and hug him like a teddy bear.

*Pull it together, Emma,* she told herself. *And say something adult sounding. Go on. You can do it.*

"Daphne—I want to help you, I do. But the police are doing their jobs, and if I get in the way, it could be really bad. I could mess up evidence or confuse a witness. Just because I was lucky the once—"

"You weren't lucky," said Pearl. "You talked to people. You worked it out."

But even while Daphne was looking at her, pleading, Emma heard Constance's warning in her head. *Don't make this any harder than it has to be.*

This was exactly what Constance was talking about.

At the same time, Emma remembered the argument she'd overheard: *Bert, how come you're so quick to say Marcie jumped? . . . Because it's obvious she jumped! . . . Oh, is it?*

"Daphne," Emma said. She hoped she sounded reasonable but not condescending, but sympathetic, but firm. It was a lot to put into one word. "You can trust DCI Brent. She's really good at what she does. I know you're hurting, but—"

"It's not about me," Daphne shot back. "I mean it is, but it's about Aunt Marcie too. I'm scared."

"Scared?" echoed Pearl. "Of what?"

"I was listening to Dad and my uncles. They were arguing after the detective left. I didn't . . . okay, I wasn't supposed to hear any of it, but you know what? You can hear anything in that house if you really want to." She paused and gave Emma a sideways glance. "So now I look like a sulky teenager or something."

"No, you don't," Emma assured her.

Daphne either decided to believe her or decided she didn't care. "They were talking, but they weren't talking about what happened to Marcie, or what to do, or anything. They were talking about . . . about how it was going to look, and whether there was anything any of them had to worry about. Aunt Marcie's *dead*, and they were worried they were going to be *embarrassed*!" She spat out the last word.

"Grief and fear do strange things inside people," said Emma, but even she was aware how stilted those words sounded.

"But what if they decide there really is something to be embarrassed about?" demanded Daphne. "What if they decide there's something that they need to cover up? Something that might help the police work out what really happened?"

"Do you honestly think your uncles would do that?" said Emma incredulously. "Marcie was their sister."

"Maybe Uncle Gus wouldn't," said Daphne. "He's a bit of a wet blanket but he's more or less okay. And maybe not Dad. Maybe. But Uncle Bert?" Her mouth curled into a sneer. "He'd do it in a heartbeat."

Emma remembered Bert, with his tan, his muscles and his (possibly) dyed hair, towering over his brothers. *And if we sit here arguing like idiots, someone is going to think something's really wrong in this family,* Bert had said. *And they'll start asking awkward questions.*

"I only met him today."

"Oh, he's a charmer." The way Daphne said "charmer"

made it somehow sound like "snake." "He's very big into being a member of an 'old family.'" She made the air quotes. "He thinks being a Cochrane is a privilege and a responsibility, and he never lets the rest of us forget it. If he knew the cops would find something that might be a stain on the family reputation—and I don't mean something quaint, like how Charles II is supposed to have had a quickie with one of my grand-cestors—but you know, something modern and grubby. He'd do whatever it took to cover it up."

"But you can't mean he'd want them to stop investigating if it turned out that . . . well, it wasn't suicide. Or . . ." Emma didn't get any further. She could see by the look on Daphne's face that was exactly what she did mean.

"So, you'll help, right?" said Pearl.

"Please," said Daphne.

Oliver leaned against her knee.

*I'm surrounded.* Emma bit her lip. "Can you . . . can you just give me a minute?"

Emma walked to the edge of the car park. Just across the two-lane highway were the stairs to the beach and the sea. Emma sat down on the top step and rested her arms on her knees. The breeze whipped her hair around her face.

Oliver, of course, was right beside her.

"What do I do, Oliver?" Emma asked.

Oliver scratched his chin. "She needs help, Emma. You like her. Pearl likes her. You'll both help her."

"But what if I mess up?"

"You'll try again."

Despite everything that had happened, Emma laughed. "It's that simple?"

Oliver cocked his head at her. "Why wouldn't it be?"

Emma put her arm around her wonderful, loyal, talking dog and squeezed. "I love you, Oliver."

"I love you too." He licked her cheek. "We should take a walk. You have been inside too much today. It's stopped raining," he added helpfully.

"Thank you, Captain Obvious."

"Corgi Obvious."

Emma laughed again and kissed his nose. She also stood up, checked for random traffic and walked back across the road to where Daphne and Pearl were still waiting.

"All right," she told them. "I will try, but that's all. I can't . . . I can't promise I'll actually find anything."

Daphne let out a long breath. "That's all I'm asking. Honestly. I'll feel better knowing there's somebody on Aunt Marcie's side, you know? Where do we start?"

Emma sucked in a deep breath. She also tried to will her hands to stop shaking. "It's more a question of when. I can't do anything before Monday."

"Monday!" exclaimed Daphne. "That's three days!"

"Two," said Emma. "And it's the soonest we'll hear anything about the autopsy, and if the police find anything in the meantime, we should know what it is before we go stomping about in the flower beds." Saying it out loud, it sounded almost reasonable, even though she was just making things up as she went along.

*"Stalling" is the formal term. I'm stalling.*

"But no matter what, Monday afternoon, I'll come up to the grange and you can show me around. All right?"

Daphne looked like she wanted to argue, but Pearl put a hand on her shoulder. "It's a good plan, Daph."

Reluctantly, Daphne nodded and Emma was able to breathe again.

Maybe by Monday Constance would have found all the answers anybody needed, or Helen would, or the board of the du Maurier society would—with or without the Hyphenated Caite. Maybe she wouldn't have to be part of this at all.

That would be the best possible outcome.

*Wouldn't it?*

# 19

TAKEN AS A WHOLE, TREVENA VILLAGE ACTUALLY COVERED a fair amount of ground. The outskirts, farms and housing estates sprawled well up into the hills. The village proper stretched along the coastline from the tourist trap of King Arthur's Castle at one end to the genuine medieval ruins that topped the cliffs at the other. But the center of the village was a few narrow, winding streets lined by white-washed buildings. Many still sported the traditional bright blue doors and pub-style signs. Some of them, like the post office and the King's Rest itself, had been standing for hundreds of years.

Genny's chip shop, the Towne Fryer, stood on a corner right on the edge of the old central village, and Emma's route home from the B&B took her right past it. The Towne Fryer was a classic chippery—just a service counter, a space for the fry baskets and warming table, and a little counter under the window where maybe three customers could sit, if they were very good friends. Genny and her family ran the shop with part-time help from not only Josh but a rotating selection of kids from the local secondary school, as well as Becca, who also helped out at Emma's shop.

"Are we going to get fish?" asked Oliver when she stopped in front of the shop. "We should definitely get fish. You did not have any lunch. You shouldn't skip meals, Emma. You have not been healthy today." For emphasis, he prodded her ankle with his nose.

"Yes, Mum." Emma laughed. Which only caused him to prod her again.

Fortunately, it wasn't the teatime rush yet and the shop was currently empty of customers. Despite everything on her mind, Emma couldn't help noticing that the covered cake stand on the service counter was empty. Emma had an arrangement with the Towne Fryer to provide a selection of bakes to supplement their menu of fried goodies. The empty stand meant the Grandma's Grand Chocolate Cake she'd delivered just yesterday was already gone. But the plate of Lemon Blue Shortbread Bars was still half-full.

*Might need to tinker with that recipe.*

Genny was behind the counter, talking with her husband, Martin. Martin was a slender, cheerful man with a round, freckled face and neatly trimmed beard. Emma had bonded with him, one pale-skinned ginger to another. They had been known to trade tips on hats and favorite brands of sunscreen. When he wasn't helping with the chip shop or wrangling the kids, Martin volunteered with the local life-saving service, something he'd done since his school days. In fact, he and Genny had actually met during her one ill-considered attempt at windsurfing.

Genny noticed Emma first. "Hullo, Emma! I was just going to call you." Genny came out from behind the counter and gave Emma a long hug.

"Thought I'd save you the trouble." Emma hugged her friend back. "Are you all right?"

"Just about. Martin's been great, as always." She flashed her husband a grin. "And Josh is a little amazing."

"He's got a great mum." Emma rubbed Genny shoulders.

"Aw. Thanks. How about you? How are you doing?"

"I don't know," Emma admitted. "I may have just made a colossal mistake."

Martin struck a pose, pressing his fingertips to his fore-head. "My husband senses tell me there's about to be a long talk here," said Martin. "Why don't you two go out-side? I'll get the tea."

"You are the best possible man in the whole world," said Genny.

"No fish?" Oliver lifted a pair of mournful eyes toward Emma.

"And could we get an order of the haddock?" asked Emma. "We missed lunch and Oliver is growing faint."

"A noble corgi never faints!" Oliver jumped to all four feet. Martin heard the bark and laughed.

"Coming right up."

Emma and Genny settled at one of the outdoor café ta-bles. Oliver took up his favorite position, right under Em-ma's chair.

"All right," said Genny. "What mistake? When? How? And with who?"

Emma sighed. "Daphne. She's asked me to find out what happened to Marcie."

Genny didn't even blink. "Why?"

"Pearl told her about the thing with Victoria last year, and Daphne said she's afraid that one of her uncles will try and cover something up— "

"Bert, I'll bet," said Genny.

"You know about Bert?"

"Oh, lord, Emma, the whole village knows about Bert. Fancies himself a regular power behind the throne. Gets most of his money from the estate and spends it like a drunken sailor. Takes all the right people to lunch, sits on all the right boards."

"He's on the council?"

Genny raised her eyebrows. "What, and risk an actual election? Not his style. He prefers buying drinks, playing golf and charming the socks off all and sundry."

That certainly sorted with Emma's brief impression of the man. Next to Bert, the other Cochrane brothers had faded into the background.

Emma wondered how Bert and Marcie had gotten along, especially after Marcie inherited all the property.

"So, I take it that Daphne doesn't believe Marcie killed herself?" Genny asked.

"That's the problem," Emma said. "She's afraid Marcie did, and that it's her fault."

"Oh, the poor girl! But why on earth would she think that?"

Emma explained what Daphne told her, about the talk with Marcie, and about turning down an inheritance she was afraid would turn into a prison for her the way it had for her aunt. In the middle of the story, Martin came out with a tray with two mugs of good, strong tea and a basket of delicious, fresh fried fish and chips. And something else.

"What's this?" Emma blinked at the pretty little salad.

"Vitamins." Martin put the dish of bright greens, carrot, strawberries and crumbled farm cheese in front of her. "With balsamic dressing. You're not the only one who can help class up the menu." He grinned, kissed Genny, tucked the tray under his arm and headed back inside.

"Emma?" Oliver emerged from under the chair to wag and give her the full tragic-puppy-eyes treatment.

"Yes, Oliver." Emma scratched his head. She also put down some fish, strawberries and carrot. Humans were not the only ones who needed vitamins.

"That's so awful for Daphne," said Genny once Emma had straightened back up. "I mean, I'm sure Marcie meant well, but . . ." She shook her head. "Maybe it will turn out to be an accident after all. That would be awful, but just . . . not quite as awful." She gestured helplessly.

"I know," said Emma. "But there was something else I didn't tell Daphne, because she was already upset and I've got no idea what it means." She leaned forward, as if she was afraid of being overheard. "Caite Hope-Johnston was in the house."

"Wait. Stop. You're *kidding*!"

"I'm not. She got in, even after Raj tried to keep her out, and she was using Marcie's computer."

"That cannot mean anything good."

"No, but it doesn't mean it was anything connected with Marcie's death."

"Emma." Genny looked down her nose at Emma, which since they were both the same height when sitting down, was a pretty good trick. "If you want me to believe *you* believe that, you're going to have to try harder."

"Well, it doesn't. It just means she was afraid of something."

"Or maybe she was looking for something."

"I suppose," admitted Emma slowly. *Maybe something to do with the missing money?*

"Have you told DCI Brent?"

"Yes. I'm not sure how seriously she took me."

"That you can't do anything about." Genny broke open a chip and examined the interior with a professional eye before she popped half in her mouth.

Emma finished her piece of fish. "I wish I knew what was happening now. I mean, with Marcie."

"Well, I'm no expert," said Genny, "but I expect our good detective will have shepherded the body to the morgue and they'll do an autopsy. And if the pathologist finds anything funny, they'll get the coroner to call for an inquest. Raj thinks it'll be a couple of days at most," said Genny.

Emma paused with a chip halfway to her mouth. "Raj does?"

Genny shrugged. "Raj enjoys a bit of fish and chips and a Jackie Chan movie when he's had a hard day," Genny told her. "Puts mayonnaise on his chips, of which I cannot necessarily approve but we all have our little ways, don't we?"

"Yes," agreed Emma blandly. "It seems we do."

"So what are you going to do next?"

"Go home and hide under the bed for a bit and wonder what got into me?"

Genny smiled. "And after that?"

"Well, I've got to go back to the grange as of Monday, don't I? I told Daphne I would."

"You mean *we've* got to go back to the grange as of

Monday." Genny made a back and forth gesture indicating the both of them. "We've got to pick up all those bins of stuff we left behind."

In the rush to get Daphne out of the way of her bickering family, they had in fact left several bins behind. "Listen, Genny, you do not want to get involved in this."

"Too late," Genny said cheerfully. "Already in."

Emma blew out a sigh. "Oh, all right. We can go after my appointment with Brian."

"Fantastic. I can take you. You'll need a chaperone, anyway."

"What are you talking about?"

Mischief sparked in Genny's eyes. "Word on the grapevine is that you are exhibiting all the signs of becoming romantically infatuated with our local auto mechanic and vintage car enthusiast."

"I am going to kill Angelique," Emma muttered.

"Who says Angelique told me? If you're going to insist on flirting during high tea in a small village, people are going to notice."

"I do not flirt."

"If you say so, but you sure do know what you like, don't you?"

Emma folded her arms. "You're awful and I disown you."

"You can't. You're addicted to my haddock."

"You're right. Darn you." And to prove it, Emma helped herself to another piece of fish.

Genny laughed. "Look, I've got to get back inside. I'll meet you here Monday, take you car shopping. And don't make any more rash promises before then, yeah?"

"Nope. All done with that." Emma crossed her heart to emphasize the fact.

Genny nodded once firmly and headed back into the shop. Emma stayed where she was, drinking tea and nibbling the excellent fried fish, and trying to make sense of everything that had happened over the past three days.

"Did I make a mistake, Oliver?" she asked. But this time, there was no answer. Emma peeked under her chair.

Oliver was sprawled on his back, legs splayed, and sound asleep.

Emma sighed. *Well, it doesn't really matter, does it?* She'd promised she would try to find out what happened. She wasn't going back on her word, especially when Daphne was hurting so badly.

But if she was honest with herself, Daphne was not the entire reason for wanting to go back to the grange. Deep inside, Emma felt like she owed it to Marcie to do whatever she could to help. As hard as she tried, she could not shake the idea she'd let Marcie down last night. She should have tried a little harder to keep her at the B&B, or asked just one more question, and then maybe everything would be all right.

Emma glanced in the window of the chip shop. Genny would tell her she was being ridiculous. So would Angelique. And Pearl.

*But, I wonder, what would Marcie say?*

# 20

SATURDAY PROVED TO BE A LONG, TENSE DAY. PEARL AND Angelique were not happy with each other. That happened sometimes. Both were strong-willed women with ideas about the business, and each other's lives, that sometimes clashed. On days like that, Emma tried to stick to her scones and stay out of the way.

The only semibright spot was the phone call from Tasha Boyd saying the board had agreed to accept their proposals, even without the tasting.

"They've agreed to the deposit amount, and I've agreed that we'll return the deposit if the festival is ultimately canceled," Angelique said.

"Any idea how likely . . ." asked Emma, but Angelique just shook her head.

That question of whether the festival would go forward threw a damper over the good news that they'd secured the job. It was not helped by the fact that, if it was all still on, they had just thirteen days to get ready.

Despite her best efforts though, Emma couldn't escape into her work today. The topic of conversation for everybody, whether they came in for a a quick bun or a cream tea, was Marcie's death. From the bits Emma picked up,

Marcie had always been well-liked but not particularly well understood. To the village in general she seemed to be a sad and somewhat mysterious figure while she was alive. Very much the lady in the tower. Now she was a quiet tragedy. Competing rumors about old lovers, new debts and other suicides in the family were chewed over along with the apple cake and ginger biscuits.

Emma hoped Daphne was staying well away from the village this weekend. She also hoped they'd hear something from the police. Or the du Maurier society.

"Not likely," muttered Pearl. "Ned Giddy practically ran the other way when I saw him in the Tesco this morning."

Emma found herself thinking highly uncomplimentary thoughts about Ned Giddy, and even Tasha Boyd. Not that she really expected solid answers yet, but any bit of news would be better than suspense and speculation.

Unfortunately, all they had by the end of the day was more silence. All the uncertainty, combined with Angelique and Pearl snapping at each other, left Emma with a feeling she didn't get very often.

"Oliver," she said as they headed up the winding village high street. "I think we need a drink."

"Excellent," said Oliver. "The pub has very good treats. There will be treats, right, Emma?"

Emma laughed. "For both of us."

There were two "locals," in Trevena. The Donkey's Win was mostly geared for the tourist trade. Emma's favorite was the Roundhead, which was roughly as old as the King's Rest. According to village legend, the original operators of pub and tavern had squared off in the Battle of Trevena during the Civil War. During that battle, the owners of the Roundhead had rolled hogsheads of beer down the hills at the owners of the King's Rest. In the present day, this was widely regarded as a waste of good beer, but it had given rise to an annual festival that involved chasing a barrel downhill.

Oliver had gotten one look at it last summer and insisted that Emma enter him in the canine version of the race.

The Roundhead was a whitewashed stone building just off Trevena's crooked high street. There was a little cobbled courtyard to one side behind a stone wall and an iron gate. The place was pretty bare-bones—a wooden bar tucked into the corner, some benches and tables all battered by age, exposed oak beams blackened by smoke from when the huge hearth was used for warmth and cooking. There was one side room that had used to be the snuggery, and now housed the obligatory television for match days. Which today wasn't, so the pub was only partway filled with regulars enjoying a quiet pint. Dale Wilson and Dev Patel, Raj's dad, sat in one corner, engaged in one of their cutthroat backgammon games.

"Hullo, Emma!" called Liza from behind the bar. "How are you doing?"

Liza Greenlaw and her husband, Sam, had taken over the Roundhead when Sam's dad retired. She was the central casting version of a publican—a big woman with a cap of gray curls, red cheeks, pale skin spotted by age and the wrist strength to twist a drunken football fan's arm behind him while she frog-marched him out the door, informing him that if he didn't learn to act like a grown-up he could do his drinking over at the Donkey's Win. Thank you very much.

Sam had held the door.

"Been better, Liza." Emma climbed up on the bar stool. "Hullo, Sam," she added as Liza's cheerful, grizzled, red-faced husband came out of the back with a bin of clean glasses.

Oliver stretched up on his hind legs and barked in greeting.

"Hullo to you too, Oliver!" said Sam. "Hullo, Emma. Some cider?"

"Yes, please."

Liza kept the pub, but it was Sam who "kept the cellar." His dad, and granddads all the way back, brewed a delicious concoction from the local apples which was to be treated with the utmost respect. Emma had learned this the hard way.

After she'd recovered, that cider had become the secret ingredient in her apple cake.

Sam poured a judicious measure out of a crockery jug and set the glass in front of her. "Cheers."

"Cheers." She raised the glass and took a careful sip. "Wonderful."

The Greenlaws kept a jar of home-baked dog biscuits on the bar and Emma filched one and held it up for Oliver to nab out of her fingers. She rubbed his ears. *Don't know what I'd do without you.* She smiled.

And looked up to see Bert Cochrane standing in front of her.

"It's Emma, isn't it?" Bert extended his hand. He had an easy, polished smile. It went with his carefully combed dark hair, his even tan and tidy clothing. Today the polo shirt was pea green and the trousers were gray twill. The shoes were elegant city loafers, and might even have been bespoke.

"Bertram Cochrane," he reminded her. "Bert. We met up at the house the other day."

"Yes, of course." Emma took his offered hand. "So sorry for your loss."

Oliver perked up and went over to give those expensive shoes a sniff.

"Petrol, rubber, antiseptic, dirt, coffee, beer . . ."

Bert drew his foot back. "Um, do you mind?" he said. "These are my good shoes."

Emma remembered neither Bert nor Frank seemed particularly happy to have the dogs around them. She wondered who was taking care of Dash now.

"Come on, Oliver." She patted her leg. Oliver obeyed, but he was grumbling.

"I wasn't going to hurt his shoes. Why did he think I was going to hurt his shoes?"

*Because under all that charm, he's really kind of a git.* "Good boy." She rubbed Oliver's head.

"Would you care to join me?" He gestured toward the table under the window.

*Well. This is unexpected.* "All right," said Emma.

Bert picked up Emma's drink and gave her a smile as he gestured for her to go first. Emma collected her bag and crossed over to the table. Of course everybody in the pub looked. The rest of the customers had doubtlessly heard about Marcie's death, and were now wondering why Bert would want to talk to Emma.

"Do we like him?" Oliver settled down beside her chair rather than under it. His head and ears remained upright and alert. "I'm not sure we should like him."

*I'm not sure either.* Emma might sometimes have her doubts about Oliver's ability to accurately read people's characters, but she harbored very definite prejudices about overly fussy humans who did not like dogs.

Bert was drinking the pale ale. He took a long swallow. Emma sipped her cider and tried to ignore the wordless, and probably groundless, suspicion stirring in the back of her mind.

*He's a little vain, that's all. Doesn't make him a bad person. Necessarily.*

"I wanted to apologize if I was a little brusque when we met back at the grange," Bert said. "You understand, I'm sure."

"Of course," said Emma. "No worries."

"And I wanted to make sure somebody thanked you properly for what you did that day."

"It wasn't that much."

"I know it doesn't seem that way, but, well, Helen was in a really bad way, and, Daphne was no better, I'm afraid."

"I'm glad I could help."

Bert was watching her carefully. Emma resisted the urge to take another drink to cover the silence. Between her time in finance, and then as an aspiring baker with a new space to kit out, Emma had been glad-handed by some of the best in the business. Daphne said her uncle was a charmer. She could believe it. He projected an air of casual confidence, and she could easily picture him being as comfortable in a London club as he was here in the Roundhead.

She also remembered Daphne's suspicion, and his brother's insinuation, that her uncle had something to hide regarding Marcie's death.

Bert smiled again. "I guess by now you've figured out I've got an ulterior motive here."

Emma smiled. She took another sip of cider.

"I understand Daphne's been down at the B and B, talking with Pearl?" Bert went on.

"They're friends," said Emma. "It'd be a surprise if they weren't talking right now."

Bert grimaced. "All right, I guess I see how that sounded. But I worry about her. Daphne loved her aunt, and what's happened . . . I know she feels horrible and she blames herself." He paused and dropped his gaze to his beer. "It's my fault, really."

"Why would you say that?"

"I should have listened better. To Marcie, I mean. But I was busy. I'm on a lot of charity boards, hospital boards, that sort of thing. It kept me too busy to see what was really going on. I've got to give Gus credit—he *tried* to tell the rest of us something was wrong, but, well, Gus has always been the type who gets himself worked up over nothing. I just didn't listen, and this was the one time I should have." He sighed and waited.

Emma made a noise she hoped would sound sympathetic, and took another small sip of cider. For someone who said he blamed himself, Bert certainly was spreading a lot of blame around to other people, like Gus.

But she also couldn't help wondering about the difference between his conciliatory tone now and the way he'd shouted at his brother the other day.

*Here's little Gus, all ready to take charge, because he's so sure Marcie left him everything!*

If that was true, it meant that Gus had almost lost out to Daphne in terms of his inheritance. Emma frowned. Strange, though. If Marcie had been planning to leave the grange to Daphne up until recently, the normal thing to do would be to leave it in trust with her parents until Daphne came of age. So, why hadn't she done that? Or if she had, why hadn't she said anything to the family?

*Or maybe I'm just being paranoid?* Emma scratched the top of Oliver's head. He licked her hand.

"I want to talk to Daphne's mother about getting counseling for her," Bert was saying. "What we don't want is her talking to her friends and getting all worked up and spreading silly rumors. You know how things are in a village. Somebody says something once, people like the story and it gets written into local lore, whether it was ever true or not."

Emma took another drink, but this time, the cider bit too hard against the back of her throat. She pushed the glass away. What she really wanted to do was glance around the pub and see who was within earshot. Bert may have been trying to warn her that whatever Daphne said to Pearl might get round the village, but she couldn't help thinking his words applied to this conversation right now. This was the definition of a public place. Anybody might overhear them.

*So why are we talking about this here? And now?*

"Are you going to ask about Rain Lady?" grumbled Oliver. "He smells a little like Rain Lady. Only less green."

*Right.* Emma steadied her nerve. "So, Bert . . . and I'm sorry, this is awful, but I suppose there's no question in your mind about what happened?"

His sigh was long and gusty. His shoulders slumped, and he looked out the window for a long moment. "You know, I've gone back and forth over it so many times, and I don't see how there could be. When Daphne rejected her inheritance, it was like she'd rejected Marcie, and so Marcie killed herself.

"God knows I feel for poor Daphne. I'm sure she had no idea what she was doing. But we're all thoughtless when we're kids, aren't we?"

Despite the cider, Emma felt a spark of anger. She remembered Daphne's helplessness as she told Pearl all her fears, as well as her reasons for refusing to tie herself to

Truscott Grange. "Thoughtless is not how I'd describe Daphne."

Bert looked at her sharply. Her answer had clearly put him on the alert. He'd been spinning a sympathetic story, and he'd been expecting her to just go along with it.

"No, I suppose not. She's a good girl, I'll say that much. Her mum's done a decent job. Maybe a bit too sporty, but what's the harm there? And Frank, he hasn't exactly gone out of his way to make sure his daughter had a connection to the family the way he should. So I guess it wasn't really her fault in the end."

"I wouldn't say it was her fault at all," said Emma. "No one should pin the family future on a twenty-one-year-old girl. It's not fair."

"I can see how it must look to an outsider," said Bert loftily. "But it's different when your family has been here for generations. It changes your perspective. That house was Marcie's life. When Daphne turned her down, well, it was like all her years of work had been for nothing. I think in the end none of us were really surprised when she . . . she took her own life."

Emma blinked. Bert sounded not only wounded but absolutely certain. "But what if she didn't?"

His head jerked up. "I'm sorry?"

"What if it's discovered that Marcie didn't kill herself?"

Bert's handsome, well-groomed attitude shifted smoothly over into pure, dismissive contempt. "This isn't anything like that sordid business with Victoria Roberts, Ms. Reed. I'd take it very much amiss if I heard you were encouraging Daphne or Helen to think it might be."

Looming while seated was not something everybody could pull off, but Bert managed it. Emma kept her expression calm, but barely.

"I meant, what if it turns out to have been an accident?"

Emma watched with a certain amount of satisfaction as Bert's measured contempt melted into a puddle of confusion.

"Oh! Yes, of course." He started to chuckle and then

seemed to think the better of it. "Sorry. Yes, I suppose an accident is a possibility. But I think we all need to prepare for the worst. Including Daphne." He had regained his poise, and his smooth charm. "I'm hoping I can count on you, and Daphne's other friends, to understand how confused she is right now and help to keep her, well, on an even keel, you understand?"

"I'm sure we'll all do our best."

"Thanks, that's all I'm asking." He finished his beer. "Well, I'm off. Good to see you again, Emma." He stood up.

"Sorry," said Emma. "Can I ask you a question?"

"Sure," he said, although there was some hesitation in that one word.

"I know it's a very awkward time, but has the family made any decisions about whether the festival is still going to happen?"

Bert looked at her blankly. Then realization dawned. "Oh. Oh, well, no, I don't . . . that is, that's not really on my list, you know. You should probably ask Helen or Gus about that." Then, a thought seemed to strike him. "Still, I imagine it's a bit of a big deal for you and your friends?"

"My partners," said Emma. "Yes, it would be. We've already put a fair amount of work into it."

"Well, how about I see if I can get an answer for you, then." He pulled out his mobile. "Give me your number and I'll let you know soonest."

There it was. The man who did business on the golf course and liked to be seen as the power behind the throne, however small the throne might be.

"Thanks so much," said Emma. They exchanged numbers. Bert waved to Liza and Sam, and headed out, whistling softly.

Emma watched him leave. Oliver did too, even stretching up to put his paws on the windowsill to see him climb into the silver BMW parked across the street and drive away.

Emma stayed where she was, playing their conversation over in her mind.

What exactly had that been about? Daphne said her uncle tried to cover things up. And yet here he was in the pub talking about the certainty of his sister's suicide within earshot of a half dozen different people.

Usually, if there was a suicide in a prominent family, uptight relatives would jump at the chance to call it an accident. But Bert hadn't done that. In fact, he'd been unusually quick to assume she'd been talking about murder.

*And to demonstrate he wasn't above a little light tit for tat.*

"He doesn't like dogs," said Oliver. "That's sad."

"Yes. That too," murmured Emma. "That too."

# 21

· · · · · · · · · ·

WHEN EMMA GOT TO THE B&B ON SUNDAY, SHE STARTED TO take herself round the back to the kitchen entrance as usual, but then she saw Angelique's husband, Daniel, sitting on the front porch. He raised a mug in salute to Emma.

"Hullo, Daniel. All right?"

"Just about," he answered. Of course, Oliver immediately sniffed his shoes and trouser cuffs. Daniel held out his hand for further canine inspection. "Hullo, Oliver."

"Salt, salt and diesel, sand and wood and fish and tea!" Oliver sat down and opened his mouth in that way that made him look like he was laughing. "It is a good morning!"

"Most intelligent dog I think I've ever seen." Daniel rubbed Oliver's head. "You could swear he understands every word."

"You have no idea," said Emma. "No trippers today?"

"Taking a couple days, in case Angelique needs something. She's still pretty rattled."

Emma had liked Daniel from the first time she met him. As a sailor, he had a firm grasp of the difference between what was really important and what was just loud and large.

"Can't say as I blame her for being upset," Emma said. "I still can't believe it even happened." She paused. "Erm, Daniel, have Pearl and Angelique had a row? Only they were barely speaking to each other yesterday."

"Yeah, they did that." Daniel put his mug down and rested both elbows on the table. "Got quite heated."

"What was it about?" she asked, and then immediately shook her head. "Sorry. I should ask them that. Never mind me."

"No, it's all right. The truth is, it was about you."

*"Me?"* Emma's voice broke and Oliver yipped.

Daniel nodded. "Angelique found out that Pearl asked you to try to get some news, or something, about poor Marcie."

"Oh, well, yeah, that happened. Sort of. But she was really just trying to help Daphne."

"I'm sure, but Angelique's a woman of strong principles. She thinks it wasn't fair for Pearl to ask, because you're renting your space from us, you see. You might feel pressured to go along, even if you didn't want to."

"Oh, dear." Emma looked toward the peaceful old tavern. "I mean, I never thought— Do you, um, think I should say something?"

"If you find the chance. But it'll probably work its own way through, maybe even by this afternoon, if my weather eye's any good." He tapped his temple.

"Well, thanks for the warning anyway. I better get on." Emma hitched her bag up on her shoulder.

Daniel raised his mug again. "Cheers. Oh, and, Emma?"

"Yes?"

"I know you've got a nose for these things"—Oliver barked—"oh, not as good as yours, old chum. But if you are going to look into the Cochranes' business, you might want to tread lightly there too."

"Any particular reason?"

Daniel stared out toward the horizon, as if scanning the sky and the sea for squalls. "That family's always had its own troubles, and always set great store by appearances. My da said he heard old Mr. Cochrane say that the modern world stopped at the door of Truscott Grange."

"Wow. That could be very peaceful, or utterly smothering."

"It could," he agreed. "But it was also pretty serious stuff. I remember how Archie Hope-Johnston started speculating on the possibility that Cochrane had made more than a bit of his money off some sharp dealings in the City. After that, old Archie started having a lot of trouble getting clients. Had to close up shop and go into partnership down in Penzance."

She paused. "Wait. Is Archie Hope-Johnston related to . . ."

"To the Hyphenated Caite?" said Daniel. "Her dad. Local solicitor before things went bad. I was at school with Caite. They tried to make out like it was just a career move, but everybody knew."

*Well. A family feud.* That could explain the origin of Caite's malice toward Marcie.

"What was it old Mr. Cochrane did?"

"Stock trader. Made a pile in the City, cashed out and retired early."

Emma let out a long, slow breath. There were a lot of ways to get rich in the City. Not all of them stood up to being examined in the cold light of day. Daniel nodded, clearly aware of the direction her thoughts had taken.

"And what happened to Archie Hope-Johnston?"

"Very bad business, that," said Daniel. "He was never able to make a go of the new position, and in the end, he hanged himself."

They both sat silent for a minute, letting those words settle between them.

"Thanks for that, Daniel," said Emma at last.

"Good luck."

*Thanks, I might need it.* But Emma didn't bother to say that out loud. The look in Daniel's weather eye told her he already knew.

\* \* \*

THE GREAT ROOM WAS EMPTY, WAITING FOR THE BREAK-
fast setup to begin. Emma automatically checked the
Reed's Classic Cakes counter to make sure everything was,
as Daniel might have put it, shipshape. Then, she crouched
down and rubbed Oliver's chin.

"Oliver, I need your help. We need to get Angelique and
Pearl talking to each other again," said Emma. "Can I
count on you to break the ice?"

"Yes! Yes!" Oliver grumbled affectionately and licked
her face. "They should be playing together, not growling.
They love each other."

"Right. So. You first, and I'm right behind you."

"Watch me!" Oliver wagged, whisked around in a tight
circle and headed straight for the kitchen. Since a corgi at
high speed is basically a little, furry battering ram, he barreled right through the swinging door.

"Oh my goodness!" Angelique exclaimed. "Oliver!"

Emma followed her dog inside. The preparations for
breakfast were already under way. Angelique and Pearl were
both at their cutting boards, chopping piles of onions and
tomatoes. A huge carton of eggs stood between them like a
barrier. Neither woman was looking at the other.

Oliver immediately went on the charm offensive. He
trotted over to Pearl and poked her firmly in the calf with
his nose. She looked down and smiled when he laughed up
at her. "Good morning to you too, boyo," she said.

Oliver yipped and bounced, and immediately raced over
to Angelique and gave her ankle a poke.

"Shameless flirt you are," she murmured. Oliver yipped
again and zoomed back to Pearl, and then back to Angelique, and somewhere in this, mother and daughter both
caught each other's gaze, and held it.

Oliver barked approvingly and bounced. And laughed.

"Emma, I'd swear you've got him doing this on purpose," said Angelique sternly.

"Oh, come on," said Emma. "How would I do that?" She

went to her station and pulled out her baking list for the morning. "Do you know," she said, "I had the weirdest conversation in the pub with Bert Cochrane yesterday."

"How so?" asked Pearl.

"He was trying his best to make sure I knew that Marcie killed herself."

"What?" exclaimed Angelique, pausing her precise onion disassembly.

"Yeah, right?" Emma flipped the page on her baking list. "I mean, given everything everybody's said about the Cochranes and how old-fashioned they are, I would have thought they'd be trying to hide that possibility as far under the bushes as they could."

"You'd think so, wouldn't you," murmured Pearl.

"And *then* he tried to convince me that Daphne's all troubled and guilty . . ."

"Which she is, poor girl," added Angelique.

"Yeah, but I think he also wanted me to snitch on her."

Pearl laid her knife down. "Tell me you're not serious?"

"Very. It was so odd." Emma paused to make sure she had everybody's attention. "I think something weird is going on up at the grange."

Angelique and Pearl looked at each other, both stubborn and wary.

"What kind of weird?" said Pearl.

"I don't know, but I'm sure it's something. And I know what I said before, Pearl, but now I think Daphne might be right to be worried." *Especially about her uncle Bert.*

"Emma, I wanted to talk to you about that," began Angelique.

"No, Ma. I should say it." Pearl cut her off, but there was no rancor in it, only a subdued determination. Oliver flopped down beside her, no doubt intending to provide furry moral support. "Emma, I'm sorry about the other day. I shouldn't have let Daphne put you on the spot like that."

"You were trying to help out a friend who is having a bad time," said Emma. "Maybe even worse than we realized."

"So what is it you want to do?" asked Angelique.

Emma looked at her baking list. She wanted to be making her scones and her biscuits, and frosting the vanilla sponges she'd made with the almond-cherry mascarpone cream. And then she had to assemble the new chocolate cake for the Towne Fryer and deliver it along with a batch of Deluxe Ginger Biscuits, which generally sold better than the lemon bars . . .

But this had to come first. "I don't know that there's anything I can do, or should do," she confessed. "Not really. Nothing's changed, and we still don't know the results of the autopsy."

"But there's got to be something there, right?" said Pearl. "Daphne's my friend, so I know I'm biased, but she's also pretty grounded. Comes from being a goalkeeper," she added. "If you can think while people are kicking balls at your head, you just don't get flustered over nothing."

"I would have to agree with that," said Angelique. "Her mother has always seemed much the same to me."

Pearl shot her mother a grateful look, and Angelique smiled at her daughter. Oliver plopped down on his hindquarters right between them, obviously pleased with a job well done.

*He's going to be insufferable for at least a week.* Emma ducked her head to hide a smile.

"How well do you know Helen?" she asked Angelique.

"Not well," said Angelique. "Mostly I know her because the girls are friends. I got the impression she wasn't comfortable in that house, or maybe I should say, in that family. She came from a very different class, and Richard and Evelyn—the old Mr. and Mrs. Cochrane—I think they tolerated her more than they welcomed her, you know?"

"Ouch." Emma winced.

"I think she stayed married to Frank as long as she did simply because she didn't want to give them the satisfaction, but I wasn't surprised when she took Daphne and moved back to Manchester."

"But she and Marcie stayed close?"

"Marcie was the only person who really treated her like a friend, instead of a nuisance," said Pearl. "At least, that's what Daphne always said. She told me she was honestly relieved when they did move out."

"But they kept coming back every year. Wasn't that a little awkward?"

"Must have been," said Angelique. "They never talked about it, of course."

"I hate to say it, but it probably got easier when Richard and Evelyn died," said Pearl.

"When was that?" asked Emma.

Pearl and Angelique looked at each other. "A while ago now. Maybe nineteen or twenty years ago?" said Angelique. "They weren't very old."

"Oh, that's right, it was a car accident, wasn't it?"

"Richard Cochrane did love his fancy cars." Angelique paused to check on the eggs baking in the oven. "And he drove too fast. That can be a mistake on these hills. He swerved to avoid a lorry coming the other way and crashed through the hedge and down the incline. In a modern car they might have made it, with airbags and all."

"Suddenly I'm changing my mind about car shopping," muttered Emma.

"I doubt you're going to be taking these roads at a hundred kilometers an hour," said Angelique. "Frankly, the pair of them were a menace. She was every bit as bad. It was a surprise, really, for such a buttoned-up pair. One of the sons, Gus, he's just the same. Seems to be a bit of a streak in the family."

"Streak?" said Emma.

"Adrenaline junkies," said Pearl. "It happens with upper-class families. The boredom gets to them and they start thrill seeking. We did a bit on it in psych class."

"Well, I don't know about that," said Angelique, "But I do know Richard Cochrane had an older brother, Steven or Samuel, or something. He died in a boat accident donkey's years ago. Tried to test himself against a northeast gale and lost."

"That's a lot of bad luck for one family," said Emma slowly.

"That's the truth," said Pearl. "Makes you think, doesn't it?"

*Yes, but think what?* Emma bit her lip.

"Enough of this," said Angelique firmly. "Whatever is happening with the Cochranes, right now, we have a B and B full of guests expecting Sunday breakfast."

"Hurray!" barked Oliver "Sausages!"

She was right, of course. It was past time to get to work. Emma bundled her unruly hair up under the billed cap she kept for the purpose.

"But, Ma . . ." began Pearl.

"No buts." Angelique pointed her spatula at Pearl. "We are not going to do Daphne, or anyone else any good by worrying away at things we can't prove or fix."

*For now.* Emma got down the mixing bowls. *But tomorrow, that's another story.*

# 22

...........

MONDAY WAS EMMA'S DAY OFF. USUALLY, THAT MEANT sleeping in, perhaps all the way to eight o'clock, lounging about the cottage, working in her new garden or catching up on her favorite cooking shows and reading new cookbooks.

Today it meant heading down to the Towne Fryer to meet up with Genny and go look at cars.

"And Brian," added Genny.

"I'm not talking to you," said Emma.

"Why not?" Oliver, who was sitting on her lap, bonked her chin. "You should talk to Genny."

Emma sighed. "Oliver says I should talk to you."

"Oliver is very sensible," said Genny.

"Genny is an excellent human," said Oliver.

Emma rolled her eyes at them both.

TREVENA TAXI AND PROWSE'S CLASSIC CARS STOOD A BIT to the southeast of Trevena proper, just past the Tesco and the town's single strip of shops but before the first of the housing estates. The place had most likely been a small farm once. Cornish hedges—walls of earth and stone topped by tangled shrubbery—fenced in the property. A squared-off brick cottage stood on one corner of the lot. The sales office with its signs for both Taxi and Garage had been fitted a bit awkwardly onto one side. There was one huge outbuilding that had probably once been a cow barn and another, smaller one that might have been the farm's workshop and storage shed. Judging by the assortment of vehicles, and the tow truck parked out front, Emma decided this was now the garage.

As soon as Genny pulled up into the rutted car park, Brian came out of the office. A shaggy collie dog loped beside him.

"Hullo! Hullo!" Oliver barked and bounced up to the much bigger dog. He and the collie started exchanging the exploratory sniffs and nips that stood in for "nice to meet you," "how about this weather, eh?" "you see the match last night?" and all other bits of human small talk.

"Well!" Brian chuckled. "That was fast. Lucy!" He whistled. "Come say hello to Emma."

Emma went down on one knee and held out both hands for Lucy to sniff and lick. "Hello, Lucy! There's a good girl." Emma rubbed her ears.

"She likes you," said Brian.

"Everybody likes Emma!" announced Oliver.

Brian laughed at Oliver's energetic yip and rubbed the corgi's head. He wore jeans and a soft blue button-up shirt with the sleeves rolled to the elbows.

Emma found herself staring at his muscular forearms. Genny noticed. Emma could tell because Genny also kicked her in the ankle.

Oliver sniffed at Brian's hands. "An excellent human," he told Emma. "But too much petrol, grease and oil." He sneezed.

Brian laughed again and straightened up. "All right, Genny?"

"Just about. What you got for us, then?"

He turned a wry grin to Emma. "Always good to have a friend along to check out your new relationships, yeah?"

"She thinks if we're left alone, we'll get up to no good," said Emma blandly.

"Well, she knows I cannot resist your wiles."

"Speaking of . . ." Emma pulled a carefully wrapped packet out of her bag. "Open it when you're alone."

Genny pulled a face. Brian just raised both brows. "I'll treasure it."

Genny rolled her eyes. "Maybe we should leave them alone, Oliver."

Oliver grumbled. "A noble corgi never leaves his human— Oooo . . . what's that?" He put his nose down and started after some scent trail. Lucy barked and bustled after him.

"Oliver!" snapped Emma. "No wandering off! There's cars here!"

"I was not wandering off!" huffed Oliver, but he did come trotting back.

"Amazing how he knows," said Genny. "My dog never listens like that."

"We had a really good training school," mumbled Emma. "Right, Brian. What have you got for me?"

"Well, I don't know yet."

Emma pulled back in surprise. Brian grinned. "I can't say what I've got for you until I know what it is you need. What do you want to do with your car?"

"Aside from drive it?"

"Yes. The kind of travel you're planning is important. If you're commuting to London three times a week, I'm not going to put you in a Range Rover. So, what are your plans?"

"Well. Obviously, errands around the village. The bus is hopeless if you've got a load to carry, and there's a good taxi but you know, the fees are ridiculous, and the driver's always angling for a bigger tip . . ."

"Guy's a prat," said Brian promptly. "I know him and you shouldn't put up with it."

"You two aren't going to knock it off, are you?" growled Genny.

"Doesn't look like," said Brian. "So, okay, errands. What else?"

"Well, general getting around, I guess. I mean, there's all these lovely farms around here and Devon, I want to be able to check out the markets and the stands, for the honey and jams and the seasonal fruits, all that."

"Are you talking a lot of hauling or . . ."

"Oh, no, nothing like that. We get deliveries of all the bulk stuff, but just . . ."

"Shopping?" he suggested.

"Shopping, and I want to see the countryside." Not to mention the jumble sales and antique shops. There was a fantastic vintage store in Trevena, and its owners, David and Charles, had become two of her best friends, but she felt the need to stretch her wings.

"All right then," said Brian. "I think I've got just what you need. If you ladies will step this way?"

Brian led them across the stubbly grass to the massive barn Emma had noticed when they first pulled in. The building was even bigger than it had seemed from the road. Close up, it looked to be nearly the size of a football pitch. Inside though, the stalls and feed boxes had all been removed, leaving nothing but a huge space with a concrete floor filled with neat rows of cars, some new but many vintage.

Emma was not a car enthusiast. Until she moved to Cornwall, she'd never even considered owning one. She hadn't even gotten her license until university. But even so, a black Rolls-Royce looming over a low, sleek yellow BMW convertible was an impressive sight.

"Wow!" Emma exclaimed. "Not what I was expecting."

"Oh, don't let the Cornwall countryman facade fool you," said Genny. "Brian's a connoisseur. Although some people around here pronounce that 'snob.'"

"Oh, come off it, Genny, you'll frighten her," said Brian.

Lucy had evidently had enough of this human standing about. It seemed that now was actually the time to play chase and bounded off between the cars. Oliver barked excitedly and raced after her.

*Dogs.*

"Well, Brian, I just hope you don't think my budget runs to a . . . a . . ." Emma waved vaguely at a low black and silver car, all curves and chrome.

"1966 Shelby Cobra," Brian said promptly.

"Yes. That. Because I may be inexperienced, but I'm not daft."

"Emma." He laid his hand against his breast. "Would I lead you astray?"

Emma turned to him. She moved two steps closer. She blinked up into his blue eyes. "Brian, you may flatter me, and you may be helping keep my shop afloat by purchasing the equivalent of a whole apple cake on a weekly basis, but when it comes down to brass tacks, you, sir, are still a used car salesman."

"Oof." Brian put a hand over his stomach. "That, madam, is a low blow. All right. Come on, then."

He led them both past the first row of vintage rarities, then past a second row of more pedestrian, and more contemporary, imports from Japan, Germany and America.

"Now this is what I was thinking of for you," said Brian.

He spread his hands toward a tiny, blocky, bright red convertible. It looked like an adorable toy beside the larger models, and Emma's heart leapt in a way normally reserved for new lemon cake recipes.

"1966 Austin Mini Cooper convertible," announced Brian. "Fully restored and upgraded. Candy apple red, all the original upholstery. Very gently used, but goes like a champion if you give her the chance." Brian opened the door. "If madam would care to have a seat?"

*I will not fall in love at first sight,* Emma told herself firmly. *It's a car, not a puppy.*

She settled into the seat. Brian closed the door. Emma put both hands on the wheel.

And instantly she imagined touring down the winding coastal roads, the wind in her hair, a scarf billowing out behind her. Oliver would be in the passenger seat, mouth open and laughing into the wind.

"What do you think?" Brian leaned down so he could smile at her through the open window.

*I am a mature woman, not an infatuated teenager,* she told herself. *I have a business degree and an accounting license. I am not impulse buying thousands of pounds' worth of automobile. Especially when it's a convertible and I live in* Cornwall, *for heaven's sake.*

"It's very nice," she admitted.

"What's the mileage like?" asked Genny. "Are the tires new? When were the brakes last done?"

Emma put a hand on the gear lever. It fitted exactly.

"Emma, stop fondling the gears," said Genny briskly. "We need to do a walk around."

"Spoilsport," muttered Brian.

Emma climbed out of the car, only slightly shamefaced. Oliver immediately pushed past her and put his paws up on the driver's seat, wagging his entire bum in excitement.

"Oh, it's you too, is it?" Genny rubbed the corgi's ears. "I knew you lot needed a chaperone. Show the girl a splash of red paint and a cute pair of headlights and she's hopeless. Come on, Prowse, open the boot. Smart!" She clapped her hands.

Emma swallowed a laugh and managed to have a serious expression pasted on by the time Brian opened the hatch. Genny kept firing questions as they walked around the little car, and Brian lobbed back the answers. He even opened the glove box and pulled out the maintenance record, meticulously kept, he claimed, by the previous owner, a little old man in St. Ives who bought the car new and only sold it when his grandkids moved to Sydney.

He was warming to this theme when a voice cut across the car barn.

"Hello, Brian! They told me you were out here!"

All three of them turned around. The barn's side door was open, and a man stood on the threshold.

It was Gus Cochrane.

# 23

"'SCUSE ME," MURMURED BRIAN TO EMMA. HE PASTED ON A much broader smile than he'd worn yet as he strode between all the cars.

"Mr. Cochrane! Good to see you."

Emma looked at Genny and Genny looked back at Emma. In silent agreement they started to stroll just a very little bit closer to the men at the entrance.

*Just looking at the cars. Genny's just helping. Not planning on listening in at all.*

But then Oliver and Lucy appeared out of nowhere and headed straight toward Gus and Brian.

"Oh, Oliver!" sighed Emma, and she hurried to call back her endlessly curious corgi.

"I was very sorry to hear about your loss," Brian was saying when the dogs, followed by Emma and Genny, reached Gus. Both the collie and the corgi started sniffing energetically around his shoes and ankles. Gus shifted backward.

"All right, Lucy, knock it off," said Brian amiably.

"Nah, she's fine," said Gus. "And this guy . . . I know you, don't I?" He patted Oliver's head.

"He's mine. Come on, Oliver." Emma whistled. "Manners."

Oliver came to stand beside her. "Too much petrol and coffee," he said. "It's not healthy. He should walk more. Also dead roses."

"Oh, hullo," said Gus. "It's Emma, right? You were at the house when . . . well, the other day. We didn't get a chance to say it at the time, but everyone really appreciated the sandwiches."

"Thank you," Emma said. "I couldn't have done it without Genny's help."

"Oh, ah, yes. Of course, you were . . . there . . . too? Again, thanks."

"I'm just glad I could do something to help," said Genny.

"Wish I could've." He shook his head. "She was so, so self-contained, our Marcie. Never wanted to trouble anybody. Just wanted to get on with it, you know? Wasn't going to burden anybody else with her troubles. I knew something was wrong, but I wasn't able to do anything in time. And now I've got to carry that." He wiped at his face. "But. We go on, right? Stiff upper lip and all that. Still. I'll admit, I'm not sorry for an excuse to get out of the house. Especially now."

"I'm sorry, has something new happened?" asked Emma.

Gus hesitated. He also jammed his hands into his pockets. "Well, I probably shouldn't say, but I'm sure everybody will know by end of day anyhow. See, Bert's been on the phone all weekend, and, well, this morning we got the word. It's official. Marcie's death has been ruled a suicide."

"I'm so sorry," said Brian.

"We all are," added Genny. "Is there anything . . ."

"No, no." Gus shook his head. "It's all being handled. Still . . . bit stuffy back at the house and all . . ." He shrugged.

Emma felt an uncomfortable tightening in the back of her neck, but she couldn't quite say why. Gus's stiff-upper-lip response was the expected thing, especially among people who venerated old-fashioned manners and keeping up appearances. At the same time, there was something off-putting about how fast Gus pulled the stoic facade over his sister's death.

"Anyway," Gus went on. "The Jag looks fantastic. I just wanted to stop round and say hello and thanks while the paperwork got together. I appreciate your rushing the repairs through." He held his hand out for Brian to shake.

"No problem," said Brian. "It's a beautiful machine. Always a treat to work on."

"Good, good." Gus gave them all a vague smile. "Well, must be off."

"Oh, Gus," said Genny. "Emma and I left some equipment and such at the grange the other day. We were planning on coming round after we finished here to pick it up. Would that still be all right?"

"Um, well, yes, I should think. You won't find me there. Things to do." He shifted uncomfortably. "Anyway. Rest of the family's all home, and it's not like this was a surprise. More of a relief, rather, to have it all official. Can get on with things now. So, it should be fine. Thanks again."

He headed out the door with the air of someone making a hasty retreat. Emma watched him climb into a low, sleek convertible painted a truly breathtaking shade of lime green. The engine roared as it started, and even from here, Emma could hear the clash of the gears as Gus backed and turned.

"And see you soon," murmured Brian as the Jaguar peeled out of sight.

Emma raised her brows.

"It is a gorgeous machine, but those early Jags are pretty notoriously unreliable, and he's got no idea how to take care of it. He just likes the speed, and the name."

Which coming from a car connoisseur was about as clear a condemnation as you could get.

"So, you see it a lot, do you?"

"The thing's practically family by now," Brian muttered. "The Cochranes have a history of being careless with their stuff." He shook his head. "You can tell a lot about people by the way they treat their machines."

"And how do the Cochranes treat theirs?"

Brian rubbed his chin. "Well, I'd guess we've had just about every one of their cars, and declared a bunch of them totaled out, for the insurance, you know. My ol' da must have totaled out three cars just for Frank before he turned thirty."

"Oh," said Emma.

"Yeah, oh. Now Bert, we barely ever saw young Mr. Bert, but then nobody else did either. He was always up in London, uni then off to the States for business school, and then back again. Now he takes his BMW to a specialist in St. Ives."

"How about Marcie?"

"Marcie drove the family car when we were younger. A Range Rover, seventies vintage. Took care of it like . . . well, like it was all she had. I'm pretty sure she even read the manual. She did everything like that. You gave Marcie Cochrane a job, it got done, and maybe overdone."

"You've got thoughts," said Emma.

Brian shrugged. "I admit, I've always wondered who told her she had to be the one to take care of that lot, if you see what I mean. Her brothers—wouldn't give you a bob for any of 'em."

"Even Bert?"

"Especially Bert. Gus, he's all right, or at least, he could be, if the other two left him alone, and if somebody would teach him how to actually drive that car. But Bert and Frank can get him to do anything, especially if they lean on him together."

A dozen questions bubbled up inside Emma, but Brian was already shaking his head and turning away. "Let's get you the keys, then, and the paperwork, and you can take that test drive."

The office was a strictly functional room, with lots of clipboards hanging on the wall and a pegboard of tagged and labeled keys. Emma signed the liability and insurance documents and let Brian photocopy her license.

"Oh, and you'll want this." He pulled a bundle of bright

green straps out from under the counter. "Dog harness," he said. "Safety first and all."

"Thanks."

He pushed the keys across the counter. "She'll take good care of you. I promise."

Genny rolled her eyes. "Good grief, Emma, you're dating the Cooper whisperer."

"We're not dating," said Emma and Brian together.

Genny snorted. Oliver sneezed.

"Bless you," said Brian solemnly. "See you soon."

Someone had brought the Mini round to front. The harness proved fairly easy to figure out, and soon Oliver was snugly strapped in. She climbed into the front seat and buckled her own belt.

"Um, Emma?" said Genny, who was buckling herself into the passenger seat. "You do know how to drive, right?"

Emma grinned at her. "Trust me."

"Right." Genny gripped the dash. Emma laughed, and started the engine.

# 24

. . . . . . . . . . . .

*THIS IS AN EXCELLENT IDEA.*

Oliver did not like the car harness Emma insisted he wear, but he decided he could humor her. Despite the straps, he sat up tall in the back seat of the new car. The dizzying wind, with its heavy, heart-pounding scents hit him full in the face. The rushing air was tinged with green and wildlife and farm animals and other dogs and warmth and sunshine. If he let his tongue hang out, he could practically taste all the berms and hedges that lined the narrow, winding roads.

He barked for the sheer excitement of it all, and Emma laughed.

"What do you think, Oliver?" called Emma.

"It is an extremely good car," he barked loudly. "We should go faster."

Emma laughed again. Then she looked over at Genny. "Stop it," said Emma.

"Stop what?" asked Genny. "I'm not doing anything. You're the one who's contemplating elopement with this car."

"Well, since you're not doing anything, you can call Daphne and let her know we're on our way."

Genny dug in her purse for her mobile. Oliver was glad that Emma had not even tried to leave him behind with Lucy and the car man. He liked Lucy. She was cheerful and not at all stuck up like some collies could be, and she had an interesting home. But Emma needed him if she was going back to the grange. Bad things had happened in that house. Emma would find out why that was. Emma was good at that, but until then, she needed looking after, whether she knew it or not.

"All right." Genny was putting her mobile away again. "Daphne says she's home and ready for us. We should go around back, like the other day."

"Got it," answered Emma. She moved the gear shift thingy and the car went a little faster. Because Emma really was the best human ever.

THE GRANGE HOUSE CAST A LONG SHADOW OVER ITS front courtyard. Emma drove them around the two corners. Oliver inhaled deeply when they passed the place where they found Rain Lady Marcie, but he couldn't pick up any trace of her anymore, at least not from here. There was just warming stone and fresh green.

Running Lady—who Emma said was called Daphne—stood in the back car park with Dash.

"Dash!" Oliver barked happily as Emma undid his harness so he could jump down and run over to the big mutt. Dash had been outside a lot since they were here last. He smelled like mud and water and crushed plants and mice and dust and a dozen other things. His coat was tangled. He answered Oliver's greetings with sniffs and happy growls. Then he flopped over on his side so he and Oliver could be nose to nose.

"Is Running Lady your new human?" Oliver asked.

Dash huffed at him. "All the humans in my house are my human! But she is a very good human. Watch!" He surged to his feet and bounded over to Daphne, jumping up to put his legs on her chest.

"Cut it out, ya big daftie!" Daphne exclaimed. But she also laughed and ruffled his ears before she pushed him back down.

"See?" Dash backed away, satisfied. Oliver shook himself and sneezed.

"I don't understand how all humans are your human. What about Rain Lady Marcie? I thought she was your best human."

Dash's ears and tail drooped. "I miss Marcie. She shouldn't have gone away like that. She was sad. Then she got hurt. I wanted to help her, but no one would listen to me."

Oliver felt his muzzle quiver. This was important. He felt it at the very tips of his paws and tail. "When was she hurt?"

"The last night. She was in her room. She was hurt. I went to get somebody, but they locked me outside. She was hurt here too, but I didn't see that part."

Oliver felt a growl building.

"Who locked you out?"

Dash told him, a mix of description and scent language that he'd have to work out how to translate for Emma later. He thought it was the bearded man—what was his human name? Gus! That was it. Gus locked Dash outside the night Rain Lady Marcie died.

That *had* to be important. But there was something else too.

"Where was she hurt outside?"

"Here! Here!" Dash galumphed toward the small side building with a whole line of doors. Oliver raced after him.

"Oliver!" called Emma. Oliver skidded to a halt. The humans were all heading into the house. She whistled. Oliver yelped impatiently.

"It's important, Emma!"

She whistled again. Dash shrugged with his whole shaggy body. "Does your human have roast beef today?" he asked. "My humans never give me beef. Well, almost never. Hardly ever. Not enough," he added.

"I don't know," Oliver told him. Emma whistled again. "I have to go."

"You do that, mate." Dash nosed him once in the side, and then turned around and trotted toward the gardens.

*Nobody calls him back,* Oliver thought grumpily. Which was not right. Dash had the whole house and all these gardens and woods to take care of. It was a big job. For a mutt, he was a very important dog. But if Emma was going inside the house, Oliver could not even think about leaving her alone.

Not even to find out where Rain Lady Marcie got hurt. Because if one of the house humans could get hurt here, so could Emma.

Oliver broke into a run.

# 25

"EMMA! EMMA!" EMMA HELD THE DOOR OPEN WHILE OLIVER hopped down the stairs into the kitchen. "Dash told me something important!"

"Yes, yes," Emma breathed. "Good boy."

Usually, Oliver understood that this meant she needed to talk to other humans now. The problem was, from Oliver's point of view, all humans did was talk to each other. He didn't always understand how sliding in a few extra words here or there could really matter.

"But Dash knows where Marcie Rain Lady got hurt!"

Emma frowned and rubbed Oliver's ears. That shouldn't be important. They all knew where she "got hurt—" out beside the driveway, under the third story window. They'd all seen her. Oliver knew it. He'd been there.

*So what's he talking about?* Emma's curiosity didn't so much itch as burn with the heat of the summer sun at noon.

The problem was, she couldn't ask him, not when Genny and Daphne were in the same room.

"How are you doing?" Genny was asking Daphne. Daphne folded her arms tight across her chest and leaned against the kitchen island. She was dressed for running in a bright pink top and electric blue leggings, but her face was pale, and she did not look like she'd slept much, or eaten much either. All Emma's baking instincts prodded at her to feed the girl a big slice of bread and butter, maybe some soup. At least a slice of cake.

Daphne shrugged. "It was not a good night. The uncles aren't talking to each other. Mum's . . . Mum's kind of a mess. Dad's trying to help, which is a surprise, but he's not very good at it. And none of them know where anything is. Mom finally got some breakfast together, cuz none of them was going to. She says Marcie should have kicked them all out years ago. Probably would have done everybody a world of good."

"We heard about the autopsy," said Emma. Oliver, distracted by some fresh scent, was sniffing around the baseboards and heading toward the pantry.

"What's that?" he mumbled. "What is it? What?"

Emma tore her attention away from her literally nosy dog and tried to focus on Daphne.

"So that's out already." Daphne tugged at her ponytail. "Uncle Bert was on the phone all weekend, rattling cages. Seems he finds it unacceptable that our public servants didn't work overtime to get him the answers he wanted."

The door to the main house opened. Daphne snapped her mouth shut. Her mother, Helen, came in carrying an empty tea mug with a spoon sticking out of it.

"Oh, hullo, Genny. Emma. Daphne said you'd be back today." She touched Daphne's arm as she passed. Helen looked tired and more than a little disheveled. She wore a loose gray T-shirt over black trousers, a stark contrast to her tall daughter's neon pink and blue. "You had some equipment and so on? You may have to dig around a bit. It's been a little chaotic the past few days." Helen set her empty mug down on the kitchen island and blinked at it.

Daphne put her arm around her mother's shoulders. "What is it, Mum?"

"Oh, nothing. Just tired," Helen said. "Bert's being particularly managing just now. Wants all the details about the obituary and the funeral finalized so it can get in the papers as soon as possible, or wherever obituaries go nowadays." She pushed her hair back from her forehead. She clearly hadn't been able to muster a lot of patience with brushes and combs this morning. "I've decided to just let him have his way."

"Because heaven knows Uncle Bert doesn't get his way often enough," Daphne muttered.

"Daphne, please. Not now."

"Then when, Mum?" Daphne stalked back to the kitchen island. "You know as well as I do that he's trying to cover something up!"

Genny eased herself back toward Emma. Emma shot a glance at the door. *Exit, stage left?*

Genny's eyebrows shot up. *Are you kidding? And miss this?*

"I know this isn't what you want to hear," Helen was saying. "But we have to face facts."

"I am facing them!" Daphne snapped back. She paced down the length of the island, before she turned around. It was like she was positioning herself to protect . . . what exactly?

"The fact is that Uncle Bert pushed to get the autopsy released as fast as possible," said Daphne. "There has to be some reason for that. You know he never does anything unless he thinks there's something in it for him."

For a moment, mother and daughter just stood there, staring each other down along the length of the antiquated kitchen. Emma felt her throat constrict.

"It's over, Daphne," Helen said. "We will miss Marcie. *I* will miss her. You just have to believe it was not anything to do with you, or your choices. It was something inside Marcie herself, and I should have seen it and I should have tried harder to help her, and I will always regret that. But it is over."

"All right," said Daphne with hollow cheerfulness. "Since it's over, I guess there's no problem with us going into Aunt Marcie's rooms now, is there? I mean, it's not like we're going to need to keep things as they are for the cops, right?"

Helen narrowed her eyes, clearly trying to see just what might be behind her daughter's words. "Who's 'us'?"

"Emma and Genny are working with the du Maurier Society. They're going to do a memorial at the festival." The lie came out so smoothly, Emma was impressed, and a little appalled. "We were going to pick out some photos, maybe some of the books."

"Daphne . . ." Emma began, but she didn't get any further.

Helen narrowed her eyes in an expression that Emma suspected Daphne had seen a lot, especially on occasions when there was a broken plate or missing homework.

"What are you doing, Daphne?"

Daphne shrugged. "Giving you an out if any of the uncles get mad that I let Emma look around."

"And why does Emma need to look around?"

"You know why, Mum," said Daphne flatly. "Because something's wrong, and I don't trust Uncle Bert."

Helen glowered darkly at Emma and Genny. Uncertainty bubbled up inside Emma. What if her rash promise let Daphne cling to some false hope rather than come to terms with her own grief?

"This once," said Helen softly. "That's it. If there's nothing to see, then it's over, agreed?"

Daphne didn't answer right away. She tugged at her ponytail and looked to Emma and Genny for support.

They both shrugged like they'd coordinated the move.

Daphne rolled her eyes, exasperated. "Okay. But, Mum, if we do find something, you have to promise to listen, yeah?"

"Yes. All right. I will listen."

Genny let out a long slow breath. Emma nodded in sympathy and agreement.

Oliver bustled back to Emma's side and bonked her with his nose. "Emma? I think I found something here too. I'm not sure, but there's something. It's leftover. But there was a lot of rain all over the floor. Also soap, and bleach."

*Bleach?* Emma looked down at Oliver. *Who'd use*

*bleach to clean a floor like this?* Something in the back of her mind shifted uncomfortably. There wasn't enough time to follow it, though.

"Oh, Helen, there you are." Frank pushed open the door from the main house. "I was looking for you."

As he came toward them, Emma saw that Frank looked like he'd slept well and taken time with himself that morning. His silvering hair was well combed, his polo shirt was fresh, so was his shave. Objectively, one might even find him handsome.

Subjectively, Emma decided she preferred mechanic/taxi driver/car salesmen.

Helen sucked in a deep breath, straightened up and smoothed down the hem of her T-shirt, obviously pulling herself together. "Yes, Frank, what is it?"

"I just wanted to make sure you were both all right. It's been kind of a rotten morning." He laid his hand on top of Helen's where it rested on the kitchen island. She looked confused. He tried to take Daphne's hand too. She actively stepped back.

Frank sighed. "All right, all right, I know what you're thinking. What am I doing? I was never there, I keep whining about what I want and I need. But I am here now and I'm *trying*, all right?"

"Sorry, Dad," Daphne mumbled. "You're right, you are and I . . . it's just all a great big mess."

"I know," said Frank. "But we're together, yeah? That's what matters."

If Emma had one stereotypical English trait, it was the deep-seated desire to *not* be wherever people were expressing private emotions. She found herself immediately searching for some excuse to make a quick exit. But Genny found it first.

"Well! We'll just get the bins from the pantry," Genny said briskly. "We'll come back later for . . . the other stuff."

"No," said Daphne, her attention squarely on Emma. "You don't want to have to make a second trip."

"What's going on?" asked Frank.

Helen was the one who answered. "The du Maurier So-ciety wanted to borrow some of Marcie's books and things for a memorial at the festival. Emma's here to help with that."

"Oh, yes, right," said Frank. "Good. I'll take her up-stairs, then, shall I?"

"No, I'll do it," said Daphne quickly.

"You were going for a run," said Frank. "You should do that. It will help you clear your head."

Daphne turned to her mother. Helen hesitated. "You know, I think your father's right. You go on. We'll talk more about this later."

Daphne glared at her mother, but Helen stood firm. There was a determination in Helen's eyes that had not been there when she walked in, and Daphne felt it, probably even more strongly than Emma did.

"Right. Okay," said Daphne. "I'm off, then." She headed out the door and up the steps to the car park.

"Well, okay." Frank looked to Helen for some explana-tion, but she just shook her head. He sighed. "Let's go, then, Emma. Genny? You coming as well?"

"Nah," said Genny. "I'm going to get the bins loaded. Emma's got it covered."

Emma smiled weakly. She didn't feel like she had it cov-ered. She felt like she wanted to yell at everybody to go away, for the truly ridiculous reason that she needed a min-ute to talk to her dog.

But Frank was already on the way back into the main house, and everybody else was watching her, so Emma had to follow him, with Oliver in tow.

What else was there to do?

# 26

. . . . . . . . . . . .

EMMA, FRANK AND OLIVER REACHED THE BEAUTIFUL FOYER,
and Emma found herself looking up at the distant ceiling
and the branching chandelier. She tried to imagine what it
would be like to live in this dramatic, silent manor house.
She expected her inner thirteen-year-old to let out a sigh of
envy.

Thirteen-year-old Emma remained surprisingly silent.
Adult Emma thought about Marcie, and how this house had
been her life's work, and all the details that would involve.

"How many staff do you normally have?" Emma asked
Frank, partly so she could focus on him again. Oliver's running commentary was making it hard to think straight. He
did not seem to have lifted his nose once the entire way
here. "Nope, nope. Emma, this is the wrong way . . . Still
the wrong way . . ."

"There's been nothing like you'd call proper staff, not
since we were kids, really," said Frank. "It was all Marcie's
show. There's a housekeeper, Mrs. Childress—she comes
in days, whenever Marcie sends, sent, for her." He frowned.
"We should probably call her. I better find the number." He
pulled his high-end mobile out of his pocket and spoke into
it. "Note: find Mrs. Childress." The machine beeped and

Frank tucked it away again. "The gardens are looked after
by a service. Marcie had some kind of system for working
out which rooms needed cleaning and when. The only time
we've got a full staff of any kind is during the festival.
Marcie had a whole set of high-end people, antique special-
ists as well as movers come in and get everything into
place. We've been fielding calls all morning."

"That's a lot of work."

His mouth quirked up. It was not a nice expression. "Oh,
don't think Marcie was doing it out of the goodness of her
heart. She got a regular allowance straight out of the estate's income, just like we do, only more so. Besides, if she
didn't want the responsibility, she could have turned it
down, couldn't she? But she didn't."

Frank spoke those last words with a flat finality, but
Emma felt the anger underneath them. He started climbing
the stairs. Emma, in the interests of keeping pace, scooped
Oliver into her arms and followed.

She also took a moment to whisper in his ear. "I hear
you, I promise, but I need to do the human things now."

"I know, I know," grumbled Oliver. "But we're wasting
time going this way! We need to go the other way!"

"We will," Emma promised him, and herself. "We really will." She raised her voice to Frank. "These are beautiful portraits," she said.

"Ancestors." Frank waved at the gilt-framed paintings
on the walls. "At least, they're supposed to be. I think some
of them may have been adopted later." He gave her a half-
hearted wink. "You know how it goes."

They reached the first floor. Oliver wriggled in Emma's
arms. "I want to see," he whined. Which really meant he
wanted to give everything a thorough snuffling. Emma
kissed the top of his head.

"The family mostly lives in this wing." Frank gestured
toward the right-hand corridor. "My brothers and I have
rooms here on the first floor. Marcie took over the top floor.
Helen and Daphne are up there too when they come to stay.
It's not really like what you'd think of in a normal house

with everybody having their own bedroom, and sharing a lounge and sitter and whatnot. It's more like a block of flats. Everybody's got their own en suite, and so on."

They'd reached the top floor. Frank was puffing a bit. Emma put Oliver down. He scampered ahead, nose to the floor.

Frank watched the zigzagging corgi for a moment, and then turned to Emma.

"So, tell me, Ms. Reed. What are you actually doing here?"

*So, this is why you wanted to walk me upstairs. You wanted the privacy.*

Emma opened her mouth to repeat the story Helen and Daphne had given out, but then she looked in Frank's eyes and remembered that here was a man who had lost his sister and who was dealing with the backlash to years of troubled relationships.

"I'm just trying to help," said Emma.

"Is that all? Really?" Frank took another step toward her. He wasn't as conspicuously powerful as his brother Bert, but he still outweighed her, and he was doing his best to loom.

Oliver felt the attempted menace too, and Oliver, of course, was not going to leave Emma to handle this on her own. He slipped between her and Frank, plunked down, and laughed at him.

Frank stared, clearly uncertain as to what to do about this cheerfully obstructive corgi.

"I'm here to help," repeated Emma. "And really, that is all."

"I want to be very clear, I will not have you upsetting my wife and daughter. They need time to get their heads around what happened."

Emma cocked her head, aware she now looked a little like Oliver. "I thought Helen was your ex-wife."

Frank refused to budge, mentally or physically. "You think what you like, but you also remember what I've said."

Emma did not look away from Frank. She did not let

herself blink. Oliver clearly felt the tension thicken, because he was on his feet now, and his hackles were rising.

"I'll remember," she said.

"All right then. Come on."

Frank turned around and started down the hallway, all
the way to the door at the end, in fact.

"I do not like how he stands around you," said Oliver.
"He needs to be more careful."

*Or I do,* thought Emma.

They'd reached the far end of the hallway. There was
another stairway here leading back down. An arched,
many-paned window let in the daylight. A closed door
waited to the left, with an identical door to the right.

"That's the office." Frank nodded toward the door on
their right. "Used to be a schoolroom and governess's quar-
ters, I think. Now, this was the old nursery before Marcie
redid it for her suite."

He opened the left-hand door. Emma stood blinking in
a flood of sunlight. Oliver barreled ahead.

As Frank had said, it really was like a flat. In fact, it was
nicer than many of the flats Emma had lived in. Marcie had
a lounge, a bedroom with both a dressing room and a bathroom attached.

She could see why Marcie had taken these rooms for
herself. For one thing, they were much cozier than the
showy rooms she'd seen on the first floor. There were three
bay windows. Two overlooked the front courtyard. One
looked to the side of the house. Each one had a curved and
cushioned window seat. Emma could easily imagine Marcie
relaxing there with a book or just her own thoughts, looking
out across the courtyard and the rolling lawns toward the
misty countryside beyond.

Marcie had made these rooms into a comfortable, homey
nest. The furniture was all overstuffed and decorated with
colorful throw pillows, quilts and afghans that made Emma
wonder if she and Marcie were frequenting the same jumble sales. A few landscape paintings decorated the walls,

separated by framed movie posters for *Rebecca*, *Jamaica Inn*, *The Birds* and *The Scapegoat*.

Oliver, as usual, was everywhere at once, determined to get his nose into all the corners and under every piece of furniture. Emma, however, found herself drawn immediately to the bookcases. There were four in all, and they were stuffed to the brim.

Emma smiled. She didn't believe in ghosts, but it was easy to feel an extra personal presence in front of a shelf of much-loved books. The covers were all battered, the spines all broken. Marcie clearly not only read these, but reread them many times.

It was no surprise that Marcie had favored mysteries, mostly the classics. There was a whole shelf of Agatha Christies, along with the entire run of Dorothy L. Sayers. Less well-known authors like Josephine Tey, Helen MacInnes and John Dickson Carr were also represented. There was a good selection of romances and historicals. Mary Stewart was there, and Mary Renault and Georgette Heyer.

But something was missing.

"Nothing by du Maurier," she said.

"Eh?" Frank was standing by the fireplace, looking at the photos that dotted the mantel.

"Sorry, I was looking at Marcie's books, and there's nothing here by Daphne du Maurier."

"Oh, oh, right. Yeah. I think they're in the office. There's another bookshelf in there. Several, in fact. I'll show you."

"Thanks." Emma looked around for Oliver. He had his paws up on the window seat and his head under the cushion.

"Oliver!" she exclaimed, exasperated. "What are you doing?"

"Investigating!" mumbled Oliver. Oliver pulled his muzzle out and dropped to the floor. "It's important! Dash told me. But there's nothing here. Maybe here?" Nose to the floor he trotted to the hallway. "Here, here, here, then where?"

"You can control your dog, right?" Frank stood at the

office door with his hand on the knob. "There are some valuable antiques in here."

"Of course," said Emma cheerfully. "He's very well behaved, really."

Frank looked skeptical, but he did open the door.

The office was a much more dramatic room than Marcie's suite had been. Flocked, burgundy paper covered the walls. China ornaments filled vintage curio cabinets—Dresden shepherds and Art Nouveau nymphs and jeweled boxes, and delicate wax flowers protected by bell jars. The furniture was all Victorian—heavy dark wood with elaborate carvings. There were brass lamps with painted shades, and the old sconces on the walls still had their etched glass shades. The computer sitting in the middle of the broad, mahogany desk looked jarringly out of place.

"This is it! This is it!" Oliver zoomed into the room, trying, as usual, to be everywhere at once. "This is where the Perfume Lady was!"

"Shhh, yes, Oliver." Emma bent down and Oliver ran up and put his paws on her knee.

"Dash was right, Emma! He was!"

"I know, I know," she murmured. "But I need you to be calm now, good boy. We're guests, yes?" She rubbed his chin and leaned in and whispered. "Stealthy, right? We're stealthy."

"Stealth," mumbled Oliver. "Yes, good. A noble corgi is stealthy."

Emma stood up. Oliver slid under the desk, almost on his belly, and stuck his nose out toward Frank. Frank stared and shook his head. Clearly the corgi confounded him. Emma hid her smile by turning in place to better take in her surroundings.

Emma tried to imagine sitting down to work here, and found she couldn't do it. It would be like trying to work in a museum display, right down to the bookcase full of ledgers, each labeled "Inventory." The one at the top left was stamped 1900.

*Wow. And I bet there's another stash of these some-where going back further yet.*

Marcie, as manager and housekeeper for the grange had clearly kept up the practice of a yearly inventory. The label on the last ledger in the case said it was from two years ago.

*Two years ago? Wait a minute.* Emma's thoughts pulled up short. She started for the bookcase, but Frank interrupted her.

"The du Maurier books are over there," he told her.

Emma blushed. "Oh, yes, right."

Like in Marcie's private rooms, the office had three tall, latticed windows, each with its own window seat. Two of them overlooked the back courtyard, the gardens and the solid bulk of the hills beyond. The third overlooked the drive where it curved around the house.

Frank was looking out the window to the drive, hands jammed in his pockets. The expensive gray fabric rippled as he clenched his fists.

Emma turned away toward the bookcases, giving him some space to himself.

Here were all the du Maurier titles she'd missed in the other room. Marcie hadn't just been a fan, she'd been a serious collector. There was a regular open-fronted bookshelf lined with the editions that were obviously for reading. A quick glance told Emma that if it wasn't the whole *oeuvre*, it was most of it, including several short story collections and some of the more obscure titles, like *The Glass Blowers*. There were biographies, books of literary criticism, and tribute anthologies.

But there were a couple of barrister bookcases as well with glass doors to protect the polished oak shelves. This was where Marcie had kept the valuable pieces.

Inside, the books were opened to display autographs or to the copyright page indicating a first edition. Individual prints of original illustrations were laid out beside them. There were several letters to and from Daphne du Maurier herself.

"Wow," said Emma.

"Yeah." Frank was still staring at the window, and the window seat beneath it. "This was Marcie's passion. She'd spend hours cruising around the Internet, looking for something new." He shook himself and turned away and deliberately walked up to stand beside Emma. His whole body was stiff, as if he was afraid to make any sudden moves.

*He's trying to get used to being in here*, thought Emma.

"Apparently some of the stuff in there is worth a real packet." Frank peered at the shelves, but Emma wasn't sure he was actually seeing any of it. "So I'm afraid we can't let you have any of that, at least not on the spur of the moment, yeah? But this . . ." He waved toward the reading shelf. "All yours. Have at. Oh, this one especially." He pulled out the battered, vintage hardback of *Rebecca*. "That was her favorite." He handed it to Emma. "But you probably knew that."

"Thank you," said Emma. "I . . ."

A phone rang, the classic double-buzz. Frank jerked his mobile out of his pocket and checked the screen.

"Oh . . . blast," he muttered. "I need to take this. Be right back."

"No worries," said Emma. Frank went out in the corridor and shut the door.

Oliver zoomed straight up to her. Emma felt her heart begin to pound.

"Quick, Oliver, you said this is the room where you saw Caite?"

"Yes, yes!" Oliver raced over to the desk. "Right here! Here! But there's more! Dash said there was and he's right!" Oliver zoomed back to the window seat.

Emma hesitated. Curiosity dragged her in two directions. She needed to look at the computer. But Oliver was at the window seat, standing up on his hind legs and trying mightily to scramble up onto the cushions. He had found something, or Dash had, and he was sure it was important.

He could be right. He had been before.

*Oh, sugarplum fairies!*

Emma set the book down on the desk, and made herself walk up to the window. She took a deep breath and looked down onto the drive. *This is where Marcie fell, or Marcie jumped.* She was normally good with heights. Despite that, she felt briefly dizzy.

*It really isn't that far down,* she told herself. As soon as she thought this, a fresh uneasiness gripped her.

It really *wasn't* that far down, but that was only part of the problem. Now that she stood here, Emma saw it wouldn't be that easy to fall, at least, not if you were standing on the floor. The broad window seat put at least half a meter between her and the sill.

*Maybe she was leaning over to open the window, maybe she'd already opened it . . . Or maybe she really was standing up on the seat and getting ready to jump.*

Oliver grumbled wordlessly, and backed off, and jumped. Emma squeaked, startled. Oliver ignored her. He thrust nose and paws between the cushions. "Here. Right here. It's bad!" He pawed at the cushion edge. "Bad!"

"Bad how?" Emma glanced at the door. No sign or sound of movement from Frank, yet.

Oliver didn't answer. His pawing grew frantic. Emma moved to pick him up, but as she did, she saw a flash of gold between the cushions.

Emma momentarily forgot about moving her dog and instead dug her fingers down between the cushions. When she pulled her hand back, she was holding an earring.

It was a lovely piece of jewelry, clearly vintage, a fan shape dripping with jet and gold beads.

Emma recognized it. It was one of the earrings Marcie had been wearing when she came to the B&B.

"Oh," she breathed. "Oh, dear."

She closed her fingers gently around the earring. She should probably put it somewhere, or give it to Frank when he came back. She looked around, searching for the other one. She was just about to reach under the cushion, but Oliver barked.

"There! Emma! Somebody's coming!" Oliver stood up

on his hind legs and pressed his front paws against the window. "Look! Look!"

"Shhh! Oliver! It's all right." Emma leaned over next to him. A lime-green convertible pulled around the circular drive.

"Oh, that's just Gus," she said. "Headed for the . . ."

*Snick.*

Slowly, the window swung open. Oliver yipped. His front paws scrabbled against the empty air.

Oliver tipped, and fell forward.

# 27

THE NEXT THING EMMA KNEW, SHE WAS TWO FULL METERS back from the window seat, staring at the open window, with Oliver clutched tight in her arms.

"That was bad," wheezed Oliver. "I'm sorry, Emma. I'm . . ."

"Not your fault," Emma whispered. Her heart was banging against her ribs like it wanted to get out. She couldn't stop seeing Oliver tilting forward over the empty air, his paws waving.

"It's okay." He licked her chin. "I'm okay, and so are you. Nobody fell. It's all okay."

"Yeah, I know." She pressed her forehead against the scruff of his neck.

"Emma, you can let go now."

"Yeah, yeah, okay." Emma sucked in a deep breath and put Oliver down. She pressed her palms against her face and tried to will herself to stop shaking.

The window hung open. The breeze blew the dark curtains back. Emma smelled the summer air.

Emma made herself walk to the window. She needed to get it shut. It was dangerous. Somebody could fall.

*Somebody already fell.* She swallowed hard.

Emma made herself lean in and look more closely at the latch. It was dangling loose. It was the kind of latch with a little bar that rested in a bracket. When you wanted to open the window, you turned the latch up and pushed the window open. When you pulled the window shut, you turned the latch and dropped that little bar into the bracket again.

But the bracket was missing. Nothing was holding the windows closed except the hinges.

She could picture what came next so easily. Marcie had arrived back home. She was tired. She was sad. She'd come into her office to drop off her bag, and she'd slumped down on the window seat and leaned against the pane.

And the latch had given way, and she'd tipped out and fallen. Just like Oliver almost had.

It had been an accident.

*Except for Caite Hope-Johnston sneaking into the house to get at the computer,* she reminded herself. *And except for Bert making so sure that everybody knows it's suicide.*

*And what about Oliver saying something's bad here?*

"Oliver . . ." she began.

"What are you doing?" demanded Frank. "Get back from there!"

Startled, Emma shrieked and whirled around. Frank stood in the office doorway, his face flushed red.

Oliver barked.

"I, uh, sorry." Emma tried to calm her heart down, but it wasn't interested. "Oliver got up on the seat, and he put his paws on the window, and it came open."

Frank swore and hurried forward. He grabbed the window latch and pulled it shut. "This house! I swear the place is held together with caulk and baling wire! But my dear sister kept saying she'd handle it. Didn't want anybody's help. She could take care of everything and she was going to, whether the rest of us wanted her to or not." He glared at the window. Then he stopped, and the color drained from his cheeks. "I didn't mean that," he said. "I don't want you to think I'm *blaming* her. Because I never would."

"No, no, of course not," Emma murmured.

Oliver barked again, but then immediately ducked his head in apology. Emma desperately wished she could ask him what he smelled that was so bad. But it was too late.

"Emma." Oliver tentatively bonked her calf. "Emma, tell him about the bad. And you dropped the sparkly!"

*What are you . . . ?* Emma looked around, confused. Oliver pawed the carpet. *Oh!* Oliver was pawing at the earring on the Persian carpet. Emma picked it up. "We found this. It was Marcie's."

Frank took the earring from her fingertips. "Where was this?"

"In between the window seat cushions."

"Oh. I expect it's been there for ages." He tucked it into his pocket. "I'll give it to Helen. She might want it. Did you find the other?"

"No, just that one." She paused. "How long has that window latch been broken?"

"I don't know that I'd ever noticed it was." He considered. "I think I remember Marcie saying last winter she was going to get somebody in to fix all the windows. It'd help with the heating costs and all. But she didn't get round to it. She decided that the roof repairs were more important." He glowered at the window again. "You don't think, I mean, that it might have been an accident after all, do you?"

"I don't know," said Emma. "I mean, it could be."

"Yes," muttered Frank. "I wish I knew—" He stopped again. "Yes. Right. Well. You pick out those books, then?"

"Oh, no. Sorry." Emma hurried over to the bookcase. She reclaimed the copy of *Rebecca* from the desk and then started pulled additional titles as quickly as she could: *Jamaica Inn*, *The Scapegoat*, *My Cousin Rachel*, and *Mary Anne* (a dark horse favorite). "This should do to begin with."

"And then some, I'd say," said Frank, striving to lighten the tone. *Stiff upper lip.* "Well, you've got a lot to be getting on with I'm sure. And so do I."

"Yes, thank you. Sorry to have taken up so much of your time."

"No, no, glad to. Well. Yes." He looked back over his shoulder to the window. "And no."

"I understand," said Emma.

Frank murmured something under his breath that sounded like *I very much doubt that,* and walked out the door.

Emma trailed behind with Oliver. She tried frantically to think of some excuse to linger in the office. She wanted to try to get into the computer. She wanted to find out what it was around the window seat that had upset Oliver and Dash so much. This room was full of answers, and all she was taking out was a stack of old books.

She was grateful Frank couldn't see her face as she followed him down the hallway to the main stairs. They met Gus coming up from the first floor.

"Oh, Frank, I was looking for you. Do you have a second?" He pointed down the hallway toward what Frank had said were the family rooms.

"Yes, sure. You can find your way all right?" he said to Emma.

"No worries," she answered brightly.

"You can call if there's anything else you need." There was an undercurrent in Frank's voice. *Call. Don't just show up again. We'll decide if you can be let in.*

"I'll do that, thanks," said Emma. "Come on, Oliver. Genny's waiting for us."

She brushed past the brothers, smiling in what she hoped was an apologetic fashion.

*Something is wrong. Something about all this doesn't add up, and I don't know what it is.*

"Oliver," she muttered, "as soon as we get out of here, we are going to have a long talk."

"Yes!" Oliver yipped. He hopped down two more stairs. "I've found out many important things!"

*That makes one of us.*

She wanted to talk to Genny. She wanted time to think. She wanted an excuse to run back upstairs to Marcie's office.

But Genny wasn't alone when Emma got to the kitchen. Daphne was sitting on a stool beside her, pouring out a fresh mug of tea.

"Are you all right, Emma?" Genny asked. "You look like somebody just took a swipe at Oliver."

"Nobody takes a swipe at a warrior corgi!" grumbled Oliver as he went to nose at the food bowl by the cast-iron stove. "Dash has eaten all the kibble again."

"Yeah, sorry." Emma shook herself. "But Oliver did almost fall out the window."

"The window?" echoed Daphne. "Not . . . the same one as Aunt Marcie?"

"I'm afraid so," said Emma. She had no idea how Daphne was going to take this revelation. "The latch is broken. It's missing the lower bracket, so that when it slipped, the window just swung open."

"Yikes!" cried Genny. "You must have been scared to—" Genny evidently realized she was about to choose a bad figure of speech and changed course. "Out of your wits!"

"For a minute there, yeah," agreed Emma. "And we found an earring too, under the cushions. It was one that Marcie had been wearing when she came to see me."

"Oh," breathed Daphne. "Well, I mean, all that says is that she was up there. We knew that."

"And that's it? That's all you found?" said Genny.

"I didn't have a lot of time. But so far, yes, that's it."

Daphne tugged at her ponytail, caught herself and brushed it back over her shoulder. "Well, I mean, I guess— Gah!" she grunted. "I was just so sure Uncle Bert must be covering something up."

"He still might be," said Emma. "I just don't understand why he'd be so anxious to call her death a suicide rather than an accident."

Daphne looked away and tugged at her ponytail. "I suppose. But it's going to take a lot more than some confusion and an earring to convince Mum. But thanks for trying. I mean that." She was trying to be polite, but she was also clearly disappointed.

"We've just started," Emma reminded her. "There's still plenty we don't know."

"Right, right." Daphne took a deep breath. "Keep calm and sleuth on?" She tried to smile. "I'd better go get a shower," and with that, she headed toward the door to the main house.

When she was gone, Genny turned to Emma. "All right, Emma Reed, I know that look. What didn't you tell her?"

"Nothing. I mean, nothing really. It's just, there is one more thing I want to check on."

"So you did find out something else," said Genny eagerly. "I knew it!"

"It's a maybe," Emma warned her. "I'm really, really not sure."

"So, tell me all about this maybe."

Emma looked over at the door to the main house. "Outside." She collected her bag and gathered up the books from Marcie's office. "Come on, Oliver!"

"Yes! Yes!" Oliver zoomed up the steps to the courtyard. He paused by the Mini, his whole body quivering, and then he made a beeline for the old carriage house. It was a low brick building with a sloping roof with wide eaves. Clearly, it was now doing duty as a garage. Even Emma could make out the tire tracks leading up to the three sets of bay doors. The doors didn't lift open, like on a modern garage, they swung open sideways. They also sagged against their hinges and could have used a good coat of paint. Various vermin had gnawed at their edges.

Oliver nosed the gravel, moving back and forth, searching for something.

"What's got into him?" asked Genny.

Premonition closed Emma's throat tight.

Oliver froze in place for one strained heartbeat, and then started pawing frantically at the gravel, just like he had at the seat cushions upstairs.

"Emma! Emma!" barked Oliver. "It's here! There's more bad!"

Without a word, Emma dumped Marcie's books into

Genny's arms and ran over to her dog. A cold, sinking feeling dragged hard at each step. Genny mumbled something not entirely complimentary and hurried to catch up.

"Bad! Bad!" barked Oliver. "Dash said it. He said! It's bad!"

"Oliver, it's okay, calm down." Emma knelt down and wrapped an arm around him. "Calm down now."

"Bad!" he barked again. "She was here!"

Emma leaned in close and rubbed Oliver's head. "What . . . what do you mean she was here?" she whispered in his ear. "Which she?"

"The Rain Lady . . . Marcie! Marcie was here!" he whined sharply. "She was dead here, Emma! Just like upstairs!"

# 28

............

EMMA FROZE. HER BREATH RASPED HARD INSIDE HER throat.

"Is Oliver okay?" asked Genny. "He's awfully agitated. Maybe he got into a patch of nettles or something?"

"No." Emma stood up slowly. She felt the blood draining from her cheeks. Her hands had gone cold. "Nothing like that."

"Emma," said Genny. "You're scaring me. What is going on?"

*How do I even . . . ?* Emma forced her mind into motion. "Um, Genny. I'm going to have to ask you to take a leap of faith with me here."

"Ooookay. Where are we leaping?"

Emma swallowed. "Can you, just, go watch the kitchen door for a second and warn me if anybody comes out?"

Genny didn't move. "Can I ask why?"

"I just need one second," she said. "And then I'll tell you everything."

"You promise?"

Emma nodded.

"Yeah. Right. Okay."

Genny, with a lot of backward glances, walked over to

the Mini. She opened the driver's side door and laid Marcie's books on the seat. One at a time.

Emma sucked in a breath and got back down on her knees beside Oliver. "Tell me again, Oliver. What did you find?"

Oliver crouched low, as if getting ready to charge. "Rain Lady Marcie, she was dead here, *and* she was dead up there! I can smell it! It's blood and it's sick and it's *bad!*"

It wasn't always easy to understand Oliver, especially when he got upset, but this time Emma was sure she grasped his meaning, or at least its implications. The problem was, she really didn't want to.

"Are you absolutely sure, Oliver?" she whispered. "I mean, it was raining hard all that night." It should have washed away any scent.

"It's dry here." Oliver thrust his nose at the gravel.

"Because we're under the eaves." Emma glanced overhead. "If the rain was falling straight down, it wouldn't have gotten this part of the ground . . . Oh, sugarplum fairies," she breathed.

Oliver sprang forward, like he was trying to trap something under his paws. "Here! Here!" He scrabbled at the gravel. "Right here!"

Emma leaned in closer. Oliver dug harder. Another few bits of gravel shifted backward. Emma saw a glimmer of gold among the loose stones.

She slapped her hand over her mouth. Because there in the mud was another earring, all gleaming gold and shining jet beads. Just like the one she'd handed to Frank.

Gravel crunched. Startled, Emma fell over onto her backside. Genny loomed over her and did not look at all sorry.

"That's it," Genny said. "I'm done playing lookout. What is going on?"

Emma scrambled to her feet and dusted her hands. She also looked toward the grange. This was taking too long. Somebody in the house would see them. Frank and Gus could be looking down from a first floor window right now.

Or Bert, wherever he was. Somebody would come to find out why on earth she and Genny were hanging about in the courtyard.

"We need pictures," she said.

"Of what?" demanded Genny. Oliver whined and wagged, and pawed at the ground. Genny bent closer. "Is that an earring?" She reached for it.

"Don't!" shouted Emma. "It's evidence!"

Genny straightened up slowly. Emma yanked her mobile out of her bag. She took a couple of photos of the earring close-up. Then she backed away, crouching down and angling the phone awkwardly, to try to make sure she could get enough of the garage and the door into the shot to show exactly where the earring was.

Genny hovered anxiously over Emma as she snapped her shots. Then, Emma fished a tissue out of her bag and used it to pluck the earring out of the gravel, then tucked it into a side pocket.

"So, what exactly is it evidence of?"

"What's evidence?" said Helen.

Both Emma and Genny jumped. So did Oliver, only he came down wrong and flopped sideways.

Helen was crossing the courtyard.

"Oh, hullo!" said Genny brightly.

Helen stopped about a meter from them. Her skeptical gaze swept across the scene. Emma felt her cheeks heating up, as if she'd been caught with her hand in the cookie jar.

"Tell her!" Oliver bonked Emma's calf. "Tell her about the bad!"

"What is the matter with you two?" Helen looked from Genny to Emma, both anger and disbelief showing plainly on her face. "You picked up something, I saw you, and you were talking about evidence."

"Um, yes, well . . ." began Emma. She looked to Genny for help, but Genny just gestured.

Emma sighed. "We found this." She pulled the tissue out of her purse and carefully opened it up. Helen stepped gingerly closer and peered at the earring.

"That's Marcie's," said Helen. "It was her favorite pair. She must have lost it the night she died. I remember her wearing them."

"Yes, I remember them too," Emma told her. "And I just found the other one up in the office, between the window seat cushions."

"If she was wearing them when she died, that wouldn't be so strange," said Genny reluctantly.

Helen wasn't listening to her. She closed the bits of tissue over the earring, as if she didn't want to look at it anymore and handed it back to Emma. "You think it means something else, don't you, Emma?"

Emma nodded, but she found it surprisingly hard to speak. Oliver lay down beside her and put his front paws over her shoes to let her know he was there for her.

"I know you don't really know me, Helen, and I know you haven't got any reason to trust what I'm about to say, but I think Marcie's body was moved."

"Are you serious?" said Genny.

"You can't possibly . . ." said Helen at the same time. "Why would anybody do that?"

Emma didn't answer. Neither did Genny.

But Helen didn't really need an answer, not, at least, after the words had time to settle in. Her face creased with consternation and anger. "You think someone tried to hide the fact that Marcie killed herself?"

"Helen, I think Marcie was murdered."

# 29

............

HELEN STAGGERED, AS IF EMMA'S WORDS KNOCKED against her with physical force. "You can't mean it."

"I'm sorry," breathed Emma. "I should have—"

Genny cut her off. "I've got an idea. Let's take a ride." She faced Helen. "Emma's considering buying the Mini here. You can tell us what you think."

Helen hesitated, but she also glanced over her shoulder at the house. "Yes, all right. Let's do that."

Helen climbed into the back seat and let Emma boost Oliver in with her. Oliver, recognizing Helen's distress, snuggled up close. Helen wrapped her arms around him and held on as if it was for dear life.

Maybe it was.

Emma backed and turned the Mini with exaggerated caution. She drove around the corner of the house, across the front courtyard, down the long drive and through the gates. She kept on driving, slowly and steadily until they turned onto the main road. As soon as the hedges pulled back enough to make a decent shoulder, Emma eased the Mini over and switched off the engine. She sat there, both hands on the wheel, staring out the windscreen.

"I'd like to get out," said Helen."

"Oh, yes, right." Genny opened the door and got out onto the shoulder, followed by Helen, and of course Oliver. Emma got out too. Helen walked up the road a few paces, so she was standing in the shadow of the earthen berm with its tangle of bracken drooping overhead.

A battered lorry rattled down the road, slowed and stopped.

"Everything all right, ladies?" called the rumpled, stubbled driver.

"Yes, thanks!" answered Genny. "No worries!"

He nodded and waved and drove on.

"All right," said Helen. Her voice was taut and her features were drawn. The ride had frizzled her hair and now the summer breeze whipped it into a shifting, ragged halo. "Emma, I need you to tell me exactly why you think my sister-in-law was murdered."

Oliver was nosing the ground by the hedge. Emma's already jangled nerves were not made any better by how close the road, and its traffic were to her back.

Another car stopped, this one a boxy, blue import. "All right, ladies? Need anything? Oh, hullo, Genny!"

"Hullo, Tom!" Genny waved. "We're fine. Thanks! Say hi to Mary for me!"

"Will do!" Tom drove off.

"Better make it quick, Emma, or somebody's going to tell Brian you crashed his Mini into a hedge," said Genny.

"Right." Emma squared her shoulders. Oliver trotted back to her side, every part of him on the alert, just in case. "I know how this is about to sound," she told Helen. "But it was my dog who knew. And yours."

"I don't understand."

"Oliver was upset by something in the office, and again by the garage. So was Dash. The last time I saw Oliver get that agitated was last year when we found Victoria Roberts, and she was dead."

"You mean, you think he smelled something?"

"I think he smelled blood in both places. And we found one earring in each place as well." She took a deep breath.

"And the day Marcie died, Caite Hope-Johnston was in her office."

"*Caite?* What was she doing there?"

"I don't know," said Emma. "But she was using Marcie's computer."

Helen said nothing. She paced back to the car. She didn't even look at Emma, or Genny. She put one hand on the hood. Emma suddenly remembered Caite standing in the rain, absorbing the news that Marcie was dead.

Oliver trotted over to Helen. He sat back on his haunches and stretched himself up. Helen rubbed his head, but didn't look down.

At last she turned around. Oliver dropped back down onto all fours. He also bonked her in the calf, trying to herd her back to Emma and Genny.

"Oliver," said Emma sternly.

Oliver ducked his head. "Sorry, Emma."

Emma picked him up and deposited him in the car. Oliver huffed and grumbled. But he also turned around three times and curled up onto the seat. Emma patted his head.

She felt, rather than saw Helen move closer to her. When Emma turned around, she was face-to-face with the other woman. Helen had flushed red, and she held herself so tightly, Emma felt sure something was about to break.

"How sure are you about this?" she demanded, her voice low and rasping. "About Marcie being murdered?"

"I'm not sure at all," Emma told her. "But we do have a whole bunch of very strange circumstances."

"You can't honestly think Caite had anything to do with it?"

"I don't know anything for sure," said Emma. "But you have to admit, you wouldn't sneak into a house where someone just died on a whim."

"No, you're certainly right about that." The breeze pushed a broad swatch of hair across Helen's eyes. She brushed it back impatiently.

"I also had a very strange conversation with Bert in the pub," said Emma. "It was before the autopsy report came out. He wanted to make very sure I knew that Marcie had killed herself, and when I asked if it could have been something else, he immediately assumed I was talking about murder. Why would he make that jump? Why not think it might be an accident?"

"Yeah, that's something that's really been bothering me too," said Genny. "Why would Bert, or anybody, want to push the idea of a suicide over an accident? It doesn't make sense."

"Actually, that's the one thing that does make sense." Helen smirked. "You see, the Cochrane family is rather famously accident-prone."

"I don't understand," said Emma.

Helen raised her eyebrows and cocked her head in mock surprise. "Richard Cochrane, Frank and co.'s father, was the second son," she recited, as if repeating a lesson she'd learned as a schoolgirl. "His older brother, Stewart, died in a boating accident. Went out on a rough sea after having had too much to drink," she added. "So Richard and his wife, Evelyn, inherited the grange. They moved in right after probate was settled, and very shortly after that, they had their four children. The current generation—Marcie, Bert, Gus and Frank. Then, when Richard and Evelyn died in a car accident, Marcie inherited."

"Now, Marcie's dead and the grange changes hands yet again," murmured Emma.

Helen nodded. "If this gets called an accident . . . well, people might start thinking how that makes three accidents in a row that changed who owns Truscott Grange."

"Which does start looking a little odd, if you stop to think about it," said Genny.

Emma thought about the argument she'd overheard. *And if we sit here arguing like idiots, someone is going to think something's really wrong in this family,* Bert had said. *And they'll start asking awkward questions.*

"But if it's suicide . . ." began Genny.

"Then it's a different story," Emma finished. "Anybody who wants to can say it was Marcie's own fault, because she had problems and didn't tell the family." She'd already seen how Bert was not above blaming the victim.

"Yes." Helen plucked a leaf off the nearest bit of bracken and twirled it restlessly by the stem. After a moment, she pitched it away. "What a god-awful mess! What on earth am I going to tell Daphne?"

Emma steeled her nerves. She walked around so she was facing Helen. "I know you didn't ask for this, and it's not fair that you're the one who has to deal with it, but this is where you are. So there's really only one question." She put her hand on Helen's shoulder. "What do you want to do?"

"I don't *know*," Helen snapped, but then she shook her head. "I suppose I ought to talk to Frank. Tell him about the other earring. Get him to go to the police with me." She shoved her hair back from her forehead. She looked like someone who had seen her world break once before, and now had to watch all those cracks opening up again. "He's been different lately. He says he's looking for a new start of some kind between us and he might just mean it this time. Life is full of surprises." She paused. "Unless Frank is in on it. But we don't even know what *it* is, do we? I mean, we think Bert's covering something up, at least Daphne does. But we don't know what that something is. But if the body was moved . . ." She swallowed. "If Marcie was killed, it could have been any one of them, couldn't it?" She stopped again. "It even could have been me."

Emma saw the exact moment Helen thought, *Or Daphne*.

"And let's not leave out Hyphenated Caite," said Genny quickly.

"Oh, lord, yes, let's not," said Helen bitterly. "So you're the one with experience in these things, Emma. What should we be doing?"

Emma rubbed Oliver's ears and tried to think. But nothing came to her.

"Well, I think it's pretty obvious," announced Genny. "The first thing to do is make sure the festival happens."

# 30

. . . . . . . . . . . .

HELEN'S FACE WENT ABSOLUTELY BLANK. "YOU CAN'T BE serious, Genny."

But as soon as Genny said it, Emma felt like her brain had been kicked into high gear. "Actually, that might be a good idea, at least it is if we can't shift the police round to the idea that Marcie was murdered. Working on the festival gives us an excuse to talk to people and to keep looking around."

"Yes, yes!" Oliver put his front paws on the window frame. "An excellent idea! A noble corgi warrior can always find what's missing!"

Oliver might tend to overestimate his own abilities, but this time, Emma had to admit he might be right. *Look at what he's found out already.*

Plus, Genny could be there, and Pearl, as well as Daphne and Helen. They could be working together to search that enormous house, to see if there was anything more to be found.

It could work.

Despite the warmth of the day, Helen wrapped her arms around herself. "Poor Marcie. She would have hated this."

Her voice trembled. Emma wished she'd thought to put extra tissues in her bag. "She spent so much time trying to make things go smoothly for everybody."

"What was Marcie like?" Emma asked curiously. "I only met her a couple of times."

Helen smiled, distant and fond. "She was quiet, but she had a wicked sense of humor once you got to know her. She went out of her way to make me comfortable whenever she was around. We had a shared love of old mysteries and soppy romances. She was a wonderful listener. When things started to go bad with Frank, she was one of the few people I could really talk to. Before or after the divorce."

"You stayed close?"

"Best mates, really. Frank liked to think Daphne and I kept coming to stay because somewhere deep down I wanted to keep us together as a family, but it was really to see Marcie. We'd talk two or three times a week, no matter where we were, and of course we're always here for festival weekend. It's a lot of fun, really."

"Are you a du Maurier fan?"

"Me?" Helen shuddered. "No. She's much too dark for me. Give me Dorothy Sayers any day."

"I'd been wondering, because of your daughter's name."

"Daphne? Oh, yes, that was Marcie's idea actually. I'd planned to name our daughter Marcia, for her aunt. Frank was okay with it, because it was a family name. But Marcie nixed the idea."

"Did she say why?"

"She said our girl should have a name that would promise a chance at a future."

Genny whistled softly. "I hadn't ever heard that bit. That's . . . I'm not sure what that is."

"I've never been sure either, honestly. But I know Marcie deserved better than she got." Helen's expression tightened. "And she does now. Can one of you loan me a phone?"

"Sure." Genny reached over the side of the car and pulled her mobile out of her bag and handed it to Helen. Helen frowned, and her mouth moved silently for a moment. Then, she punched some buttons. Another car passed, and slowed.

"All right?" called the driver, a tiny, dark woman with bright, white hair. "Oh, hullo, Genny!"

"Hullo, Mrs. Singh! Yes, everything's fine, thanks." Genny smiled and exchanged thumbs-ups.

Helen was holding the phone to her ear. "Hello, Caite? Yes. Helen Dalgliesh."

Emma raised her eyebrows, and both she and Genny turned to face Helen.

"No, everything's fine . . . well, yes. But I know you've been wanting to hear from us, and the family has decided that the festival should go forward. What?" She pressed two fingers against her ear. "Sorry, I'm out in the garden. Yes . . . yes. That is everybody's decision. We think it'd be the most appropriate send-off for Marcie. I know there's not a lot of time, so I'd like to help out, if I can. I've got all Marcie's notes and so on—at least, I know where she kept them." Helen paused, listening. "Yes. Wonderful. Then we can count on seeing you tomorrow? Good. We'll expect you and the board then. And we'll have Angelique and her people there as well . . . Yes. I do. Good. Thank you." She said goodbye and she hung up, and handed Genny's phone back.

"There. Done."

"What will you do if any of the brothers object?" It was strange how quickly Emma had come to think of them as a collective, like bricks in a wall. She resisted the urge to start humming Pink Floyd tunes.

"I can handle them," said Helen. "But I'd better get started on it."

"Do you want us to drive you back?" asked Genny.

"It's not really all that far, I'll walk. You should get going before the other half of Trevena comes by."

She turned away, but Emma stopped her.

"Helen?"

"Yes?" She looked back over her shoulder.

"Are you sure about this?"

Helen straightened up. For the first time that morning,

Emma could see the confident woman who knew her own worth and her own strength. "You know, I am. Maybe if it was just me, it'd be another story. But this is about Marcie, and Daphne."

Emma nodded. *I understand that.*

They said goodbye. Helen started walking up the road, back toward the grange and all its secrets.

Emma and Genny climbed back into the Mini. Oliver scrambled up into Emma's lap. Emma wrapped her arms around him and rested her head on top of his.

"Hey!" Genny put her hand on Emma's shoulder. "Are you all right? Do you want me to drive?"

"No, I'm okay." Emma wiped at her face, embarrassed to realize that her eyes were watering. Oliver twisted around and licked at her chin.

"I'm right here, Emma."

"You sure you're okay?" said Genny. "Because I'm not so sure I am. Anyway, here's what we're going to do. We're going to get Brian his car back before he sends out a search party. Then, we all go home and get over the shakes, which I know you're going to have, because I'm getting them now. Then, I'll call Pearl and Angelique."

"What am I going to be doing while you're calling them?"

"Calling DCI Brent," said Genny. "You're going to have to eventually. Might as well be now."

"Yeah, you're right." Emma rubbed Oliver's back. "I just wish we had something more to show her than one earring." *Because I do not fancy explaining how it was a couple of dogs who worked out that the body got moved.*

"Well, we'll cross that bridge when we come to it. You sure you're okay to drive?"

"Yes, Mum." Emma boosted Oliver across to Genny's lap and started up the engine. With exaggerated care, she checked the mirrors and pulled back out onto the road. Oliver barked happily and opened his mouth to laugh at the passing scenery.

"So," said Genny as they rounded the first bend. "What do you think really happened?"

That was an excellent question. "I don't know," Emma admitted. "There's just too many pieces. The only thing I'm sure about is that somebody moved Marcie's body. I mean, we've got the earrings—"

"And the bad!" yipped Oliver.

"In two different places. "Plus Oli . . . that is, Oliver was acting like he'd smelled something wrong in the kitchen, and when I looked at what he was fussing over, I thought I saw signs that somebody had used bleach to clean the floor."

"Bleach?" said Genny, incredulous. "That's a wooden floor in that kitchen. You can't use bleach, it leaves a dark stain."

"Erm. Right. Exactly. That's what I thought. But you do use bleach . . ."

"If you want to obliterate bloodstains," Genny finished for her. "You're talking to a woman who dismembers fresh fish on a daily basis. I could write you a book on cleaning products. Also hand soaps."

"So somebody moved the body through the kitchen. But which direction? Upstairs to downstairs, or downstairs to up?" Emma shifted her grip on the steering wheel and eased the Mini around the sharp corner and onto a broader stretch of road that wound between neatly fenced fields.

"That broken window latch has to mean something." Oliver stood up on Genny's lap, mouth open and tongue out to catch all the wind rushing by. Emma felt a twinge of guilt. She really should have him in his harness. Genny, experienced dog owner that she was, kept a firm hold on him.

"It means something," agreed Emma, thinking about the broken latch. "But what? I mean, at first, I thought that maybe somebody'd tinkered with it deliberately, so the window would open if Marcie leaned on it, but I mean, the window seat is pretty broad. It wouldn't be that easy for anybody to fall, even if they were sitting on it."

"And it wouldn't explain why there was blood or a lost earring down by the garage," added Genny.

"So maybe the latch is a distraction," said Emma. "Maybe somebody actually killed Marcie in her office. But then what? If they just pushed her out the window that still doesn't explain what we found by the garage or the kitchen."

"How about this?" said Genny. "Somebody kills Marcie in the office. Then they carry her body down to the garage. The plan is to drive her body away, maybe throw it off a cliff or something. But halfway through, they get a better idea and just drop it under the window."

Emma slowed down and stopped. This far in the country, traffic jams were infrequent, but when they did occur, there were probably sheep involved. Right now, a woolly white drift clogged the road, with Arthur Wolstead holding the gate so his border collie could herd them all through.

"Clem! Clem!" barked Oliver urgently. "There's one getting away! Clem!"

"Shhh." Emma patted Oliver's head. "It's rude to tell others how to do their jobs."

Genny laughed. "You have a rich and wonderful fantasy dialogue going with him, don't you?"

Emma laughed heartily.

The sheep cleared, Clem barked, Arthur waved and Emma drove on.

"You know, Genny," she said, "the more I think about it, the more I think leaving the body under the window was a good idea. Not only does it make everybody think about suicide, but the rain would mess up all the evidence, wouldn't it? It was really pouring that night. Fiber and hair and DNA . . . all that, it'd all be washed away. If somebody had been handling the body, there'd be no way to tell."

"And it'd mess up the body temperature, so it'd be harder to determine time of death," Genny added. "You're right. It would be a good idea. In a horrible, cold-blooded sort of way."

Emma turned the Mini into Brian's car lot and parked.

Genny agreed to stay with Oliver while Emma went into the office.

Brian sat at his desk, marking up invoices and running numbers through the calculator. He looked up when the bell rang over the door.

"Hullo!" He smiled to see her. "How was it?"

Emma mustered a smile of her own. "Handles like a dream. I had fun."

"Fantastic," he said. "Only I was just about to call. Mrs. Singh came by and said it looked like maybe you'd run into a hedge up by the grange."

*Villages.* Emma rolled her eyes. "No, sorry. That was just . . . Oliver needed to take care of business."

"Ah. Right. Should have known. So, thumbs-up from you. What's Genny say?" He nodded out the window. Genny was standing by her little van, texting someone on her mobile. Oliver was frisking around Lucy, clearly daring the bigger dog to try and catch him.

"She's giving us a moment," said Emma. "But I have her permission to tell you that the car seems to be in decent shape and does not represent an immediate hazard to life and limb."

"I'll have to thank her for the vote of confidence," said Brian blandly. "So." He rested his elbows on the counter. "Is that a yes?"

This really was, she reflected, the worst possible time to be flirting. She was exhausted from everything that had happened up at the house and all the suspicions that had come home to roost inside her.

At the same time, she didn't want to discourage Brian. She liked him, and she liked having someone to tease and banter with.

"Weeeeelllll . . ." Emma leaned against the counter. Oliver was right. Brian smelled like oil and petrol. But she could probably get used to it. "I will have to think about it, and check the budget and all, but at the risk of sounding too easy, there's probably a yes coming along pretty soon."

"I suppose I can live with that." His smile softened and he studied the countertop for a minute. "But you know, Emma, I wouldn't be doing my job if I didn't try everything possible to woo you over onto the side of that lovely Mini there."

Emma steeled herself, trying to get ready to explain she was tired, that she had to go home, that she needed time to catch her breath because Marcie Cochrane might have been murdered.

He lifted his gaze again. "What are you doing Friday night?"

"Friday? Erm . . . nothing."

"It's movie night at the library. They're showing *The Italian Job*, the original, with Michael Caine, and about a dozen Mini Coopers."

He was asking her out on a date. A real date. With popcorn and sitting together in the dark. She stared at him.

Brian saw her surprise, and his face fell. "Did I say something wrong?"

"No, no, no. I just . . . it's been kind of a long day. And, yes, sure, I'd love to. But I warn you, I have to get up really early on Saturdays."

"I'll have you home by curfew, promise."

Emma smiled again. This time it felt real. "All right then. I'll see you Friday. I'm usually done by six."

"See you at seven then? The movie isn't until eight thirty. We'd have time for dinner. Maybe at Claudia's Bistro?"

"Sounds brilliant. You can pick me up at the King's Rest."

"Super." He straightened up. "And, Emma?"

She'd turned halfway around, and now she turned back. "Yeah?"

All the flirtatiousness had left Brian's demeanor. "If something's going on . . . I'm a first-rate listener."

Emma's heart squeezed, just a little. "Thanks," she said softly. "And, yes, something is going on. And I will tell you. Soon. At least, I think it'll be soon."

For a minute, she thought he was going to make a joke,

but he seemed to think the better of it. "Right, then, see you Friday."

They said goodbye and Emma walked out to where Genny was leaning up against the van.

"I've got a date," said Emma.

"Interesting timing," said Genny.

Emma shrugged. "Funny old thing, life."

At the same time, she had to admit, the prospect of having something as ordinary and pleasant to look forward to as a date with an attractive, age-appropriate gentleman did a lot to lift Emma's spirits. It was certainly a welcome relief from the realization she had agreed to go back to a house where a murder might have been committed by persons yet unknown.

*It'll be all right,* she told herself. *It's not like I'll be on my own.*

All the same, she found herself hugging Oliver a little more tightly on the way back home.

EMMA INSISTED SHE COULD WALK WHEN THEY REACHED THE Towne Fryer, but Genny waved this suggestion off.

"Nancarrow's right on my way home, and you've been through enough today."

Emma found she couldn't argue with this. In fact, it was kind of a relief to just settle back and let someone else be in charge of deciding where to go for a while.

"I texted Angelique and told her that the festival is officially on," said Genny as they drove up the narrow highway which skirted right around the curve of Trevena proper.

"Did you also tell her Marcie might have been murdered?"

"Not yet. I figured that's the sort of thing that goes over better in person."

"Probably right." Emma patted Oliver restlessly.

Genny gave an uneasy sideways glance. "And you are definitely going to call your detective friend?"

"I just wish I knew what to tell her. I mean, the last time

I talked to her, she hinted really hard that I should not be mucking around in Marcie's death."

"Well, whatever you're going to tell her, you should probably get it figured out fast, Em."

Because they'd pulled round the bend in the road, and now Nancarrow cottage was in view. A battered, blue Range Rover sat in the driveway, and leaning against it, like she had all the time in the world, was Constance Brent.

# 31

IN A BRIEF MOMENT OF PANIC, EMMA CONSIDERED ASKING
Genny to keep driving. But she was already too late. Genny
pulled into the grassy drive. Constance pushed herself
away from her car and stuffed her mobile into her bag.

Genny stopped the van and rolled the window down.

"Hullo, Genny," Constance said amiably. "Hullo, Emma.
We need to have a little talk, yeah?"

"Sure, just let me unbuckle," said Genny.

"No, sorry, I meant with Emma."

Genny glanced at her to see what she wanted to do.
Emma pulled her nerves together and nodded. "It's okay,
Genny."

"Well, remember, I'm right on the other end of the phone
if you need anything."

"I will." Emma opened the passenger side door. Oliver
immediately ran over to Constance, bouncing up and down
and barking his hellos. Constance laughed and bent down
to rub his chin.

"Hullo, Oliver. Who's a good dog?"

"Emma, why do people always ask that?" Oliver licked
the detective's hands and gave her a thorough sniff. "Am I

supposed to name all the dogs? Except maybe Caesar. Caesar is not a good dog."

Despite everything, Emma had to swallow a laugh. But her sense of humor bled away when Constance straightened up again, and Emma had to meet the detective's serious blue eyes.

"Coming in?" Emma asked. She also dug in her bag for her keys. She'd never lost her London habit of locking her door when she went out.

"Yes, thanks," said Constance. "You know, I'm starting to think Genny doesn't trust me."

"She does, really. She's just protective."

"I noticed."

Emma snapped on the front room light. Constance looked around curiously. The cottage had originally been one room, and still mostly was, but was divided into distinct spaces. The garden-side part was a lounge area. The part toward the front of the house was the dining area, with the kitchen sort of tucked into the space behind the chimney.

"Nice place. Cozy. Love the garden." Constance, escorted by Oliver, went over to look out the back door.

"Thanks."

Emma had never had so much as an allotment before, and she was reveling in her garden. When she'd moved in, the walled space behind Nancarrow was nothing but weedy grass and a pair of scraggly yew bushes. Over the spring, she'd spent much of her spare time working to transform it, with the help of a whole cadre of enthusiastic local gardeners she'd met over tea and cakes.

Instead of flowers, though, Emma had gone for a big kitchen garden. She had rows of vegetables coming up—carrots, beetroot, Swiss chard, kale, three kinds of beans. There was an herb patch as well—lavender, rosemary, thyme and dill. She'd even put in a pair of fruit trees—a pear and an apple, one in each corner.

Objectively, this was a lot of work for a place she was just renting, but whenever she looked out the back and saw her harvest in the making, she couldn't work up any real regret.

"Can I get you anything? Tea?" Emma propped open the back door for Oliver. He'd been inside a lot today.

"Do you have any coffee? It's been a long day."

"Coming right up."

Emma had hoped that making the coffee and pulling out the remains of the chocolate babka she'd baked yesterday would give her time to think. But Constance followed Emma into the kitchen. While Emma set the coffeemaker going and unwrapped the babka, Constance folded her arms and leaned against the doorjamb.

"I hear you've been up to the grange today."

"Yeah." Emma focused on cutting generous slices of the chocolate-swirled brioche and laying them on a plate. "And I want you to know that I was absolutely planning on calling you."

"Well, you wouldn't be the first."

"Sorry?"

"We've been fielding phone calls about what happened at the grange all weekend." Constance was trying to maintain her nonchalant attitude, but it was definitely fraying at the edges. "And by we, I mean my governor, at least mostly."

"I'm guessing they were about releasing the autopsy report?"

"So you've heard. You are one for picking up the local gossip, aren't you?"

"People talk to you when you give them cake." Emma handed Constance the plate of babka.

"I can see your point." The detective took the plate over to the Arts and Crafts–style dining table. Emma had found the beautiful linen runner at a Christmas jumble sale. "Then I guess it's safe to assume you've heard about the autopsy results?"

"Yes. Nobody seemed surprised."

Emma put together a tray with cups, spoons, milk jug and sugar bowl. The coffeemaker beeped, and she added the carafe. Her nana Phyllis would have been appalled at the makeshift coffee service, but Emma figured Constance was the sort to value speedy caffeine delivery over the formalities.

"Want to hear an interesting fact?" said Constance as Emma carried the coffee tray over to the table.

"Sure."

"Women are really bad at suicide."

"Oh? Really?"

"Yeah." Constance pulled out a chair and sat down. "See, women think about what will happen when they're found. So they try to make sure it doesn't look . . . well, too bad. They take pills, or try to drown or suffocate themselves. Methods that won't make a mess, yeah? Now, men, they don't care. Blow their brains out, hang themselves, whatever. Their means are usually much quicker and more successful."

"Oh," said Emma feebly.

Constance nodded in acknowledgment of this feeling. "Nobody actually likes having the homicide detective to dinner."

"Really?" said Emma. "Why do you suppose that is?"

"Can't imagine." Constance chuckled, and she and Emma fixed their coffee in silence. Constance poured a lot of milk into her coffee. Emma was surprised. She was under the impression that all detectives took their coffee coal black and strong enough to burn a hole through the table linens.

Constance took up a big forkful of babka. "Oh, lord, this is brilliant. More of yours?"

"Mmm-hmm." Emma also added a generous dollop of milk to her coffee and a spoonful of sugar.

"You are a dangerous woman to know."

"You know, coming from you, that's a double-edged comment. So." Emma planted her elbows on the table. "What are you really here to talk about, Constance?"

"Technically, I'm here to issue a warning."

"I thought you might be."

"Not my idea this time," Constance told her. "It seems there's certain parties up at the grange who took an exception to your presence there today. It is thought by some you might be trying to stir up trouble." Constance sipped her coffee. "Would they be correct?"

"No," said Emma promptly. "I wasn't trying to stir up anything at all."

"But I'm guessing trouble was stirred nonetheless?"

Emma drank some more coffee, and added some more milk to what remained. It was a habit her brother, Henry, never stopped ragging her about. "Nothing but pure milk by the time you get to the bottom," he said. "Makes no sense at all."

"Can I ask you something, Constance?"

The detective waved her fork. "You can always ask. We are here to assist the public."

"Do you really think Marcie Cochrane killed herself?"

Using the edge of her fork, Constance methodically cut the remaining bit of babka into tidy squares, and then cut the squares into smaller squares. She frowned in concentration, utterly absorbed in dismantling Emma's sweet bread.

"I don't like to talk about what I think, if I can help it," Constance said. "What I *know* is that one Mr. Bertram Cochrane was driving my superiors stark raving mad all weekend with his phone calls. And then at eight thirty a.m. today, my boss handed me a report, duly signed by himself and the assistant coroner for Devon and Cornwall, stating that Marcia Cochrane had jumped out a third story window in her home and died as a result of injuries sustained in the fall, and that was the end of all police involvement and thank you very much."

"And you don't agree with that?"

"You're quick. Most people find me entirely opaque. No, I don't agree. In fact, I think something very different happened."

"Why?"

"Because her face was smashed in. Not just cracked, like it would have been from a fall from that height, but smashed."

Emma nodded, remembering. She also might have turned a little green.

"Sorry," said Constance. "Do you need a minute?"

"No." Emma swallowed. "I'm fine. Do go on."

"There's also the strange affair of the missing handbag."

"Sorry?"

"We had a look around her room, her office, her car, the usual places, and there was no sign of a handbag."

"Huh. That's . . . odd."

"Yes, I thought so too. But my superiors remain unconvinced. They think that Marcie might have gotten rid of it herself."

"Well, maybe, I mean, if she was trying to hide something."

Constance narrowed her eyes. "Do you know what she might have been trying to hide?"

"Well, not for sure, no," said Emma. "But, there was an accusation. Some money went missing from the du Maurier literary society, enough that they couldn't pay their catering deposits. Marcie was the treasurer, so she got blamed."

"Hmmm." Constance took another swallow of coffee. "Now, I didn't know that."

"I can't see anybody killing themselves over a few thousand quid, honestly."

"You'd be surprised," said Constance. "But in this case, I think you're right. You see, after the report came out, I went and had a little talk with the so-called pathologist."

"Wait a minute, I thought you liked our local pathologist." In fact, Constance had once described the pathologist as an amazing old broad of thirty years experience dealing with unexpected deaths up and down the Cornish coast.

"The chief path is off on holiday, and her assistant is some new bloke who is very keen." She said the last word like it left a bad taste in her mouth. "So keen, in fact, that he doesn't want to stay tucked away here on our lovely seacoast and thinks that kissing up to his superiors is the way to get a posting in Manchester or London."

"Oh."

"Yes. Very much oh. Anyway, I did, after about a half hour of trying, get him to admit that, while most of the injuries on the body were consistent with a fall from a window, the injuries to the face were surprisingly severe." She paused. "I asked would they be consistent with Marcie having been struck in the face with some blunt object. He assured me that if she had not been found lying on her face under a window, he might have reached that conclusion. But she was, and I could read all about it in the official report, case closed and I'm a very busy man."

Emma added more coffee and milk to her own mug. She looked out the garden window. Oliver, she noticed, was sitting on the edge of the new vegetable patch. At first she thought he might be on guard against his local nemesis, a fox that had no respect at all for personal boundaries. But then she realized he was exhibiting a perfectly natural reaction to this very long day. Oliver was sound asleep in the afternoon sunshine.

*Wish I was there with you, corgi me lad.*

"So, what I'm wondering"—Constance pulled Emma's attention away from her peaceful garden and dog—"is did you see anything at the grange that might shed some light on this particular little mystery?"

"Erm," said Emma.

"Are you about to tell me you paid attention to everything I said before, and just went up there to get your catering things and come straight back home."

"The thought had crossed my mind."

"Right. Well, we can just skip past the part where I say I don't believe it, and you protest your innocence and all that."

"Erm, yeah. Sure."

"Good. What did you find out?"

Emma swallowed. "I think you're right. I don't think Marcie fell. Or I don't think she just fell. I think she was killed, and the body was moved."

Constance turned and leveled her with a hard stare. "Would you care to tell me why you think this?"

"You won't like it."

"Try me."

This was exactly the situation she'd wanted to avoid, but she couldn't see any way around it. So Emma took a deep breath and chose her words very, very carefully. "My dog smelled something by the garage that got him really upset. He's only been that agitated a couple of times before, and that was when we . . ."

"Found a body," Constance finished for her.

Emma nodded. "He had the same reaction in the office upstairs and I *think* I maybe saw some signs that somebody'd been trying to clean the kitchen floor with bleach."

"Go on," said Constance.

"So, I was wondering if maybe Marcie was killed in her office, and then the murderer carried the body downstairs, maybe thinking to hide it, but got the idea to put it under the window and make the whole thing look like suicide."

Constance considered her babka for a moment. "No," she said. "Wouldn't work. If Marcie was hit in the face, there'd be spatter and, well, a number of other things you don't want to hear about over pastry. I did have a look round that office. Nobody on their own would have been able to do that level of cleaning without it being noticed."

"So, maybe she was killed down by the garage and they took the body upstairs to push it out the window?"

"Messy," said Constance, "but doable, if you wanted to go with the appearance of suicide and you were smart enough to realize the damage the rain would do to any trace evidence."

"So, um . . . what do you think they, um, used?"

Constance blew out a sigh. "Hard to say. To damage her face like that, it'd have to be something heavy, that's for sure. Or something with a handle, so they could swing it. A cricket bat, maybe, or a wooden plank, or a shovel. Something like that." She paused. "I don't suppose while you were comforting your agitated dog, you might have found some actual evidence? Maybe something I could take to my superiors?"

"Well, there're the earrings."

"Are there?"

"Um, yes. Sorry. Here." She went and got her bag and dug the tissue out. "I took a picture, on my phone when I found it. Here." She pulled out her mobile.

She showed Constance the photos. Constance flicked back and forth through them several times. Then she took the tissue and dropped it into her own, much larger bag.

"This doesn't mean much," she said. "She could have lost it any time."

"Except it's one of the earrings she was wearing when she died, and we found the other up under the window seat cushions in her office, and the window latch is broken," she added.

"Broken? How?"

Emma described the missing bracket, but her voice trailed off.

"You look like you've had a thought," said Constance.

"Yeah, I did, kind of. What if the killer knew about the broken latch, and they carried the body up to the office, and just, sort of, left it there? Propped up on the window seat or something?"

"Knowing the window would open under the weight, sooner or later, and the body would fall on its own. Which would give them the time to be somewhere else when it did?"

Emma nodded.

"It's a thought," said Constance. "But it's not the kind of detail somebody's going to think of on the spur of the moment. Which tells us that somebody planned this murder well ahead of time. Maybe even tampered with the latch deliberately."

Emma wrapped both hands around her coffee and tried not to shudder.

Constance was silent for a long time after that. When she turned her gaze back to Emma, anger sparked behind her calm blue eyes.

"Emma, I cannot believe I am about to say this. But I need your help."

# 32

. . . . . . . . . . .

IF CONSTANCE HAD A HARD TIME BELIEVING SHE WAS SAY-
ing those words, Emma had an equally hard time believing she heard them. But she made herself take a deep
breath.

"What can I do?"

"You can find some excuse to get yourself up to the
grange again. Talk to the family. Make a pest out of yourself. Let Oliver run about. Find out whatever you can."

"Erm," began Emma.

"I know, I know." Constance cut her off. "Believe me, I
know, and if I had any other choice, I would not even dream
of asking. But my boss's boss has made it clear that the case
has already been closed. Permanently."

Emma thought about Bert, and about how sure Daphne
was that he was covering something up, and about the way
he'd talked in the pub. He'd already made up his mind it
was suicide, or at the very least, he'd made up his mind that
that was the story he wanted everybody to believe.

"I do not like string pullers," said Constance. "I especially do not like murderous string pullers. It's going to
take me some time, and a few favors, and . . . well, never
mind that. It's going to be a job to get any kind of investiga-

tion opened, and by then, all kinds of things might have been tidied away."

"But, I mean, you can still just talk to people, can't you?" asked Emma. "Off the record, or something?"

"I could," agreed Constance. "But there's a catch. I'm an officer of the law. Any evidence I turn up outside of the confines of an official investigation is going to get thrown out of court so fast it'll make everybody's head spin. But you"—Constance pointed her fork at Emma—"are a member of the public. If I'm acting because you have come to the police with a concern, that's an entirely different story."

Emma swirled her coffee and watched the tan waves rise and fall. Her gaze strayed back to the garden and Oliver sleeping peacefully in the afternoon sun.

"Will you help me?" asked Constance.

"Well, as it happens, Helen Dalgliesh has decided she wants the du Maurier festival to go forward. So I'll be spending quite a lot of time up at the grange helping out with that. So, naturally, if I hear anything or find anything out about Marcie and what happened, I'll just have to report it, won't I? My parents always told me we should do whatever we can to help the police."

"Well." Constance sat back. "Amazing how that all worked out."

"Yes, isn't it?" Emma drank her coffee, then added more milk.

"Right. Time for me to start harassing my bosses." Constance got to her feet and Emma started to stand, but the detective waved her back. "No, never mind, I can show myself out. Oh, and, Emma?"

"Yeah?"

"We need to be very, very careful about this," Constance said. "I could lose my job, and you could get charged with interfering in an investigation, yeah?"

"Yeah."

"So we never had this conversation."

"What conversation?" asked Emma mildly. "We're friends. I invited you over for coffee. And babka."

"Knew I liked you." Constance slung her bag over her shoulder and walked out the front door.

Emma sat where she was for a while. Then she picked up her coffee mug and went out the garden door. She sat down on the grass beside Oliver, who was still asleep on his back. She stared at her tomatoes and beans, breathing in the scents of lavender, rosemary and the distant salt tang of the sea.

Oliver's ears twitched. His body stretched and wriggled and in the next instant, his eyes popped open and he rolled over.

"Hullo, Emma!" He shook his head and scratched. "What're you doing?"

"Oh, Oliver," breathed Emma. "We are in real trouble."

"What trouble?" He sprang to his feet and also wagged his bum, which kind of spoiled any guard dog vibe he might have going. "Where?"

Emma shook her head. "Never mind. I'm hungry. Are you hungry?"

"Yes! Yes! What's for dinner?"

Emma smiled, and together they headed for the kitchen.

For an hour or so, she lost herself in chopping and mixing and tasting. All the events at the grange were real. She and her friends had all been dragged into them, or jumped into them, depending how you looked at it. And she really had just been asked to help Constance look for reasons to open an official murder inquiry into Marcie's death.

But for this moment, she was going to set that aside. She was safe in her cozy home. She had her best fur friend with her, and she was going to cook, and she was going to relax and get her head together.

In the end, she had a lovely fry-up of sausage, peppers, mushrooms and tomatoes. She toasted some of the bread she'd bought yesterday at the village co-op. Oliver supervised, as always, and Emma made him eat his kibble before she agreed to let him have some sausage and tomato.

"I'm going to get another lecture from the vet about your diet."

"We need to take more walks," said Oliver. "That's how you take care of sausage."

Emma sighed. There was no arguing with corgi logic.

After the dishes were done, Emma took her tea, and the remaining slice of babka she'd decided to keep for dessert, and went over to her chaise lounge. This had become her favorite way to spend an evening at home—stretched out on the old fainting couch under her diamond-paned window, Oliver on her lap, watching the sun set over the sea. Unfortunately, a quiet evening with the sunset was not on the docket for today. When they were both settled, Emma took a deep breath, picked up her mobile and dialed Angelique's number.

"Hullo, Emma," said Angelique as soon as she picked up. "We heard from Genny that you had the detective there." Oliver, of course, slid up into Emma's lap and barked.

"Hullo to you too, Oliver!" laughed Angelique. "Well, if he's sounding so chipper, you two must be all right."

"Yeah, mostly," said Emma. "Did Genny tell you what happened at the grange today?"

"She did. Pearl is here too. Okay if we put you on speaker?"

"Yes, of course."

There were some shuffling noises on the Delgados' side. Oliver took advantage of the pause to resettle himself so he was draped across Emma's stomach, ready to listen in, or be scratched along his spine. Or both.

"Can you hear us all right?" said Angelique.

"Loud and clear."

"So what happened with Constance?" asked Pearl.

*The last thing I expected.* Emma laid out her suspicions.

"Is this the part where I get to say I told you so?" asked Pearl. "Because I told you so."

"I think Daphne actually gets to say that," said Emma. "And, yes, you were both right. Whatever happened to Marcie, someone is trying to cover it up." Then she told them how Constance had asked her to keep her eyes open while they helped get ready for the festival.

"Not the circumstances I'd want for taking this job," said Angelique.

"That's because you are a rational individual." Emma leaned back on her chaise. "What are we going to do?"

"Well, you've already said what you're going to do," said Pearl. "The question is, how soon are you going back to the grange? And do you want me to come get you, or should we leave from here?"

"Um, Angelique, are you okay with that?" asked Emma. "I mean, if Marcie really was murdered, the killer might very well still be at the house." It was not something she'd let herself think too much about before, but it seemed important to point out just now.

"Pearl is an adult," said Angelique. "She gets to make her own decisions."

Emma wasn't sure her voice would have stayed as steady if she'd been talking about her own daughter, no matter how adult.

"Well, I'm going," said Pearl. "Daphne needs help, and so do you, Emma. So does Raj, who has got to be pulling his hair out over this. Besides, if we pull off the festival gig, both our businesses benefit. But, Ma, if you don't want . . ." Her words trailed away.

"No, Pearl." Emma could picture Angelique shaking her head. "Trevena is our home. If we can do something to keep a . . . person from getting away with this, whatever it turns out to be, then we will do it."

Emma felt heart and hope swell. "You're both kind of amazing, do you know that?"

"Thank you, Emma," said Pearl. "You always had good judgment. Now. What's the plan?"

"I don't know that there is one, except to get up to the grange and keep our eyes and ears open."

"And noses!" mumbled Oliver. "Well, as open as you can, because, you know, you don't pay enough attention to the smells."

"Oliver doesn't sound happy about any of this."

"Oh, no, he's very excited." Emma scritched his neck. "He's going to get to spend lots of time with Dash."

"Yes, Dash!" Oliver yipped. "He is an excellent dog. He will be a big help, I know he will."

They talked some more, about who they could get to cover the cake counter and whether Angelique and Genny could handle the tea service while Emma and Pearl (and Oliver!) did what they could up at the grange.

It was almost eight thirty by the time they hung up. The room was dim. Only a thin salmon-pink line of daylight showed above the sea. Emma didn't move to turn on the light.

"We're lucky to have friends like Angelique and Pearl, Oliver," she said. "And Genny."

"Yes!" He licked her face enthusiastically. "And you!"

"And you, Oliver!" She kissed his nose. "And you. Listen, corgi me lad, these next couple of days are going to be really important."

"Don't worry, Emma! I'll be right there!"

She couldn't help smiling. "I know you will. In fact"—like Constance, she couldn't really believe she was asking this—"I'm going to need your help."

"Yes!" Oliver jumped to his feet, which pressed hard against her chest and stomach and made Emma squeak.

"Sorry, Emma!" Oliver flopped back down, which made her go "oof!" instead. "What can I do? What?"

"Do you think, maybe, you can get Dash to show you around the house and the grounds? Maybe see if there's anything you can find? Anything that's out of place and maybe smells like Marcie?"

No one would think twice about a pair of dogs nosing about the grounds. Probably. Hopefully.

"Yes! Yes! Something is missing and I'll find it!" Oliver barked and wriggled with excitement. "Only, there is one thing you should know."

"What's that?"

Oliver put his head down on his paws and looked up at

her with his most soulful eyes, so that she would know that whatever came next was really not his fault. "If you want Dash to do something, you're going to need to bring more roast beef."

Emma laughed and hugged him. "Okay, Oliver. Roast beef all 'round. I promise."

It was getting late, but not late enough to head to bed. Emma felt restless. She knew what she should be doing. She should be pulling out her cookbooks and getting serious about the festival menus. Hyphenated Caite would doubtlessly be going over any plans with a microscope and have plenty to say if they weren't up to snuff.

But Emma's mind wouldn't settle.

Marcie's books sat in their stack on her tea table. She put her mug down, switched on the overhead light and picked up *Rebecca*. It was a hardback copy, but the cover was battered and the jacket was long gone. She held it loosely in her hand, curious to see where the book would open.

Not only did the book fall open in her hand, a small square of paper dropped out onto Oliver's back.

"What's that?" Oliver shook himself. "What's that?"

"I don't know." Emma picked up the paper. But it wasn't paper. It was a business card. Very nice quality card stock with gold and black embossed print.

MINCHIN, PRICE & LITTLE
LEGAL SERVICES

There was an address, email and phone number, of course. Emma turned the card over in case there was something written on the back. Nothing.

"What is it, Emma?" Oliver sniffed at the paper and sneezed. "Dusty."

"Yeah, it's been in there for a while." It must have been what Marcie had at hand when she'd last been reading the book. Emma shuddered to think of all the kinds of things she'd used as bookmarks.

She looked at *Rebecca* again to see what page the card had fallen out of. It was page 270, she noticed, right at the end of a chapter.

Emma felt all the hairs rise on the back of her neck.

Somebody had used a pencil to underline two separate phrases.

The first was: *There never was an accident.*

The second was: *I killed her.*

# 33

THE REST OF EMMA'S EVENING WAS SPENT ON THE PHONE, coordinating with Genny and Becca, while texting updates to Pearl and Angelique. She left *Rebecca* closed on the table, with the business card marker in its place.

*It doesn't necessarily mean anything,* she told herself. It's two lines in an old book. They could have been put there any time.

Except that two separate accidents had caused Truscott Grange to change hands—when Stewart Cochrane died in a boating accident and again when Richard and Evelyn Cochrane died in a car accident. And Constance had said Marcie's murder might have been planned in advance. In fact, she seemed to think it would have had to be, because of all the details.

And if somebody was planning a murder, Marcie, who was smart and careful and thorough, as well as a fan of mysteries and Gothic suspense, might have suspected she was in danger. She might have wanted to leave a message.

*There never was an accident. I killed her.*

Despite being in her own warm bed, and having Oliver's solid comfort beside her, it took Emma a long time to fall asleep that night.

\* \* \*

"SO, HOW ARE WE GOING TO WORK THIS?" ASKED PEARL as she and Emma buckled themselves into her little blue Fiat so they could drive to the grange. She had to speak loudly to be heard over the wind. Oliver was already buckled into the back seat. He'd given up protesting about his harness as soon as Emma pointed out that they could keep the windows down.

"I've been trying to think," said Emma. "When I talked to Constance yesterday, she thought that Marcie's murder was planned out, not just a spur-of-the-moment thing."

"But she does think it's murder?"

Emma nodded. "It looks like Marcie was killed down by the garage and her body moved up to the office, and either she was pushed out the window or left to fall. That latch might have been deliberately tampered—" Emma stopped. Pearl had gone a shade of greenish-gray around the gills. "You all right?"

"No, not really," said Pearl. "I've got three brothers too, like Marcie. I'm trying to imagine how messed up it would all have to be for one of them to plan to kill me." She shuddered.

"I know how you feel," said Emma. "I've bickered with my brother, Henry, my whole life, but we still love each other. If I really needed him, he'd be here." She shook her head. "But it doesn't necessarily have to have been one of the brothers. There's still Caite. She's got a motive."

"Her dad? Yeah, I heard about that. So awful."

"And we know she can get into the house if she wants to."

"So, you're thinking, what? Caite hits Marcie over the head, drags her body up the stairs and props her up against the window and gets out without anybody hearing or noticing?"

"Well, it was a dark and stormy night, and it's a big house."

"But if she can do all that, why doesn't she take care of whatever it is on the computer at the same time?"

"Frank said that Bert and Gus were still out when he went to bed. Maybe they came home while she was in the house and she got spooked before she was finished."

"But, hang on." Pearl frowned. "They'd find her finger-prints, wouldn't they? I mean, if they looked."

"Which they didn't, because Bert pushed to get Marcie's death ruled a suicide. But even if they did look, Caite's in and out of the house all the time at festival weekend; it wouldn't be that strange to find her fingerprints all over."

"Pants. You're right." Pearl stared out at the road for a minute. "You know, I wish we could do like in an Agatha Christie novel and gather all the suspects in one room and say 'But it was you, Monsieur Malfeasance, who poisoned Lady Innocence!'"

"I'm pretty sure nobody's ever actually done that."

"Yeah, but it'd be easier, wouldn't it? I mean, as it is, we *know* what happened, at least sort of, but how do we prove it?"

"Maybe," said Emma, "we start with where Marcie was that night, before she got to the King's Rest. If we can find out what she was up to, maybe we can work out who wanted her dead."

"You know," said Pearl slowly, "we don't know where anybody at the grange was that night. We've only got Frank's word on it that he was the first one home."

"No, you're right. We should probably try to find out more about that too, if we can."

"You're not sounding very confident."

"I don't expect the Cochrane brothers are going to be really happy to talk to us about the night their sister died."

"Well, we'll just have to get creative, won't we?"

# 34

...........

THIS TIME, THEY PARKED OUT FRONT. PEARL AND EMMA grabbed their bags and briefcases. Oliver hopped out, stretched and yawned and immediately began snuffling around the gravel. Dash appeared as if by magic, and soon he and Oliver were capering enthusiastically around each other.

Before the dogs had finished their energetic canine greetings, two more cars pulled up the drive. Emma recognized Caite's silver Saab. The other was a black, battered four-door. Doubtlessly Brian could have identified the exact make and model, even from a distance.

The cars parked. Caite, looking freshly washed and pressed, climbed out of the Saab. John and Tasha Boyd, along with Ned Giddy climbed out of the other car.

"Oh, fantastic! You're here too!" said Tasha. The little gray-haired woman beamed all over her round face. "I can't tell you how delighted, and, yes, I'll admit it, relieved we all were that you agreed to take the job. Oh, and did your mother tell you we spoke and she confirmed the deposit cleared?" Pearl nodded. "Excellent! Now I feel like we're actually going to be able to move forward, just as Marcie would have wanted."

"Getting her way one last time," remarked Caite, who

sounded neither delighted nor relieved. "I'm sure she's pleased, wherever she is."

The rest of the board looked awkwardly at each other. Ned Giddy rubbed his hand across his shining scalp. "Yes, well, I think—"

Ned did not get a chance to let them know what he thought; the grange's front door opened and Helen came outside. Today, she'd had time and energy to put herself together. She wore a yellow silk, summer-weight sweater and immaculate black trousers. Her hair was pulled back in a pair of French braids, and probably sprayed into place within an inch of its life.

Emma had the impression that this tailored, styled look was meant to be like armor. No one was getting through Helen's chinks today.

"Good morning!" Helen said to all of them. "Thank you so much for being here."

John Boyd was the one who went up and took her hand. "We're the ones who should be saying thanks, Helen. You didn't have to do this."

"Well, John, I think I did. For Marcie," she added. "We're in the sitting room. I think you all know the way?"

Emma paused to kneel down and give Oliver one more head rub. "Remember what we talked about," she whispered to him. "Be a good boy."

"A noble corgi warrior is always good," Oliver grumbled. Dash shoved his way to Emma and thrust his big, wet nose at her hands.

"Dash wants to be sure you brought the roast beef," Oliver informed her.

*Great. The world's only trust-but-verify dog.* But Emma let the mutt smell her palms. He must have been satisfied, because he gave her hands a good, slobbery lick as well.

"He says you're a good human," said Oliver.

Emma rubbed Dash's head. "Tell him you guys need to stick to the grounds, and come when you hear me whistling."

"We will! We will!" Oliver said stoutly. It might have been Emma's imagination, but Dash looked uncertain about all this. The bigger dog evidently decided this was more than enough standing about, and took off at a run.

Emma grinned and tried to push down her worries. She turned around, only to find Caite waiting alone on the steps.

"My goodness, Emma. You do love your dogs."

"We always had them growing up," said Emma. "A place never quite seems like home to me unless there's a dog in it."

"I'm sure," said Caite with cold pleasantry. "And, by the way, congratulations. I'd say you and your friends have managed things quite nicely."

"Thank you." Emma ignored the edge on Caite's words. "I'm well aware we weren't your first choice."

Caite's smile was thinner than the glaze on Emma's lemon cake, and twice as tart. "Oh, no, don't mistake me, Ms. Reed. I'm the last one to criticize doing what it takes to get ahead."

Emma looked at Caite's smile and her artificially smooth face, and found that she had no patience left for this particular dance.

"Caite, can I ask you something straight out?"

Caite cocked her head curiously. "Of course."

"Why did you want to sabotage the festival?"

"You know, you should have asked Marcie that. When you had the chance, of course."

Emma felt her brows lift. It normally took years of dedicated practice to achieve that level of offhand disrespect. "But you were the one who didn't want to find a caterer," Emma reminded her, as pleasantly as possible.

For Caite, this seemed to be just a little too much. "I wanted to find a good, experienced caterer," she snapped. "Not a gaggle of Marcie's friends, or her niece's friends. She'd already stolen enough of the society's money. I didn't want us paying for any little extras she might have arranged as well."

Despite her resolve to remain calm and professional, Emma's jaw dropped. "You really think that's what's going on?"

"I'm sure I don't know. How could I? No one's going to tell me anything."

"But you're sure she was stealing from the society?"

Caite drew herself up. She was a tall woman, and with all her perfect grooming, the effect was impressive. "It could only have been her or me. And it wasn't me."

"But why would Marcie do that?"

She huffed out a sigh. "Because despite her reputation as some sort of wonder worker, the grange was in trouble. The family was losing money hand over fist."

Emma drew back, shocked. Caite's air of smug satisfaction brightened into triumph.

"There. Now you know. And I imagine the rest of Trevena will know soon as well."

"What did Marcie ever do to you?" Emma breathed. "Or is this all about your father?"

"Ah, here it comes." Caite's jaw tightened. "Hyphenated Caite—and, yes I do know about that nickname, thank you—is just jealous and vengeful. You have no idea what the Cochranes' whispering campaign did to my family. My father was destroyed, professionally and personally. My mother was left alone and devastated. Still." She straightened up, lifting her chin and her nose. "Mustn't grumble, must we? After all, obsessing over the past isn't healthy is it? Who knows, it might even make you push somebody out the window.

"And, yes," Caite went on before Emma could draw breath. "I did notice how closely that little scene matched the one in *Rebecca*, and I have no doubt you'd love to cast me as wicked Mrs. Danvers. For the record, however, I did not do it. I didn't need to. I knew things were falling apart without my help."

"Then why did you sneak back into the house the day she died to get to her computer?"

For the first time, Caite seemed genuinely caught off guard. Emma was sure she heard teeth grinding. "Who told you that?"

"Somebody saw you." Emma was amazed at how smoothly those words came out.

Caite slowly walked down the three steps to stand nose

to nose with Emma. "I was *trying* to prove that she was the one doing the embezzling," she hissed. "I was tired of being suspected, and now that she's dead, I didn't want the legend of her saintliness to get in the way of everybody remembering she was also a thief."

Emma folded her arms. "So what exactly happened with the money?"

Caite sighed impatiently. "Three checks were cashed, without the board's authorization or knowledge. They were all signed by Marcie. She insisted that someone must have gotten hold of the checkbook and stolen checks out of the back and forged her signature."

"That's a common scheme," said Emma. "It used to be more common before online banking."

"Well, then, you'll be pleased to know the second theft was much more up-to-date, and rather simpler, as I understand it. *Someone* opened up an online payment account and attached it to the society bank account, siphoned off the funds, then closed the online account. The end. But to do that, you not only need the check routing numbers but you need authorization to withdraw funds. The people who had that authorization were Marcie and me."

"There could have been identity theft involved. Maybe somebody got hold of Marcie's ID when they stole those checks . . ."

"In London that might happen, but this is Trevena. No one can possibly impersonate Marcie here."

"But it didn't have to happen here," said Emma. "If you use Barclays or NatWest or another one of the major institutions, the thief could have gone through a branch in Treknow, or St. Ives, or even London."

Caite frowned. "I hadn't considered that."

"They might not have had to go to a branch at all. If you can sweet-talk the right clerk, it could have all been done online and over the phone."

Caite was silent.

"Somebody had to have pointed this out. I mean, I'm no expert, but these are pretty standard tricks."

"Yes, *somebody* did point this out," Caite admitted. "At least some of it."

Emma strongly suspected that "somebody" actually meant "Marcie." "But you decided not to believe her."

Caite sucked in a shuddering breath. "This has gone on quite long enough," she said. "You are supposed to have work to do, and I know that I do."

Caite marched back up the stairs and through the doors. Emma followed much more slowly.

WHILE EMMA AND CAITE HAD BEEN HAVING THEIR DISCUS-sion on the front steps, something at least as intense had obviously been happening in the sitting room. Helen stood in the farthest corner whispering rapidly with Bert. The minute Emma walked in the door, she could sense the tension radiating off him. The Boyds and Ned moved about the other side of the room, plugging in laptops and setting out notepads and binders, and very obviously trying not to make too much noise.

Pearl and Daphne were standing right by the door, clearly trying to decide whether they should try for a quick, and quiet, escape.

Caite frowned and sailed over to the board members. Emma sidled over to the girls.

"Hullo, Emma," breathed Daphne.

"Hullo, Daphne. What's going on?"

"Seems we weren't expected quite this early," said Pearl.

"And Bert's upset?"

"Been on a tear all morning, actually," Daphne muttered.

"What for?"

Daphne glanced toward her mother and uncle, and tugged on her ponytail. Then she pulled her mobile out of her back pocket and typed something. She passed the phone to Emma.

Emma read:

*They can't find Aunt Marcie's will.*

# 35

THIS WAS GOING TO BE AN EXCELLENT DAY.

Oliver did not forget for a moment that he was on an important mission for Emma. But that was no reason not to enjoy himself. It was a lovely day and this place was so huge! Okay, it was probably going to rain soon, but for now, the wind was just brisk. Fresh green smells; wild smells; sun-soaked smells; thick, loamy, decaying smells piled on top of each other so that Oliver barely knew which way to turn first.

"Keep up! Keep up!" Dash galloped ahead.

"You keep up!" Oliver sprinted ahead, stretching his long body the whole way out. "Come on! Come on! Dash! This way!"

"Where are we going?" Dash paused to thrust his nose under a flowery bush. "Huh, huh, that's new!"

Oliver joined him, plunging his nose deep into the rubbish and then backing away. The only problem with outdoors was it tended to get stuck on his nose, and that made it harder to understand new smells properly. "Emma says we need to explore. We need to find anything that smells like Rain Lady Marcie."

"Your human is strange."

"All humans are strange," admitted Oliver. "Emma herds them back together and makes them play nice."

"Huh, huh." Dash sat down and scratched his ear hard. "Well, she has good snacks."

"She'll have more snacks if we can find the Marcie smells," Oliver said.

Dash shook his head until his ears flopped. "She's smart too. I don't know how you taught her to understand so much. My humans never hear me when it's important."

"I told you, Emma is special. Where should we look first?"

Dash put his nose down and cast around in several directions. "Don't know. Nothing here. Well. Lots here, but not Marcie."

Dash was right. Oliver nosed around through the grass and the stones and the winding, layered trails of smells. So what to do?

He considered. Humans had patterns. They had territories. Emma had all her favorite spots, even just in the house.

"Is there a favorite human spot?" asked Oliver. "A best trail?"

"Oh!" Dash pricked up his ears and tail. "*That's* what you mean. Why didn't you say so? We'll go to the pond. Let's go!"

Oliver barked happily. It was chaotic progress, but that was okay, because it was fun too. Dash ran, and loped, and stopped to investigate the new things. They flushed a whole bunch of birds who all said rude things as they flew away. There were rabbits too, but they were too fast to bother chasing for more than a little way.

A big, saucy crow flew down and stood right in their path. Dash barked. The crow stretched out its shiny black wings and thrust its long beak forward. To his embarrassment, Oliver backpedaled and fell sideways.

The crow laughed loud and harsh, and flew away.

"I know that one," muttered Dash. "Look out for him. He's a troublemaker."

"I can tell." Oliver barked, but the crow was long gone.

Pretty soon, they came to a dirt path that ran through a patch of old trees. A snake slithered away under the ferns, hissing angrily about its disturbed nap. The wind freshened and Oliver smelled water and decay.

And a human.

Oliver bounded ahead of Dash, who growled impatiently. Oliver ignored him. The tree shadows gave way to sunshine and the pond.

It wasn't anywhere near as big or as interesting as the sea. It was a still, flat, dark body of water, more like an enormous puddle than anything else. Patches of reeds and peppery-scented weeds and sweet flags lined much of the shore. One of the Cochrane humans stood at the very edge of the water. He had a big stick in one hand, and in the other he held a bundle of something.

"Gus! Gus!" barked Dash. Gus started at the sudden noise. Dash bounded past Oliver and leapt up, planting his paws on the human's chest and making him stagger.

"Dash!" the human shouted. "Get down, you stupid dog! Come on, down!" He shoved Dash's paws off his chest, but he also rubbed his head and ears in a friendly way. "That's enough now. About scared the life out of me, you did!"

Now that he was closer, Oliver realized that the stick wasn't a stick at all. It was a digging thing for the garden, like Emma used sometimes. Shovel! That was the name. Or spade maybe. Oliver had never really been able to tell the difference. They were seldom interesting. Now, the bundle. The bundle was very interesting. He nosed the dirty underside. It was hard to tell what it might be. It had a long strap, but a bulgy bit at the end. It was a human thing, not a plant tangle or old animal. It smelled like clean dirt. It must have been buried somewhere.

It smelled like something else too. It smelled like . . . like . . .

"Watch out, boys!"

Oliver yelped and jumped back. Gus swung his whole body around and threw the bundle out into the pond as hard as he could. Dash barked, and splashed right into the water.

Oliver followed, only not as far. A noble corgi could do anything, if he really had to, but swimming was hard.

Gus whistled. "Leave it, Dash! Leave it!"

Oliver was confused. He climbed out of the water and shook himself hard. Humans didn't throw things unless they wanted them back. That was not how the game worked.

*This is very strange.* He would definitely have to tell Emma, just as soon as he got back.

# 36

. . . . . . . . . . .

EMMA READ THE SCREEN MESSAGE ON DAPHNE'S PHONE again. *They can't find Aunt Marcie's will.* Her gaze went from the words to Daphne's serious expression.

Pearl mouthed, *"Are you serious?"*

Daphne nodded.

Across the room, Helen raised her voice. "Sorry about that, everybody."

Daphne snatched her phone away and stuffed it into her pocket.

"My fault entirely," said Bert smoothly. "I just forgot you'd all be here so early. But best of luck. Helen. You'll let me know if there's anything I can do to help." He touched her elbow. Helen shook him off.

"I'm so sorry we have to descend on your house at a time like this, Bert," said Caite. "I know you and your family would much prefer for this to be a private time."

"Yes," said Bert. "But of course, this is what Marcie wanted, and so we really should go forward. No better way to say goodbye."

It had been a long time since Emma had watched two equally insincere people engaged in a smile-and-stare down, but Bert and Caite were giving it their all.

Bert broke away first. He gave the gathering a stiff little nod and left. Emma knew she didn't imagine the sigh of relief that echoed around the room.

Tasha and John immediately sat down at the oval marquetry table and started opening their laptops and notepads. Ned Giddy pulled up a chair and thumped a festival tote bag filled with three-ring binders down on the table.

"Well," said Helen to Caite. "Looks like you've got everything in hand here. I'll just steal Emma for a bit, if that's all right?"

Caite frowned. "We were going to finalize the catering arrangements."

"Pearl has the menus and the cost breakdowns," said Emma. In fact, they'd strategized about how one of them could keep the board busy while the other took some time to look around the house. Now might be the time to put that plan into action.

Caite sighed. "Well, I suppose that's all right then."

Pearl pulled out a chair and Emma left with Helen and Daphne.

As soon as they'd gone far enough down the hall that Emma was sure they couldn't be overheard, she asked, "What was going on with Bert, Helen?"

But Helen didn't answer until they all reached the foyer. When they got there, she spread her hands out to brace herself against the central pedestal table, like she needed to keep her knees from collapsing, or herself from breaking something.

"Mum?" Daphne put an arm around her. Helen leaned her head briefly on her daughter's shoulder.

"It's all right, Daph. Bert's just being himself. Very put out that I didn't make sure he remembered that the festival people would be here today."

"And here I thought he was just cross because he couldn't find Aunt Marcie's will," said Daphne.

"What?" Helen pulled away. "Who told you that?"

Daphne shrugged. "I heard Dad and Uncle Gus talking about it yesterday."

*Because you can hear anything in this house if you want to.* Emma found herself looking around uneasily. Somebody could be listening to them right now.

"Uncle Bert sent Gus to the solicitors yesterday to get the will," Daphne went on.

Of course, thought Emma, it would have to be Gus, because he was Marcie's heir, and the solicitor would only give the will to the heir or the executor. And if Marcie hadn't gotten around to changing her will to Daphne's favor yet, that heir should have been Gus.

"Anyway, it seems Uncle Gus came back empty-handed," said Daphne.

"And you didn't *tell* me?" Helen's voice broke. She slapped her hand across her mouth, and looked around. But the room stayed still. They were the only ones there.

*Probably.* Emma shifted her weight uneasily.

"I thought there must have been a mistake," said Daphne defensively. "I mean, Uncle Gus isn't the sharpest knife in the drawer. Besides, you weren't exactly in a mood to talk anymore when you got back yesterday."

"Yes, well, that's true."

Emma remembered how yesterday Gus had come to take Frank away for a second. Was that when he told Frank something was wrong? She mentally squinted at the memory. Had Gus been struggling to maintain a casual expression, or was that just her imagination overwriting her actual memory?

"Anyway, Uncle Gus told Uncle Frank that Aunt Marcie didn't make a will after all. Or at least that's what the solicitor said."

"No will? That's ridiculous," said Helen.

"What happened then?" asked Emma.

"Well, Uncle Bert came in, and he about hit the ceiling." Daphne tugged on her ponytail, and then pushed it over her shoulder. "Said he was going to call the solicitor and demand some answers. Then he left, and then Uncle Gus complained about how he was going to have to sign up for extra therapy sessions. But Uncle Frank wanted to know if

Gus knew anything about where the will was. He really got into it. Said they needed to present a united front against Bert, or Bert would just bulldoze through everything. Gus said he'd love to, but he didn't know anything. He was really unhappy," she added. "He wanted to get out of there."

"Speaking of," said Helen. "I haven't seen Gus all morning."

"I saw him drive past when I was on my run earlier," said Daphne. "I don't think he's back yet."

"I still don't believe Marcie didn't have a will," said Helen. "It's been years since her parents died. She would never be so careless."

"You've gone very quiet, Emma," said Pearl.

Emma rubbed the back of her neck. She thought about the solicitor's card she found in Marcie's copy of *Rebecca*.

"Yeah, well, I just . . ." She swallowed. She wished they were somewhere more private. "I agree with Helen. Someone as careful about loose ends as Marcie would leave a will."

"Probably there's a copy in her office somewhere," said Helen.

"We could—" began Daphne, but then an idea seemed to strike her. "How about you go check the office, and I'll keep an eye out to make sure nobody sneaks up on you?"

Helen gave her daughter a long, hard look. The look Daphne returned was one of complete innocence.

"Right, yes. Good idea," she said slowly. "Emma?"

"Right," Emma agreed. "We should look at her computer, and maybe see if we can find anything in the desk."

"If Bert's left us anything." Helen started up the stairs. "We can stop at Gus's rooms on the way. I think maybe we should talk to him without the others listening."

*That's probably a good idea,* thought Emma. Then she thought of something else.

"Helen, can I ask you something?" said Emma as they started up the stairs. "Why did Marcie pick Gus to inherit? I mean, before Daphne?"

Helen sighed. "I suppose because of the three of them,

he was the one she got on with the best. He tried, at least. Helped out with the yearly inventory, advocated for allowing the house to be used as an event venue, tried to get the others to stop grousing about the du Maurier festival."

*Oh, yeah, right,* Frank had said. *You spent all those years sucking up to her for nothing, yeah?*

They reached the first floor landing and turned down the right-hand hallway. "I would have thought that once Daphne came along, Marcie would have redone the will in her favor," Emma said. "Or at least so you and Frank would hold the property in trust."

Helen didn't answer. She just walked all the way down to the far end of the hall. And she knocked on one of the last doors on the left and waited.

Emma waited beside her. As she did, she realized these quiet, dim corridors with their dark paneling and closed doors were beginning to get on her nerves. She wished for daylight, and noise.

*And maybe fewer secrets.*

"Gus?" Helen called. "Gus, you there?"

There was no answer. Helen shrugged. "Not back yet."

"I wonder where's he gone?"

"Probably he just wanted to be elsewhere. Gus is like that."

*I'm not sorry for an excuse to get out of the house. Especially now.* Gus had said that when he came to pick up his Jaguar from Brian. "Not one for confrontation, then?"

"No. Never. Well, not until recently. When I was first married, Gus was always trying to sweep anything difficult under the rug. I'll say this for his therapist, he's at least started standing up for himself."

Helen walked out onto the landing for the back stairway. She paused, staring out the window. The day outside was turning gray. Emma wondered if it was going to start raining again.

"Are you okay, Helen?" asked Emma softly.

"Yes, fine. It's just—" In the watery daylight, her face was all hard lines and shadowy planes. "It's ridiculous is what it is," she said. "I still have trouble talking about the Cochranes. I left a dozen years ago, but—" She smiled weakly. "No matter what happens, they're still Daphne's family, aren't they? I wanted her to be able to come to her own terms with them. I still feel like I can't air the dirty laundry in public."

"I understand," said Emma.

"Marcie never talked much about how she came to be the one to inherit, but she did sometimes. And by sometimes, I mean when she'd had a fair amount to drink. We'd always split a bottle or two of white wine when the festival was over." She smiled sadly. "We'd sit in one of the big downstairs rooms with all the old furniture and stuff, and get comfortably sloshed. She'd talk about growing up here and how her parents would have these serious talks with her about her responsibilities. You see, Richard and Evelyn, they knew that the boys were all, well, extraordinarily careless with money. They excused it. Boys take longer to mature, they said. Boys need to sow their wild oats. All that . . . stuff. They said—everybody said—they'd settle down in time.

"Until then, it was Marcie's job to take care of them. For the whole family's sake." Helen leaned back against the railing and folded her arms. Emma remembered how Daphne struck that exact pose down in the kitchen. "It was all so absurdly out-of-date, but there it was. She was the oldest. She had the brains and the common sense. She was the one who had to make it all right. They were all counting on her."

"The modern world stops at the gates of Truscott Grange." Emma whispered the words, but Helen heard her anyway.

"It certainly did for Marcie. She never finished uni. She just stayed home and took care of things."

"But she didn't give the place over to them, because she knew they'd make a mess of it?"

"She strongly suspected, that's for sure." Helen pushed herself away from the railing. "They all live on their credit cards. Frank and I fought about it the whole time we were married. But with everything that's happened, I can't help thinking it might have been better for everybody if she'd just told them all what they could do with the family name and the family home and walked away."

Emma felt herself frown. "Helen, did Marcie ever say anything about leaving the grange to . . . you?" If Marcie's brothers were hopeless, and if she meant the property to eventually go to Daphne, leaving it to Helen in case the unexpected happened made more sense than leaving it to Gus.

"Me? I never even thought about it. Much, anyway. I thought there might be a couple of pounds coming our way, and there's a tea set I'd like to have." She paused for a moment, clearly trying to sort out her own feelings. "I know this is going to sound ridiculous, but the house never stopped being a kind of fantasy for me. I mean, nobody actually lives like this, do they? My home is a flat in Manchester. Six rooms, if you count the loo. I might have lived here for all those years, but somehow the grange never became real to me, so I never thought about owning it."

This made no sense. None. Marcie was practical. Marcie was careful and thorough. Marcie had been responsible for a major enterprise for *years*, and she'd never completed the arrangements to pass it on when she died?

All right, people did not like to think about their own deaths. One of the things Emma had learned when she was still in finance was that people did in fact leave large estates in a state of absolute chaos rather than spend time dealing with the fact that they were not going to live forever.

But Marcie did deal with it. She had talked about it. She had wanted her niece to have a choice that had been denied to her and she was taking steps to make it happen.

And now Marcie was dead and there was no will, and her three brothers finally got to be in charge.

Unless there was a will, and she just hadn't wanted those brothers to know about it ahead of time.

# 37

...........

EMMA AND HELEN CLIMBED THE STAIRS TO MARCIE'S OFFICE.
Neither of them were surprised to see the door was already
open. Bert stood behind the desk. He had a stack of folders
out and he was sorting quickly through them.

Helen knocked on the doorjamb. Bert jerked back.
"What the . . . What do you want?"

"We need Marcie's festival lists," said Helen. "And
we've got the memorial to work on and—"

Bert cut her off. His normally perfect hair was tousled,
like he'd been running his hands through it. "This is a really bad time, Helen."

"Is something wrong?" asked Emma.

The oldest Cochrane brother stared at her, like he
couldn't work out who she was, or how she came to be here.

"I don't . . . I just can't have you here right now," he
stammered.

"You can't?" said Helen in mock surprise. "It's not like
it's a crime scene. We'll just be a few minutes. You can
keep on with . . . whatever it is you're doing." She was
clearly daring him to say what he was doing.

Bert set the folder he was holding down on the stack,
and then he pressed both hands down on top of the whole

pile, like he felt he needed to hold them down or they'd all be snatched away from him.

Emma let her gaze rove around the office all around him. Daphne had predicted he'd be tearing the place apart, and she was right. The desk was piled not only with folders but with envelopes and bundles of paper. A number of the inventory ledgers had been pulled out from their bookshelves and stacked on top.

The window was open. Emma's stomach lurched.

"Look here, Helen." Bert struggled to put some of his usual charm into his voice. "I understand you want something to keep yourself busy, but I am dealing with real problems that are going to affect the entire family."

"What kind of problems?" asked Helen sweetly. "Can I help at all?"

"No!" he snapped. Helen drew back. Bert sighed and ran his hand through his hair. "No," he repeated. "Really. This is . . . this is private family business and I just need to get on with it."

"That family includes my daughter," Helen reminded him.

"Yes, your daughter." Bert said the words like they strangled him. "Not you."

Helen's whole body tensed. Emma stepped just a little closer to her. She thought Helen would back down now. Bert was not just impatient. A red flush of anger showed under the collar of his polo shirt.

Helen, however, was not done.

"We're not going to get in your way," said Helen. "We just want to get into Marcie's computer. I don't suppose . . ."

"I don't know how much clearer I can be, Helen!" Bert cut her off with a single slashing motion. "Whatever it is you want is just going to have to wait."

"No, I'm afraid I can't," said Helen. "I've got work to do too."

That red flush started creeping up Bert's neck. Then, much to Emma's surprise, a grin broke out across his handsome face, and he chuckled.

"Okay, Helen, I get it. You want to let us know you're

going to look out for your interests too. But let's be clear, all right?" His grin broadened. The false bonhomie sent a chill up Emma's spine. "This is not your house, and what happens here is really not your business, you know."

"But it is my business," insisted Helen. "My daughter . . ."

"Yes, yes, it's all about your daughter." Bert sighed sadly. "The daughter you used to try to pull Frank away from his family. And when that didn't work, you divorced him, but you couldn't quite make yourself let go, could you?"

He spoke perfectly reasonably, and somehow it was that gentle, sad tone that turned each word into ice.

"You used poor Marcie to keep your foot in the door here, and you used Daphne to keep Frank on a string. But you left us, Helen," he said softly. "And it really is too late to come back. I'm so sorry if you regret your disloyalty now that Marcie's dead but . . ."

"Bert." Frank's voice cut through the room.

Helen and Emma whirled around. Bert jerked back half a step. As soon as he saw it was his brother, he straightened up.

"Hullo, Frank," he said. "Sorry if you heard that. I was just . . ."

"Get out," said Frank. He walked forward until he stood just inches from his taller, broader brother. But in that moment, Frank was the one Emma was afraid of.

"Sorry, old bean," said Bert softly. "You do not tell me what to do."

"Actually, I do," replied Frank harshly. "I'm telling you to leave my wife alone."

"She's not your . . ."

Frank's face hardened. Emma was not sure exactly what Bert saw in Frank's expression just then, but he hesitated.

"She's using you, Frank, and the sooner you work that out, the better off we'll all be." Bert leaned in close. "You need to decide which side you're really on."

"Maybe I already have," said Frank.

"Then I'm sorry for you," replied Bert. "Because that's going to mean that from here on out, you're on your own."

Bert picked up the stack of folders and stalked out of the room. Frank stepped aside to let him pass.

"I'm sorry, Helen. You shouldn't have had to hear that."

"That's all right, Frank." Helen hung her head. "It's good to know where I stand."

"Bert doesn't speak for all of us." Frank put his hand out, almost touching her, but not quite. "He certainly doesn't speak for me."

"He was right about one thing though," said Helen. "I'm not your wife."

Frank's hand dropped. "No. I'm sorry. I just . . . it was a slip. I just want, for this once, to try to make things better for us. You, me and Daphne. That's all." He spread his hands to show they were empty. "Nothing up my sleeve this time. I swear."

"I believe you."

Frank grinned. It was an expression of pure relief, and something else Emma couldn't quite name.

"Well, I'll let you get on with things. Give a shout if you need me."

"We will," said Helen.

"Oh, Frank," said Emma. "Sorry, but do you know where Gus went this morning?"

"Gus?" Frank looked surprised. "No idea. Why?"

"Just curious," said Emma. He probably didn't believe her, but she didn't have a better answer.

"Well, if I see him, I'll let him know you were looking for him." He smiled easily, and for one minute, he looked even more charming than his older brother.

# 38

. . . . . . . . . . . .

AS SOON AS FRANK SHUT THE DOOR, HELEN TURNED TO Emma.

"Sorry you had to be here for all of that."

"It's not your fault," Emma assured her.

"I did love him once, you know," She brushed her toe across the spot where Frank had been standing. "When I left, I even asked him to come with me. I said the three of us could make a fresh start somewhere else. At the time, I didn't realize what I was really asking was for him to choose between me and his family. Of course he couldn't do that."

"It's natural to have regrets at a time like this. Give yourself time."

"Yes. You're right. Now." Helen brushed her sweater down. "Now. We have work to do, before Bert comes back and tries to throw us out bodily."

"Helen." Emma hesitated. "I was wondering if you had any idea where Marcie might have been that last night."

"Oh, gosh. You know, that detective asked us about that. And I didn't know." She snapped her fingers. "But it would be in her planner. Marcie put everything in that planner. I don't know why I didn't think of that at the time."

"You were a little upset." Emma paused, and tried to keep her voice casual. "Um, do you know where she kept it?"

"It must be in the desk somewhere." Helen opened the central drawer, and then the first of the side drawers and then the second. "I'm not seeing it, though. Maybe Bert took it."

"How about her handbag?" said Emma. She hoped the question did not sound as awkward as it felt. She didn't know why she couldn't just bring herself to say that Constance hadn't been able to find Marcie's bag, but she felt it was important to keep as much of that conversation as she could confidential, for now anyway.

"Oh, of course," said Helen. "Let me just see if we can get anything out of the computer."

Helen sat in Marcie's desk chair, and started typing on her keyboard.

"Sugar," she muttered. "It's password protected."

"Try 'password,'" suggested Emma. She started flipping through the folders Bert had left behind.

"You're kidding."

Emma shook her head. "Most common password in use, right after 'one, two, three, four.' Birthdays are also high on the list. People just aren't that creative."

Helen typed and Emma flipped.

Marcie was clearly a woman after Emma's own heart. She saved all her papers and her correspondence. Every folder was neatly labeled. A number of them had dates. Here were the fuel bills for the last five years, and here were the gardening services, and laundry services . . .

"Nope. Not that. How about 'du Maurier'?" Helen typed as she talked. "Or 'Rebecca'?"

*And bingo!* Emma pulled out a pile of folders labeled *Bank Statements—Grange.*

Caite said that the grange, and Marcie, were having money issues. If that was true, the evidence should all be right here.

Emma pulled the files out of the stack, and paused. "Try 'Manderley.'"

Helen typed. The screen beeped and flashed to life. "You got it. Manderley. Now, let's see . . ." She moved the mouse, clicking on the screen icons. "Oh, here we go. Calendar. Huh."

"What is it?" Emma leaned over to peer at the screen.

"The whole month. It's blank." Helen scooted sideways so Emma could get a better look.

She was right. The electronic calendar page had the dates listed, but there were no appointments, no notes. Nothing at all. Not even the du Maurier festival.

"What about last month?" Emma reached over for the mouse, and clicked backward to the previous month.

That page was crammed with entries. Phone calls, lunches, deadlines for the house and herself. Big, bold entries saying things like ONE MONTH TO FEST!!

"Well, that's not strange at all," Helen murmured.

Emma clicked the mouse, past the current month, and into the next. That was blank too.

"No," she said. "Not at all." She straightened up, and another idea struck her. "Helen, where's Marcie's mobile?"

Helen looked at her blankly. "I don't know. I imagine it's with her handbag as well."

"And where's that again?"

Helen opened her mouth, and closed it again. "I . . . I don't know."

"So, so far we're missing her will, her planner, her mobile and possibly her handbag. That's a lot."

"Yes, it is rather, isn't it?" murmured Helen. "Makes you wonder what else has gone walkabout, doesn't it?"

*Yes.* Emma turned to survey the office. *It certainly does.*

"Helen—" she began but a sudden squeal of laughter cut her off.

"Gah!" remarked Emma.

"Oh, for heaven's sake . . ." Helen pushed away from the desk. Then, to Emma's surprise, she went over to the fireplace and knelt down. "What are you two *doing*?"

There was silence.

"Erm . . . Helen?" began Emma.

"Sorry." Helen got to her feet. "It's the vents. When they finally put in the central heating back in the forties, they installed all these floor vents, and didn't pay much attention to the fact that if somebody's standing in the right place, the sound travels right up into the room overhead. You don't notice it much, because most of the house is empty these days."

"So that's how Daphne keeps hearing things."

Helen nodded, chagrined. "She spent a lot of bored rainy days working out the best eavesdropping spots."

"So, what room's down there?" asked Emma.

"Gus's," said Helen. But before she could say anything more, footsteps thumped outside the door. Daphne burst into the room, followed quickly by Pearl.

"Look what we found!" Daphne brandished a colorful square. "Oh my God, I cannot believe this!"

"What were you doing in your uncle Gus's room?" demanded Helen.

"And why aren't you meeting with the board?" demanded Emma.

"Because we're finished and finalized," answered Pearl calmly. "Updated cost breakdown approved, margins for overruns approved, preliminary menu approved, new tasting time arranged, at the King's Rest this time," she added. "I've sent you and Mum an email. We can go over it tonight."

"So, she decided to help me search for clues," said Daphne. "And I think we found a big one."

Pearl plucked the square out of Daphne's fingers and handed it over to Emma.

It was a photograph. There was Gus, in his everyday uniform of polo shirt and khakis. And there was Caite Hope-Johnston, in twinset and pink beads, looking surprisingly relaxed.

They had their arms around each other, and they both looked shockingly happy.

# 39

HUMANS, OLIVER HAD OBSERVED, STOOD AROUND A LOT, even when there weren't other humans to stand around with. Emma said it was because sometimes humans needed to think.

Gus seemed to need to think now. He stood at the edge of the pond, staring out at the water where he'd thrown the bundle. Dash was splashing in the water at the edge of the pond. He'd found something in the water and was wrestling it out.

It was a branch.

"Look! Look!" Dash barked. The human only glanced over. Oliver bustled up to Dash and sniffed at the water-logged stick. But it was very dead and not really that interesting. He didn't understand what Dash was getting so excited about.

Gus turned away from the pond, put the shovel on his shoulder and started trudging up the path.

"Gotta go!" Oliver told Dash, and he turned to bound after the human.

"What? Why?" Dash caught up and bumped Oliver in the side with his muzzle. "He's only going back to the house, and we haven't gone halfway round the place yet."

"I know, I know," panted Oliver. "But I need to stay with the human."

"You do?" Dash pricked his ears forward, confused. "What for?"

"He's acting strange. I need to be able to tell Emma about it. It's important."

"You and your human are the strange ones."

Oliver wanted to stop and bark at him. He shouldn't talk like that about Emma. *Or me.* But he remembered in time that they were friends. "You go on if you want to. I'll meet you back at the house."

"Okay, as long as you save me some roast beef!" Dash yelped, and then headed off back to his new, old, branch.

"Well, hullo," said Gus as Oliver caught up with him. "Lonely?"

Oliver barked. It didn't really matter what he said, of course. This man was not Emma, and he wouldn't understand.

"You need to get yourself a lady friend," said Gus. "Trust me, makes all the difference. Even when there's trouble. It is all worth it." He was quiet for a minute. "At least, I hope it's worth it. And I hope she thinks it's worth it."

All at once, the human had stopped walking. They had come to a little clearing. There was a path here, but it wasn't used much. There was a wooden building too, and Gus was fussing with the door. Oliver went up and smelled sweat and there was something else. Something . . .

"Go on, give us some room." The human nudged Oliver sideways. Whatever he was doing with the door, it worked, because he got it open, and went inside.

Curious, Oliver followed. It was a tiny building, and dark inside despite the sunshine. There were lots of wood and metal things. Oliver smelled steel and pine and rust and spiders and something else.

Gus leaned the shovel against the wall. Oliver sniffed around the dirt floor.

*There's something. There's something . . . What is it? What is it?*

This was frustrating. The new smells Gus brought—
water and mud and dirt and sweat—were getting in the
way. But there was another smell, one that he was sure he
would recognize, if only it was a little stronger. It was
something that he tried hard to explain to Emma, but he
wasn't sure she ever understood. Sometimes there was a
smell that was so faint, or so old, that all it felt was *familiar*.
Some deep down instinct told him it was important, but not
why. Or even where it was. It was here somewhere, though.
Somewhere close . . .

"Come on, Oliver. That's enough. Let's go." Gus nudged
him toward the door. Oliver barked, and tried to get around
him. This was important. He was sure it was . . .

"Now, Oliver!" The human grabbed his collar. Oliver
whined and scrabbled, but Gus pulled him out, then kicked
the door shut behind them both.

"Sorry," he said, as he turned to fuss with the door
again. "But I've got things to do." He slid something into
his pocket.

Just then, the wind shifted a little. Oliver whipped
around. Another human was coming up the path. A man;
he smelled like soap and coffee and the house, and the
people in the house and . . . and . . .

Gus turned around and yelped, suddenly frightened.
"Frank!"

"Gus!" shouted the other human. "There you are!"

The other human was Gus's family; it was easy to tell by
the smell. He wore more of the perfume stuff, a confusing
mix of chemicals and alcohol, than Gus did. Although, now
that Oliver noticed it, Gus had a little bit of smell like dead
roses on him. Oliver wondered if that was important. Or
maybe it was just a family trait. Without thinking, he went
over to sniff Frank's ankles.

"Oh, for God's . . . Get back, dog! Go on!" he snapped.

*Not a nice human.* Oliver skulked back to Gus. He suddenly missed Emma. Maybe he should just leave these two
here and go find her. He already had a lot to tell her.

"What are you doing out here?" Gus was asking.

"Looking for you!" growled Frank. "Where've you been all morning?"

"That's my business. How'd you even find me?" Gus was having trouble with his hands. He put them in his pockets, and took them out, and tucked them under his arms, and then tugged at his shirt.

"I saw your car in the garage. I thought you might have not wanted to come inside yet, so I was heading down to the pond."

"Yes, well, you know." Gus folded his hands under his arms again. He was very nervous. But so was Frank. Frank was sweating, even though he was just standing there. "I hate confrontation. My therapist says that's common in youngest children. We're always trying to please everybody."

"I thought that was middle children."

"You as well. We're all still trying to win approval from our parents."

"Our parents, in case you hadn't noticed, are dead."

"Makes it that much harder, doesn't it?"

"Yes, all right. Leaving all that." Frank's voice was tight too, and harsh. "Has Wilkes been able to tell you anything about the will?"

"No. He hasn't." Gus pulled his shirt down again, and shoved his hands in his pockets again. "As far as they're concerned, there isn't one."

"I can't believe that! Marcie had to know what that would mean! Years of probate, maybe even court cases. And God! All the *money*"—he practically whined the word—"tied up for ages! She wouldn't just . . . leave it like that."

"Maybe she meant to get around to it, but she didn't get the chance."

"She had years!" shouted Frank.

"She had a lot going on!"

Oliver barked. He couldn't help it.

"Christ, Gus, can't you do something about that damn dog!"

Gus made a low, growling noise. "Go on, Oliver. Go home." He shooed him away. "Go on."

Oliver backed away, unsure what to do. He did want to go. He wanted Emma. He didn't like the way these men were acting with each other. But this might be important.

A noble corgi always found a way. Oliver zoomed away up the path, and then dove straight into the underbrush, and stopped. He lay flat on his belly and strained his ears.

"Look, Gus, I don't want to argue with you," Frank was saying. "We need to try to work together, especially now."

Slowly, one little bit at a time, Oliver inched forward. Leaves and grass tickled his ears, and made him blink.

"Do we?" Gus said.

Oliver found a good spot. He could smell the two of them from here, as long as the wind was blowing. He stretched out his nose and his ears as far as he could.

"I keep telling you," Frank was saying. "If Marcie really didn't leave a will, the estate is going to be tied up for years! We won't be able to get at a single penny!"

Gus shrugged. "Maybe it's not worth it anymore. Maybe it's time to just . . . walk away."

"You are kidding. After all these years? After . . . everything . . . ?"

"Yes, Frank, after everything. I mean, look at us!" He spread his hands. "Look at where we are. We're *brothers* and we're wondering if one of us went and killed our sister. I bet if I said right now that I think it was Bert, you'd go along!"

"I would," said Frank. "Gladly. Because, as it happens, I'm sure one of us did kill Marcie, and you and I need to think very hard about exactly what that means."

Oliver did not like what these humans were doing.

Gus raised his hand toward the other man, fast. His whole body said he was angry. Frank swatted Gus's hand away.

Oliver barked, he couldn't help it. Gus jumped, startled.

"Oh, for heaven's sake," groaned Frank. "Can't you do something about that blasted dog?"

Oliver tried to scamper backward, but Gus spotted him.

"All right, Oliver, go on!" Gus waded into the underbrush. "Go on home. I'm sure Emma's looking for you. Go on."

Oliver ducked out of the way, grumbling. Not that Gus was paying any attention. He was trying to herd Oliver toward the house. He wasn't very good at it.

Oliver was annoyed. He didn't actually want to stay with Frank, or Gus, but they might be saying, or doing, something important. Unfortunately, it was pretty obvious whatever that important thing was, it wouldn't happen while he was there.

Oliver yipped at Gus, and Frank, to let them know they were being rude, and darted back into the undergrowth. Gus didn't follow.

Frank said a few more rude things.

"You and dogs, Frank," said Gus.

"It's not my fault. I'm allergic. I don't see why I should have to live through a week of clogged sinuses . . ."

"There's these shots you can get, you know. My therapist says—"

"Please, Gus, spare me what your therapist says right now."

They were walking away. Oliver hesitated, then he turned and started snuffling the ground until he found his own trail, and trotted back to the shed.

It was possible the humans might do, or say, something important. But Oliver knew for certain there was something important in that shed. He might not be able to find out what the humans were doing. But he could find out what was in the shed. At least, he could try.

Because there was one little problem. All that fussing Gus had been doing with the door. He'd been locking it.

Oliver scrabbled at the door to the shed. He stretched up as far as he could and batted at the hasp, and the lock. He dropped back down and barked at it. It wouldn't do any good, but it made him feel better.

Oliver sniffed around the shed. The bottoms of the walls were jagged. Things had been gnawing here. Mice, and a rat, and squirrels had all been chewing at the wood at various times. An idea struck. Nose down, Oliver circled the shed.

There.

Just what he'd been looking for—a jagged hole, bigger than the others. Not quite big enough to get in through, but an enterprising corgi could fix that.

Oliver started to dig.

# 40

............

HELEN TOOK THE PHOTO OF THE INCONGRUOUSLY HAPPY Caite and Gus out of Emma's hand. "It must be an old picture. Gus doesn't have a girlfriend. Let alone—" Words failed her and Helen just waved the photo.

"Doesn't look old," said Daphne, obviously swallowing a laugh. "Looks like just yesterday."

"But Gus doesn't . . . He couldn't," said Helen. "If he was dating Caite, Bert would never let us hear the end of it."

"Which could explain why nobody heard the start of it," said Pearl.

Emma nodded in agreement. She could just imagine what Bert would think about his brother dating someone who had spread uncomfortable rumors about the Cochranes.

"I just can't believe, I mean . . . *Caite*?" breathed Helen.

"We can't do this here." Emma felt the space between her shoulders tightening, like somebody was already staring at her back. *I am really starting not to like this house.* "Somebody might hear us. I'll meet you down in the kitchen."

"Meet us?" said Pearl. "But . . ."

"Because you're going to put that picture right back where you found it," said Helen. "Now."

"Mum—" Daphne tried.

"Daphne"—Emma cut her off—"you have to get that back to wherever it was before Gus gets home."

"Oh, yeah. Right." Daphne plucked the photo back out of Helen's hand and tucked it into her side pocket. "Meet you all in the kitchen."

THE KITCHEN WAS, THANKFULLY, EMPTY WHEN EMMA, HELEN and Pearl got there. After a minute's hesitation, Emma dropped the folders she'd filched from Marcie's desk on the counter, grabbed a hand towel out of the drawer and used it to prop open the door to the outside, just in case Oliver came back. Her nerves were very much on edge. Maybe it was from being in Marcie's office for so long, or finding out that so many important items had gone missing.

Or because of Bert's casual dismissal of Helen's place in the family, or Frank's sudden willingness to try to take on his larger brother.

Or because Caite Hope-Johnston, who resented Marcie to the point where she was ready to accuse her of theft, seemed to be in a relationship with Gus Cochrane.

"I cannot believe you girls went rifling through other people's things," Helen was saying.

Pearl looked thoroughly unapologetic. "We thought we might find a clue about Marcie's death. And we did. And anyway, we're not the only ones making off with things." She held up the folders full of bank statements Emma had collected.

"That's evidence. I hope." Emma took them out of Pearl's hand, and put them back on the counter, and put her handbag on top of them. She also went and switched on the electric kettle. If they were making tea, no one would question what they were doing in the kitchen.

"So's that photo," Pearl pointed out.

"What could a relationship between Gus and Caite have to do with Marcie's death?" Helen demanded.

"It does help explain how Caite was able to get into the house," admitted Emma.

"And we know she and Marcie hated each other. Well, she hated Marcie anyway," said Pearl. "What if Marcie found out she and Gus were a thing? What if she threatened to cut Gus off if he kept seeing her?"

"I can't see Marcie doing that," said Helen.

"But I can see Gus thinking she might," said Emma.

"And Caite as well," said Pearl. "What if Caite wanted the estate? I mean, until just recently, everybody thought Gus was in line for it, right? They might have wanted to kill Marcie before she had a chance to change her will."

That was a very ugly idea. Emma shivered.

The door from the main house opened and all three of them straightened up abruptly. Daphne came in, and waved them all back. "Just me."

Helen sagged against the counter. "I am really starting to hate this."

"I know the feeling," said Emma. She wished Oliver would come back. Had sending him out with Dash been a mistake? She shook herself. Oliver was smart, and he was a good dog. He was fine. Maybe a little distracted out in the patch of woods, but fine.

"Do you want to go home?" Daphne asked her mother.

"Yes," said Helen. "But we can't. At least, I can't."

"Well, I'm not leaving you here on your own." Daphne hugged her mother and gave her a quick kiss. "So we'd better just work out what's going on as quick as we can."

"Well, I'll tell you what," said Pearl. "I think Bert better hope that will gets found."

"Bert?" said Emma. "How do you figure?"

"Bert is used to being able to boss his brothers around," said Pearl. "With Marcie out of the way, he might figure he'll be able to take charge of the estate, and the money. That's a serious motive."

Daphne swore, and then blushed. "Sorry, Mum."

"No, that's all right. So, what do we do?"

Emma looked at the door to the outside. Then, she went to the door to the inside of the house and listened for a minute.

"Emma, you're making me nervous," said Pearl.

"I'm making myself nervous," she admitted. "But, Helen, I've got a question. Who are the family solicitors?"

"Able and Wilkes," said Helen promptly. "I spent goodness knows how long dealing with them during the divorce. Why?"

"I didn't want to say this earlier, but when I was looking through Marcie's copy of *Rebecca* last night, I found a business card for a law firm tucked in the pages. A different law firm."

Pearl whistled. "You think Marcie kept the will with somebody else?"

"I think it's possible," Emma said. "She knows her brothers are not happy that she controls the estate. She tried to keep her conversations about the future with Helen and Daphne quiet, because she knew they'd kick up a fuss. And she knows Bert drinks and golfs with all kinds of people. She might have got worried somebody at the old family firm might let something slip over the port." *Especially if she was afraid that one of them was plotting her murder.*

"So, what firm was it?" prompted Daphne.

"Some three-name firm. I didn't bring the card—" Emma searched her memory. "Minchin! That was one name. I remember that, because it was the nasty boarding school headmistress in *A Little Princess* . . ."

Daphne and Pearl had their phones out before she could finish and were typing madly at the screens.

"How about this?" said Pearl. "Minchin, Price and Little? They're over in Camelford."

"Yes! That's it!" exclaimed Emma.

"I'm calling." Pearl stabbed at her screen.

"No, it has to be Daphne," said Emma. "They won't talk to you—you're not in the family."

"Oh, right." Pearl handed her phone to Daphne.

That was when the door opened.

"Oh, hullo!" Tasha walked into the kitchen. "There you all are." She looked from one of them to the other. "Am I interrupting something?"

"No, no," said Emma.

"Just talking about who we could get to help with service on the festival weekend," added Pearl. "Daphne thought some of her mates might be interested in a little extra cash."

Daphne tucked her phone into her pocket. "I'll text later."

"Oh, well." Tasha hesitated, but then clearly decided that believing them was easier than not. "I was coming down to see about some tea. Oh, great minds think alike," she said as she saw the kettle already plugged in.

"How are things going?" asked Emma.

"So far, disastrously." Tasha sighed. "Do you know where the cups are in this museum?"

"Of course." Emma started opening cupboards and handing down mugs and the Staffordshire ware teapot with its brightly colored pansies.

"What's wrong?" asked Helen. "Can I help?"

"I wish you would," said Tasha. "The crew is here, and we're starting to get the public rooms set up. People love seeing the house all dressed up in its best, especially during the masquerade. But there's a whole set of things we can't find—some of the good paintings, the silver Lamerie tea set, one of the William Morris tapestries. Caite is about to explode. Ten days to go, and we're all at sixes and sevens."

Daphne snorted, but at least had the grace to look apologetic, and to start helping with the tea things. She even went and got a packet of McVitie's ginger nuts from the pantry.

"Once more into the breach." Tasha picked up the tray. "You sure everything's all right here?"

"Fine," said Helen a shade too quickly, and Tasha noticed. She narrowed her eyes a little, but thankfully didn't ask.

Emma held the door for her.

As soon as Tasha was gone, Daphne yanked the phone out of her pocket, touched redial and held it to her ear and waited.

Emma's gaze drifted to the window. She wondered where Oliver was. Had he found anything? Or had he forgotten he was even supposed to be looking and spent the time chasing mice and rabbits in the gardens with Dash?

Somebody must have answered at the law firm, because Daphne straightened up. "Yes. Hello. My name is Daphne Cochrane. I think my aunt, Marcia Cochrane, was a client of yours? Oh. Thanks."

"*Switching me over*," Daphne mouthed. Then she spoke into the phone again. "Yes, hello, Mr. Minchin. Yes. Oh, you heard? Yes. Thanks. We're going to miss her a lot. I'm calling about Aunt Marcie's will? You do? Oh, great." She nodded vigorously at them all. "Well, obviously we'd like to get a copy as soon as we can. Aunt Marcie doesn't seem to have kept a copy here at the house. Maybe you saw . . . oh. Uh-huh. So who would the executor be? Oh? Yes. I can get hold of her right now. Yeah. Of course. Right. Thanks." She rang off.

"They have the will," Daphne announced. "The executor will need to go pick it up, and they'll need a copy of the death certificate."

"Who's the executor?" asked Helen.

"Uncle Gus," said Daphne. "And you, Mum."

The women all stared at each other. Emma opened her mouth, but whatever she'd been about to say was cut off by a faint but very familiar, high-pitched bark.

"Emma!"

"Emma!"

Emma threw open the back door and ran up the steps. She knelt down and held her arms out. Oliver bounded straight into them, licking her face enthusiastically. "Where have been!" Emma hugged Oliver hard. "I was worried!"

"I found things!" he barked. "Marcie things! There was a bundle, and Gus threw it in the pond, but he didn't want it back, and then he went to the shed, and but the important thing is there's more bad!"

Emma grabbed his paws so she could help him balance on his hind legs and look him in the eye. "Whh . . ." She gulped and glanced behind her. Everybody was still talking in the kitchen. "More bad?" whispered Emma.

"Yes, in the shed. With the digging things! I'll show you!" He stopped. "Except the Gus man locked it."

"Yes, yes, okay. We'll work that out. Soon." She rubbed his head and settled him back down on all fours.

Constance said Marcie must have been hit with something with a handle to provide momentum. Like a cricket bat or a wooden board.

*Or a shovel.*

Could Oliver have actually found the murder weapon? Emma's heart thumped, but she wasn't sure if it was from excitement or fear.

It took some doing, but Emma schooled her face back into something like a neutral expression and led Oliver back into the kitchen.

Which was when the kitchen door opened and Caite strode in.

"What are you still doing here? I thought you'd all left."

Oliver yipped. Pearl moved to grab the open folder off the counter, but not fast enough. Caite had already seen it.

"What are you doing with that!" she demanded. "These are private family papers! I knew something like this would happen!" Caite spat. "I tried to warn—" But she stopped without saying the name. "You don't care about the festival and you don't care about this job. You're just up here to try and play Miss Marple and spy on . . . this family!"

Emma tensed, but Daphne answered before she could. "I'm surprised you're that upset, Caite. From the way we talked before, you didn't seem like you would care very much what happens to us."

"You have no idea what you're even talking about," said Caite coldly.

"Actually, she does," said Pearl. "And it's all right. I'd be surprised if you didn't feel conflicted right now."

"Yeah, I mean, being in a relationship with Gus when you've spent years blaming his family for your father's death. That would confuse anybody." Pearl's tone was utterly bland.

Caite stared at them, very much looking like a rabbit that's spotted a fox. Then she snatched the folder up off the counter and stormed out.

Pearl whistled, a long, low sound. Helen just folded her arms and stared silently out toward the car park.

"Yeah," agreed Emma.

"You'd almost think she had something to hide there," said Daphne.

"You mean aside from the fact that she's dating a member of a family she's hated for years?" asked Emma.

"Yeah, actually," said Pearl.

"Funny, I was just thinking the same thing." Because Emma was also thinking about Caite sneaking in to get to Marcie's computer, and the missing appointments, and the missing handbag, and the missing planner.

And she was thinking about Caite being so suddenly and abruptly sick when she heard the news of Marcie's death.

Then she thought about what Oliver had told her. She'd been so focused on the possibility that he'd found the murder weapon, she'd almost missed the other part—that he'd seen Gus throw something into a pond.

"You don't really think Caite did it, do you?" Pearl was saying softly. "Killed Marcie, I mean?"

Gus had thrown something into the pond. Gus had locked up the shed that might contain the murder weapon. Caite had risked sneaking back into the house to get to Marcie's office.

"I don't know," said Emma. "But I do think she's trying to cover it up."

# 41

IN THE END, IT WAS DECIDED THAT EMMA AND HELEN WOULD
be the ones to visit the solicitor's office in Camelford, while
Pearl and Daphne stayed at the house to fend off awkward
questions, work out festival details and keep searching for
information. After much persuasion, Emma convinced
Oliver that he was needed to help Dash guard the girls.

As they drove through the looming green hills, Emma
allowed herself to put the troubles at the grange behind her,
at least for a while. She even convinced Helen to stop at a
little roadside pub that looked like it had been there as long
as the hills had and split a ploughman's lunch and a pot of
very strong tea. They talked about small things—Emma's
plans for the summer, how Daphne's football team really
was hoping to make it to the finals next year. Emma could
tell just by looking at her that Helen had needed this small
break at least as much as she had.

Refreshed, and determined, they got back into the car
and headed out.

The offices of Minchin, Price & Little proved to be in a
venerable slate-roofed building right off Camelford's winding high street. Whoever had been put in charge of their
interior decorating had clearly decided the wood signaled

the correct level of solidity and stability for a law firm. The rooms were wood paneled, the furniture was all heavy oak, or at least oak veneer. Even the coatrack at the entrance was bentwood.

The chirpy, middle-aged receptionist took their names and bustled away into the interior of the office. A moment later she came back and said Mr. Minchin was ready to see them, if they would step this way, please?

Mr. Minchin's office continued the theme of oaken stability, and so did the man himself. The truth was, he looked more like he should be a bouncer at a nightclub than a solicitor in a sedate, book-lined office.

When Emma and Helen filed in, he heaved himself to his feet. "Ms. . . . erm . . . Dalgliesh?"

"I'm Helen Dalgliesh." Helen held out her hand for him to shake. "This is my friend Emma Reed."

"Ms. Reed." Mr. Minchin had the kind of overly soft handshake big men sometimes used with women. "Well, now, please sit down."

Once they'd gone through the formality of taking Helen's identification and her copy of Marcie's death certificate, Mr. Minchin pulled a long file folder out of his in tray.

"I admit I was very surprised and very sorry to hear about Ms. Cochrane's death," he said. "I'd just spoken to her last Thursday. Tell me, has any decision been made about the sale?"

"The . . . I'm sorry," stammered Helen. "What did you say?"

"The sale of the grange. Ms. Cochrane was working with an estate agent from Christie's, at our recommendation—" He paused. "You have no idea what I'm talking about, do you, Ms. Dalgliesh?"

"No," said Helen. "I mean, Marcie had recently talked with my daughter and me about the future of the estate, but she hadn't mentioned the possibility of selling Truscott Park."

"Was this a recent decision?" asked Emma, partly so

Helen could have a minute to recover. She sounded rattled, and Emma couldn't blame her.

"Ms. Cochrane initially approached me about six months back. She said she wanted to explore the possibilities. It was just last week, she let me know she had decided to move forward."

"Right after she talked to Daphne," murmured Helen.

"Yes, she mentioned that," said Mr. Minchin. "And I believe she had an appointment with the agent recently."

"Recently?" said Emma. "Could it have been Friday?"

"Possibly," said Mr. Minchin. "I'm afraid I don't remember the exact date."

Emma sat back in the comfortable club chair, stunned. At the same time, it all made sense. Marcie was a planner. She knew there was a good chance Daphne would decide to turn down her inheritance. So, why not have her plans in place in case that happened?

"I'm sure we'll want to be talking with the Christie's agent," said Emma, pulling on her office manners. "Do you happen to have the name?"

"Yes, of course." He flipped open a leather portfolio and pulled out a business card. "That's the number there."

"Thank you," said Emma. "Can you tell me, did Marcie have any other papers with you?"

Mr. Minchin obviously was not entirely comfortable with Emma doing the asking. He looked to Helen. Helen nodded.

"There was an estate inventory as well. I have it here." He unlocked one of the lower desk drawers and pulled out a leather-bound ledger. Emma was not at all surprised to see it was stamped with last year's date.

*And now we know where that got to.* She'd noticed last year's inventory was missing the first time she'd walked into the office.

"And here, of course, is the will." Mr. Minchin opened the folder in front of him, took out a sealed envelope and laid it on top of the ledger.

"Thank you." Helen pulled the ledger and the envelope toward her with both hands.

"I'm sure you'll want some time to familiarize yourself with the document, but we are ready to help with any questions you might have. Administering such a large estate raises special issues."

Emma recognized the light in the man's eyes as the glowing reflection of pounds sterling.

"Thank you," Emma said. "I'm quite certain we'll be in touch soon." She stood and Helen stood with her. "We appreciate all your help."

They exchanged some final polite pleasantries, and Mr. Minchin walked Emma and Helen to the door.

As soon as they climbed back into the car, Helen shoved the ledger into Emma's hands, ripped open the envelope and unfolded the long, thick pages of Marcie's official last will and testament. She scanned the lines of legal script, breathing like she'd just run a marathon.

"She didn't, oh, no, she didn't." Helen let her head drop back against the seat's headrest. "Oh, Marcie, you *idiot*!"

"What is it, Helen?" asked Emma, but Helen just pushed the will into her hands.

Emma's eyes swept over the legalese, until she got to the words "the bulk and residue of the estate, including all real property . . ."

"Oh," she breathed.

Helen nodded. "She's left it to Daphne after all. And me."

And in the stroke of a pen, or at least of a keyboard, had turned Helen into Likely Suspect Number One.

# 42

. . . . . . . . . . . .

"HOW COULD SHE DO THIS TO US?"

Helen sat in the parked car with her hands on the steering wheel. Outside, the shadows from the hills and the crowded buildings had already cast the street into twilight.

Emma read the will slowly. There was no question about what it said, or what it meant. Daphne and Helen between them owned Truscott Grange and Truscott Park.

"Daphne told her she wanted nothing to do with it!" said Helen to the windscreen and the world outside.

Emma flipped back to the first page of the will. "She had this written last year. Obviously, she didn't get a chance to update it before she died."

Helen pushed herself straighter. "Last . . . ? But I thought she had named Gus . . ."

"That's what everybody keeps saying." Emma folded the will back up and tucked it into the envelope. "Did you ever hear *Marcie* say it?"

Helen opened her mouth, and closed it. "I . . . I don't know. I know I heard Gus say it. And Frank. And Bert, of course."

"Of course." Emma tapped the envelope against her hand. "Maybe it was easier for Marcie to let them think

that. I mean, why give them one more reason to complain?"
She stopped. "Or to hassle Daphne."

"Oh, yes." Helen rubbed her head. "And they would
have, whatever Daphne had decided to do. But what about
the rest of it? Was she really thinking of selling the place?
Without telling anybody? I mean, I know she didn't like
confrontation but that seems pretty extreme."

"I know how to find out." Emma paused. "Do you have
a pound coin?"

"Ummm . . ." Helen dug into her handbag and came up
with a gold-and-silver coin. "Yes?"

"Good, give it here." Emma held out her hand.

"What am I doing?" asked Helen as she dropped the
coin onto Emma's palm.

"You've just hired me." She put the coin on the dash-
board and pulled out her phone and the card Minchin had
given her. She dialed the number and waited while it rang.

"I've hired you for a quid?"

"I'm a licensed accountant," Emma told her. "There's
rules." The ringing had stopped. "Hullo?"

An actual receptionist answered, and put her right
through to William Drinkwater. Emma imagined herself in
a board room in her best black suit, briefcase in hand, and
said, "Good afternoon, Mr. Drinkwater. This is Emma
Reed, financial representative for the Cochrane estate. I
understand you were in discussion with the late Ms. Marcia
Cochrane about the sale of Truscott Grange and Truscott
Park?"

"I'm sorry. Did you . . . that is, Ms. Cochrane is de-
ceased?"

"Unfortunately, she is. I am acting on behalf of the estate. I can fax you the relevant documentation, if required,
or I have some photos here I can email you, or I can refer
you to her lawyer, Mr. Minchin." Emma crossed her fingers
that the willingness to provide the paperwork would short-
cut the actual need to provide it.

Mr. Drinkwater let out a long breath. Something rustled—
paper or cloth, maybe both. "Well. We will of course need

all that. May I ask, does the estate plan to move forward with the sale?"

"That is still being decided. I'm reaching out today to get an understanding of how matters were left between your agency and Ms. Cochrane."

There was a pause. Emma could practically hear the estate agent's brain ticking over, trying to decide whether he should stick to the rules or appear cooperative with someone who had the power to help him to what was going to be a truly outstanding commission.

Mr. Drinkwater evidently decided to try for a middle course. "I suppose I can tell you that things had advanced pretty far. We found a buyer who is quite excited about the property, even though Ms. Cochrane had not completely made up her mind to sell. Until last week that is, of course." *Until she'd talked to Daphne.* "We arranged for them to attend an upcoming festival to be held at the grange so they could see firsthand how well it functioned as an event venue."

"And that would have been last Friday?"

"Yes, we had a supper meeting and she confirmed she was ready to go forward with the sale of the house, and a considerable portion of the adjacent property. If there's any question . . ."

"No, none. We're just double-checking on the status of events. Thank you for your time. I'll have Mr. Minchin's office fax over the documentation, and let me give you my email, in case you need to get in touch." Emma rattled off her address. Mr. Drinkwater expressed his condolences, and said he'd keep an eye out for the documents, and looked forward to working with the estate executors.

They said goodbye and Emma rang off.

"You're good," said Helen.

"Talking business is my superpower. Along with cake," said Emma. "But at least that explains why Marcie was so anxious that everything be perfect at the festival this year. She wanted to impress these buyers."

It also explained where she was the night she died, and

why she'd kept it secret. Emma bit her lip. As it turned out, Marcie had been keeping a lot of secrets.

Marcie had started laying plans to sell the ancestral home months ago, without telling her brothers. Or anybody else. The quiet planner. The one who believed she could handle anything on her own. She'd set the process into motion, after she'd had a will written, so that whatever Daphne decided about the estate, all the brothers were formally disinherited. Emma wondered if there'd been another will before this one, and if that one really had named Gus as the beneficiary.

*And if there was and if it did, what changed last year? Was that when she found out Gus was seeing Caite? Or was it something else?*

Emma looked down at the inventory in her hands.

"What am I going to tell Daphne?" Helen was saying. "Good lord, what am I going to tell any of them?"

"We'll think of something," murmured Emma. She flipped the ledger open and scanned the neatly written pages.

Helen noticed, and cocked her head sideways. "What do you suppose she gave that to the lawyers for?"

"I don't know yet," said Emma. "But if Marcie was leaving it with her lawyer, it must have been something she didn't want her brothers to see."

Helen craned her neck trying to read over Emma's shoulder. "Wait, what's stuck back there?" She reached across and plucked at a bit of paper that stuck up out of the book.

Emma stuck her finger in between the pages and flipped them over.

What turned up was a screenshot of a website that had been glued into the ledger. An auction website to be specific, advertising an elaborate silver tea set for immediate sale.

At the time the printout had been made, the bid was more than Emma's rent on her cottage for a month.

"I know that set . . ." began Helen.

Emma turned the page. It was another screenshot for the same auction site. This time advertising an "exquisite miniature circa 1800, believed to be by Richard Cosway, favorite artist of King George IV . . ."

"That's the Prinny!" exclaimed Helen.

"The what, I'm sorry?"

"It's a miniature of the Prince Regent. Apparently, one of the Cochranes was a favorite, at one point."

"I thought that was with Charles the Second."

"Yeah, well, him too. The Cochrane ladies were pretty popular company for a long weekend. What's it doing for sale on the Internet?"

Emma turned the page. This screenshot was for a William Morris tapestry.

"What is going on?" Helen breathed.

"Is this the tapestry Tasha said was missing?" Emma asked.

Helen nodded. Emma closed the book. "Well, we can save everybody some trouble now."

"And I guess we know why Marcie didn't want Frank and the others to see this." Helen rubbed her forehead. "I knew the estate had money troubles, but I didn't know she'd been selling things off to try to make ends meet."

"Well, she was going through a lot of trouble to keep it secret."

"Selling the contents of the house, then selling the house and not telling anybody about any of it." Helen blinked at the windscreen. "That's a lot. Makes you wonder what else she'd been hiding."

*Yes,* thought Emma. *It really does.*

# 43

. . . . . . . . . . . .

THE DRIVE BACK TO THE GRANGE WAS A QUIET ONE. HELEN
pulled around back. As Emma climbed out to open the garage door for her, Helen put her hand on Emma's arm.

"Please don't tell anybody the details about the will," she
said. "At least not yet. I want a chance to talk to Daphne first."

"That's probably a good idea."

Emma opened the garage door and then stood back so
Helen could pull into the bay. Behind her, Emma heard the
familiar clamor of happy barking.


HELEN WAS COMING OUT OF THE GARAGE. EMMA STOOD
up and faced her, trying to force her face back into something like a neutral expression.

Daphne and Pearl were both in the kitchen when Emma
and Helen walked in. Daphne was at the sink, taking a long
swig from a water bottle. Pearl was perched on a stool at
the counter, with a notebook and a three-ring binder open
in front of her. She was scrolling on her mobile with one
hand and making notes with the other.

Dash was there as well, curled up on his blanket. Oliver
seemed to think this was an excellent idea and went over to

nestle down with him. Dash flopped his feathered tail over the corgi's back.

"Hullo, Mum." Daphne lowered the bottle. "Did you get it?"

"Yeah, we did. Daphne, can we talk a second?"

Pearl raised her eyebrows toward Emma. Emma shook her head.

"Sure." Daphne snapped the cap back onto her bottle. "Upstairs?"

"Good idea."

They both exited up the back stairs. As soon as they were gone, Pearl laid her mobile down.

"What happened at the solicitors?" asked Pearl.

"Well, we found Marcie's will. I expect that's what Helen's telling Daphne about right now. And we found this." Emma put the ledger down on the counter and flipped open to the screenshots of the missing antiques.

"Well, looks like Marcie had a method."

"What do you mean?"

Pearl dug into her stack of binders and papers and pulled out two identical ledgers. "I found these. Last year's inventory wasn't the only place Marcie was hiding things."

Like all the other grange inventories, these ledgers were stamped with their respective years. One was for 1976, and the other for 2000.

"Wait," said Emma. "Didn't Marcie's parents die in 2000?"

"And Stewart Cochrane died in that boating accident in 1976." Pearl passed Emma the ledger. "Seems Marcie was taking an interest in the family accidents."

Emma flipped open the pages. Several news clippings had been pasted in, blurred copies of newspaper articles, tracking the grim progress of the boat going missing and eventually washing up on the shore, with Stewart found trapped belowdecks. There were charts of the currents and tides, as well as a weather report from the day.

"Pretty dark for a scrapbook," muttered Emma.

"Not as dark as the other one." Pearl opened the 2000 ledger.

Emma was already sure what she'd see, and she was right. It was more clippings, this time coverage of the "tragic accident that claimed the lives of local Trevena residents Richard and Evelyn Cochrane." Here there was more information. Not only had the news accounts been included but copies of the autopsy reports, the police reports and the inspection of the car showing no signs of mechanical failure. Someone had carefully underlined the concluding section: driver lost control of the vehicle. Alcohol determined to have been a factor in crash.

Someone had also added a question mark.

*There was no accident.* Emma remembered the underlining in the copy of *Rebecca.*

"Where did you find these?" asked Emma.

"Right on the shelves with the others. Hidden in plain sight."

Just like the message inside *Rebecca.*

*If it was a message.*

# 44

............

PEARL PULLED OUT HER MOBILE.

"I'm texting Daphne," she said, her fingers already tapping the screen.

"Good idea," agreed Emma. "She should know about this."

"And maybe we should get upstairs?" Pearl typed as she talked. "At least find the rest of the board?"

"You go ahead. I'll be there in a minute."

Pearl must have caught something in her expression, because she glanced up from her screen. "Are you all right, Emma?"

"Yeah, yeah. I just . . . there's a call I need to make," she finished. As an excuse, it sounded pretty lame.

Fortunately, Pearl didn't seem to notice. "Right." She finished her own text and tucked her mobile into her pocket. "Meet you in the sitting room."

The door closed and Emma rounded the counter. "Psst, Oliver!"

Oliver was on his feet immediately. He must have jostled Dash, because the big mutt lifted his head and looked distinctly annoyed. Oliver just yipped and scampered over to

Emma. She crouched down and let him put his paws up on her knees.

"Quick, Oliver. Tell me exactly what you saw this afternoon."

"I saw Gus!" Oliver barked. "That is, we saw Gus, because Dash was there too!" Dash huffed, and dug his nose into the folds of his blanket. "But he got distracted by a branch, but I didn't and . . ."

Emma suppressed a groan of frustration at this corgi digression. "Okay, you saw Gus," she said quickly. "You said he was standing by the pond?"

"Yes!" yipped Oliver. "He had a bundle, and a shovel. I think he dug up the bundle. I didn't get a chance to look. Should I look?"

"Maybe later. What kind of a bundle was it? Was it, like, clothes?"

Oliver hesitated. His ears drooped. "I don't know. Sorry, Emma. He didn't hold it for very long. He just threw it. All the way into the center of the pond. Dash tried to go after it, but Gus said leave it." He paused. "It had a long handle."

A bundle with a handle? Emma bit her lip. *What could . . . wait!* "Was the handle, like, maybe a strap? Like on my handbag?"

"Yes!" said Oliver excitedly. "Yes, like that!"

That could make it Marcie's missing handbag, maybe with her mobile and her planner. Emma felt her chest tighten. "Okay. Then what?"

"Then Gus went to the shed, and he put the shovel inside, and I smelled something, but he wouldn't let me stay, and then the Frank man came."

"Wait. Frank was there?"

"He said he was looking for Gus, and he found him. He must be a smart human. Not a nice human, but smart. You have a hard time finding—"

"What did they talk about?" asked Emma quickly.

Oliver scratched his chin and then his ear. "I didn't understand it all. He was worried about not finding a thing, even though he could find Gus. He said they needed to stick together because of the Bert man. And Gus was worried about Marcie being dead, and then Frank made him shoo me away and they walked away, and I couldn't hear anything else. Sorry, Emma!"

"No, that's okay, Oliver." She hugged him. "You did great."

"I can show you where the shed is!" He barked. He also licked her chin. "It's close! Sort of. We can go now!" Oliver bounced over to the outside door. "Come on, Emma!"

Dash barked and Oliver barked back. "She is not!"

Emma was about to answer, but her mobile in her pocket vibrated. She swore under her breath and pulled it out. A new text lit up the screen. It was Pearl.

*Helen facing down uncles. Marcie's room.*

"Oh, sugar!" Emma stuffed her mobile into her pocket. "We'd better get up there."

Both she and Oliver took the stairs at a run.

The ground floor was bustling. They passed Tasha directing young men in work clothes where to put tables and chairs. Nobody even seemed to notice as Emma hoisted Oliver into her arms and ran up the main stairs. Well, she started out running. By the time she reached the first landing, it was more of a trot, and by the time she reached the top it was just short of a stumble. She put Oliver down and drew a ragged breath.

"They should put water bowls at the top of these stairs." Oliver shook himself. "You should tell them."

"Will do. Shortly." Emma gasped. "Right." She hurried down the hall as best she could, with Oliver bouncing beside her.

"What were you thinking!" The door to Marcie's room was open, and there was nothing to muffle Bert's shout.

The Cochranes were ranged across the room. Bert was standing all but toe to toe with Helen. Bert's calm had obviously deserted him. His face was flushed red and for a moment Emma was afraid he might raise his hand. Daphne was right beside her mother, and from the way Daphne was watching Bert, Emma guessed she thought so too. Pearl stood at her friend's shoulder, one hand jammed in her back pocket, ready, Emma realized, to pull out her mobile if needed.

Frank stood by the fireplace, watching the others with all the intensity of a football fan with a bet on the match.

Gus, on the other hand, looked like he was about to burst out laughing.

Oliver started to charge into the room, but Emma caught him by the collar, and pressed on him gently to sit. The last thing this family quarrel needed was a corgi invasion.

"I can't believe you did this without telling us!" shouted Bert.

"That I did it, or that Marcie did?" inquired Helen. "Because I didn't do anything except find the papers she had drafted."

"Well, I think it's bloody marvelous." Gus slid between her and Bert and shook Helen's hand. "Congratulations, and I'm sorry. For both of you." He touched Daphne's shoulder. "Bit of a white elephant you've won here, but—"

"Thanks, Gus," Helen said, uncertainly.

"Couldn't wait five minutes to start sucking up again, could you?" muttered Frank.

Now Gus did laugh, once, sharply. "Jealous?" With apologies to Ned, Emma thought he sounded positively giddy. "You should be. She did it, our big sister, didn't she? Pulled the rug right out from under all of us, and good for her! You hear that, Marcie?" he shouted toward the ceiling. "Good for you!"

Pearl and Emma looked at each other. Pearl tipped her hand toward her mouth in the universal sign for "Has he had one too many?" Pearl shrugged.

"I'm surprised to hear you so happy about it all," Bert said coldly. "After you went through all that trouble to make sure you'd inherit sooner rather than later."

The overflowing humor drained straight out of Gus's manner. "What?" he croaked.

"I think I was quite clear."

"No, you were not." Gus walked up to him. "You say that again."

"Will you all just stop it!" shouted Daphne.

What they all did then was stare at her, including Helen.

Daphne planted herself in front of her mother, clearly ready to block whatever might be coming in. "You want to know why Aunt Marcie left this place to me and Mum? This is why." She spread her arms to indicate all three of the brothers. "This, right here. This mess is your fault for being such a bunch of gits! Not Mum's, not Marcie's and not mine! Yours!"

"Daphne, I really don't think . . ." began Bert.

"And I really don't care!" she roared. "Come on, Mum. Pack up. We're getting out of here."

"You can't!" sputtered Bert. "Frank, will you explain to your daughter that we have to settle this?"

Frank raised both eyebrows and mouthed, *"Me?"*

"Unfortunately, Bert, Marcie already settled it," said Helen. She turned around. "Pearl, do you think there's room for Daphne and me at the King's Rest tonight?"

"I happen to know there is," said Pearl cheerfully. "Come on, Daph. I'll help you pack."

Helen nodded to the three brothers and followed the girls out. Emma did the same, only more awkwardly, and with Oliver trotting alongside.

"You want some help too?" she asked Helen when she caught up.

"Yes, thanks," she said.

Pearl and Daphne disappeared into one of the left-hand rooms. Helen opened a door directly across the hall. On the other side was a comfortable bedroom. The Victorian-era furniture made it feel a little overfull, but it still had a kind of bed-and-breakfast charm to it.

Helen hauled her suitcase out of the big standing wardrobe and dropped it on the four-poster. Emma unzipped it for her, and Helen pulled open the dresser drawers and started loading her clothes into the case.

Oliver nosed around the new room. "Ooo, what's that?" he muttered and went down on his belly so he could slide under the bed.

"Should you let him do that?" asked Helen.

"Probably not," sighed Emma. "But he needed a bath anyway."

Somebody knocked on the door. Emma glanced at Helen, and then went to open it.

It was Ned Giddy. He stepped tentatively into the room.

"We heard, that is, I've been sort of . . ." He gestured helplessly. "I got the short straw actually. I'm here to find out what's going on."

"Family squabble," said Helen tersely. "Nothing you need to worry about, just yet anyway."

"Right, right, of course." Ned rubbed his scalp. "Well, then. I've done my bit. But really, Helen, we just want to make sure you're all right."

Helen mustered a smile. It wasn't very enthusiastic, but it was genuine. "Thanks, Ned. Tell Tasha and John I appreciate it, and I'm sorry about all the fuss."

"Will do," he said briskly. "Right, then. Just show myself out." This he did by stepping backward and closing the door.

Emma opened her mouth.

"Emma, please don't ask me what we're going to do about the festival."

"I wasn't going to. I was just—"

Somebody knocked on the door again. Helen threw up her hands. The door opened, and Frank leaned in.

"Well, Frank," sighed Helen. "I assume you want to weigh in on all this?"

"Not really," he said. "I think it's a good idea you get out for a bit."

Helen pulled back, surprised. "You do?"

"Yes, I really do. With this news about the will and all, and all the uncertainty around what happened to Marcie, things are not going to be exactly peaceful around here for the next few days. You and Daphne are better off out of it."

"Thanks," said Helen softly.

"And who knows? Maybe I'll get myself out of bed and

meet you down there for one of Angelique's famous break-fasts. If that'd be okay?" he added.

"Yes, sure. If you want."

"Thanks." He paused, and held out his hand. "Friends?"

Helen hesitated. "All right. We can try anyway." She shook his hand. The smile she returned was small, but it was genuine.


AFTER FRANK LEFT, HELEN FINISHED PACKING IN A HURRY. Emma got the distinct feeling she wanted to make her escape before another interruption arrived.

Oliver crawled out from under the bed, sneezing mightily and looking sheepish. His normally white patches were now a mottled gray.

"Oh, it is so bath time for you, corgi me lad."

Oliver shivered and tried to look pitiful. Emma just shook her head.

"Ready in there?" called Daphne. Emma opened the door. Helen heaved her suitcase off the bed and all of them, including the very dusty Oliver, started down the hallway toward the front door.

"Can we stop for some takeaway?" Daphne hitched her bulky rucksack up on her shoulders. "Only I forgot to get any lunch."

"No worries," said Pearl as they started down the stairs. "I texted Ma. We're covered."

Down in the foyer, Gus was standing with Caite. They were whispering frantically at each other. Then, all at once, Caite looked up. Emma thought she was looking at them, but she wasn't. She was looking past them, above them in fact.

Emma twisted around to see Bert looking down from the second floor. Caite drew herself up like she was coming to attention. She put her hand on Gus's shoulder.

Gus turned, and he looked up as well, meeting Bert's gaze and not flinching at all. Frank came out of the shadowy hallway too, and stood next to Bert.

*Choosing sides?* wondered Emma.

Caite whispered something in Gus's ear. He nodded, and touched her hand. He straightened his shoulders and made a mocking bow toward his older brothers, complete with a sharp click of his heels. Then, Gus turned and followed Caite out the door.

Bert made a move like he was going to charge down the stairs, but Frank caught his arm.

"Don't," he said. "You'll only be making things worse."

Bert shook Frank off. "It doesn't matter. He'll be back; he just doesn't know it yet."

But Emma remembered Gus's expression just before he turned to follow Caite and found she wasn't so sure. Because that was the look of a man who finally realized there really might be such a thing as freedom.

# 45

. . . . . . . . . . .

PEARL SAID THAT ANGELIQUE HAD THEM COVERED AS FAR as dinner was concerned. To Emma, "covered" did not begin to describe it. What waited for them in the B&B's garden was a feast.

Angelique and Daniel had put up the Private Party sign at one of the big picnic tables in the garden. There was fresh plaice poached in tomato broth and chilies, coconut rice and beans, a dish of cabbage and carrots cooked with yet more chilies, and a pile of fried dumplings.

Genny was there too. "It's father-sons night at our house," she said. "Otherwise known as Martin and the boys get pizza and watch some movie with a lot of explosions while Mum gets the night off."

She brought a huge beetroot and fennel salad. "Since this time somebody else cooked the fish."

"I feel bad," said Emma as she pulled up a chair. "I didn't bring anything."

"You brought all the news," said Genny as she settled down at the table. "So spill."

"Oh, no," said Angelique firmly. "Not until after. Look at these girls." She gestured toward Pearl and Daphne. "They're practically fainting."

Emma found she was not in a mood to argue.

Oliver, of course got his bowl of kibble. He tried the fish, but politely declined, after the chilies made him sneeze, and shake his mouth, and paw his nose.

Emma tried very hard not to laugh. She failed.

Not to be left out, Daniel had decided to show off his own baking skills for the occasion. At the meal's finish, while Angelique set up the tea things, he produced a sticky toffee pudding so good that Emma announced she was going on strike until he gave her the recipe.

She was sorry when the last crumbs were scooped up and the cups refilled. Not because it was delicious, which it was, but because for a moment, she'd been able to set aside everything that had happened at the grange and simply be with friends. But now all her worries were starting to creep back in. She couldn't help wondering what was happening back at the grange tonight with Bert and Frank left to themselves inside that dark, silent house. She wondered where Gus was, and if he'd decided to come back or—and she could barely believe this was a real possibility—he had gone to stay with Caite.

And then there was the question of what Oliver had really discovered in the shed and how was she going to get in there to find out?

Daphne offered to help Daniel with the dishes. As they were all piling them into one of the B&B's bins, Helen drained her mug of tea.

"I think I'm going up to bed," she told them. "I could really use a minute's quiet. Thank you for the dinner. It was magnificent."

Everyone wished Helen good night. Daphne kissed her mother on the cheek and followed Daniel into the kitchen, carrying a stack of dessert plates.

"So." Angelique poured herself another cup of tea. "From what Pearl says, you all had an interesting day."

"That's one way to put it," said Pearl. She gestured toward Emma with her tea mug. "You first?"

Emma hesitated. Oliver, ever on the alert for her mood

changes, pawed at her jeans. Emma scooped him into her lap, and he snuggled down. Emma scritched his ears and was rewarded by a gigantic, and rather dog-breathful, yawn.

"Well," she began. "When we got there this morning, the family was in kind of a state—"

"A positive tizzy even," drawled Pearl. Emma waved her off.

"—because nobody could find Marcie's will. Turns out, she'd hired her own solicitor without telling the family. It further turns out she'd had a new will made just last year, and it left everything to Helen and Daphne."

"Wait," said Angelique. "I thought Daphne had turned the inheritance down."

"She did, but this will was made before she and Marcie had that conversation."

"Huh. Seems a bit backward," said Genny.

"Well, that would depend, wouldn't it?" said Angelique. "Is she actually trying to give the grange to somebody, or does she just want to keep it away from somebody else? Maybe Marcie meant the will as a temporary measure. Something she could do until she had a better solution."

"There's a thought," said Pearl. "Makes you wonder what happened last year."

"Well, we know one thing that did," said Emma. "Somebody started quietly selling some of the grange's more valuable antiques."

"That'll get the family knickers in a twist," said Genny. "How do we know this?"

"Marcie left the evidence with her solicitor, the one who drafted the will."

"Are you sure it wasn't Marcie who was selling things off?" asked Pearl. "And trying to hide it from her brothers? I mean, we've heard the grange was having money troubles."

"It's possible," said Emma. "But if that's true, then it means something changed in this balancing act Marcie had kept up for years."

"So we're back to what happened last year?"

"Well, something else that happened was a change in Gus's relationship status," said Pearl.

"Gus is seeing someone?" said Genny.

Emma nodded. "Gus is seeing the Hyphenated Caite."

Genny's eyes bulged as she tried to hold back a spit take. "Hyphenated Caite and *Gus*?"

"It's true," said Pearl. "There's pictures. At least one. And they left together today."

"Wow." Genny shook her head. "Well, you know what? Good for them. I mean, she's an absolutely awful person, but he's nobody's prize either. Maybe they'll take the edges off each other."

"Two wrongs making a right?" suggested Pearl with exaggerated innocence.

"I'd agree with you, Genny, except"—Emma paused, trying to collect her words—"I'm starting to wonder whether they might be working together."

"What do you mean?" asked Angelique.

"What we did not find was Marcie's handbag, her appointment planner or her mobile."

"That's a lot to go missing," said Genny.

"What has also gone missing is a whole month's worth of Marcie's appointments off her computer, and we know that during that time she met at least once with an agent from Christie's real estate."

"Real estate?" exclaimed Angelique. "She was going to sell some of the land?"

"She was going to sell off the land," said Pearl. "And the house. The lot, or at least most of it."

"Impossible. Bert would never let her," said Genny immediately.

"How could he stop her?" asked Pearl. "The place was hers."

"Yeah, tell Bert that." Genny waved her mug at Pearl. "Or Frank," she added.

"Maybe she tried," murmured Angelique. "Maybe that's why she's dead."

Genny pulled a face. "Oh, lord. You're right. I'd believe that as a motive for either one of them."

"I think it was a motive for Caite and Gus too," said Emma. "I think Caite deleted the information on Marcie's computer and stole her handbag so no one would find out about those meetings with the estate agent."

"But why would she?" asked Genny. "What could it matter that Marcie wanted to sell?"

"Because," said Pearl slowly, "everybody, including Gus, thought Gus was supposed to inherit—"

"So if Marcie was going to sell the grange, that would have been that," said Angelique.

"And if Gus had found out about the sale, he would have had a very strong motive for murder," added Pearl.

Emma swallowed. "And so would Caite."

# 46

· · · · · · · · · · · ·

"OH . . . MY," BREATHED GENNY.

"But why would Caite get involved with something like this?" Angelique frowned and swirled the dregs of her tea. "It's a terrible risk. I know she didn't like Marcie, but despite what they tell you on the BBC, literary society politics seldom lead to murder."

"How about for revenge?" said Emma.

"Revenge?" said Genny.

Emma nodded. "Caite blames the Cochrane family for her father's suicide. And she might be right."

"Wait, what?" said Genny. "I hadn't heard this one."

Angelique nodded. "Her father, Archie, was a lawyer and he found out that Richard Cochrane had been profiting off some shady deals in the City," Emma told them. "Archie made the mistake of saying something about it. Richard took exception and started a whispering campaign. Archie lost his firm and had to accept a position out of town. He never recovered."

"That's awful!" Genny looked down into her tea. "Honestly, I never thought I'd be sorry for the Hyphenated Caite, but that really is too bad."

"It's also a motive."

"I can see it," said Genny. "She seduces poor Gus—"

"Ew!" exclaimed Pearl.

"Needs must," Genny reminded her. "And she thinks he's going to inherit the property, right? So she does what she has to, and when she's got him, she plans Marcie's murder. She makes it look like suicide, so Gus will be able to inherit right away—"

"And also not suspect her," said Pearl.

"Right," said Genny. "It also removes the possibility of a messy inquest or risk of a police investigation. Living well in the house that used to belong to the people who destroyed your family is the best revenge."

"Look, I've got to say, as a motive, it's nice and simple," mused Genny. "But we can't be sure it was Gus. None of the brothers would want Marcie to sell. Partly because they love to boast about the ancestral home, but really because they couldn't be sure she would share the profits."

Pearl set her mug down. "I hadn't thought of that. She could have just tossed them all out the door and gone off to St. Kitts with the cash."

"I don't think Marcie would do such a thing," said Angelique.

"But what would the brothers think?" put in Genny.

Angelique nodded. "That would be the question, wouldn't it?"

"And there's signs that Marcie was becoming disillusioned with the Cochranes as a whole," said Pearl. "Not only did she know somebody was stealing from the estate—"

"If she wasn't the one doing the stealing," said Genny.

"Right, but say she wasn't. Say she found out that one of the brothers was. She was also digging into the old accidents—Stewart Cochrane's boating accident and her own parents' car accident. Maybe she found out, or thought she found out, that they were something more than accidents. I found two ledgers in her office, with press clippings and reports and all that, about both accidents."

"That's a stretch," said Angelique. "I never heard anybody say anything about old Mr. Cochrane's accident being anything other than a bad combination of a fast car and Irish whiskey."

"Yeah, but things can get covered up," said Pearl. "And the Cochranes are good at that."

"As everybody knows," added Genny.

"So, maybe Marcie did find out something," Pearl went on. "And maybe she decided she doesn't want any part of this legacy anymore."

"That I could believe," said Angelique. "The straw that broke the camel's back."

"It's a good theory," said Pearl. "But honestly, if it's any one of the brothers, I'm betting it's Bert. He's the long-term planner, and family is everything to him. Well, okay, family reputation is everything."

"Important distinction, that," agreed Angelique.

"And Bert's the one who pushed to get the death declared a suicide as fast as possible," said Emma. "And if he'd found out from the family solicitor there was no will that they knew about, he'd know he had a chance to inherit at least some of it. At the very least, he would have assumed that he would be able to bully Gus more easily than he'd been able to bully Marcie."

"But we need to think about Frank too, don't we?" said Genny. "He's always been in Bert's shadow. Wants to be the big man, but he's never quite been able to make it work. Maybe this would be his chance. Save the house for himself and his whole family."

"Possibly," said Emma. "Or maybe he's helping whoever did it, and plans on turning them in later."

"That'd be a risky strategy," said Pearl.

"Well, Frank's not the smartest of that bunch," said Angelique. "He's spent years believing that Helen is going to come back to him." She shifted in her chair.

Genny sucked in a sudden breath.

"What is it?" asked Pearl.

"Well, I hate to say it, but that's another possibility."

"Oh, you are not thinking it was *Helen*?" said Pearl.

"Of course I'm not," said Genny quickly. "But other people might. Maybe she decided she wanted the place for herself. And she was Marcie's best friend. That makes her one of the few people who might have known the will was already written in her favor." She paused, and went on more slowly. "Then, when Daphne turns down the inheritance, Helen decides it's too much to just throw away. I'm not saying I believe it," Genny added. "But if and when this goes to the police, they're going to be looking right at her."

"What do you think, Emma?" asked Pearl.

Emma laid her hand on Oliver's warm back. He was asleep, his nose tucked under one paw.

"I think it's weird," she said.

"Weird how?" asked Angelique.

"None of this stuff adds up. Not really. We know Marcie died. We know her body was moved. We know that the way she was found looked like suicide. But the latch on the window was broken, maybe tampered with. And these ledgers with all the information about the other important accidents in the Cochrane history are left where anybody can find them—"

"Thank you very much," said Pearl.

"Sorry. Bad choice of words. Add that to all the things that went missing, with Marcie's handbag, and the schedule on her computer. I mean, for a situation that's supposed to look like suicide, really it couldn't look much more like murder if you tried."

"So what do you think happened?" asked Genny.

"I don't know," said Emma gloomily. "I wish I did. But I don't."

Pearl pushed her tea mug away from her. "I've just had a very nasty idea."

"Well, out with it," said Angelique.

"The bank theft, from the du Maurier society . . . could Caite have done it herself?"

"Easily, assuming she told me the truth about what happened," said Emma.

"So, what if that was part of the setup? To make Marcie's death look like suicide?"

"To make it seem that since the estate was in so much trouble, Marcie robbed the literary society, and when that wasn't enough, she fell into despair and killed herself?"

"After destroying the evidence of her theft," Pearl pointed out.

"It's a stretch," said Emma. "But I mean, maybe."

"It wouldn't be that hard," said Pearl. "Caite follows her home the night of the murder, kills her, and then she puts her up at the window and gets out of there."

"With or without Gus's help?" asked Genny.

"Either way," said Pearl. "We already know she could get in and out of that house on her own."

"I thought you were Team Bert."

Pearl shrugged. "A girl can change her mind, can't she?"

"Marcie was a pretty substantial person," Angelique reminded her. "I can't see Caite moving her body on her own. And somebody cleaned up the trail."

*And then hid the murder weapon in the shed and tossed the handbag in the pond,* thought Emma. Assuming that was what Oliver saw happen. It was certainly possible.

"Then she did it with Gus's help," said Pearl. "Gus finally wanted to be able to lord it over his brothers, and Caite wanted to take everything away from the family that destroyed hers."

"But wait," said Angelique. "If Caite was there that night, why not take the handbag and all then? Why wait until the next day?"

"Maybe she got interrupted? Or she didn't think about it?" Pearl shrugged. "I mean, there was kind of a lot going on."

*There's a lot going on now.* Emma drummed her fingers against the table. "We're missing something," she said. "What we've got now doesn't add up."

Then, she yawned, loudly enough that Oliver kicked and woke himself up with a snort.

"What? What?"

"Oh, gosh." Emma covered her mouth. "Sorry!"

"Well, that says it all," said Angelique. "It's past time we all got some rest."

"But, Ma, it's not even nine o'clock . . ." began Pearl.

"No buts. If you feel moved to go over this . . . evidence all night, that's fine, but Emma needs to get home. No one is going to do anyone any good if they're falling asleep in their tea."

"I'm afraid you're right," said Emma sheepishly.

"I'll take you back." Genny got to her feet. "I was thinking of heading home myself. I'm sure most of the explosions are over by now and the worst of the junk food is all cleaned up."

"Thanks, Genny." Emma set Oliver down on the floor. "Let me just go say good night to Daphne."

Emma, with Oliver following, headed for the kitchen, but before she got there, she saw Daphne, sitting just outside the gate, arms around her knees, staring out at the car park. Oliver whined and wagged, and Emma pushed open the door.

Oliver bounced up to Daphne. Daphne rubbed his head, absently.

"I didn't see you there," said Emma. "Um, I guess you heard all that?"

"Some of it," said Daphne. "You know, when I asked you to find out what really happened to Aunt Marcie, I never thought it'd go like this."

"I'm sorry." Emma sat down beside her.

"I mean, I really did think maybe Bert did something, yeah? But I didn't think there'd be all this circling round and wondering and being afraid. And I really never thought I'd have to worry that somebody might think it was me and Mum."

"We'll figure it out," said Emma.

Oliver put his nose on Daphne's knee. "Will you?" she breathed. "You promise, old chum?"

"Emma promises," whined Oliver. "That's what's important."

Emma sighed and rubbed his head. She just wished she felt half as sure.

# 47

GENNY DROPPED EMMA AND OLIVER OFF AT NANCARROW with another stern admonishment that she should go straight to bed.

"I mean it, Emma," Genny said firmly. "No Marpleing after nine p.m."

"Marpleing?"

"You know what I mean."

"I do, and I think I should be worried about that."

When they got inside, Emma dropped all the ledgers on her kitchen table and stared at them. She reached out to flip one open. Oliver, who evidently decided that he should be acting *in corgi parentis*, bonked her calf.

"Nope, Emma," he said sternly. "Bed. You need to rest. Bed now." He bonked her again.

Emma laughed and threw up her hands. "All right! All right! Bed!"

But first there was a very long, very hot bath and a good curl up in bed with the computer and Season 3 of The Great British Bake Off.

She was asleep before they announced the winner of the signature bake.

* * *

WEDNESDAY WAS NOT A TEA SERVICE DAY. SO NORMALLY
Emma let herself sleep in until the luxurious hour of seven
a.m. Today, however, habit and leftover worries shook her
awake at six.

After she let Oliver out into the garden, Emma decided
she'd earned herself a proper breakfast and set about fixing
a genuine meal—a piping hot cheese and herb omelet with
buttered toast and marmalade and, yes, sausages for both
her and Oliver. As she sat down with her plate and a cup of
her favorite second-flush Darjeeling tea, she pulled the first
of the Truscott Grange ledgers off the pile and opened it to
the screen shot of the silver tea set.

Emma took a bite of toast, and savored the bittersweet
marmalade. She also squinted at the bid amount and the
sale date for the tea set. She groped for a pencil from the jar
she kept on the table, and stuck it behind her ear, just in
case she needed to make notes.

Then she flipped open the folder of bank statements and
started leafing through them.

Oliver slid back in through the doggie door and trotted
over.

"What're you doing, Emma?" He put his front paws up
on the coffee table so he could see better. "Are you Marpleing? Because Genny said you shouldn't."

"I'm not Marpleing. I'm accounting."

"Oh. That's all right then."

"And there's sausages."

"Hurray!" Oliver yipped and made a beeline for his
kibble bowl.

Emma chuckled and went back to flipping through the
account pages. Marcie had been one for notes too, and
clearly she hadn't believed in relying solely on electronic
bank statements. She'd religiously printed out her records,
and just about every deposit or withdrawal had some kind
of annotation.

*Rent, W.F*
*Rent, A.G.I*
*Frank, monthly*
*Gus, monthly*
*Bert, monthly*

So. The brothers were all on allowances. But evidently they weren't shy about coming around and asking for more.

*Frank, clothing*
*Gus, car repair*
*Bert, greens fees*
*Bert, club fees*
*Bert, tailor*
*Bert . . .*

Emma stuffed another forkful of omelet in her mouth and went and got her calculator. Oliver plunked himself down beside her chair. "You're going to be here awhile, aren't you?"

"'Fraid so." Emma rubbed his belly. "There's numbers to crunch."

"Are they good numbers or bad numbers?"

"They're less confusing than the humans who made them."

"Oh, well." Oliver rolled over onto his back. "That is good."

Emma smiled and gave his belly another rub for good luck, and went back to crunching.

At ten thirty, Emma's phone rang.

"Yeah?" She stuck the phone between her ear and her shoulder.

"I hope you've got something good," said Constance.

"You're the one calling me," she reminded the detective.

"Only because you haven't called me."

"Sorry about that."

"You're forgiven. If you've got something I can use with my boss."

Emma surveyed her tidy piles of bank statements. "I don't know."

"Can you be more specific?"

Emma leaned back and stretched her legs out. Oliver had fallen into a post-sausage nap sprawled out on his back.

"Okay. Here goes." Emma told Constance about the marked-up copy of *Rebecca*, and the solicitor's card, and the ledgers with all the articles and reports about the earlier tragic deaths that had lead to the grange's changing hands. She told her about the visit to the solicitor's, and about the will, and how Helen and Daphne were set to inherit the grange. She told her about the blanked-out appointment calendar on Marcie's computer, and Gus down by the lake, tossing what might have been the missing handbag into the pond.

"There is something going on with that lot," said Constance decidedly.

"Is that your professional opinion?"

"It is. I just wish there was something I could do about it."

"Well, we're not done yet," Emma told her.

"Oh?"

"Yeah, it seems somebody's been selling off some of the grange's antiques. And Marcie kept a record of it, but she wasn't doing the selling."

"You're sure?" Emma could picture Constance sitting up a little straighter.

"Fairly sure. I'm staring at her bank statements, and the grange's bank statements, interestingly, and I've got a list of what's gone missing and—"

"Do I want to know how you got all that?"

"Helen Dalgliesh hired me to act as her financial representative, and since she's one of the estate executors, as well as a legatee, I get to look at the estate accounts."

"Are you serious?"

"Thought you'd be pleased."

"Oh, I am, I am. Very much so. Do go on, legally authorized representative person." There was a rustle and a creak, like Constance was leaning back in her chair.

"Well, you know, as her financial representative, I'm not supposed to be telling you any of this without permission—"

"Emma, did I mention time's getting on and I had to call you? Not in the mood for teasing."

"Right. Sorry. Well, the antiques were all sold online. I've got the approximate dates. But unless she had an account we haven't found yet, the money from the sale was never deposited, either in her personal account or in the estate account. So where'd it go?"

"I am breathless with anticipation."

"I don't think it was Marcie who was selling off the antiques at all. I think Marcie caught somebody else doing it, and she kept the records as proof."

"Why?"

"Just in case that other person decided to kick up a fuss when she told them she was selling the whole estate. Remember, Marcie was in control. She didn't have to have anybody's permission to sell, and she didn't have to share the profits. The brothers are all living off their allowances, and handouts, and they all have very expensive habits. If their income from the estate went away, they would all be in serious trouble. Marcie had to know that."

"Phew. That is a serious motivating factor, that is."

"Money makes the world go round," sighed Emma.

"Well, keep digging, but—" Constance hesitated. "Maybe be a little discreet, all right?"

"Why?" asked Emma. "Is something wrong?"

"Nothing I can't handle, but just . . . be careful."

"Because that's not going to make me worried at all," Emma muttered.

"Sorry. Listen, I have to go." Emma heard paper rustling. "I'll give you a call around eight tomorrow, all right?"

Emma agreed, they said goodbye and rang off. Beside her, Oliver snorted in his sleep and pawed anxiously at something. Emma chuckled, and rubbed his tummy again.

Then she thought of something, picked her mobile up again and dialed.

"Trevena Taxi." Brian answered on the second ring.

"Good Morning, Brian, I thought you'd be out with the spanners and things."

"Wish I was, but paperwork waits for no man." She heard the sound of paper flapping and she pictured him waving a stack of invoices by the phone. "What's going on? You're not going to back out on me again?"

"No, no, I will be there. Friday night. Six sharp."

"That's good, because, some people are saying it's getting pretty tense up at the grange."

Emma's eyebrows raised. "Some people?"

"I was grabbing a bite at the Roundhead, and ran into Ned Giddy."

*Villages.* She sighed. "Well, yeah, he's right. There's some special drama brewing. And that's why I'm calling."

"Oh?"

"I need a favor. It's pretty huge."

"At your service, ma'am."

"Can I borrow the car?"

# 48

AT LEAST, EMMA REFLECTED, SHE WAS USED TO BEING UP
with the sun.

Emma had arranged a short-term rental agreement with
Brian over the phone yesterday, and he even agreed to show
up with the taxi at her place first thing in the morning to
drive her down to the garage.

She greeted him with scones.

"Is this a thank-you, or a bribe to keep me from asking
too many questions?"

"You're learning," she said. "And I'll tell you later."

Brian shrugged. He also ate an orange and vanilla scone
in two bites.

Now, she was driving down the narrow roads in the
Mini with the top down. She had to admit, having Cornwall's early morning air in her face was almost as good as
an extra cup of coffee. Almost.

Oliver, of course, was in his element.

"Faster, Emma!" he barked from the passenger seat.

"Constance will arrest us if I do that!"

"What's arrest?"

"Trust me, we don't want to find out!"

Although, technically Constance could arrest them for

what they were about to do now too. Because, technically, they didn't have permission to be here at the grange, and they really didn't have permission to be poking around in the (locked) shed.

THE GRANGE WAS DARK. EMMA TENSED UP AS SHE SLOWLY drove around back, like she was trying to will the car to tiptoe.

"I left my briefcase, I wanted to come back for it, sorry," she whispered to herself. "I left my briefcase, I wanted to come back for it, sorry . . ."

She eased the Mini Cooper into the little muddy niche beside the garage where it would be harder to see from the house, grabbed her rucksack and unbuckled Oliver.

"Okay, Oliver, we're being stealthy, right?" she whispered. "I need you to show me where that shed is."

"Yes, yes!" Oliver huffed. "It's this way . . ." He cast around for a moment. "No. This way." He took off at a steady and, Emma hoped, confident trot.

Emma crossed her fingers, slung her rucksack across her shoulders and followed.

OLIVER'S PATH TOOK THEM AROUND THE EDGES OF THE garden and into the walnut grove and the tangled bit of "wilderness" on the far side. They were about halfway through when Emma heard a loud rattling. She ducked instinctively. An ink-black crow swooped right overhead, cawing.

"Hey!" Emma yelped, and then bit her lip.

"That crow is extremely rude," sniffed Oliver. "You watch out for him, Emma."

"Can you try to make friends with the wildlife next time?"

"A corgi always tries!" he insisted. "You need to talk to the crows."

*No, thank you,* Emma sighed.

All at once, Oliver broke into a run. "Here, Emma! Here!"

Emma hurried to keep up. They were on a dirt path and the shed stood right at its edge. It was a weathered wooden building not much bigger than a walk-in closet with a battered tin roof. A rusted padlock on an equally rusted hasp held the door shut.

Emma tugged it once, just in case. The lock rattled, but didn't open.

"What do we do now?" asked Oliver.

"I need you to keep watch for me."

"Yes!" Oliver growled. "The crow might come back!"

"That too. But I was thinking more about any of the humans from the house."

"Oh, yes. Of course." Oliver turned his back to her, planting himself square in the center of the path.

When Emma was growing up, her family had lived in a row house that dated from early in the twentieth century. One day, she managed to accidentally lock herself in the loo and lose the key down the drain. Her mother, who believed in professionals, had wanted to call a locksmith. Her father, who was a bit tightfisted, had slipped a butter knife under the door, and talked Emma through the process of dismantling the hinges.

Her brother, Henry, had looked on, all the while predicting this could only lead to trouble.

The experience taught Emma two important lessons. The first was never put the door key on the side of the sink. The second was that doors were not as solid as people thought. You just had to look at them the right way.

Emma squinted at the padlock hasp. She unzipped her rucksack and pulled out the brand-new screwdriver kit, which her friend Rose up in London had given her as a housewarming gift, and the oil can, which was only about a quarter full. Nancarrow had a lot of squeaking hinges.

"Now then," Emma whispered to the hasp's screws. "You'd best come along quietly . . ."

It took all the remaining oil, and a whole lot of cursing. And there was a pause to call back Oliver because the rude crow had put in another appearance, and this time it brought friends. For a minute Emma was afraid they might try reenacting a scene out of *The Birds*, and found herself wondering if the shed roof would be solid enough to keep them out.

But the crows evidently decided it wasn't worth the trouble. They took themselves off in a flurry of wings and what Oliver assured her was very rude cawing. Without the distraction, Emma was able to get the last screw undone with only a moderate amount of swearing.

The hasp came away from the shed wall. Emma tucked it into her pocket along with the screws and opened the door.

Oliver zoomed straight past her.

"Here!" he barked. "It's here! Right here!"

"Shhh! Oliver!"

"Sorry, Emma."

The morning was brightening around them, but the inside of the shed was pitch-black. Emma had planned for this and fished her pocket torch out of the rucksack.

Oliver was scrabbling at a tangle of old shovels, spades and gardening forks. Emma took a steadying breath, and stepped inside. She shone the torch down to where Oliver was, and the beam caught a gleam of brighter silver among the wooden handles and dirt-encrusted blades. Emma tiptoed closer and leaned in.

It was a golf club. Rusty patches stained the steel handle. *It'd have to be something heavy, that's for sure.* Constance's words came back to her *Or something with a handle, so they could swing it. A cricket bat, maybe . . .*

Emma made herself point the torch down closer to the floor. The club had a round, brown, blobby handle, or foot, or whatever the technical term was for the bottom bit that you actually hit the ball with.

*Did that make it a wood?* Emma asked herself.

*We'll let the experts work that out,* she answered herself, and reached for her mobile. All at once, Oliver whipped around and zoomed back out the door.

"Oliver!" On pure reflex, Emma darted after him.

Oliver was bouncing up and down to say hello to Dash. Evidently, in his excitement, he'd forgotten about being stealthy, or about keeping a lookout for humans from the house.

Bert was standing in the middle of the path. He was dressed in a thin black T-shirt, running shorts and high-end trainers. He was breathing hard and sweat gleamed on his forehead.

"Well, well." He smiled. "What's all this, then?"

Emma remembered her carefully rehearsed line about her briefcase. *So much for that idea.*

"Erm. Sorry . . ." she began.

"Turns out Dash is good for something after all. Led me right here. Maybe you can let me know what kind of treat he should get."

Bert brushed past her to examine the spot where the hasp used to be.

"A little light breaking and entering to start the day, Emma?" he inquired.

"Yeah, well, this does not look good, I know."

"It looks like somebody's in a spot of trouble, if you ask me."

"Well, yes and no," said Emma. "You see, I've just talked to Detective Brent . . ."

"Oh, good," said Bert. "Did you tell her about the part where you're trespassing?"

Emma closed her mouth.

"And breaking and entering." He shook his head. "And, what else?" He looked around them. "Maybe you were thinking about planting evidence?" His dark eyes gleamed. "Oh, wait, I've got a better one! Planting evidence with the cooperation of Detective Brent, with whom you've just been talking!"

Emma's heart thumped. "You've got to be kidding me."

"Maybe." Bert's smile broadened. "But maybe not. After all, you are on my property, and you did break into my shed. And you were the one who pointed out this does not look good."

"Actually, it's Helen's property now," Emma reminded him, and herself.

This fact did not seem to worry Bert at all. "That has yet to be conclusively determined," he said. "You know, I've been talking to people about you, Ms. Reed, and that business last year with Victoria Roberts." Bert took two steps forward. Oliver stopped his frisking with Dash and bounded over to Emma's side. He put up his ears signaling with his whole body that he was on high alert.

"Now," Bert went on pleasantly, "I don't know what kind of stories you've been telling Helen and Daphne, and frankly, I don't care if you get a kick out of playing Nancy Drew or Miss Marple or Sherlock bloody Holmes. But you do not do it on my land, or with my family, or I will see you in court, where you will get to find out exactly what kind of story I can spin. Understand?"

Oliver growled. Emma nudged him with her leg, silently willing him to calm down.

"Yes," she said to Bert. "I understand."

"Good." All Bert's cheerful urbanity returned as if he'd suddenly thrown a switch. "Then I'll walk you back."

With Bert beside her the whole way, Emma walked toward the house. Bert kept a half step behind her, just at the edge of her peripheral vision. Which set her teeth, and her nerves, on edge.

She was pretty sure he knew that.

It was a relief to see her little red Mini. Emma boosted Oliver into the back, climbed into the driver's seat and closed the door.

Bert leaned down and rested both elbows on the doorframe.

"Now," he said pleasantly, "unless you're with somebody else from the festival, I don't want to see you, or that damned dog, on this property again, all right?" He tapped the doorframe twice as he straightened up. "Have a nice day."

With Bert standing and watching, Emma started the Mini, and backed and turned until she was pointed to the drive and headed toward the main road.

She didn't look in the rearview. She knew he was still there.

PEARL, ANGELIQUE AND GENNY WERE ALL IN THE KING'S Rest kitchen when Emma got there. Breakfast service was under way, not to mention the prep for tomorrow's tea service. Oliver had spotted Fergus the Irish setter in the B&B's garden, so she opened the gate to let him out to say hello.

"Where've you been?" demanded Angelique as Emma hung her bag on the hook beside the door. "We were getting worried."

Emma collapsed onto the kitchen stool, planted her elbows on the counter and her face on her hands. "I've been out making an enormous mistake."

"You went and bought that car, didn't you?" said Genny. "I told you . . ."

"That was not the mistake," mumbled Emma.

"Then what was?" asked Angelique.

Emma looked toward the door. "Are Helen and Daphne down yet?"

Angelique shook her head. "Not yet."

"Okay. I went up to the grange."

"On your own?" exclaimed Pearl. "What for?"

Emma sighed. "I thought I'd found the murder weapon."

"*What?* Why didn't you tell me!" cried Pearl.

"Or me!" added Genny indignantly.

Angelique poured a mug of tea and put it down in front of Emma.

"Thanks." Emma took a long swallow. "I didn't tell you because I wasn't sure." *Oliver's not right every time.* "And because somebody might have moved it, and because you would have wanted to come with me and you would've gotten in trouble too." *And I couldn't have you around while I needed to talk to Oliver . . .*

"Oh, don't tell me you got caught," said Pearl.

"By Uncle Bert." Emma took another swallow of tea.

"Oh . . . sugar." Genny put a hand on her shoulder.

"Yeah," agreed Emma. "He threatened to have me arrested for trespassing, and breaking and entering."

"He can't," said Pearl.

"And to accuse me of planting evidence, with DCI Brent's help."

"Oh—" began Genny.

"Sugar," finished Emma. "Yeah. He told me not to come back. At all."

Pearl leaned back against the counter and shook her head. "I hate to say it, Emma, but that is rather bad."

"Yeah, I'd noticed."

"What are you going to do?" asked Angelique.

Emma watched the steam rising from her tea for a long moment, "We've got to come up with something else, something convincing that Constance really can take to her boss."

"And fast," said Angelique. "If I was Bert, I'd be making sure the evidence is in the bottom of the pond with Marcie's handbag."

"Yeah," said Emma gloomily. "I've thought of that."

"Well, we've got a lot," said Pearl. "We just have to work out how it all fits together."

"And I know where to start," announced Genny. "If Emma's right, somebody's been selling antiques out of the grange. And that means we need . . ."

"David and Charles!" they all said together.

# 49

. . . . . . . . . . . .

EMMA WANTED TO TALK TO DAPHNE AND HELEN. SHE wanted to lose herself for a couple of hours in the normalcy of baking scones and doing the other prep work for tomorrow's tea service. But Bert's calm, cheerful threats had left her rattled and angry. She was not going to give him any extra time to make trouble, if she could avoid it. So she grabbed her bag, whistled for Oliver and headed out down the street.

The shingle over Vintage Style was painted with a motorcycle with a fedora hanging off the handlebar. It was still well before opening time, but Emma knew the Kemps were always in early. When she pushed on the handle, the door swung open smoothly, ringing the string of bells overhead.

"Mar-ooow!" The shop's big orange cat, Cream Tangerine, rose to all fours on the wooden counter and glowered at them. Well, at Oliver specifically, as Oliver plunged in ahead of Emma, zipping around like he wanted to be everywhere at once.

Back in the day, the shop had been a dry goods store. It still had the long wooden counter where fabric and ribbons would have been measured and cut. Drawers and cubbyholes lined the wall behind it. Each cubby held a single antique: a glass-shaded lamp, a lacquered jewelry box, a spectacularly tacky canalware pot or a vintage stuffed elephant on wheels. A large sign on the counter read SEE SOMETHING YOU LIKE? JUST ASK FOR ASSISTANCE! WE ARE HERE TO HELP.

"Be right there!" called a man's voice from the back.

"It's me, David!" Emma called back.

"Hello, Cat!" Oliver reared onto his hind legs and craned his neck to try to see up to the countertop.

Whatever the cat said in reply made Oliver huff, "Cats." He dropped back onto all fours and continued his very important investigation of the shop.

"Good morning, Emma!" David strode out from the back office and gave her a warm hug. Oliver, of course, had to come over at once for a pat and a chin rub. David, of course, obliged, and did not seem at all distressed at slightly muddy corgi paws on his neat trousers. "How are you both doing? Charles?" he called back over his shoulder. "Emma's here!"

"And she'll understand I'm busy!" came the curt reply.

"Impossible." David waved dismissively.

David was a stylish little man with sparse white hair and an unapologetically flamboyant manner. Today, he wore a green sports coat and white turtleneck with a white pocket square and baggy tweed trousers. He and his husband, Charles, had become two of Emma's best friends in Trevena.

"So, is there something I can help you with? Oh, you know, I just found the *dearest* little Blue Italian pot for your collection . . ."

"Actually, I came to see if I could get some information."

"Information?" David raised both bushy white eyebrows. "I am intrigued."

"And, erm, maybe we could go into the office? It's . . . kind of delicate."

"I am intrigued." David crooked two fingers. "Come along."

The office was tidy in a very old-fashioned kind of way.

All the furniture was wooden, including the file cabinets. The decorations on the walls were mostly framed maps, with the exception of one very strange picture. It was a black-and-white photo of a pale man in a skimpy bathing suit, stretched out on his belly on the seat of a vintage motorcycle.

"The fastest man alive," said Charles, without looking up from his screen.

"Sorry?" Emma blinked.

Charles swiveled his wooden desk chair around. He was a tall man, with a somewhat long and horsey face. Where David might turn on a bit of a flamboyant act for customers, or just because he was feeling puckish, Charles was never anything but his own, slightly dour self.

"You were wondering about the photo."

"How'd you know?"

"Because everybody does. It's Rollie Free, setting the world speed record on a Vincent Black Shadow motorcycle, 1948. It made him the fastest man alive."

Emma peered at the picture. "Oh! The Black Lightning, like on your sign."

"Got it in one," said David. "We have a bit of history with that make of motorcycle, Charles and I."

"Didn't you tell me once Charles kidnapped you on his motorcycle?"

Charles coughed. He also moved Cream Tangerine off one of the chairs at a round table that took up the corner of the office not occupied by desks or filing cabinets.

"So, Emma, what can we do for you?" David sat in the other chair with Cream Tangerine cradled in his arm. He proceeded to gently stroke her back and ears.

"I've married a Bond villain," Charles muttered.

"And you love me for it," replied David. "You were saying, Emma?"

Oliver, of course, was not going to be left out of the proceedings. He trotted over and pawed her knees. "Up, Emma? Please."

The cat yawned.

"Ignore the cat," said Oliver. "She's rude."

"Of course she is," murmured Emma as she gathered him up onto her lap. "She's a cat."

"I'm sorry?" said David.

"Um, nothing. Sorry. Um . . . I guess you know about what's been going on at the grange?"

Oliver put his chin on the table and twitched his ears at the cat.

Tangerine, very pointedly, looked away.

Husband and husband exchanged a meaningful glance. "Well, there has been a lot of talk," said David.

"Don't tell me you're involved in all that mess, Emma?" asked Charles.

"Just helping Helen and Daphne," Emma told them. "There's some question with the accounts, and the inventory."

David cocked his head skeptically at Emma. "What sorts of questions?"

Oliver stretched his neck out as far as he could, keeping his whole attention on the cat. Tangerine stared at him. Oliver huffed.

"Well, that's part of what I wanted to talk to you about," said Emma. "Have either of you heard anything about Marcie Cochrane selling off some of the antiques from the grange?"

"Well—" began David.

All at once, Oliver yipped. Tangerine squeaked, and leapt off her owner's lap.

Oliver pulled his chin back and let his jaw drop open, panting happily.

"Oliver!" scolded Emma. "Now *that* was rude."

"I'm sorry, Emma!" Oliver looked up at her with his big brown eyes. "Really!"

Emma sighed. She also kissed his nose. "Sorry," she said to David. "He's usually very well behaved, which is good because I'm clearly a terrible disciplinarian."

"You're not, Emma!" barked Oliver.

"Oh, no worries, no worries." David brushed at his shirt.

"I'll give Tangerine some extra chicken at dinner. She'll get over it."

"The cat gets chicken, Emma," said Oliver. "You should listen to your friends about how to feed your . . ."

Emma did put Oliver on the floor. Oliver was about to slip under Emma's chair, but he clearly got a look at the Tangerine, who had flattened herself under David's seat, and he decided a strategic retreat might be in order.

Emma folded her hands on the tabletop. "I'm sorry about this, guys. But I wouldn't be asking if it wasn't important."

"Well—" began David again.

"Client confidentiality," snapped Charles.

"No," said David firmly. "Marcie never did."

"So if it wasn't Marcie, then who was it?" asked Emma.

Charles grimaced. "Not very subtle, are we?"

Emma shook her head.

David contemplated her for a long moment, like she was a vintage bit of glassware with just the tiniest little crack in the side. "There's been a rumor running about that Marcie's death might not have been a suicide, no matter what Bert's been telling people."

"Yeah, I've heard that," said Emma.

The men gazed at each other. Emma could practically feel the thrum of the wordless communication passing between them. Finally, Charles sighed.

"Someone from the grange did come to us," he said. "And they did ask for help to sell some vintage items, including a magnificent silver tea set. But quietly. We were happy to help, and it looked like everything was going fine, until it came down to the paperwork."

"How was that a problem?" asked Emma.

"Well, my dear," said David. "You may not realize this, but some people try to sell us antiques that strictly speaking aren't theirs."

Emma laid her hand on her chest. "I'm shocked, sir, shocked!"

"I'm sure," drawled Charles. "But where it gets especially frustrating is some of them try to use our shop because we're old friends of the family, and they assume we won't ask awkward questions."

David folded his arms across his chest, "But, as it happens, it's a dangerous game, isn't it? If it does turn out that those items didn't belong to the seller, or if the seller didn't have permission from their family, say, and we don't have the paperwork to cover our personal backsides, well, it just gets bad for everybody, doesn't it?"

"Yeah, I can see that," agreed Emma. "And I take it this person was not able to provide the paperwork."

"As it turned out, no. They assured us they would sort it, but they left and never came back."

"Did they say why they were selling the stuff?"

"Well, it was indicated that the family was having some money difficulties that they wanted to keep quiet." David narrowed his eyes at her. "You look skeptical."

Emma sighed. "Well, let's just say, I've done a bit of digging. Yes, the estate was having money problems, but they weren't the kind that would be solved by selling a few antiques, even for the prices listed. It would have been a stopgap and it would have been messy, and Marcie—"

"Messy was not her style at all," David finished for her.

"So, who was trying to sell the antiques?" Emma asked.

"Emma." Charles looked down his long nose at her. "Do you really need to know?"

"Yes, I do. And so do the police. And please don't tell anybody that last bit. It could get . . . people into a lot of trouble."

"Right, well. Not to put too fine a point on it . . ." began David.

"It was Frank," said Charles.

# 50

"DAD!" CRIED DAPHNE.

They were in Helen's room at the King's Rest. It was a simple, neat room, a little small, maybe, but the big window with its view of the beach and the sea kept it from feeling claustrophobic.

Helen sat on the bed, her arms wrapped tightly around herself. Daphne couldn't seem to make herself sit down. She just leaned on the back of the desk chair.

Emma understood how Helen felt. Her own nerves still hadn't settled down from this morning. She couldn't escape the feeling that they were running out of time to find out what had happened. Every member of the Cochrane family knew now that they might be in danger, and Emma was sure every one of them would be looking for their own way out.

"Why would Frank need money?" said Helen. "Marcie gave him everything he wanted."

"He came to the shop to ask them directly," Emma told her. "There's no way they could have made a mistake. He tried to offer them the silver tea set for sale, but when they asked for a provenance, he went away and did not come back."

"I don't . . . *why*?" Helen threw up her hands.

Emma shook her head. "I don't know."

"Maybe Aunt Marcie threatened to cut him off," said Daphne. "He had to find an alternate supply."

"I suppose it's possible. Oh, lord." Helen pressed both hands to her cheeks. "And I was halfway to believing he'd really changed."

Daphne plopped down next to her mother and put her arm around her shoulders. "Not your fault, Mum."

Helen patted her hand.

"But that doesn't mean Frank's the one who killed Marcie," said Helen. "I mean, whatever his reasons for doing it, Marcie was keeping quiet about it, wasn't she?"

"Keeping family secrets. That was part of the job," growled Daphne.

"I'm really sorry about this," Emma told them both.

"Not your fault," said Helen.

"You were just . . . you were trying to do me a favor," said Daphne. "If anybody's sorry, it should be me."

"You need to get back to work and we need to talk."

"Yeah. Come down when you're ready, all right? I know . . . whatever you decide, if you need anything, we'll help however we can."

"Thank you."

Emma closed the door softly on her way out and trotted downstairs.

"Emma?" Oliver had waited down in the great room for her. "You look sad, Emma."

She was sad, and tired, and nervous. But more than that, she was restless. She should be ready to prep ingredients for finger sandwiches and check off varieties of cake slices. Instead, her thoughts kept circling around everything that had happened just today.

Something was nagging at Emma, but she couldn't put her finger on it. It was like two ideas were trying to drift toward each other, but she couldn't clearly see either one yet.

Emma made it to the kitchen on autopilot.

"Listen, I need to run home," she said to Angelique and Genny. "I've left all the ledgers and bank statements from the grange up there. I need them."

"What for?" asked Genny.

"I don't know," Emma admitted. "But there's something. Something I read, or something I saw. It's bothering me."

"Go on, we've got it covered here," said Angelique.

"I'll be back in less than a half hour." She grabbed her handbag off its hook and headed out the door, just barely remembering to hold it open for Oliver.

NORMALLY, OF COURSE, EMMA WALKED BETWEEN THE King's Rest and Nancarrow, but since she had the Mini, and she didn't want to waste any time, she buckled Oliver into the passenger seat, and pulled out of the car park.

The road to her cottage didn't have a lot of traffic, and it was the sweet spot of the morning, when the farmers were already at their fields or out making their deliveries, and everybody who had to be in a shop or office was well on the way. So she had the road to herself, and was able to make it home in under ten minutes.

"Be right back, Oliver." Emma jumped out of the car and hurried into the cottage.

She swept the pile of accounts into her briefcase, and for good measure added all three ledgers and headed back out.

"Right." Emma dropped her case and bag into the footwell of the passenger side and started the car. She turned it round and headed down her bumpy drive. "What I hope is . . ."

But Oliver cut her off with a sharp yip. "Emma! Emma! Something's burning, Emma!"

"What the . . . !" Emma exclaimed. She could smell it now, a scorched rubber and hot metal smell.

It was a smell she knew perfectly well from her time in the city.

*Car crash.*

But they hadn't seen anything on the way up from Trevena. *Must be farther up the hill.*

Emma turned the car uphill and shifted into second. The road from Nancarrow didn't have hedges, but it was a winding, narrow strip of blacktop between wide ditches and stone walls. Oliver, of course, was sitting up tall in the passenger seat, sticking his nose as far into the wind as he could.

"Faster, Emma!"

"Not here!" They were just coming to one of the road's more dramatic bends, with a dip thrown in for good measure. When they rose back out on the other side, the road straightened and Emma saw the source of the acrid stink.

It was the lime-green Jag. Its front end was plowed right into the stone wall. Gus sat beside the car, his head in his hands.

"Oh, no . . ." Emma gripped the steering wheel and downshifted as fast as she could manage, while guiding the little car over onto the negligible strip of dirt between the road and the ditch.

"Stay here, Oliver." Emma climbed out. She checked the road nervously for traffic, but it was empty.

"Gus?" She touched his shoulder.

He lifted his head and looked up at her. "Oh. Hullo."

His hands dangled between his knees. What hair he had was sticking up on end. There was a dark smear on his forehead, but there wasn't any blood, at least not that she could see.

"Are you all right?" she asked. "What happened?"

"Caite's dead," he whispered. "That's what happened. Caite's dead."

# 51

..........

"OH NO," WHISPERED EMMA. "OH, GUS, I'M SO SORRY."

"She was hit by a car," Gus said, more to the ground between his knees than to her. "Last night. Hit and run. I was supposed . . . we were going to have breakfast. Not that she actually ate breakfast. She was careful about her weight, you know? We were going to have tea, though." He made a strangled little laughing noise and then pressed the heel of his hand against his left eye. "I'm sorry. I'm sorry."

"It's okay." Emma knelt down beside him and put a hand on his shoulder. "It's all right. You loved her."

"Ridiculous, isn't it?" He gasped, clearly trying to hold back a sob. "I mean, after everything my family did, was doing to her, and there we were, sneaking around like a couple of teenagers."

Emma swallowed and looked at the road again. Still no cars. She looked back at the Mini and at Oliver, with his front paws balanced on the window frame, craning his whole body to try to see what was going on.

*I wish I knew.*

Caite was dead. Caite had walked off with Gus yesterday. Caite had accused Marcie of stealing. Caite was out for revenge for the ruin of her father's life.

Caite was one of the people who might have killed Marcie.

Gus was one of the people who might have killed Marcie. Gus had believed he was going to inherit, and he might have found out Marcie was planning on selling the grange. Gus and Caite might have been working together, or at the very least, might have been covering up for each other.

And here she was sitting by the roadside trying to find some way to comfort him.

"Gus," she said gently. "You need to go to the hospital. Just to have them check you out."

"No."

"Come on, you might have a concussion, or whiplash, or something . . ."

"I said no!" he shrieked. Back in the car, Oliver barked.

Emma closed her mouth. She forced herself to start thinking. There were things you should do at a time like this. The first was stay with the vehicle and call the police. But she did not like this situation, or this spot. She wanted to get Gus to the hospital, but at this point, she'd have to drag him. Or sit on him while she called the ambulance.

Emma bit her lip and pulled out her mobile. She touched Constance's number, but it went straight to voice mail.

"Yeah, it's me. Call when you can." She rang off, and touched another number.

"Hullo, Brian?" she said as soon as he answered. "There's, been an accident. Not me," she added quickly. "Gus Cochrane. He's done a header with the Jag and he's going to need a tow. Only, we're not in a good spot, and he doesn't want to go to the hospital. I'm going to take him back to the grange."

"Okay, no worries," Brian answered. "Where are you?" Emma told him. She heard the sound of scribbling. "Right. I'll make it work, and I'll have the truck out there in twenty minutes. You sure you don't need a ride?"

"No, I've got this great new vintage car. We'll be fine." She hoped he didn't hear how strained her voice was or realize how overwhelmed she felt.

Emma rang off and faced Gus. "Come on," she said. "Let's get you home."

"Yeah," he breathed. "Home. After all, where else am I going to go?"

She helped him to his feet. He put a hand on the Jag's door, like he was saying goodbye.

"Don't worry. Brian's on his way," she told him. He nodded, but didn't say anything.

Emma shifted Oliver from the passenger to the back seat. Gus buckled himself in with shaking hands. Emma wished she had a blanket, or something, to give him. He was more than likely in shock.

She pulled out onto the road again, backing and turning at the farm gate so she could head down in the direction of the grange. Gus stared out the windscreen. He barely even blinked.

Worried, Emma searched around for something to talk about.

"Gus? How did you and Caite get together?"

"Well, it was my idea, wasn't it?" he said heavily. "Not getting together, but . . . I'd decided I didn't want anything more to do with all the family secrets, yeah? I wanted . . . I wanted to clear the air. And, honestly, I wanted to take Bert down a few pegs."

"Bert?"

"Swaggering around the place, telling everybody how they should act, because we're Cochranes. I thought if I could just show him how little being a Cochrane actually meant, he'd give up all the posturing and preening. And I thought, Caite could help. She could tell me the story about her father and . . . everything that happened there. I wasn't sure she'd go along, but she did.

"So, we started digging into Dad's time in the City, and my parents' car accident, and then kept on going, all the way back to Stewart and his 'boating accident.'" He made the air quotes. "And, somewhere along the line, the working dinners turned into just dinners and the drives to look things up or talk to people turned into just drives and . . ."

He shrugged. "I'm not sure which of us was more surprised." He stared mournfully at the ruined car. "She loved the Jag. Said it made her feel seventeen again. We'd drive for hours up the coast, talk about all the things we wanted to do. Leave Trevena, start fresh away from the grange and, well, everything."

Emma tried to picture Caite in a convertible, the wind in her hair, driving up the coastline, maybe stopping at a lovely little pub, or at least a chic little wine bar. It was not easy.

"Gus," said Emma carefully. "We found some printouts hidden in Marcie's office . . ."

"Oh, yeah. Those. Marcie caught us. Well, me. I was at the library, going through old newspaper records and I'd forgotten it was one of her book club days and . . ." He shrugged again. "I told her what I was doing, and why. That I was done with the secrets and covering up. I wanted freedom. Peace. I thought she understood. I even thought she and Caite might start . . . getting along. But then this stuff with the society money happened, and, well, that was the end of that."

Which would at least explain some of Caite's fury. Not only was she in a relationship that defied expectations, it looked like her boyfriend's sister was stealing money.

"So this all happened last year?" said Emma.

"Yeah," answered Gus. "Why?"

"I think Marcie did understand. That was when she made her will in Daphne's favor, and started looking into selling the grange."

"Yes," said Gus. "I know."

"Did she tell you?"

"Oh, no. She was too used to not telling any of us anything. My—" He stopped himself. "I was at Claudia's Bistro. I'd just dropped Caite off home. And I saw Marcie there, with a strange man. The bartender's a mate of mine, and he told me."

"But you didn't tell anybody?"

Gus shook his head. "Just Caite, and I knew she wouldn't

tell anyone. I knew what would happen if word got out and I thought . . . well, actually, I thought she was doing the right thing."

Emma nodded. "Maybe you inspired her to try to start a new life."

"Or maybe I got her killed." Gus shoved his hair back with both hands. "She should have talked to me! I would have helped! I . . . but, she couldn't, could she? I was dating Caite, and Caite thought Marcie was stealing from the du Maurier society. She said Marcie was doing it to make her look bad and force me to choose sides. I tried to tell her Marcie wasn't like that, but Caite wouldn't believe me."

"Was Marcie stealing?" asked Emma.

"No, of course she wasn't! I don't know what happened to the money, but it wasn't Marcie."

They'd reached Truscott Park. Emma turned onto the long drive up to the grange. "Did Caite think you killed Marcie?" she asked.

Gus closed his eyes. "She told me she stole Marcie's handbag and deleted the appointments off her online calendar. She told me she was afraid I'd be accused of killing Marcie. It wasn't her fault. It was all that trauma with her father. My therapist—" He stopped. "Anyway. She was trying to help me."

There it was. Caite heard that Marcie was dead. She had been afraid that Gus had killed her, because Marcie was going to sell the grange. So, she'd tried to cover up evidence of the sale, because she thought she'd also be covering up Gus's motives and keeping suspicion away from him. The murder was carefully planned, but Caite was acting hastily and out of fear. That's why it looked clumsy. Because it was.

"What was it you threw in the pond?" Emma asked Gus.

"Marcie's handbag. Caite had buried it in the walnut grove. Hadn't done a very good job of it."

"So you were trying to help Caite too."

"Speaking of not doing a very good job," he breathed.

"The police are going to need to know about that."

"Yes. I suppose they are."

They broke the tree line on the drive, and the grange came into view. That was when Emma saw why Constance hadn't picked up her phone.

Trevena's miniature police cruiser and Constance's battered, blue Range Rover were both sitting in the grange courtyard.

# 52

............

EMMA PULLED INTO THE COURTYARD AND PARKED. GUS turned toward her, his face haggard.

"Did you know?" he croaked. "That the police were here?"

"No, I didn't. I promise."

"Well," he said, and Emma heard a hollow echo of the giddiness that had taken over just yesterday. "I guess we'd better get going, then."

He climbed out of the car. Emma knew that the expected thing would have been for her and Oliver to just drive away. She was not, however, about to let expectations stop her, and she wasn't about to let Gus walk in there alone.

Quick as she could, she unsnapped Oliver's harness.

"Should I get Dash, Emma?" he asked. "I think we need help."

"Not yet, good boy." She put him down. "Just . . . stick close."

"I'm right here, Emma!"

The two of them ran to catch up with Gus just as the grange doors closed behind him.

Emma couldn't tell if Gus noticed them following. He didn't look back. He didn't even break stride. He just kept walking straight down the central corridor to the sitting room. He gripped the door handle and yanked it open.

"Well, well!" he chirped. "Here we all are!"

He was right. All the Cochrane brothers were now present—Bert was there, changed back into his normal outfit of polo shirt and slacks. Today's shirt was blue. He stood by the fireplace.

Frank stood by the windows, a dark silhouette in the unexpectedly bright summer sunshine that streamed in from the gardens.

As Gus, Emma and Oliver walked in, Constance got up from the sofa. Raj was already standing, his cap tucked under his arm.

"Gus," said Bert, and the same time Constance said, "Mr. Cochrane."

Then, they both noticed Emma. Bert smiled.

"Well. That didn't take long, did it?"

"Sorry," said Emma. "I thought it'd be better if we got him home."

"Yes, of course it is," said Frank. He hurried forward and pulled out one of the chairs from under the marquetry table, which was still piled with festival flyers. "Gus, sit down. You look like you've been in a train wreck."

"Car wreck," Gus said, and he did sit. "Afraid the Jag's had it this time."

"You were driving your Jaguar this morning?" said Constance. "When was this?"

"You don't have to say anything, Gus," said Frank.

"In fact you shouldn't say anything," added Bert. "I've called Wilkes. He's on his way."

Gus ran a shaking hand through his thinning hair. "What is this? What's going on?"

"It's about Ms. Hope-Johnston's death," Constance told him.

"Seems there's CCTV footage," said Frank.

Emma felt her hands clench around nothing at all. This was unusual. Unlike London, Trevena had very few cameras around.

"The village co-op was having some problems with a sneak thief," Constance went on. "Unfortunately, we weren't able to review the footage until this morning."

"And what did you see?" breathed Gus.

"That's enough," said Bert softly. "Really, Gus. It's for your own good."

Constance moved. She circled the chair so she put herself between Gus and Bert. "Mr. Cochrane, can I have a look at your hand?"

"Don't . . ." began Bert, but he was talking to her back, and neither Constance nor Gus was actually listening. Gus extended his hand to the detective, palm up.

"Hmm . . ." Constance cocked her head. "Interesting. You've got a chained heart line, you know. Says you've been unhappy, and depressed. Bit sensitive, and you have a hard time trusting."

"Well"—Gus curled his fingers tight—"that sounds about right."

"Your Jaguar has been identified on the video leaving the scene of Ms. Hope-Johnston's accident," said Constance softly. "As you can imagine, we need to ask you some questions about that."

"But I wasn't driving last night," said Gus. "I mean, I was, but . . ."

"August Cochrane," said Constance. "I need to caution you here. You do not have to say anything, but it may harm your defense—"

Bert cut her off. "Gus, you really need to stop talking now. Wait for the solicitor. There'll be a lot less to sort out later."

But Gus didn't pay any attention to either of them.

"I dropped Caite off at her place," said Gus. "After everything that happened at the grange—with finding the will and Helen and Daphne leaving—I wanted to stay with her. But she said she wanted to be alone. She needed time to think."

Raj, Emma noted, had very deliberately faded into the background. But he also had his notebook out and was scribbling busily. Oliver went over to snuffle his ankles.

Emma patted her leg to signal him to come on back, and Oliver obeyed. Raj gave her a quick glance of thanks.

"So I stopped at the Donkey's Win for a drink, and I came home," Gus was saying. "I went to my room and I stayed there. I thought about going to a hotel, but"—he shrugged—"it must have been around nine, nine thirty."

"Can anybody verify this?" asked Constance.

"Yes," said Bert immediately. "I can. He got home around nine, and he was home all night."

Constance turned to the remaining brother.

"What about you, Frank?" she asked. "Can you verify what your brothers have said?"

"Of course he can," said Bert. "He was home too."

Frank put his hands into his pockets. He looked from Bert to Gus and back again. He seemed perfectly calm, even, Emma thought, ever so slightly satisfied with the scene around him.

Emma shivered.

Gus must have caught something in the quality of the silence. He lifted his head. His eyes narrowed.

Frank's expression shifted to a slow, sinking regret.

Emma felt the hairs on the back of her neck lift up. *What are you doing, Frank?*

"There's a problem, Bert," Frank said. "You weren't home all night last night."

Emma sucked in a sharp breath. The sound made Oliver sit up abruptly, and plop onto his hindquarters.

"Frank?" said Bert sharply. "What the hell are you doing?"

Frank ignored him. Instead, he faced Constance. "Are you sure, Detective? About the Jag showing up in the video, I mean?"

"We've got a very clear shot of the license plate," she answered. "And you have to admit, the car itself is fairly distinctive."

*Yes, it is.* Emma frowned. Oliver was scratching his chin, hard. *Why would you take* that *car to kill somebody? Especially somebody you knew?*

Frank was turning toward Bert now, his expression sad, but his body language—there was a disconnect between the way he walked and the sadness on his face. It was too smooth, too assured.

"I'm sorry, Bert," breathed Frank. "I can't let you do this."

"I'm not doing anything!" Bert shot back.

Emma looked to Constance to see if she had noticed anything was wrong with Frank's attitude. But the detective's face was absolutely stony. Whatever she was thinking, she was giving none of it away.

"I couldn't sleep last night." Frank was speaking to them all, but he kept his attention fixed on Bert's face. "We'd had a shake-up here, like Gus said, and, I was up thinking about, well, life in general, and my life in particular. My bedroom overlooks the gardens. I saw Bert come out of the house and go to the garage. I watched him pull out in the Jag. I remember thinking it was strange that he'd be taking it. It's really Gus's car."

"And you're sure it was Bert?" said Constance. "It would have been dark by then."

Frank nodded. "It's easy to tell them apart from the window. Bert's got a lot more hair."

Everybody was looking at Frank and Bert. Nobody was looking to Gus, except Emma. She saw his expression shifting, from fear, to resignation, to comprehension.

"Frank?" Bert was saying. "What do you think you're doing?"

But Frank just met his brother's wide, confused gaze, and slowly shook his head.

*He's enjoying this,* thought Emma suddenly. *He's having* fun.

"Bert, you were the one who took the Jaguar out last night," said Frank. "You killed Caite Hope-Johnston, and I'm ready to swear to that in court."

# 53

............

ALL AT ONCE, GUS SHOVED HIMSELF TO HIS FEET. HIS EYES were red, his face pasty gray. Moving like a much older man, Gus walked past Frank, straight up to Bert. He opened his mouth. Raj tensed. So did Constance.

Frank just stood back, relaxed and smiling.

"You told me I should drop her," Gus croaked. "You said she was going to make trouble for everybody!"

Raj moved uncertainly toward Constance. But Constance held up her hand, gesturing for him to stay put. She kept her eyes fixed on the brothers.

"No, Gus." Bert fought to put on a smile, to be calm, to be charming. "I was happy for you. I swear! I wished you both the best."

But Gus didn't seem to hear him.

"This whole disaster is your fault!" The force of his shout balled up both Gus's hands. "Yours! None of this would have happened if you hadn't been such a . . . a . . . bully! You resented Marcie because she owned the grange. You did everything you could to undermine her! You wanted to be in charge! You thought if you controlled the property, you could control the rest of us. But Caite was onto you." Gus grinned at him, and Emma felt herself shrinking back. "She told me you were just trying to get your hands on the grange. Following in the family tradition, she said. I bet . . ." Gus grinned suddenly. "I bet you even checked with the solicitors weeks ago to find out if there was a will."

"Yeah, that'd be just like you, wouldn't it?" whispered Frank.

"And when they said there wasn't any, you figured you had a fighting chance to get your hands on the grange, if you could just get Marcie out of the way."

"You lost your minds," said Bert firmly. "Both of you."

"No," said Gus. He sounded exhausted but steady. "I've made up my mind."

"Listen to me, Gus, Frank. Think about this. You do not want to do this. You haven't got the nerve. Either one of you."

Gus didn't bother to answer him. Instead, he turned around to face Constance and Raj. "You need to drag the pond. Right near the middle. You'll find Marcie's handbag there."

"And how do you know about this?" inquired Constance pleasantly.

"Because I threw it in there."

She arched her brows in an expression of mild surprise. "Because?"

"Because Caite stole it. She was trying to cover up what Marcie had been doing the day she died." He held up his hand. "And before you ask, she was doing it because she thought I'd killed Marcie."

"Did you?"

"No," said Gus. "No. I knew she was planning on selling the grange, and I was glad. It was the right thing to do."

"He told me that," said Emma. "On the way here."

That may have been a mistake, because it reminded Bert that she was there. He looked directly at her. If looks could kill, Emma knew she would have been dead as several dozen doornails.

If Constance noticed, she didn't give any sign. "Well, I

think this is a conversation we really ought to be having up at the station. I'm afraid I'll have to ask you all to come with us. We'll be able to take your statements, and you can have your solicitor meet us there," she added to Bert.

Bert shook his head. To Emma's surprise, he chuckled.

"You don't know it yet, Detective, but your career is over. I'll have your badge, and I'll have your head," he added to Emma; and then he gave her a particularly nasty smile. "And your little dog too."

"Wait!" shouted Emma.

Everybody was looking at her, and Emma blushed beet red. *What am I doing?*

"Emma?" said Constance, her voice studiously bland.

"Erm." *Take it back,* she told herself. *Say sorry.*

But she couldn't. "I . . . think. No." She took a deep breath and straightened her shoulders. "I know we're missing something."

Bert threw up his hands. "Oh, here it comes. Are you going to start waving around a bloody knife and yelling '*J'accuse!*'?"

"Are you, Emma?" inquired Constance.

"No. But—"

But what? Whatever it was, she needed to think of it fast. Then, she did. Emma held up both hands.

"Please. I . . . just one second." Emma turned on her heel and bolted out the door.

She raced down the corridor to the front door, not caring if anybody followed. But of course somebody did.

"Emma! Emma! What are you doing, Emma?" barked Oliver.

Emma shoved her way out the front door, then stopped. "Oliver," she gasped. "I need you to go find Dash, all right? Just get him up to the sitting room."

"Okay, Emma!" Oliver wheeled around. "Do we need help now?" he asked.

"We need backup," she said, and ran out the door.

"Right!" Oliver bounced down the top steps and nosed at the gravel, and charged off to the left.

Emma found the doorstop and kicked it into place so neither she nor the dogs would be shut out. Then she hurried to snatch her briefcase out of the Mini, and ran back.

Constance was at the sitting room door, holding it open. "Well?" she said. "What did you find?"

"I object to all of this," said Bert. "It's bad enough that we're being accused . . ."

Emma didn't listen. She dropped the satchel onto the marquetry table. A whole stack of festival posters slithered to the floor.

"We'll get those later," said Constance.

Emma pulled out the three ledgers and the folders of bank accounts.

"You want to tell me what I'm looking at?"

"Inventories," said Emma. "Every year, there's an inventory made of the contents of the grange. This was for the year Stewart Cochrane died in a boating accident." Emma flipped open the ledger for 1976 to the newspaper articles. "And this was the year Richard and Evelyn Cochrane died." She opened 2000's book.

Constance leaned close and ran a finger down the first article for 2000. "Marcie was looking into the family accidents?"

"No," said Gus. "Caite and I were. But Marcie found out."

"Probably put ideas into her head," said Frank. "I mean, you were hoping to find out that Dad had killed Stewart to inherit the grange, right?"

This was too much for Bert. "You can't say that!"

"Believe it or not, I can't," said Gus. "I mean, I admit it. I thought we'd find out it really was murder, but there's no signs, not for them, not for Uncle Stewart. Those were accidents. Nothing more."

Emma watched Frank. That uncanny assurance she'd noticed before slipped, just a little.

"So why did Marcie keep all this?" Constance waved her hand over the ledgers.

"That's what I've been wondering," said Emma. "And why did she keep it in her office? The information she really wanted to keep safe, she left with her solicitor. That's in here." She opened last year's ledger to the screenshots.

Constance ran one finger down the page displaying the tea set for sale. "Very nice."

"Marcie found out somebody was stealing from the estate. This was her proof."

"And this somebody was?" asked Constance.

Emma lifted her gaze to the middle of the Cochrane brothers. "Do you want to tell her Frank, or should I?"

# 54

· · · · · · · · · · ·

OLIVER FOLLOWED HIS NOSE INTO THE GARDENS. IT WAS A warm day. The bees were buzzing and all the flowers were in bloom. A hundred different smells blew past on the fresh breeze. But Oliver made himself ignore them all. There was only one trail he needed to follow.

He found Dash asleep in the shade of a sprawling hydrangea bush.

"Dash! Dash!" Oliver barked.

Dash peeled open one eye. "Go away!"

"No!" Oliver poked his muzzle at Dash's front paws. "Wake up!"

Dash snapped at him, sending Oliver scuttling backward. "What is the matter with you, corgi?"

"I need your help! Emma needs your help!"

"Oh. More Emma." Dash rolled over onto his other side and curled himself up so he could lay his tail on his nose.

"No, Dash! She needs your help now! Marcie, your human, needs your help."

"Marcie's gone," mumbled Dash. "She can't need help."

"But we know why she's gone! We know who took her away!"

Dash lifted his head. "You know?"

"Emma knows! She's there now. She wants to tell every-body, but she needs our help!"

Dash shook his ears and laid his head back down.

*Oh, no!* What was he going to do? Emma needed him back in the room with the people. She needed Dash. But Dash wouldn't move.

*A noble corgi does what he must.*

"There's roast beef!" barked Oliver.

Dash's ears cocked up. He climbed to his feet and ducked his head down, so his muzzle was close to Oliver's. The big mutt pulled his lips back, just enough to show a few teeth. "You better be telling me the truth, little chap."

"You have to come." Oliver thrust his nose at Dash's flank. "You have to!"

Dash shook himself. "Where?"

EMMA WATCHED FRANK, AND HAD TO RESIST THE URGE TO bite her fingernails like a schoolgirl.

His dark eyes had gone cold and assessing. She wanted to believe she saw that he was nervous, that she'd scored some kind of hit on whatever he was holding back, but she'd just be kidding herself.

"How'd you find out it was Frank who sold the antiques, Emma?" prompted Constance.

"I talked to the owners at Vintage Style, and they said Frank had come in, asking to sell some antiques."

"Oh!" Frank exclaimed. "Is that what this is about? Yes, I did go to David and Charles. And they should have told you it was because Marcie asked me to *and* that I didn't have the proper paperwork. I thanked them, came home, told Marcie, and she said she'd sort it out. Obviously, she'd decided to try for a more anonymous method." He waved at the ledger.

"But there's a problem," said Emma. "I went over the estate accounts, and Marcie's personal accounts—"

Bert evidently decided that he'd been left out of the con-versation long enough. "You mean you stole private pa-pers," said Bert. "Do go on."

"Actually, I didn't," said Emma, finally feeling like she was on steady ground. "Helen asked me to help her and Daphne sort things out."

"You?" Bert sneered.

"She's an accountant as well as a baker," said Constance. "Never judge a book by its cover, or a cake by its icing, I suppose."

"Accountant or no, she's still wrong about me stealing from the estate," said Frank calmly. "I didn't need to. I'm a day trader, and I do pretty well, which after my pretty worthless time at uni would have surprised my parents no end," he added blandly. "And, yes, I have my allowance off the estate, and, yes, I admit it, I did make some extra draws now and then, which you probably saw in those accounts." He shrugged without taking his hands out of his pockets. "Why would I need to steal?" *Yes, why?* Emma looked to Constance. "Why does anyone steal?"

The detective pursed her lips. "Personal circumstance," she said. Her gaze roved across all three of the brothers, and Emma. Emma wondered what she was looking for. "There's maybe three types of thieves. There's your Jean Valjeans—the ones who steal because they're desperate and it's the only way they can figure to get by. There's your habituals. They're the nasty, organized ones. It's all business with them. Then there's the thrill seekers."

"Sorry?" said Emma.

"They're the white-collar thieves. They're in it for the excitement. It can be anything from stealing a lipstick from the chemist's or ten thousand from a stock fund. They don't really need it; there's just some part of them that wants to know they can get away with it."

"So, it's the adrenaline?" *Like driving fast cars or sailing in bad weather.*

"And to show who's boss," said Constance. "If you're taking whatever you want, you're the strong one, aren't you?"

Emma looked at shattered Gus. She looked at grim, de-termined, confident, Bert. And Frank. Frank who was trying to bring his ex-wife back, and who she was sure had stolen from the estate he was living off.

She thought about what Brian had said, about people and their cars. How Gus wanted the speed, but he was careless. How Bert wanted the prestige, and the control. But Frank, Frank was the one who liked the rush.

Frank sighed dramatically. "Detective, I appreciate a good fairy story as much as the next person, even when I'm being cast as the villain. But shouldn't you ask whether Ms. Reed can prove anything she's saying?"

"It's a fair question, Emma," said Constance. Her meaning was very clear. *I'm giving you a lot of latitude. I need you to give me something back.*

Emma pulled the stack of bank accounts out of their folders. She flipped through the pages, mentally adding up what Frank was drawing in addition to his allowance.

*Where on earth did it all go?* she asked herself.

*Never mind that,* she answered herself. *Just think about the numbers. The numbers don't have motives. They don't tell lies. The story is right there in the numbers.*

And it was. On the very last statement.

*Bert, green fees . . .*

*Gus, Jag repairs . . .*

It was the by-now familiar list of the brothers' expenses that Marcie had noted down and confirmed every month, except for one thing.

There was nothing for Frank.

Emma lifted her head.

"Marcie cut him off," she breathed.

"Which him?" asked Constance.

"Frank," said Emma. "Marcie found out Frank was stealing from the estate, and she cut him off, and then he killed her."

Frank raised his eyebrows.

Bert groaned. "Marcie killed *herself.* Why the hell are we even listening to this?" he demanded.

"Because I find it very interesting," said Constance. "Go on, Emma."

"But he didn't just plan to murder Marcie," Emma went on, her certainty growing with every word. "He planned to frame Bert for it."

Bert froze. "You cannot possibly be serious."

"It's the only way it makes sense," said Emma. "From the start, I kept thinking that Marcie's death looked like both a murder and a suicide. There she was at the bottom of the window. She could have fallen or jumped. Except, the body had been moved, and the window latch had been tampered with, and it looked like maybe Marcie had been afraid she'd be killed, and she was trying to leave clues behind, in the inventories from 1976 and 2000. But she'd left the other ledger—last year's—with the evidence that the estate was being robbed with her solicitor. And why would she be so cryptic about it? Marcie wasn't cryptic. She liked order, and certainty." She held up the sheaf of bank accounts.

"My sister loved drama," said Frank.

"She loved *reading* about drama," countered Emma. "In real life she was methodical, and cautious. Look at how she kept her records." She spread the statements out across the table like a deck of cards. "Everything's annotated. Look at how she handled the estate's future. She had plan B all set to go before she talked to Daphne about plan A." Her heart was beating hard. Thoughts were tumbling into place, but too fast. "She knew it was falling apart, despite everything she'd tried to do. Gus was ready to accuse the family of multiple murderers in their past. Daphne was headed off in her own direction. And you, Frank, you were robbing the place. Bert was spending what money there was like a drunken sailor. She'd had it. She was going to put an end to it."

*Like Mrs. Danvers in* Rebecca. *She told me she sympathized. This is why. She knew the house was the trap that held them all, and she was going to get rid of it.*

"You knew Gus was dating Caite." Emma was speaking straight to Frank now. "You decided you could work with that. You were the one who stole the checks, and Marcie's

ID, and used them to rob the du Maurier society. You knew Marcie would suspect Caite and Caite would suspect Marcie, and the feud would go public. Which would help set Caite up as a suspect when Marcie did die.

"You tampered with the latch on her office window. Then you waited for a storm to come through, so the rain would help cover your tracks. You waited by the garage for Marcie to get home that night. You used one of Bert's golf clubs to kill her—"

"*What!*" roared Bert.

"You took her body upstairs and leaned her against the window, so she'd fall, helping with the suicide illusion. But you didn't fix the latch, because it was a piece of evidence you wanted to be found. And then you put the club you used in the shed where it was sure to be found sooner or later. You could find it yourself if you had to."

"Aren't we just a little too clever?" demanded Bert. "You forget, I caught you planting that particular bit of 'evidence'"—he paused to make the air quotes—"just this morning. Or maybe you got so excited with your storytelling you forgot."

"I didn't forget." Emma faced Constance. "I was coming back to the Grange because I'd forgotten something. Oliver got away from me. He must have dug himself into the shed and got stuck. So, I unscrewed the padlock hasp to get him out. Bert found us, and I wanted to explain, but I didn't get a chance."

Bert snorted. "Are you going to believe that?" he demanded of Constance.

"You can look," Emma told her. "He dug a big hole in the dirt out back of the shed."

Constance gestured to Raj, who made a careful note.

"The thing is, Bert, you're smart," said Emma.

"Thank you so much," Bert drawled.

"But you're also a control freak."

"Hey!" exclaimed Bert.

"No, that much she's got right," said Frank.

"I'll say," added Gus.

"So, there's no way Bert would be stupid enough to use one of his own golf clubs to kill his sister and then keep it around. And Gus wouldn't be stupid enough to use the most recognizable car in Trevena to kill his girlfriend, and then go out and crash it the next morning. That was all you, Frank, using your brothers to get what you wanted.

"When Caite tried to hide the fact that Marcie was trying to sell the estate, she thought she was covering up for Gus. But because she didn't know what the plan was, she didn't realize that everything she did made it look more like Gus was the murderer, not less."

But Frank had stepped in and blamed Bert, and incidentally, saved Gus. So now, Gus owed him.

Frank chuckled. "And now, for your next trick, you're going to tell me what I want."

"You want Helen back," said Emma. "And Daphne."

The humor in Frank's face faded. "Do not bring them into this."

"They're in it," said Emma softly. "You keep calling Helen your wife. You can't admit she divorced you, and you can't admit it was your fault."

"That's because it wasn't my fault," Frank dragged the words out from between clenched teeth. "It was Marcie. She couldn't get herself a family of her own, so she had to destroy mine!"

Emma shook her head. "Marcie had nothing to do with it. You want to be the one in charge. You want to win, and winning includes getting Helen to admit she made a mistake leaving you. But she did leave you, and she doesn't want to come back.

"You don't know anything about my wife!"

"But to be in charge, and to get Helen back, you'd need to get rid of Marcie, and Bert, and you'd need to keep Gus on a string too. So you had to murder her, and frame your one brother, and get your other brother involved in the cover-up." Emma took another deep breath. "Marcie wasn't just the victim. She was the prop."

Bert was staring at Frank. "Well, Frank?" he breathed. "What do you have to say to that?"

"I say it's complete nonsense," said Frank. "You can't possibly believe any of it."

Constance responded by gathering up the bank statements and tucking them back into their folders. Then, she stacked the folders on top of the three ledgers. "I think," she said, "that it's past time that we took this discussion over to the station. Now, I'm going to caution all of you. You do not have to say anything—"

"But it's ridiculous!" snapped Frank. "She's just making it all up! She's another one of these little drama fans trying to get attention! Detective, you cannot possibly plan to listen to her!"

Constance turned. Constance raised her eyebrows.

"Frank," said Bert. "You need to shut up now."

"Good God," breathed Gus. "She's right, isn't she? You did it. You killed Marcie."

"If you will all come with me, gentlemen?" Raj moved forward, hands out to shepherd the men into the corridor. Bert scrubbed at his face, probably swearing into the palm of his hand. Gus was pale and as visibly shaken as when Emma had found him by his ruined car.

Frank looked at them all.

Frank ran.

He dove forward, past Constance and Raj. He tore open the door and bolted into the corridor.

And toppled right over Oliver and Dash.

"Oliver!" shouted Emma.

But Oliver just rolled, shook himself and bounced up, unhurt. Frank scrambled to his feet, or tried to. Oliver yipped a warning, and Dash leapt. He collided with Frank, and they both went down. Dash flopped his whole body across Frank's chest.

The big loyal mutt threw his head back and howled.

Everyone was crammed in the corridor now. Emma scooped Oliver up into her arms and hugged him hard.

"Emma." Oliver squirmed. "Emma, there's a problem."

"What problem? Good boy," she added, just in case.

She didn't need to worry. No one was paying attention to them. Raj and Constance were hauling Frank to his feet. Constance was patiently repeating the caution, and this time it looked like she was going to make it all the way through. Bert and Gus were standing shoulder to shoulder, finally fully realizing just what had happened to them all.

"But, Emma," whimpered Oliver, "we might be in trouble. You see, I promised Dash there'd be roast beef."

# 55

IT WAS THE NIGHT OF THE DAPHNE DU MAURIER LITERARY
Festival Masquerade Ball, and Truscott Grange was alive.

The whole grand house blazed with lights. Guests in
colorful costumes wandered from room to room, admiring
the artworks, the displays of first edition books and each
other's costumes. The dining hall had been converted into
a small ballroom and a jazz quintet played the equivalent
of the Hot 100 from the nineteen thirties. An instructor led
giggling couples through lessons in the two-step, bunny
hop, foxtrot and a rather businesslike waltz.

Emma and Oliver stood in the dining room, which had
been furnished with small tables and chairs, so the guests
could sit and drink and talk and enjoy what the program
listed as "Manderley's Luxury Tea" with its variety of
sandwiches, scones and cakes. The ginger-lime angel cake
had been the hit of the evening. So had the seafood sandwiches.

And she was going to have to go back and get another
tray of Black Forest minis.

Emma had come as Mrs. Danvers in a plain black dress
with a tidy white apron. She'd pulled her hair back into a
severe bun with the aid of an entire box of hairpins plus

more hair spray than she'd used since 1990. Oliver submitted to a white bow tie being attached to his collar. So far, it had stayed where she put it. The fact that she was slipping him chicken on a regular basis might have had something to do with it.

Dash had made himself entirely scarce after sneaking up to a table and wolfing down three roast beef finger sandwiches with horseradish cream.

"I still say you owe me an apology," murmured Pearl beside her.

Pearl was in a gorgeous white beaded dress with a handkerchief hem and yards of fringe. A matching headband with a bright red rhododendron flower decorated her hair.

"For what?" demanded Emma.

"You went and got all the suspects together in a room and announced who the murderer was, and you didn't invite me," she complained.

"Us," corrected Genny. Genny'd chosen a corseted serving wench costume, complete with ruffled cap. "You should have invited us."

Emma grinned at her friends. "I wanted to, really, but Gus crashing his car kind of moved up the whole timeline. But maybe next time."

"Next time what?" asked Angelique. She was dressed as Cleopatra, complete with a tall, Egyptian headdress. Daniel, Martin and Josh were all down at the King's Rest, making sure things were running smoothly, so the women could cover the festival.

"Next time I'm going to make more chocolate sponge," said Emma. "I think we're going to run short."

"I don't believe you," Angelique told her. "But I have to say, I think we've done ourselves proud." She put her arm around her daughter. "Good job, my girl."

"Good job, all of us," said Pearl.

"There you all are!" Ned Giddy bustled up to them. He'd dressed in a monk's habit, complete with a rosary dangling from the rope belt. "I've been looking for you. The board has asked me to express our thanks to you for putting together a wonderful event under, well, let's call them less than ideal circumstances. And we want you to know we will be calling on you first next year."

"Thank you so much, Mr. Giddy." Angelique shook his hand. "We will be looking forward to it."

A man in an old-fashioned chauffeur's uniform, complete with flat cap and gray jodhpurs strolled into the room. *Brian.* Emma felt herself smile.

"And now I need to get that fresh tray of cakes," said Emma. "If you'll excuse me?"

"Uh-huh," said Pearl. "We see you, Emma Reed."

"Nothing to see here," she told them.

"Keep an eye on her, Oliver," laughed Genny.

"Genny should know I always keep an eye on you," Oliver grumbled.

Emma ignored them all.

"So glad you could make it, Mr. Prowse," said Emma as she reached Brian.

"Wouldn't miss it for the world," he told her, and he smiled. "Did I remember to tell you I do a mean box step?"

"Never on the first date," Emma whispered back.

"But this is our second date," he reminded her.

Which was true. The first date had gone extremely well, despite the fact that it came right after Frank's arrest and Emma spending an entire day at the Devon and Cornwall police headquarters giving an official statement. The bistro dinner had been lovely. They sat out on the patio so Oliver and Lucy could stay with them. They shared a dish of lamb chops braised in wine and wild mushrooms, roasted potatoes and leeks, and strawberry meringue roll for dessert. Emma teased Brian about how long it took him to choose the wine. Brian teased Emma about her detailed dismantling and analysis of the meringue.

The movie turned out to be a lot of fun. Michael Caine swaggered, planned and swashbuckled his way through a series of mishaps and the wildly extended car chase between the English thieves and the Italian police, and multiple Mini Coopers gave their lives to the cause.

*I could get used to this,* Emma had thought as they strolled down Trevena's winding high street, and she didn't even feel a nervous twinge when she did.

Now Emma looked up at Brian. He had a nice face. And Oliver liked him. And he did very good banter, and did not like sweet popcorn. These are all indications of trustworthy character. She also had the growing suspicion he might be a thoughtful kisser. She was aware she'd like to test that theory.

Maybe on date number three, when they'd be a little less likely to have someone, say, Constance Brent, sauntering toward them, at what had to be exactly the wrong moment.

Constance wore a black tricorn hat, a flamboyant red coat and white shirt with trailing lace at the sleeves and throat. A red scarf hid the lower part of her face, but her blue eyes twinkled.

"A highwayman, Constance?" laughed Emma. "I like it. It suits you somehow."

She pulled the scarf down. "Yeah, my boss thought it was appropriate. Seems I've been stamped as a loose cannon, and she's not happy."

"Please don't tell me she thinks the case won't hold up in court?"

They'd already had the inquest. The coroner's jury had returned a verdict of willful murder. Frank was currently in HMP Dartmoor, awaiting trial.

"Oh, no. It'll all hold up, thanks to the bank accounts and Gus and Bert's cooperation. It was just . . . well, there is *supposed* to be a proper procedure in a murder investigation."

"Oh. Well," said Emma. "I guess next time I'll just remember to stay out of it."

"Too right you will, Emma Reed. Or you will be answering to me." Constance touched her hat brim to Emma and Brian, and strolled away.

"Now," said Brian. "It must be time for you to be taking a break. I can get us a table. I hear the food is kind of amazing."

Emma smiled. "All right. Just as soon as I get the cakes refilled."

Brian stepped back and bowed, sweeping off his cap. Emma fixed her face in a haughty stare and sailed on past. Brian chuckled. Emma's stomach did the fluttery thing, but this once, she found she didn't mind.

Emma started toward the door to the hallway. She kept her ears open to the bits of conversation as she skirted the tables, because honestly, what was wrong with a little eavesdropping?

"Are we having fun, Emma?" Oliver poked her with his nose. "Only I think I might be having more fun without the bow tie. Do we need the bow tie? Because . . ."

Emma laughed. "All right. All right." Out in the corridor, she crouched down carefully and unclipped the tie from Oliver's collar.

"Oh, there you are."

It was Helen, with Daphne and, somewhat to Emma's surprise, Gus as well. Mother and daughter were both in classic evening dresses, and Gus made a perfect escort for them in his white tie and tails. They looked like they could have stepped off the set of *Downton Abbey*.

"It's a beautiful evening," said Helen. "Marcie would have loved it."

"She would," murmured Bert.

*Bert?* Emma stood up slowly, at the same time as the family turned around, all of them equally surprised.

Bert stood in front of them, also in white tie, like Gus. He met his family's stony glares seriously, but without, Emma noted, his usual smooth self-confidence.

"I didn't know you were going to be here," said Helen. Bert hadn't been home since the inquest. The story of how he'd pushed through the original conclusion of suicide had been gone over in detail. By the time Gus got off the stand, he seemed to have aged by a couple of decades.

"I'm sorry. I'm interrupting," he said.

"Like you care," muttered Daphne. "After how you tried to cover up what really happened."

"I know you'd probably rather I'd stayed away," said Bert, "but I wanted to hear the memorial for Marcie and Caite. And I wanted to say—" He took a deep breath. "I wanted to say I've been wrong. About a lot of things. For a long time. And I know it's past time for me to start making amends."

This was greeted with skeptical silence. It was Gus who broke the standoff first.

"It's not just you," said Gus. "We all made too many mistakes for too long."

"So what are you going to do about it?" asked Daphne flatly.

"Work it out," said Bert. "With, I hope, the help of my family." He paused. "Who knows? Maybe I'll try this therapist Gus is always talking about."

Gus's face lit up. "Really?"

Bert nodded. "Really." He smiled; it was soft, but it was genuine. "What do you think, Helen?"

"Well, we'll have to see," said Helen. "All right, Daph?"

Daphne looked from Gus to Bert to her mother. Then, slowly, stiffly, she nodded.

Emma slipped away. There was eavesdropping, and then there was intruding.

"Where to next, Emma?" Oliver bounced beside her, snapping at the dust motes shimmering in the chandeliers' light.

"It's dinner and dancing for us, corgi me lad," Emma told him.

"Hurray!" yipped Oliver. "Chicken!"

# ACKNOWLEDGMENTS

At the end of every book, I find I owe a lot of people a lot of thanks. Top of the list are my fabulous and patient editor, Jess, and my agent, Lucienne, my eternally helpful writer's group (you know who you are), but most of all my husband and son, who have never failed to support me and my writing.

I also want to thank all my readers, whether you've come to this series via the other cozies I've written, or are finding my work for the very first time, thank you all! If you want to know more about the books and their author, please search for Jennifer Hawkins Author on Facebook or Twitter. Be sure to click on the link to sign up for the newsletter!

Ready to find
your next great read?

Let us help.

**Visit prh.com/nextread**

Penguin
Random
House